The Black Guard

QUEST FOR THE INVIOLABLE MAN

By Kas Smith

www.kassmith.com

To be notified of new releases please sign up for my mailing list. I promise no spam. You will only receive emails when a new title is available. For an added bonus, I will randomly select 200 subscribers to receive a free copy of the next release.

Dedication

Firstly, I'd like to thank my mum. She's been the fixed point, the lighthouse in my stormy life. Being her son is my greatest honour.

I dedicate this book to every boy trying to find their way in the world, and every man who at some point has lost their way.

Finally I'd like to say thank you to those who have helped to make this possible by actually taking the time to read my early drafts and provide me with invaluable feedback. James – unwavering in your support, an honour it is to stand by your side brother. Keli – whose beautiful heart loves the flawed man on the outside enough to see the great man within. Laurence, Frank and Justin - my friends and brothers-in-arms in the battle of life. Helen, Lola, and last... D Frost – humbly I thank you all.

And now...let the legend of the Black Guard begin.

Table of Contents

STAR

Not To Scale

KEPLER TERRA

GAIA MAJOR

GAIA MINOR

EARTH   LUNAR 1

GLIESE-EDEN

BIOSPHERE-9

UNITED EARTH

BIOSPHERE-12

Distance from Earth

Lunar1 (closest): 384,400 km
Biosphere-9: 4.367 light years
Gliese-Eden: 23.62 light years
Keplar-Terra: 1,200 light years
Biosphere-12: 27 Billion light years
Gaia Major: 10 Billion light years
Gaia Minor: 10 Billion light years
Hope: 45 Billion

Kas Smith

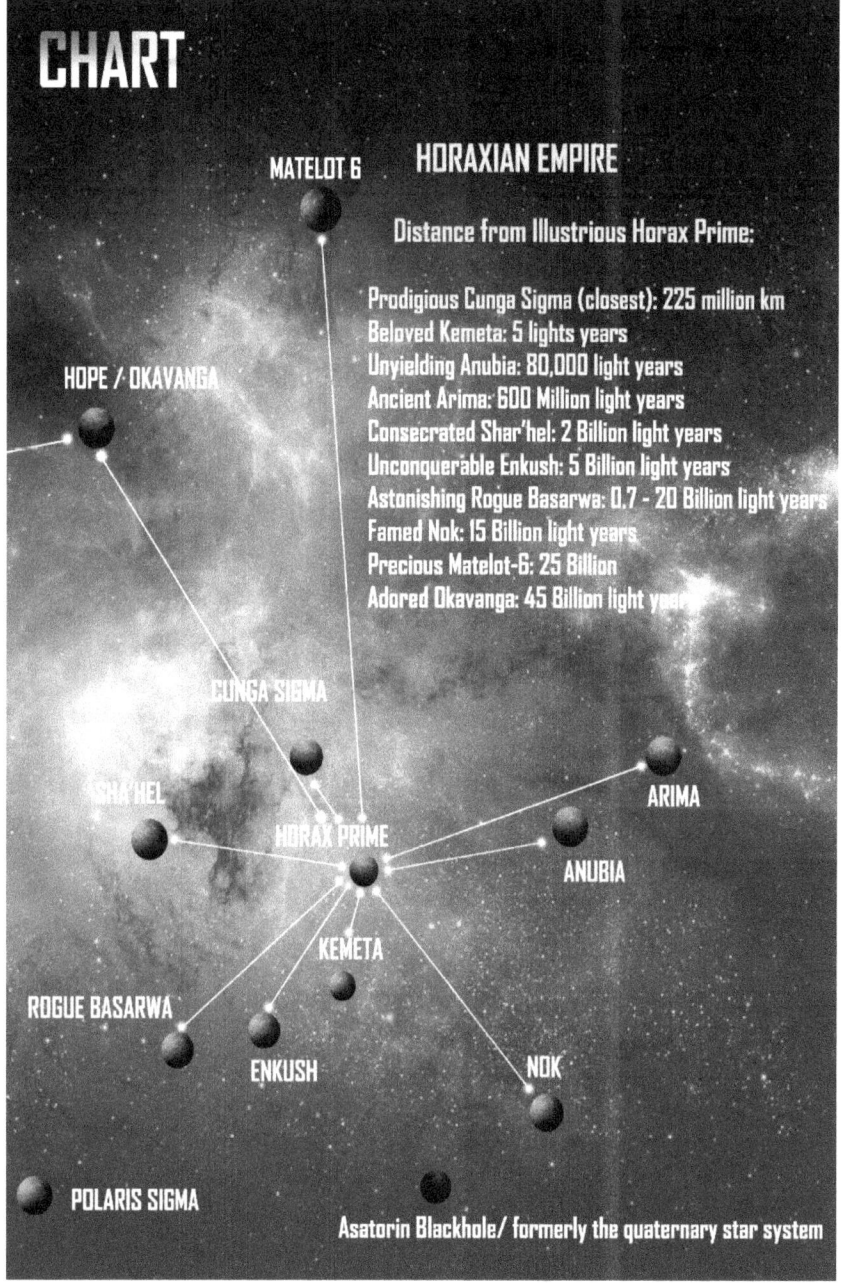

CHART

MATELOT 6

HORAXIAN EMPIRE

Distance from Illustrious Horax Prime:

Prodigious Cunga Sigma (closest): 225 million km
Beloved Kemeta: 5 lights years
Unyielding Anubia: 80,000 light years
Ancient Arima: 600 Million light years
Consecrated Shar'hel: 2 Billion light years
Unconquerable Enkush: 5 Billion light years
Astonishing Rogue Basarwa: 0.7 - 20 Billion light years
Famed Nok: 15 Billion light years
Precious Matelot-6: 25 Billion
Adored Okavanga: 45 Billion light years

HOPE / OKAVANGA

CUNGA SIGMA

SHA'HEL

ARIMA

HORAX PRIME

ANUBIA

KEMETA

ROGUE BASARWA

ENKUSH

NOK

POLARIS SIGMA

Asatorin Blackhole/ formerly the quaternary star system

Prologue

The Rise and Fall of Man – scribed works of Dr. Henreyorufulonjaro

Horaxian Imperial Calendar Year: 12430. Entry: 852 - Paradise Lost

In the historic year 2159 AD of humanity, mankind lost hope.

It was only seven years earlier that we Horaxians celebrated in the discovery we were not alone. The intelligent alien race called Homo sapiens colonized their corner of space and had made contact with us. Although Homo sapiens and Horaxians inhabited many celestial bodies, planets adequate in their natural form for the preservation of life had rarely been found.

But one dire day would change...everything. Two years after first contact was made, a planet was detected. One which measured twice the size of their precarious and precious Earth and even more profoundly rich in life. Lying perfectly within the "Goldilocks zone," their rather peculiar colloquial term for a circumstellar habitable region in space, it was a natural paradise without need of terraformation. No extreme inhospitable temperatures and rich, healthy breathable air, absent of hostile life forms, with limitless edible food in natural form and liquid water. Only their sacred Earth before mankind had poisoned it with their blindness, and our divine and illustrious Horaxian Prime were similar but dare I say, both were frivolously frail compared with the beauty of this heaven amongst the stars.

Yet I empirically observe, whether it be two Serengeti lions over territory, two ancient tribes struggling over superior hunting grounds or two superpowers' ambition to secure strategic resources, that the tragedy of Earth's spawn to fight in pursuit of preservation and desires, regardless of enlightenment, morality or spirituality, regrettably transcends space, race and time.

Tensions grew. Both races fought for sovereignty over this cosmic paradise. We Horaxians named it Adored Okavanga. The humans called it Hope. Eventually it was divided and contentiously cohabited. Then one fatally fateful day, a neutron bomb detonation deep within Adored Okavanga's Horaxian borders killed two million of our people, approximately two hundred and fifty thousand Homo sapiens died from the radiation fallout. A blanket of radioactive clouds shrouded the planet, rendering it no longer habitable. Our new home was gone.

Their Hope...was lost.

Both races blamed each other and soon after, out of mutual fear and hatred, war broke out over which empire would be dominant throughout the stars. A war that would last twenty-three years.

Chapter One - The Fabric Of Tragedy's Seams Sown

It navigated through the stars like an artificial whale migrating across a cosmic ocean. Crafted in an oblong shape, with the eloquent merger of black and silver segments running along its length complementing its hull. At its center, port and starboard, spun two metal rings revolving around each other that bore resemblance to the theoretical rings of an atom's shell.

The bold inscription *"Ploiarion"* shone across its bow, illuminated by hull lights. On its bridge, Captain Mensah stood on the alert as he had been for hours, at the edge of his smooth, circular command console. The joys of life had abandoned this once exalted soldier a lifetime ago. The suffering of over two decades of war with the Horaxians had become for him a carcinogen. His signs and symptoms were the war's outcome; inconceivable, irreplaceable and inescapable loss, both for mankind and their Horaxian adversaries. The cause of this cancer, the source—mutual fear and hatred. All accumulating into one regrettable act— the destruction of Hope twenty-three years ago, and for him there could only be one cure. That cure became the reason why he joined the expedition project. He would have spent the rest of his day reminiscing on all that had been lost, watching on while the half dozen crew members manning his bridge, dressed in their white uniforms, performed their duties. But a major alert notification shattered his concentration.

"Captain Mensah," called a dark haired, clean-shaven officer. On the shoulders of his shirt rested a black epaulet with three gold stripes and circular motif. Officer Ambrose held the rank of staff captain, second in command of the vessel.

"Sir, I've just picked up an emergency communiqué. It appears to be from Earth Command." Something on Staff Captain Ambrose's screen caused the officer to pause a moment, then his lips parted open as his facial expression altered. He rose from his seat and walked up to the captain's ear.

"Sir, it's a priority code Avalon," he whispered.

Captain Mensah's face turned to stone.

"Isolate the transmission. No one outside this bridge must be informed," said the man assigned to command and pilot one of humanity's most precious possessions to safe habitable worlds. His tall physique and thick, overgrown, black moustache added to his demeanor of authority, already denoted by the white and black hat which casted a shadow over his brow. Until now, things were going well for such a perilous journey. Yet in all his years of warfare, Mensah had only ever received one priority Avalon, and that resulted in the last time he ever laid eyes on the planet Hope. "Listen up people. We've got a code Avalon," said Captain Mensah, addressing the bridge crew, then he turned back to Staff Captain Ambrose. "Relay the message."

"Captain, we've been sent space coordinates," Mensah revealed. "There's also a request that we intercept and retrieve an object."

"What kind of object?"

"Unspecified, sir."

The captain stared at his second in command puzzled. "That's it?"

"Wait, no Captain, but the rest of the message is encrypted and DNA encoded."

"For whose DNA?" Ambrose snapped back.

"Unknown, Captain. Just ran a genetic fingerprint scan and it doesn't match anyone on this ship."

Captain Mensah looked down to scrutinize the coordinates on his own console. "Those coordinates will take us close to Horaxian territory; dangerously close. This could jeopardize our mission." The left side of his face scowled at the thought of the Horaxians, of the lives lost under him while he once held the rank of battleship commander, and of the aspirations that would be shattered if they were to be discovered. "Must be one of their traps," he rubbed his hardened face with his coarse hand.

"Negative, sir. Message has been authenticated," said Staff Captain Ambrose.

The priority code had been designated after the atmospheric processor of the same name that reduced half of North America to a wasteland at the turn of the century. To Mensah, the irony of its title was sickening.

A young scrawny first officer addressed his superior. "Captain," said Bailey. "If we intercept, we'll be dropping in right at the border of the Matelot star system, there's nothing for a civilian vessel there. The message was probably destined for a military ship. Whatever this is, it's most likely outside of our scientific directive."

"Even if that's true, we're not authorized to ignore a code Avalon." Mensah paused in contemplation. "Put us on an intercept course, First Officer."

"Aye, aye, sir."

***

With stealth, Ambrose's ship drifted along the edges of the Horaxian Empire billions of light years away from Earth. Only a few of these majestic vessels had ever been built. It was an ark. Stored safely on board were the genetic material of all forms of Earth life; zoological and botanical, as well as nine hundred personnel and millions of human embryos in cryopreservation. Humanity feared the imminent demise of Earth and its colonies, and the arks were their only insurance of survival.

Along with organic cargo, the ark stored geological specimens, art, literature and cultural artifacts which once existed in the museums of old Earth, including detailed records of every field of study—from engineering, to economics, and much more. All so that when the ark reached its destination and began re-sowing the seeds of life, it did not have to start from the beginning. The vessel's smooth finish and aesthetic dimensions seemed to go beyond its functional requirement. Clearly its architects had more say in the design than pragmatic engineers.

Up until now, the *Ploiarion* headed towards the recently discovered exoplanet which scientists believed could be a new Hope, a new Earth. But now, tensions on the bridge elevated due to the ship's new course, though Captain Mensah maintained an unwavering stance.

"I don't care how important this thing is. Maintain maximum safe distance away from Matelot-6."

"Captain, we've found something," said First Officer Bailey, concentrating on his smooth, splendid white console's screen that outputted an ISAR radar image of space. "Starboard, approximately five hundred and forty thousand kilometers away and closing."

"On screen!" commanded Mensah.

The first officer executed commands on his terminal, which changed the view of space on the bridge-wide observation screen and then amplified it.

"What is that?" asked Second Officer Cannington. The youthful, blonde haired man at the flight controls had just laid eyes on a small dark object roaming across the vast stellar emptiness.

"Can't make out what it is, but these are the correct coordinates. Could just be an asteroid or debris," said Staff Captain Ambrose.

Though Captain Mensah's eyes were more impaired by old age, experience made his perception far sharper than his second in command. He focused as the object drew nearer. "Asteroids don't have smooth surfaces and sharp corners."

"Derelict Horaxian craft, perhaps?" pondered Ambrose.

"Sir!" Interrupted Cannington. "The unidentified object is cuboid in shape, approximately ten meters by three meters by one meter. However, long range scanners are unable to identify its physical properties."

Bailey, the scrawny first officer on the helm controls, spun towards Mensah. "Captain, the object is moving faster than drift speed and it's headed towards Horaxian space. If we wait for further intel from command, we may lose the opportunity to retrieve it."

"Bring us in close. We'll grab it with the arm." Mensah turned to his staff captain, who looked anxious. "Whatever it is, it's definitely artificial."

***

A black, rectangular-shaped object became partially illuminated by faint starlight. It appeared metallic in composition and had unusual, indistinguishable markings. In front of the object's path, the *Ploiarion* closed in and locked pincers of a robotic arm on to the object. Once inside the cargo bay's bright white walls, lined with heavy loading vehicles and metal transport crates, the arm then eased the object down onto the shiny surface. Amongst the gathering of crewmen in the cargo bay, three wore hazmat suits and carried a barrage of handheld sensor equipment. However, most of the crew present were the ship's security detail armed with rifles in grey armored, pressurized suits. From a secured observation room with a view of the cargo bay via a thick glass wall, the captain, staff captain and first officer looked on anxiously.

"All right," said the captain, "I want every area of this object scanned. Need to know what we're dealing with here." The investigation team in the cargo bay heard his every word via the ship's speaker system.

"Radiation levels are non-lethal," said Tawran, the lead crewman in the yellow hazmat suit. He stood closer to the object than his two colleagues in white protective uniforms.

"Non-lethal? There's no radioactivity or EM radiation at all," said Castillo, the female crewman, wearing one of the white hazmat. "No electric charge, no lethal emissions, no temperature reading whatsoever."

Captain Mensah responded from the dark observation room. "What do you mean no temperature readings? You're standing right next to it. Is it hot or cold?"

"At the least, it must be cold, sub minus two hundred degrees Celsius drifting in outer space," said Staff Captain Ambrose.

Castillo felt a sense of embarrassment as the ship's second in command's statement was irrefutable, so she checked her instruments again. "I can't feel or detect anything. It's like it's not even there. The mass spectrometer can't identify the properties of the object, but it's definitely not human, sir. I can tell you that for sure."

"Perhaps some kind of Horaxian weapon?" Staff Captain Ambrose asked.

The Tawran interrupted. "It could possibly be a weapon, but Horaxian? I seriously doubt it."

His presumption intrigued Mensah. "What makes you so sure, Tawran?"

"Sir, although our scanners can't detect the object's properties, by analyzing the structure of the deposited cosmic elements this artifact appears to predate all Horaxian technology, and all of Horaxian civilization itself. I'm not talking millions, no, I mean by billions of years," replied crewman Tawran. "Captain, it's older than the Earth itself."

"These inscriptions are remarkable," said the third man in the white suit, referring to the hieroglyphic markings impressed in the object's surface. "I've never seen anything like this before."

"Wait a minute!" Castillo stopped, alerted by an alarm on her sensor. "Vital scanners have just picked up a lifeform ping from inside the object. Origins unknown. The object seems to be interfering with my scanners."

The other two Hazmat crewmen took in deep breaths. As the sweat accumulated on their brows, a sudden low pitch sound emanated from the object. The top section of the cuboid began to alter, fading from black to grey until it became transparent.

"Captain Mensah, are you seeing this?" said Tawran.

"I gave orders...touch nothing."

"It happened all by itself, sir." The lead investigator then crept toward the artifact and leaned over to see inside it. The object's grey internal gas obscured its contents but as it swirled around inside, the man made a startling discovery. "There's something in here. It's humanoid," his voice elevated in pitch. "Can't tell whether male or female, but I'm not seeing any movement."

"I need a visual, now, right now." The captain ordered, his forearms tensed up upon the revelation.

"Activating optical probe," said young First Officer Bailey. As he spoke, he pressed the touch screen keypad which controlled a multi-jointed, mechanical apparatus containing an orbed head. The orb responded by extending its metallic neck towards the object. An engineer within the observation room operated a console that received the relayed footage from the robotic neck. He streamed the video of the artifact onto a main viewing screen.

"Zooming in now, Captain." The observation room engineer said, enlarging the image of the alien object.

The men in the room focused on the monitor screen, analyzing the unidentifiable body. Through the grey blurring mist inside the cubiod, a body-suit became exposed. The armor appeared flexible in its fabrication, a carbon-fiber-reinforced polymer material that looked designed for the wearer's precise fit. The black suit however, looked worse for wear. Some parts were totally broken away and some had egg shell-like cracks and evidence of severe blunt force trauma impacts. But the internal mist rendered the face belonging to the body still beyond sight.

"Whatever it is, it looks dead to me," said the third crew member in full white protective gear, examining the lifeform in the cargo bay.

"Negative, electrocardiography is identifying what it determines to be cardiac cycles," said Castillo as she remained focused on her life scanner. "There's nothing on the cryobiological scans, so it's not frozen, but the heart beats per minute do indicate that *if* it is human, it's in some form of unconscious state."

Captain Mensah leaned closer to the monitor screen, squinting his eyes. He analyzed the blood stained and broken black suited armor. "The cracks in the suit look like bullet fractures...it must have been in a war." As he spoke, the smoke thinned around the humanoid's torso and revealed glimpses of an insignia etched on its breast plate.

"Stop!" ordered Captain Mensah. "Pan the arm towards the left chest area."

Staff Captain Ambrose also fixated on the insignia. "That's an Earth military emblem!" His eyes then opened wide at the sight of a white symbol on the right shoulder of the suit. It protruded three centimeters outward of the shoulder plate's deltoid region. "That mark on the right shoulder, does that resemble...a sword. Wait..." Ambrose came to a frightful realization.

"It's a Black Guard," interrupted Captain Mensah as he came to the same conclusion.

"Oh my God!" said First Officer Bailey. His mouth hung open.

Shock silenced the personnel of the vessel. All who were seated in the observation room rose to their feet. It seemed obvious they had all heard of the Black Guard, but an indecision descended over the subject of what to do about this stranger.

"The Sword in the Dark," whispered Ambrose. "We need to get him out of there, sir."

"Negative!" the captain ordered. "Bailey, I want more armed guards down here on the double."

"Aye aye, sir."

"Sir!" said Staff Captain Ambrose, edging closer to his superior. "I believe the DNA encrypted message we intercepted was for this man. It would make sense. No one has DNA records of the Black Guard. It's all classified."

"That may be true," said Captain Mensah. "But if he is a Black Guard, we need to confirm his SPU is activated and fully functional before we let him out."

Ambrose nodded in agreement, yet still frowned. "The thing that puzzles me is, you rarely ever see a lone Black Guard. They're always in a unit. So where's the rest of them?"

"All I know is, without the SPU, we've just brought a living weapon on board this ship," said Ambrose, refusing to take his eyes off the monitor screen. The armed to the teeth security detail standing guard in the cargo bay, now seemed inadequate as he watched their bodies jitter while holding their rifles even tighter.

Suddenly, audio distortions and radio static filled the ship's speaker system. The crew in close proximity to the alien object tried to shield their ears as the noise increased to almost deafening in their vicinity.

"What's going on?" Ambrose shouted as the hazmat suit team began to back away.

The sound came to an abrupt stopped, and then a voice called out.

"Ark vessel personnel of the *Ploiarion*. This is Symbiotic Program Unit Eve6676214." The unknown female voice on the ship's comms system spoke with a pacifying tone, absent of emotion. Although for AI, her voice mirrored a human being's fluidity of speech, for Captain Mensah, its composure gave away its artificial form. The voice spoke again. "I am within the alien pod but I have taken over the ship's communication systems so that we may make contact with you. Captain Mensah, the man inside the pod is the Black Guard Nephilim squadron officer commander."

"The Hawke!" The words escaped the ark captain's lips in a whisper.

"Good God!" uttered Bailey. The captain's first officer was no good to anyone now, so frozen by the discovery he couldn't follow an order even if he wanted. The security detail raised their weapons and looked at one another, foreheads sweating. More of them poured into the cargo bay in full tactical gear.

"Please stand down," said SPU Eve6676214. "We have no hostile intentions."

Upon her request, the captain nodded at his second in command, who then told the security team to stand down. With cautious hesitation they lowered their weapons.

"Is he alive, SPU Eve6676214?" the captain asked.

"Affirmative, Captain! I have commenced termination of his stasis, inducement of his body's homeostasis will soon begin." The SPU had a distinguishable accent, exotic, creole-based but faint.

"We picked up a transmission from Earth Command requesting us to intercept this artifact," said the captain. "Along with a DNA encrypted message for an unidentifiable recipient. Were you aware of this?"

The Symbiotic Program Unit gave no response and the crew looked around at each other, unsure of what to do next. The ark's captain tried once again. "Please respond, SPU Eve6..."

"Apologies, Captain Mensah. I momentarily accessed your vessel's communications log. Affirmative, your encrypted messaged is indeed encoded for the commander's DNA, only he can decrypt it. But negative, we were unaware of its existence. While the Black Guard commander drifted in stasis, I transmitted a distress beacon to Earth, which is how Earth Command was able to notify you of our location."

"That explains why we were sent here, but why the top secret message?" Captain Mensah asked while staring at his staff captain.

"You can ask him yourself, Captain," replied SPU Eve6676214. "The commander is now conscious. May I open the pod doors?"

The captain paused a moment and glanced around the room at his crew. He saw the eagerness in their faces to lay eyes on the object's contents, but he also distinguished that it was fear which fueled their anticipation. He felt the mountainous weight of his own yearnings and walked out of the secured room. Ambrose and most of the room's personnel followed behind him into the cargo bay. "SPU...you may proceed."

"Acknowledged, Captain Mensah, and thank you."

"We may have just opened Pandora's box," said Ambrose.

As grey gases began to vent from the object's lower section Mensah whispered in his executive officer's ear. "Order security to increase the luminosity of all the lighting on the ark. Now! We must not let him anywhere near a darkened area of the ship or the control systems for the vessel's lights." Mensah translated the returned expression on Ambrose's face, his second in command thought he was insane. If only Ambrose had seen what he had seen, he would be afraid of the dark too.

A low pitch hum then reverberated against the cargo bay's hull and the transparent top side of the cuboid dematerialized. The exhaust smoke obscured the surrounding area. The crew members wearing hazardous materials suits and the security detail all crept farther back.

The silhouette of a man emerged through the smoke, followed by glowing blue eyes. A third bright spot turned the grey smoke to blue around the head area. Soon after, the Black Guard revealed himself through a veil of mist. Although his body remained hidden within his black, molded, six foot three armored suit. The thinning smoke exposed the source of the third light. The man held what looked to Ambrose like an electronic cigar through his protective mouth grill, which contained a blue tar substance. His black helmet, both protecting and concealing the man's face, looked irreparably crushed on the whole of the right side. Similar to the spider webbed cracks of a damaged window.

It didn't take long for the ark's crew to notice the blood stains that covered the mysterious man's armored chess and torso. The captain observed that the blood appeared dried. The bleeding must have stopped long before and simply not been cleaned, and most likely...it was not his blood. Captain Mensah cleared his throat, then opened his mouth to speak but halted, as if he'd lost his voice. He tried again.

"Welcome aboard, Major. Do you require medical assistance?" asked the captain. The SPU did not reveal the Black Guard commander's other rank, but certain things, even only heard once, a military veteran never forgot. Mensah stood bold, yet as terrified of the man then as when he had first laid eyes on him.

The Black Guard remained silent but with an eerie calmness. He shook his head, indicating "No!" His shoulders were globed, his chest pushed up in an almost robotic posture. But the damaged helmet remained the focal point, inducing the gravest concern for the crew. It disguised everything, his thoughts, his expression and most worrying, his intent. They were only mildly comforted by the fact the man appeared unarmed, although a peculiar white object attached itself to the left of his waist-side, as though glued to his suit.

"You look in pretty bad shape." said Captain Mensah. Judging by his broken armor, whatever battle the Black Guard was engaged in he had lost.

The Black Guard then moved his left hand and gripped his transparent cigar, puffing out some greyish blue smoke. After exhaling, his helmet's mouth grill snapped close. "We're alive!" He uttered in a deep chilling voice that seemed to linger in the air.

"We have a code Avalon message for you. Please follow me to the briefing room."

Both men walked through the open internal hangar bay door towards a nearby room, but the Black Guard moved with a slower pace, more mechanical. Staff captain Ambrose and the security detail trailed behind. As they arrived at the debriefing room, Mensah opened the door and turned to the Black Guard.

"Could you tell us what that alien object is and what you were doing in it, Major?" he asked in a respectful tone.

The concealed man shook his head sideways in response.

"Very well." Mensah's good sense told him to abandon the subject. "We've established a secure room for you. You can access the message via the terminal."

The Black Guard commander nodded and proceeded inside with an abundance of calm in his pace. As the door closed, the captain whispered the last names of two of the security officers and gestured with his head for them to come over.

"I need you stationed here,' commanded Mensah. 'He doesn't leave your sight. Do you understand me?"

"Yes, sir!" both men replied.

"Not a lot that's going to do," Ambrose uttered.

"To the bridge," ordered the captain as he and his second in command marched off.

Minutes later, back on the bridge of the magnificent ship, an air of concern still enveloped the ark's crew.

"Hurry this up, Cannington," the captain growled. "I want to see and hear everything in briefing room two." Anxiety caused by the Black Guard's presence had also infected Second Officer Cannington and he struggled with the simple task of activating the briefing room's surveillance.

"Could that really be him, Captain?" asked a helmsman. But his question went unnoticed due to Second Officer Cannington's interruption.

"Sir, none of the surveillance cameras and monitoring systems are functional in briefing room two. The hard lines appear to be connected but are not responding, and radio frequency channels are being jammed by interference."

"Damn it...it's his SPU," snapped Ambrose. "Try to un-jam it."

"Sir, isn't this guy, well, like a hero?" asked First Officer Bailey, manning the helm.

Captain Mensah seemed a little annoyed by the junior officer's comment. "The Black Guard are like a nuclear bomb. It will help you win a war, but you wouldn't want to keep it in your living room."

"I thought their suits were forged to be near impregnable?" pondered Ambrose. "What could have done that kind of damage to the Black Guard commander?"

As they attempted to unravel the enigmatic man, a notification alarm on Bailey's console alerted the bridge. "Captain, we've just picked up an alarm on life monitoring, someone's vital signs just suddenly dropped."

"We have been experiencing glitches recently. It's probably another false positive. Still, send a medical team to check on whoever it is," Ambrose ordered.

Another alarm sounded off, similar to the last, both metronomic.

"Wait, I've just picked up another alarm, a crewman's vital, IDing now...sir, it's security officer Anderson's. The first was security officer Ramlapore's."

"Are they dead?" asked Ambrose.

"Negative, but something's going on," replied the Helmsman.

"It's the Hawke," said Captain Mensah.

***

The ark's elegantly curved corridors, designed to enhance this last marvel of human ingenuity, had now become the scene of a brutal event. No longer in the briefing room, the Black Guard had a one handed grip around crewman Anderson's neck, lifting him high off his feet against the corridor wall. His cryptic black helmet stared down the corridor instead of focusing on his victim. After enough of the crewman's air supply had been cut off, he allowed the heavy body to drop lifeless to the ground. The Black Guard moved down the ship's corridor with purpose, not running but at a constant jog that never broke rhythm, like a machine piston.

Another crew member patrolling the corridor witnessed the lifeless crewman on the ground and the attacker closing in towards him. He realized the futility of escaping a Black Guard at this distance, or any distance for that matter, and chose to go down fighting, sprinting towards the assailant.

The Black Guard waited for the crewman to commit himself. With adrenalin overpowering his fears, the crewman swung wildly. The mystifying man seized his moment. Stooping low, he delivered a straight punch to the solar plexus that incapacitated the crewman, leaving him struggling to breathe. Only one strike was needed, anymore would violate the Black Guard commander's principles of warfare.

His arm remained extended, and after a brief moment of immobility the victim fell to the ground. The vessel's security chief saw the combat in the corridor as he turned the corner. He immediately pulled an alarm lever activating a loud ship-wide alert as the assailant jogged towards him. The chief then reached for his sidearm and let off four rounds at the Black Guard, but the skilful attacker dodged the bullets, evading two shots by sliding side to side and adjusting his body at angles; he evaded the other two shots with a roll. As he rose, he grabbed the white, metallic object which clung to the side of his body suit that bore likeness to an ancient sword handle, minus the blade. Within a hundredth of a second, the object altered itself. First, the guard and pommel enlarged and altered its shape, then a long, white blade extracted from the guard. With this, he stabbed the security chief straight through his thigh. As the chief toppled, the Black Guard held his body to stop him from falling. He attacked with little effort or emotion in his body language, and far from out of breath.

Two more of the vessel's security team appeared, dressed in full tactical gear, and both wasted no time in firing their assault rifles. As their fingers squeezed down on their triggers, their target responded by throwing his sword into the shoulder of one of the men, piercing his armor. His screams of pain were drowned out by uncontrolled weapons fire. Still holding the body of the injured security chief he had stabbed, the Black Guard lifted the man up in front of him; using the body as a shield from the weapons fire, he moved in for the kill. They witnessed his strength as he threw the body into the air and onto the armed guard firing from meters away. They both fell on the ground on top of each other.

Pouncing onto the other crewman who had his sword still stuck deep within his shoulder, the Black Guard knocked him out cold with one blow to the face, and withdrew his sword. Then he walked up to the two crewmen laying on one another and knocked the only one still conscious clean out.

***

On the bridge of the ark, pandemonium had broken out as the alarm triggered by the fallen security chief sounded off continuously. Captain Mensah, unaware of the extent of the Black Guard's carnage, leaped from around his command console. "Cannington, I want a comms link, all decks, all channels, red alert."

The second officer pressed hard on the keys of his computer console in a panic. "Aye Captain, you're now online."

"Crew of the Unified Earth ark vessel *Ploiarion*, all hands, this is your captain. We are now at red alert. We have a Black Guard on-board this ship. He's to be treated as an enemy hostile and apprehended at any cost."

The computer console at the rear of the bridge came to life. The bridge crew were chilled by the blood-washed face of one of their crewmen on screen, his raised right hand trembling as he snapped his head around, petrified of what may come upon him.

"Captain, we're being ripped to shreds down here," he said, hyperventilating in hysteria. Captain Mensah heard automatic gunfire getting louder in the background, then an unknown force knocked the frightened man away from the screen view. The Black Guard centered the screen, bizarrely calm and composed, his broken helmet stained by fresh blood.

"Crew of the Unified Earth Ark vessel *Ploiarion*." The toneless, low, echoing voice of the Black Guard resonated throughout the ark's entire speaker system "Abandon ship, immediately. This is not a request. This is your only warning." He cut the comms link, leaving a blank black screen.

"Damn it...where the hell is he?" shouted Mensah.

"Sir, he's almost at the bridge," said Ambrose.

"Coordinate all security personnel to his location. Scratch apprehending him. Lethal force is authorized. Take him out before he kills everyone!" screamed Captain Mensah, desperation creeping into his voice.

Back along the main corridor the Black Guard stood motionless, drenched in blood, sword handle tightly held but the blade no longer visible. Close to a dozen firearms held by defeated crewmen scattered the ground. He had no need of their blood-splattered weapons. He could kill everyone on the ship with his bare hands. With an inhuman calm, he listened to the sound of men approaching from multiple directions, fully armed and intending to kill.

"They have surrounded us," said the voice of the SPU Eve6676214. With each of her words a rectangular, protruding component at the bottom of the Black Guard's neck plating flashed sporadically with green lights and stopped when her voice stopped.

"Eve, override the ship's navigation systems. Take us to Matelot-6. But first, deactivate all of the vessel's lights."

Out from the shining sword hilt, a white blade extracted once more. This time it's movement was slow, morphing like the flow of water around rocks, until it reached full length. As the men came upon him, all the lights in the corridor concurrently turned off. Multiple screams and weapons fire resonated and illuminated the body-filled, bloodied corridors. The carnage rung out within the dark, but with every second that passed fewer and fewer cries were heard. Until only darkness remained.

Chapter Two - The Curse Incarnate

Fifteen years later...

In the mess room of the United Earth vessel *The Odysseus,* Lieutenant Adcox sat alone, whirling his spoon and playing with his curdling food. After a week in deep space, the young man in his mid-twenties grew disgusted of the freeze dried ration packs special ops Unit Forty Two lived off. He daydreamed of the natural pomeracs he adored, grown in the greenhouses of Biosphere-9, mankind's stellar space city.

Yet, despite its cardboard taste, he felt grateful for the privilege of a somewhat full belly as he cast his thoughts towards the constant food riots and drought on Earth. Even with a tenuous peace treaty ending major combat operations between humankind and the Horaxians, the fallout of war kept paying terrible dividends. At least for mankind. No famine nor pestilence threatened those within the Horaxian Empire. Adcox ate while he gazed at the three dimensional digital projection of the Horaxian imperial planets that jumped out of the data-slab's screen laying on the table. His obsession in discovering which one they were headed to consumed him, more than he consumed his sustenance. Colonel Bronze, his commanding officer, had yet to share any information of this mission with his men. The junior officer was still getting used to being a part of the team, having recently been transferred. From what everyone had told him, the level of Bronze's secrecy on this mission was something to be concerned about. To ease his mind and the grotesqueness of his rations, he felt that a bit of light reading to familiarize himself with the Horaxian planets would do a world of good.

None were ideal, but undisputedly, some were a far worse destination than others. He took note of each one as the display cycled through them. Matelot-6 came up first. The database included past Horaxian worlds. Matelot-6 was obliterated in Earth year 2182, fifteen years past, when the Black Guard stormed the ark vessel prior to the ensuing colonial massacre. At least that was the rumor. In the depths of space, no one ever knew anything for certain, especially surrounding the Black Guard. He began eliminating destination improbabilities. Their Scholar world of Cunga Sigma rotated on screen. Once it schooled the brightest minds of the empire. But now this planet's rich history and people were gone. Ten billion lives taken, exterminated more precisely, by something unequivocally evil. All that remained of the Horaxian presence were their desolated, broken statues and architectural ruins that towered through the skies. He could rule this one out. The evil that resided on Cunga Sigma now...they wouldn't be headed there, not without a quarter of United Earth's entire fleet.

He felt confident enough to rule out Basarwa as well, a Rogue planet inhabited by the Horaxians. It had no fixed stellar orbit and drifted between the gravitational pull of the Hora star and its two neighboring stars. Adcox read what he was already aware of, that the people of this barren brown rock lived within vast subterranean cities, protected from the planet's zero atmosphere. The Rogue's unusual celestial movement placed it too far away to be a likely destination.

"Show me Horax Prime," said Adcox. His taste buds cursed for a beverage to wash down his excuse of a meal. Accepting his voice commands, a new planet rotated on the hologram. Lying at the heart of the Hora star system, this spinning rock had been described by humans who had the opportunity to see it decades past as magnificent. The most

Earth-like of their worlds and full of natural resources. Being bestowed the honor of prime world, it had been minimally affected by the horrors of war compared with their other imperial planets. No humans had been allowed to set foot on the prime world since the war broke out, and although mankind were no longer adversaries of the Horaxians since the year of the Matelot-6 massacre, the Horaxians were big on tradition. Still, that didn't mean they weren't heading in close vicinity to the planet.

"Continue planetary rotation," he commanded the tablet. A big red globe spun and centered the display. Anubia. Two-thirds of this planet were disease infested swamp lands and its inhabitants were the closest genetically to the Arimans, the ancestors of the modern day Horaxians. Physiologically strong and bred solely for a life of combat, even at the best of times Anubia was not the place for diplomacy. Although, it wasn't ambassadors being sent into the Horaxian Empire. Unit Forty-two were stellar marines. Whatever he and his commandos were needed for, it had the potential to get grizzly. Unfortunately, he couldn't rule this one out, even if his elevated body temperature wanted him to.

The software cycled to the next planet. With more emotions than deductive logic, Lt. Adcox ruled it out as well. The Arima Nation was an environment where survival depended upon superhuman strength and will to endure the unimaginable. A toxic atmosphere covered most of the planet, along with surface temperatures which swung too cold and hot for the lifeforms of Earth to exist, and hundreds of miles per hour winds. From this inhospitable world the cradle of Horaxians existence spawned. Now with centuries passed, Horax Prime established and other worlds populated with societies raised to new technological epochs, much of the Horaxian's link to their ancestral people had been severed. Rarely was there interstellar travel to Arima other than for scientific research, and the aboriginal people themselves chose to remain in isolation. There was simply nothing worth going there for that he could think of. In fact, cosmic dust wouldn't land there if it had a conscious.

His eyes expanded on the orb that displayed next which was split in half by a white borderline. The planet, once a symbol of unity, looked breathtaking even in a simulated model. One half of the planet was called Okavanga, its Horaxian name. The other half, mankind had labelled Hope.

"We should have overcome our differences," he said aloud. Adcox had always dreamed he could have lived on the paradise lost. One could lose themselves in the footages of its landscape and breathtaking flora and fauna. The quadrillion dollar question remained unanswered. Who had set off the detonation that extinguished its beauty forever? With decades passing, still neither mankind nor the Horaxians claimed responsibility. It had now been fifteen years since the Matelot-6 massacre which led to the mostly honored ceasefire, and thirty-eight years since the Hope bombing. But the Horaxians sure knew how to hold a grudge.

Adcox's slim upper body jolted back, then forward in rhythm to the ship's dramatic change in speed. "Looks like Zomo has depowered the string engine." He thought. The string core, a marvel of ingenuity, had allowed mankind to traverse through the vast distances of the stars utilizing string theory to fold space-time. We'll be running on antimatter from now on, he figured. This changed everything. Antimatter propulsion at this course and heading would place them on a route to only two planets.

One was Sha'hel, a rugged avian Horaxian subspecies. The classification wasn't entirely accurate, since the Sha'helians' only major resemblance to birds were their wings, and even those took more the shape of prehistoric lizard wings of old Earth. But the name stuck. His hand flicked the holo-map past two dead Horaxian worlds, Nok and Enkush, stopping at the only remaining planet, Kemeta. It was the Horaxian's industrial powerhouse and center of technological advancement. Yet without the heat created by its immense power generation, the cities would freeze over. "It has to be Kemeta," he uttered.

Lieutenant Adcox's indulgence, however, was cut short by the echoes of authoritative footsteps that disrupted his concentration. They emanated from outside the metal walkway. The door slid open and a scarred man with a black eye-patch over his left eye stood at the entrance, choosing not to enter the mess.

"Hi, Captain," said Adcox.

Although Captain Michael Lewalski was a veteran of war well into his fifties, his solid structure could conquer men half his age. His main scars were horizontal lines running across his pale face. It looked as though something with six claws made a good attempt at ripping his head off. "The colonel wants to see you on the double," said the raspy voiced Lewalski.

"Is it bad, Captain?" asked Adcox, in a common British accent, accompanied by a handsome chiseled jaw.

"He just wants to tell you what an honor it is to have you in the field with us." The old marine gave Adcox an unusual smile, a rare act for most old men of his time...the few that were left.

"Really?" The young marine had started to believe that the colonel disliked him. He wasted no time hustling out, the commanding officer was not a man to be kept waiting.

Away from the mess room, Adcox arrived at a mechanical door and paused for a moment. He questioned whether he should offer his condolences to the colonel for the recent loss of his wife. But he didn't know if the rumor was true, as the colonel never spoke about his private life to anyone except his executive officer Lewalski, and it would be even more foolish to ask the perpetually foul-tempered captain. He decided it was best to refrain from the topic as he pressed the notification tone.

"Come in!" A stern voice behind the door called out.

Adcox entered into a somewhat tidy stateroom despite being overfilled with documents and books. The stateroom served both as sleeping quarters as well as a personal office with a sink and medicine cabinet in the far right corner. On the other side of the quarters sat a man behind a desk. He hadn't much grey hair left on his aged head, quite dissimilar to Adcox's low cut, full head of black hair married with a good sharp hairline. The old man was yet another battle-hardened soldier who'd made a name of himself over many years.

"Colonel Bronze, you wanted to see me, sir?" Adcox said saluting the old man at attention.

"Negative, Lieutenant!" said the wrinkled Bronze. His face, more particularly his stare, gave away his horrifying experiences. A large, grotesque scar ran vertically along his left cheek reaching all the way up to the crown of his head. Multiple smaller, permanent facial scarring disfigured the right side of his face. He must have been a casualty of a fragmentation explosion. Adcox focused on his left ear; the top half was missing, as if it had been cut off. Good looks had abandoned Bronze a lifetime ago.

"Oh, apologies, sir. I was misinformed," said the young officer seeing the colonel engaged in reading a book.

"I ordered that you attend my quarters. I didn't *want* to see you. Sit down, laddie."

To Lieutenant Adcox, the old marine's thick Scottish accent only added to his chilling presence. Colonel Bronze was raised in the Scottish community settlement in the human colony of Kepler-Terra. First called Kepler-62f by scientists a century ago, the exoplanet lay twelve hundred light-years away from Earth in the constellation of Lyra.

As the colonel read more lines of his digital book in silence, the younger man sat and glanced around, noticing the varied subject matters along the spines of the countless books in his superior's metal cabinets. It was a rare moment for him. He hadn't seen real books outside of a museum. Three stuck out as they were of a similar nature: *Advanced Interstellar Warfare,* the *Art of War* by Sun Tzu and in the colonel's hands, *The War Magna Carta* by Shando the Grand.

"I get the feeling you're a well-read individual, Lieutenant?" said the old man, still refusing to look at him.

"Well, nothing as heavy as some of the stuff you have here, sir."

"Given the same amount of intelligence, timidity will do a thousand times more damage…"

"…than audacity," said Adcox finishing off the colonel's quote. "That's Von Clausewitz I believe. I was more into ancient history and mythology, sir. I was also fond of civil rights leader Martin…"

"There's nothing *civil* or *right* about mankind's current situation," said Colonel Bronze, cutting Adcox short.

"Right!" Adcox agreed. The aromatic smell of the rosemary scented incense burning on the desk helped to reduce his increasing heart rate.

"Lieutenant Adcox, ever since you transferred a week ago certain matters have taken away my attention and I've not had a chance to discuss a few particulars with you." The colonel placed his book to one side and picked up a digital tablet no thicker than three pieces of paper. "I've just been reviewing your service record. You were given this assignment essentially based on the recommendation of Corporal Manning. But let me ask you, at the time of the battle of Unix Caffar, what exactly were you doing?"

"Unix Caffar, errmm...I was transferred to logistics, bringing much needed supplies to the troops. It was a pretty intense war...so I heard, sir."

"So you've heard?" said the astonished colonel. "I was shot eleven times, spent two days on the floor of a cargo bay choking on my own bloo..." A coughing fit stopped his angered rant, causing all of his body to spasm on each reflex. Adcox saw that the colonel had broken out in sweat despite the cold air of the room. He first noticed a similar occurrence a few days ago.

In an attempt to steer attention away from the battle, Adcox hurried to change the subject. "Err...before that I was posted on Biosphere-9 as second in command of base security of region sixty."

"Guard detail?"

"Not exactly..."

"...but effectively?"

"Effectively, yes, sir." Adcox acquiesced.

"Lieutenant, have you ever lost anyone?" Bronze paused, his voice sunk to the lowest depths the young man ever heard. He lost himself in the moment. Adcox felt he sensed pain in the old man's words, rumors about his wife could be true.

"Yes, sir."

"I mean, anyone under your command?" asked the five foot, eight inch Bronze. He rose up from his seat to stare at the head-high shelf of documents with his back turned to Adcox.

"No, sir."

"Ever seen a man's lungs explode as he instinctively tries to inhale and hold his breath while he's blasted out of a pressurized ship under fire?

Adcox paused then responded. "No, sir."

Bronze turned and came up close to the handsome young man's face, his own contrasting. "Have you ever seen a Polymorph...up close?" he rested both hands on his desk and Adcox felt the colonel's breath on his face. The young officer had always felt awkward looking directly at the colonel because of his blood shot eyes. But it was even more difficult after he'd just brought up the Polymorph. Adcox paused in fear at the thought of what had been asked before responding.

"No, sir!"

"Aye! Of course not, if you did, you'd be looking as pretty as me." The colonel eased back. "What about combat experience?" Bronze's screwed up face was already unimpressed before receiving a response.

Adcox looked more uncomfortable now as he stuttered on his words. "Well eerrr...sir, I've completed nine months intensive combat drills in emm...camp Trinidad as part of my officers training but as of yet, I've not errr...not gotten the opportunity to...to prove myself in combat."

"We've been in a state of war for thirty-eight years laddie, you've not gotten an opportunity..."

Adcox understood why Colonel Bonze restrained himself from continuing his sentence. Being renowned as the bravest of the brave, the young man's words were unfathomable to him, like a foreign language. The lieutenant knew he had exposed what the CO had suspected all along.

"A clear pattern is emerging here," said Bronze. "Basically...you're a disgrace."

Adcox opened his mouth but struggled to find a response.

"Look, this is a special ops unit. I understand Command has a shortage of special forces operators, so you were ordered here based on my request for a junior officer, although it was for an *experienced combat* junior officer. But it's obvious you don't have the stomach for war. If I had my way, cowards like you would be castrated. I've lost a kidney, deafness in one ear, had three toes blown off and I've lost over five thousand of my men protecting people like you. Now I've put in a request to have you transferred as soon as this mission is over and we're back on Earth. I don't care how much of a manpower shortage I have. What I really would like to do is put you on a shuttle pod to Earth immediately, but right now I need all hands on deck." The colonel came close to Adcox once more. "Basically, at the next available opportunity you will be relieved. Do you have a problem with that, Lieutenant?"

"No, sir!" Adcox shook his head, his face was laded with gloom.

"I thought as much. Doubt you would have said you'd rather die. Now I won't hang you out to dry. I've already drafted a request for your next post to be a nice cosy desk job. Would this be satisfactory?" Bronze said in a condescending tone.

"Yes, sir." Adcox replied looking downwards, not feeling man enough to hold the older marine's gaze.

"I figure it would be...you're *dismissed.*"

He saluted his superior and walked toward the stateroom door. The sound of Colonel Bronze's voice halted him from leaving.

"Adcox...this mission coming up, I need everyone sharp and ready for the fight. Even you."

"Sir, yes, sir!" said Adcox as he left the quarters.

***

Five hours had passed since Adcox's meeting with the Colonel and most of Unit Forty Two had congregated in a briefing room. The room had rows of benches and a projection screen for presenting data, which happened to be military offensive strategies plotted in great detail.

Adcox sat in the room right next to another man known as Corporal Kevin Manning, the electronics expert of the team. Manning excelled beyond measure when it came to electromagnetic wave propagation theory, technology and applied sciences in the field of combat. But rarely was the corporal called anything other than Tronics, his nickname given to him by Adcox since they were teenagers.

"You still hauling around that piece of junk?" Adcox asked Tronics, referring to the unconventional weapon the twenty-nine year old black male's attention fixated on as he conducted repairs. The hi-tech gun had a long, slim shape, and was mostly silver except for parts of the butt and magazine, which were transparent and allowed red flashes of electricity to be visible inside. On the front protruded two metal prongs. Tronics had dismantled the weapon's middle compartment, exposing multiple wires connected to a small circuit board. He used an electronic probing apparatus of his own construction to conduct the repairs.

"I've adjusted the refractive index, allowing my particle accelerator laser to have a more focused beam. Thus creating a longer range intensity," said Tronics, scratching at the black bandana he wore on his head. His estuary English dialect was surprising thick at times, often dropping the "t's and "g's in his phrases.

"That's perfect," said another man in the room. "Just what I needed to barbeque my burgers." He had a plastic eye socket containing a blue artificial pupil and his tight-fitting black t-shirt revealed a cybernetic right arm. Sergeant "Ballistic" Hasselberg was one of the oldest on the team at the age of forty four. Although hardened through the trials of war, he still had a light hearted nature compared with his fellow aged warriors who had become drained of joy and humor. Similar to Tronics, no one referred to the sergeant by anything other than his alias, Ballistic, which was a mismatch to his off-combat humorous demeanor. It all changed once he entered the theatre of war; they often wondered if he enjoyed fighting a little too much.

"Hey Sergeant," Adcox called out to the big man, "I heard you've had your arm blown off a few times?" Since he transferred to Unit Forty Two a week ago, he'd been waiting to ask him about his implants.

"Five times, LT. It's my lucky bowling arm," said Ballistic, smiling. His thickly bearded face revealed an upper row of metal teeth.

Tronics smiled. "You should get them to attach my laser to your forearm next time they put humpty dumpty back together again." Having fought alongside Ballistic for a few years, he understood the sergeant's cool tempered manner that existed out of the combat zone and knew he stood a better chance of getting away with jokes on the colonel himself than Ballistic when he became battle crazed.

On a separate row of black benches were two other marines. The one sitting down peacefully was Flying Officer Hitomi Zomo, the youngest team member at the tender age of seventeen. Zomo hailed from Lunar Japan, a subcontinent of Lunar 1. Earth's moon had been completely terraformed and colonized. Adcox had already been informed that despite her youth, little escaped her in the realms of fighter vessels and ground vehicles. Humanity required children of these troubles times to learn advanced capabilities early on in their development. Her generation had grown up knowing only war.

Next to her, Private Oluseun Akerele used two rows of benches to do a dips workout. The tribal scarred Akerele was a native of Earth, although he'd lived on the human extragalactic planet Gaia Major for most of his life.

Ballistic smiled at Tronics' piss-take using only the right side of his face and continued where he left off, retelling stories of his injuries. "Got gangrene in my legs from trench foot fighting in the swamps of Anubia. Had to amputate them."

"No more ballet classes," said Zomo. Her tiny size looked even smaller next to the man she teased.

Ballistic ignored her and continued. "My eye, that was from being too close to their imperial knight's favorite, a Horaxian vault grenade. Hell, I couldn't see much out of it before anyway," said the bald Caucasian male as his round jaw unfit for modelling chewed on a ration pack that looked frozen solid. Adcox wondered why he had heard the stories about his arm, feet and eye before, but never anything about his metal teeth.

"When's the colonel going to show up so we can get this briefing over with?" said Zomo.

"I've had enough meetings for one day," Adcox responded.

Ballistic chuckled to himself. "I heard the boss really chewed you out. I told him to lay off you, some men just have a lot of estrogen in their system. It's not your fault," as he mocked the young officer, the others joined in laughter.

"Yeah, look at Zomo," said Private Akerele.

"Piss off!" she replied.

"Don't take it personally, Adcox," said Akerele. "They say the old man's inability to smile is a neurological condition called Moebius syndrome. Others say surgery after an explosion paralyzed his facial muscles."

The younger generation were fortunate, they could still smile and laugh in these dire times because war was all they knew. Colonel Bronze was one of the few old enough to have witnessed peace and prosperity. One no longer smiled once they've had such priceless gifts taken from them, along with all they held dear, and left haunted by what had been lost.

Adcox finally identified the emblem on the cap which Private Akerele wore. It was a vintage Arsenal souvenir from the ancient football team of Earth's more peaceful past. Neither the tallest nor the heftiest man in the room, still the twenty-year-old private's bare chested presence revealed his ripped upper torso.

Akerele finally completed his exercise. "I'm just hoping the colonel will tell us what we're doing out in Horaxian space. I hate being anywhere near these guys."

Zomo, donning a military short cut, turned to address Akerele. "I'd rather be out here than on Earth or any other world. All kinds of diseases are breaking out on Lunar 1. Kepla-Terra hasn't received any water shipments from Earth in months."

"Forget Kepla-Terra," said Tronics. "My wife says the UK's turning into a giant Gaia-Major refugee camp."

As his last words were spoken, the briefing room doors slid open and in stepped Captain Lewalski. The colonel and Lewalski had served together for over thirty years and the group knew that wherever the captain stood Bronze was never far behind.

"Attention females, officer on deck!" he ordered, standing near the door at attention himself. The rest of the team instantly rose to a salute.

As quick as they did so, the menacing figure of Colonel Bronze walked in. He remained in front of the doorway with a strong air of authority.

"At ease, men!" commanded the Colonel. They all sat back down, giving him their full attention. "Put that junk away, Corporal," Bronze said to Tronics, seeing him reach for his technological contraption. The aged soldier often had to discipline his electronics expert but the corporal's indispensable expertise frequently saved the team in combat. Tronics complied with swift obedience, inducing Adcox to slyly smirk at Bronze's mirroring remark.

"All right, listen up," said Bronze. "A lot of negotiations with the Horaxian Divine Council took place in order for this mission to be approved."

Akerele raised his artificial right hand. "Sir?"

"Go ahead, Private."

"Could you tell us what exactly we're doing here in Horaxian space?"

"We are on route to Kemeta."

"I knew it!" Zomo whispered in Akerele's ear.

Colonel Bronze continued. "We have been assigned to make contact with someone who may prove vital to both mankind and the Horaxians. Now I cannot at this point reveal certain particulars of the mission as this is all highly classified. But I feel it necessary for the safety of this unit, that I break protocol and reveal his identity. The man we are going to the planet to retrieve is former Nephilim Squadron Officer Commander, Major Keegan Hawke."

The team's reaction suspended the Colonel's speech; a fusion of gasp, sighs and confounded expressions. Some were in awe, some in complete shock. Adcox's brow knotted with intrigue and excitement while Tronics' had a smile of great eagerness. But the younger team members Akerele and Zomo looked bewildered.

The executive officer, Lewalski, turned and squinted his eyes at his superior. "I thought Major Hawke was dead, colonel?"

"Sorry sir, but who is this man?" Zomo asked. "The name sounds familiar."

Bronze's facial features couldn't hide his disappointment in her inexperience. The colonel took a deep breath and spoke. "When we were at war with the Horaxians, we were not always winning, as propaganda may have led you to believe." He rested his rear end on a desk. "They outnumbered us. Their capacity to learn quickly rendered our superior technology ineffective. They were more... *dedicated* to victory."

Captain Lewalski interjected. "When you kill a soldier's entire family if he deserts his post, as they do, it *would* create a more disciplined army."

A brutal imperial regime fueled the engine of the Horaxian war machine. Summary executions and severe punishment had forged a previously unconquerable army. Colonel Bronze nodded his head in agreement with Lewalski's words and continued on. "Most of the twenty-three years of war was a stalemate. Eventually, when resources dwindled, we were on the back foot of the battle of attrition. As with many dire times in the history of warfare, we turned to science. A special ops unit was commissioned, commanded by Major Hawke. They were called...the Black Guard."

"Black Guard!" Uttered Zomo, her jaw locked open, finally understanding the gravity of the situation.

Bronze continued. "Everything involving the Black Guard was kept top secret. I can tell you for certain that they were not normal men. The most logical explanation was that they were either augmented, genetically engineered clones, or cyborg killing machines. Some claimed they were neither, that the Black Guard was something else entirely. But that was all purely speculation. It's widely believed they single handily turned the tides of the Horaxian war for us. Now, if you were lucky they were surgical..."

"And if you were...unlucky, sir?" asked Akerele.

"They killed everything that moved...everything."

Captain Lewalski grimaced as he spoke. "They were known as the Sword in the Dark. Some tough SOBs, I tell you that. Zero survival rate missions and they came out without a scratch. Have you ever seen the aftermath of a Black Guard assault? It was worse than a midsummer's medieval Mongolian massacre."

The colonel coughed before continuing his speech. "Eventually, even Earth Command became uncomfortable with their manner of warfare, as they were somewhat of a double edged sword. Then, one day, they vanished without a trace. Records state that fifteen years ago a distress beacon was intercepted, by an ark vessel named *Ploiarion*. They had found an unknown alien object and inside that object was Major Hawke. His Black Guard comrades were MIA, whereabouts still unknown. Then, for reasons also inapprehensible, the Black Guard commander took control of the ark and flew it straight into the atmospheric processor of the Horaxian remote lunar colony on Matelot-6. The crash created a chain reaction which decimated the entire moon. Killing all one billion inhabitants, including the nine hundred and thirteen human ark ship personnel. Only one person survived..."

"The Hawke!" Captain Lewalski answered.

"That's impossible!" Akerele uttered.

"Those Black Guard Nephilims were straight-out monsters," said Ballistic, as he pulled out a device similar to a drill chuck key and inserted it into a small chuck lock hole in his cybernetic arm. He then turned it clockwise to tighten his mechanics. His opinion of the Black Guard shocked Adcox, coming from a man that enjoyed warfare as much as he did.

"Aye!" said Colonel Bronze. "He was eventually found months later, drifting in space within the same alien object, and was promptly court-marshaled, dishonorably discharged and imprisoned. Hawke's Black Guard unit was shut down. And that, ladies and gentlemen, was the year the Polymorph appeared."

The colonel paused on his last words. His face soured, as it would if he had bitten into a piece of rotting meat. "With the Polymorph proving too formidable for mankind and the Horaxians, both signed a peace treaty. There was, however, one condition for peace. Major Hawke was to be handed over to the Horaxians. He was paraded through the streets, tried as a war criminal for genocide and presumed executed...until now."

"We sold him out!" stated Adcox.

The colonel's wrinkled forehead creased up when he heard his lieutenant's choice of words. Before having chance to retort, Ballistic spoke out.

"Presumed executed? So if he's alive, Colonel, then where the hell's he been for the past fifteen years?"

Colonel Bronze paused. "The Abyss!"

The marines all spoke at once in disbelief, like a choir without harmony. Akerele and Zomo stood up as if to walk out of the room. Adcox turned white, Tronics began biting his bottom lip and even Ballistic, the craziest of them all, leaned back in his chair, taking a moment to digest Bronze's words.

"He's better off dead," said Akerele.

"Sir, I can't go in there," said Zomo.

Adcox never got the impression that Zomo was the type to refuse an order from the colonel, at least not in public. He also noticed she used the word "can't."

"Boss man," Tronics called, "that place is a tomb. We can't seriously be going in there?"

"Sit down!" ordered Bronze. Akerele and Zomo fell in line. "We don't know if he's even alive as nobody has ever returned from the Abyss. But our orders are to go in, find Major Hawke and bring him out. Now not all of you are old enough to have seen what a Black Guard is capable of. So I warn you, even though Hawke's been rotting away for fifteen years I need everyone to stay sharp, don't even blink around this man. He is an infiltration and escape expert, an assassination specialist, master tactician, the ultimate warrior and if he's still breathing, he's the most dangerous man alive."

"Sir!" said Adcox raising his hand.

"What is it Adcox?" asked Bronze, annoyed just by the junior officer's voice.

"What do we do with him once we have him? I mean, I know you said it was classified…"

"Yes Lieutenant, that's what I said. All I can divulge is that the powers that be are deeply concerned about his connection to the mystery alien object he was discovered in, and that the fate of two worlds could depend on this man."

Tronics and Adcox shared a glance of fascination. Bronze stepped towards the center of the room and continued.

"Now, although the Horaxians have signed off on the mission, they don't trust us and they're sending their own team which will rendezvous with us within the next three hours."

The colonel's words were met with a fusion of negative remarks as the marines waived their arms in annoyed gestures. Tronics kissed his teeth in disapproval. Adcox knew from past conversations with Tronics that Ballistic will be the most outraged.

The sergeant shot up off his seat. "I don't want any of those stinking Horaxians on my six, for them to gun me down and say it was an accident."

"Killer B's right, boss," said Tronics. "Humans and Horaxians have never co-oped for a good reason. They don't like us, we don't like them, and somebody always ends up getting killed."

"Stow it, marines!" said Colonel Bronze.

"Sir, this is a raw deal," Private Akerele added his piece. "And what about wages? Are we getting paid extra for this?"

Ballistic hadn't finish expressing his displeasure. "I'd trust a Horaxian about as far as I can throw one with a fractured hydraulic wrist, a broken cybernetic arm and dislocated pneumatic shoulder."

"I said stow it, stop your whining!" the colonel nearly reached the top of his lungs before his men finally quieted down. "I don't want to have another friendly fire incident with you, sergeant. I had to save your metal arse from the stockade the last time. General Baizan has given specific instructions. Anybody that disobeys orders or jeopardizes this mission will be court-marshaled most promptly. You'd be better off dead than if he gets his hands on you. Are you feeling me?"

"Sir, yes, sir!" they confirmed in a chorus.

"Before the Horaxian team arrives I want everyone suited up and armed. Akerele, prep the cargo bay. Zomo, once you're in gear I want you to remain on the bridge. You're dismissed!"

Upon Bronze's last words, Captain Lewalski hustled the team into action. "You maggots still here? Hop, skip and jump, stop, drop and roll let's go ladies, and don't be flattered Zomo. A Horaxian trooper has more female in him than you. Get your rear to the bridge."

Those that didn't before started moving with a purpose.

"Lieutenant, Corporal," said Colonel Bronze, calling Adcox and Tronics by rank.

"Yo!" replied Tronics. He quickly corrected himself before it was too late. "I mean yes, sir."

"Don't play around with me boy. Both of you get your arses to the armory, comms me when you're there."

All the marines cleared the room, leaving Bronze and Lewalski alone. The two senior officers took the opportunity to speak freely.

"Jesus, Mike," Bronze said to his old friend. "It's like all the good soldiers bloody died off in the Horaxian wars. All that's left now are pensioners like you, and bedwetters like Adcox. The kid's moist."

"Go easy on him, Bronzy. He's a good kid, he was just born in the wrong century. A Greek tragedy; Homer would have wrote stories about him. But I doubt he'll make it back from the Abyss anyway, and even if we do, by the way things are going we'll all be dead within a year."

"How many wars we've been in Mike?" asked Bronze without glancing in his captain's direction.

"Last time I checked...we've been in all of them. Last time I checked."

"Well, we can't win this one. We need soldiers to win wars. I don't know about you, but a squadron of Black Guard would come in handy right about now."

"I'm feeling you," said Lewalski.

Chapter Three - Unification Problem

Weapons lined the walls of the dim, yellowish armory. Most were variances of assault rifles racked on metal rails, but there were also sidearms, shotguns, machine gun pistols and large grenade launchers. On the left wall hung the ammunition boxes, bullet belts and an assortment of other military accessories. Adcox and Tronics sat carrying out the tedious task of creating a check list of the weapons and securing them.

"Brother, is all this really necessary?" Tronics commented as he picked up an assault rifle.

"Decommissioning the weapons?"

"Yeah, I mean, I know the old man doesn't want to take any chances with the Black Guard, but I could have just locked the armory down."

"Electronically yeah perhaps, but he'll still get in. The Black Guard commander's an infiltration specialist." Adcox grabbed the weapon Tronics had just finished decommissioning and placed it on the rack. "Remember your pops used to tell us stories about them? That they were incredible, each one was like over seven feet tall, fearless and super strong. He used to always repeat Churchill's words, that never in the field of human conflict was so much owed by so many to so few." Adcox's more common Southeast English accent now became apparent. It rarely came out aside from when he spoke to his long-time friend.

"I remember," replied Tronics, "they were like superheroes to us. Problem was, as much as they were strong, they were unstable. I swear they killed a lot of people, many they weren't supposed to."

"I wonder where's the rest of them?"

"Huh?" said Tronics.

"Bronze said the rest of the Black Guard were MIA. I wonder what happened to them?"

"Who knows, all I know is this guy is supposed to be deadly with just his bare hands, so I see why the colonel doesn't want him to get hold of any weapons," Tronics said. His thoughts shifted. "Hey, what did the colonel call you in for? Did the old man ask you to marry his daughter?" He grinned.

Adcox sighed. "No, more like I'm a gutless coward that doesn't deserve to wear a uniform, and he's right. Bloody hell! Kev why did you recommend me? You've known me since twelve, I'm not a fighter. If we weren't at war, I'd be in some piss poor office pushing buttons all day and making sure the fridge has milk."

Tronics laughed. "Well, technically a gun trigger is a button."

"I'm being reassigned after the mission."

Tronics' tone lowered. "Look D, you're one of the smartest guys I know. In your own, *special* way you're even smarter than me. Once the colonel sees you in action, he'll change his mind. Trust me, rubeboy!"

"The only action he'll see is my bowels detonating a thermal nuclear explosion in my pants. Hey, is the colonel sick or something?

"Brother, everybody's sick. Amanda never lets the kids out the house, it's too dangerous. There's too much disease and food riots. I'm trying to relocate them to Lunar 1. They'll die if they stay in the UK, or anywhere else on Earth."

Adcox was moved by his friend's words and phased out for a second. "We ruined Earth. No one wants to live there anymore," he said.

On a speaker system they both heard Lewalski's husky voice. "Attention maggots, we've got Horaxians approaching our bow. All crew report to the cargo bay immediately."

Tronics spoke as they rose up on to their feet. "All right, let's hope those bowels of yours hold up."

***

Most of the team were gathered in the observation room, which was in view of the cargo bay via protective, super fabricated glass. The soldiers were suited up in their grey-camouflaged combat suits minus their helmets. All except Tronics were armed with standard issue solar 506 assault rifles with underslung forty-eight millimeter explosive shell launchers. Bronze and Lewalski's armored bodysuits were worse for wear, faded in color with rusting at the creases. Indentations from weapons fire and patched metal sections indicated some quick-fix welding repair work. The sight of it was an astonishment to Adcox, since the metal in their suits were imbedded with nanites that repaired most damages. Obviously the smart metal could get overworked.

At the other side of the glass, Adcox and Ballistic waited inside of the cargo bay. Both had their helmets on as their suits were pressurized to protect them from the decompressed hangar bay conditions.

Tronics, who sat at the observation room's computer console, maintained his gaze on radar signatures on the screen. "Five Horaxian personnel shuttle pods incoming. One kilometer and closing in fast."

Adcox picked up Tronics' every word, despite the thick glass separating the men, courtesy of the team's communication interlink inbuilt into their armored suits.

"Open the cargo doors," ordered Captain Lewalski.

"Acknowledged, Captain!" said Akerele and complied.

The cargo bay doors slid open with a deep, bassful hum, and Adcox and Ballistic watched the five objects getting closer from the backdrop of space.

"Why are they using pods?" wondered Adcox. "You would have thought they would have wanted us to board their ship?"

"I don't care!" replied Ballistic. "I'm going to brace you, LT. One wrong move and I'm going to light these scumbags up like a solar flare."

Adcox had yet to be in a combat situation with the sergeant, but he believed that he was witnessing Ballistic's light hearted nature diminishing and the emergence of his infamous alter ego.

Bronze spoke out on their comms link. "Only attack on my orders, Sergeant."

"Five by five, sir." Ballistic said. Adcox looked at the sergeant, unconvinced of his obedience despite the man's respect for his commanding officer. Especially when he sighted the words 'die slow Horaxians' written on the front of his suit.

Something on Tronics' handheld electronic device held his attention. The Personal Digital Analysis slab, silver in color and flat, was equipped with a variety of sensors and it had detected something out of the ordinary. "Boss man, I've hack...I mean, I've connected up to the ship's antenna relay and conducted a spectral analysis. There's an unusually high level of interstellar transmissions emanating from Kemeta, and long range sensors have detected two Horaxian warships heading our way from Horax Prime."

"Two warships?" said Akerele with concern.

"If they've mobilized their fleet, it can only mean trouble," said Lewalski as he leaned in to check Tronics' analysis. But he was incapable of making sense of the sinusoidal waveforms on the device's screen.

"Stay on it, Corporal," Bronze commanded.

"Here they come," said Akerele.

As the five shuttle pods neared the ship, Adcox and Ballistic raised their weapons. They distinguished the grey and red hull of the pods being propelled by antimatter thrusters, exhausting gases from their rear. The pods, which were spherical in shape but with a flat base, drifted inside the docking bay at a constant speed and as they entered their reverse thrusters cut off. Symmetrically they fell to the ground.

"Recompress the bay," ordered Bronze.

"Sir, recompression has commenced," said Akerele.

A few moments of silence passed and made Adcox's stomach churn. There was always something about being in the presence of someone smarter than him that made him uncomfortable. He could deal with greater knowledge or experience but the Horaxians were different. They could understand and speak human language with ease while humans required neural implant translators that did a poor job. Their technology was inferior to mans when first contact was made, but now it greatly surpassed their own. Mankind had to concede that in some ways it was biologically outmatched.

He watched as the doors of all five pods opened in synch and shrouded in a light mist five humanoid creatures climbed out. Anthropomorphically, they were similar to Homo Sapiens in height, weight, kinesics and kinesiology but to Lieutenant Adcox their skin had a majestic blackness. Unlike the sub-Saharan people of Africa, who may vary with shades of brown, this black was different: rich, absolute, and totally void of any color. Their hair was also different, a bright white, similar to aged human hair that has lost its pigmentation.

Three of the Horaxians wore dark blue armor and sported a short head of hair. Faint red tribal markings spiraled throughout their faces. Their hair ran in a line down their necks snaking into their armored suits.

Out of the five, two were distinctively different; one of the two had the physiology of a female human and wore a silver body suit. Her long white hair was tied in one thick braid which extended down to the back of her knee. With exact precision, every ten centimeters, gold metal bands with decorative patterns were wrapped around her single braid. The other alien present stood out due to his hefty red and black armor which had unique ornamental sculptings protruding out. The shoulder area had extra thick decorative plating with two metal chains in the middle that held the crimson colored left and right shoulder plating together. The big male's massive red helmet covered the face entirely, making him even taller, taller than the average man and all other Horaxians present.

As soon as the aliens stepped out of their pods, they pointed their right arms up towards Adcox and Ballistic. All accept one, the female. Attached to their right forearms were sizable metallic gauntlets. On top of the gauntlet rested two gun barrels separated by eight centimeter spacing and blue targeting lasers were positioned in-between the barrels. The lasers projected narrow beams of light upon the heads of the two men, and a high pitched ring indicated all their weapons were armed.

Adcox was startled, but Ballistic simply looked annoyed. "Get those beams out of my face," shouted the half metal man.

"Horaxians, this is commanding officer Colonel Bronze of the United Earth vessel *Odysseus*. I'm ordering you to drop your weapons and stand down." Bronze's demand rang out on the speakers of the hangar bay.

Captain Lewalski stared at the Horaxian male who towered far above the rest due to his disproportionally large head guard. "They brought an elite-shakan. Not good."

No mere Horaxian could become an elite-shakan, the Horaxian Imperial guard. Only the strongest males of chosen blood from planet Anubia could receive the honor. Once bestowed, their lives must be devoted only to serve the empire. They gave up their fortunes, family and possessions. Anubianite warriors were most revered for their fighting ability; no soldier, human nor Horaxian, would voluntarily choose to go up against one.

The big Horaxian stepped toward the two marines in the cargo bay with his arm weapon aimed high. "Souwrak! Orders you dare bark to us?"

The other Horaxians, looking equally angered, also moved closer, but with less confidence. The female however, remained calm, despite being the only member of the alien group without a weapon.

Bronze was forced to repeat his orders. "Hold your positions and lower your weapons immediately. Stand down!"

"You stand down!" Another Horaxian yelled. Now closer, Adcox saw that his skin and hair had a hint of blue, a feature of the Horaxian aging process.

"I'm going to drop this guy any minute, Colonel," Ballistic said, aiming at the approaching large male.

"You are on my ship. Lower your weapons. This is your final warning," Colonel Bronze shouted.

Adcox glanced behind and noted that his team all had their solar rifles in hand and ready to storm the cargo hold. He estimated that the mutual aggression would have escalated into an inevitable firefight, as with numerous previous accounts of Human-Horaxian contact. In a brief pause in the tension, he made a dangerous decision. First, he lowered his rifle, he then pressed the button that unlocked his helmet. His helmet motors retracted the top-head protective plating and transparent face guard with a low pitched churn, exposing his face.

"Easy, Sergeant. Please, put it down," said Adcox.

"I don't think so, pal," said Ballistic, his eyes hooked on the helmet of the approaching elite-shakan.

"Trust me, please, put it down." Adcox placed his hand on Ballistic's rifle.

"Tronics, what the hell is your friend doing?" uttered Captain Lewalski.

Colonel Bronze shook his head like a disappointed father. Ballistic showed reluctance and resisted the downward force of Adcox's hand on his solar rifle, but eventually he complied. The Anubianite Horaxian, who's broader frame surpassed the big man's, displayed no gratitude to the humans' show of respect and kept his weapon arm raised. "So, it is death you desire, then allow Jei'Gun to..."

"No Jei'Gun, we come in peace," said the female Horaxian. Her words were enough to stop the male from his intentions.

The elder Horaxian spun toward the female. His face twisted up in disgust. He then turned and stared at Adcox with a grim intensity. Adcox fixated momentarily on his nose, which had two hardened ridges running vertically along its length like all Horaxian males.

With his pause of contemplation, the elder raised his open palm above his head. "Pack...at ease."

They all lowered their hand cannons. Jei'Gun, the elite-shakan warrior, the last to do so.

"Well, that went well," Tronics remarked to the rest of the team within the observation room.

"Shut up!" said Lewalski.

"Aye aye, Capo!"

The elder male stepped closer to the marines and looked up at the colonel, snorting his broad Horaxian nose. "I am Atomu. Birthed on the Prodigious Cunga Sigma. The Wise Axe That Cuts Deepest, I am...Alpha. By Horaxian law, this vessel must be inspected before allowed entry into Kemetan atmosphere. Defy law unopposable and approach, and you will be destroyed."

"You may inspect our ship, Alpha," said the Colonel.

"Let us proceed Bronze, Colonel. Little time we have."

***

The Horaxian society followed a highly class based structure. With an elitist monarchical rule, they had amassed an empire of star systems stretching outwards from within the Hora galaxy cluster. A king ruled each world and the empire itself was governed by the Great Supreme King. They once established thousands of stellar military bases in a perimeter surrounding their galaxy clusters, roughly two thousand four hundred and sixty bases before the wars. Now only a few remained.

Horaxians themselves were not so militantly extreme until a movement led by the High Apex, Commander Cagn, started gaining power with his radical ideals. Through his leadership, the empire quickly rivalled the technological advancement of humanity and with their larger population, they began to win the war against mankind.

Throughout time, the planet *Odysseus* approached was one of great importance for their stellar kingdom. Kemeta was once a frozen world. Due to the difficulties of terraforming—the immense power, resources and inherent costs required to make it habitable—it would have been left icy and barren. But its vast quantities of antimatter, held in natural form by its unique magnetic field, compelled the Horaxians to create a mining colony. Upon the discovery, the then Great Supreme King sanctioned it to be transformed officially into the fifth world of the empire.

As they neared Kemeta's orbit, both Horaxian and human teams stood opposing each other within the *Odysseus'* briefing room, separated only by the middle desks. You could cut the tension with an axe as both sides surveyed one another. Adcox noticed that the blue targeting beam of the elite-shakan's arm-cannon still remained active, ready in a moment to fire. As the alpha of the alien team, Atomu addressed the marines oozing with confidence as he stepped in front of the wide strategy touch screen.

"Scarce are Horaxian ships currently within sector. That is why we must use your ship for journey tasked. Let me present my warriors: Nanonramu," Atomu pointed to the only Horaxian with two black antennae protruding from his forehead, a physical feature unique to Rogue Basarwans. Living for generations in a subterranean society had robbed them of good vision and reduced the size and ability of their noses and eyes. The antennae functioned as their primary sensory organ collecting particles in the air and also, they generated sonic images of their surroundings via echolocation. It also enabled them to detect scent.

Atomu continued. "Birthed on the Astonishing Rogue Basarwa, the Blade of Death. Kaya Maghan." He pointed at another, "Birthed on the Illustrious Horax Prime—the Dark Star, a ruthless killer. Makes me proud." Atomu grinned in admiration for his warriors.

"We may have to write these names down, sir," Tronics suggested to the colonel under his breath.

"Watch it, Corporal!" Colonel Bronze said, his index finger pointed at the tall marine's face. Bronze turned back to the Horaxian leader. "Please continue, Alpha."

Luckily the Horaxians failed to identify Tronics' comment for the sly insult it was.

"My sub-alpha, Jei'Gun, a Horaxian elite-shakan name renowned. We are honored to have him upon mission. He is our combat specialist. Birthed on Unyielding Anubia, Power Made Flesh, bravest of soldiers. However, he will not disarm his weapon in human presence."

This was the first time Lieutenant Adcox had ever seen an Anubianite but he had heard all the stories of their fighting skills and genetic strength. Each warrior's muscle pre-training rivalled a professional powerlifter and further enhanced by bionic armor. Jei'Gun's presence made his stomach churn. Unlike the others he still wore his helmet which completely covered his face. It nearly touched the room's ceiling.

"The female," said Alpha Atomu. "She is not a member of my pack. She is just medic."

The female edged forward with eagerness. "I am Doctor Hatshepsut, I am a biologist and exobiologist in advance genetics research including human anatom…"

"She is a mere scientist impudent that speaks out of turn," Atomu said, irritated by her outburst. "But little I can do since she is citizen, a Caroo of all, unbound by military command, and medic was requested to ensure health of…the one." A deep frown cut into Atomu's face at the thought of Caroos. They were the noble lords of Horaxian society. The empire's rulers all descended from this royal bloodline. The majority of the Caroo resided in aristocratic regions of Horax Prime in relative luxury. Born on Cunga Sigma, Atomu's path was one far from splendor. His fortitude in the field of combat elevated him to the military echelons most of common birth never received. His tribulations gave him an innate hatred for those who possessed status without it being properly earned.

"The one...you mean Major Hawke?" asked Zomo confused by Atomu's reference.

"Do not speak its name!" Nanonramu shouted shaking with rage. Jei'Gun growled also in response. Every Horaxian in the room's body moved in a knee-jerk reaction to Zomo's comment. On Nanonramu's world, the Black Guard commander and his squadron of Nephilim were as mythological as vampires and werewolves to man. His antennae became erect from its lowered position and stiffened at the sound of the Black Guard's name.

"Souwrak!" Kaya Maghan uttered in outrage, all humans were well familiar with this common insult to their race.

"To us," said Atomu. "It is known as 'the cursed one,' of all humans the most hated. There was but a time where the mere mention of that unsanctified name could spawn your demotion or worse. I, Atomu, have lost an entire mega pack of five hundred to merely one of your demon Black Guard. Impossible it is, to kill an enemy you cannot see."

"Well, one race's butcher is another's hero," said Ballistic.

Jei'Gun released another scornful growl aimed at Ballistic and the man smirked with satisfaction.

The female, Hatshepsut, drew Adcox's attention and he observed something he had never noticed before in the brighter light of the cargo bay. It seemed outlandish, he thought his eyes were playing tricks on him...because she was glowing. He placed it down to his mystification of the doctor since he had rarely ever seen Horaxian females. Their imperial army was composed overwhelmingly of males and his inexperience combined with a life away from combat had meant that he had seen few Horaxian males in real life either.

"All right, quick roll call," Colonel Bronze felt obliged to introduce his men in return and ease the tension.

"This is Captain Lewalski my executive officer. Flying Officer Zomo, vessel specialist. That there is Corporal Manning, our technology expert known as Tronics."

"Birthed in Hackney, London." Tronics said comically but with a straight face.

"Shut up!" Lewalski ordered, arms folded. The claw marks that ran the length of his face aided and abetted the team's default opinion of his foul mood. With the captain's tendency of using his fist as an instrument of discipline, Tronics knew now his leeway for joking was over.

"Aye aye, Capo!" the corporal said with a genuine serious face.

The Colonel continued pointing at each of his team as he reeled their names out. "Sergeant Hasselberg AKA Ballistic, weapons expert. Private Akerele, Demolitions."

"And what of...him?" Alpha Atomu said as he stretched his hand out towards Adcox.

"The scared pup," said Jei'Gun sniggering.

"Alpha speaks!" Barked Atomu to Jei'Gun.

"Lieutenant Adcox," the colonel informed.

Atomu could not believe his poor eyesight, so he trod closer to Adcox to get a better look at him. He inspected the young man from the top of his pristine, low level haircut, down to the immaculate condition of his suit of armor. The sight made the aged warrior's jaws part. Not a single scratch was on it. "The boy is of age, yet his face without scars. Unblemished, as pretty as a juvenile Cungan girl."

Kaya Maghan and Nanonramu laughed, prompting Ballistic to respond. "I'm glad you find that so funny. What ain't funny is us tracking your warships heading our way! What the hell is going on?" Ballistic fixed his gaze directly into Alpha Atomu's eyes.

"At ease, Sergeant!" said Bronze.

Ballistic had hoped to offend the Alpha, but Atomu's face altered in a different way. "...deep space scouts have confirmed, Horde swarm heads towards Beloved Kemeta."

Concern stifled all life in the room and their faces absorbed their anxiety. Adcox took a deep breath and exhaled, then noticed Akerele rubbing the back of his neck as his lips tightened. He then saw how Lewalski instinctively gripped his rifle as if to launch an attack. The Horde, or simply "Horde," was what the Horaxians called the Polymorph, and its more simplistic reference caught on with most of mankind.

"Holy crap!" said Zomo.

Adcox translated her outburst to mean, "Let's get the hell out of here."

"Unlikely it is," said Atomu, his tone subdued, "planetary forces can withstand attack, Beloved Kemeta will be destroyed."

"How long?" asked Lewalski.

"Perhaps eight hours. Perhaps less," Nanonramu said.

"Sir, recommend we abandon the mission," Akerele requested.

Tronics agreed. "Colonel, we don't want to be chilling here when the Horde comes."

"Cowards!" snapped Jei'Gun.

"I've got my orders, and you have yours," said Colonel Bronze to his men.

"Mr. Bronze," Hatshepsut called out in her tranquilizing voice. "The Abyss is a Labyrinth hazardous, extending miles underground. To locate and track down subject is a task perilous and problematic. Developed I have, a device experimental in attempt to detect the DNA of Horde but I have reconfigured it to detect Horaxian and Homo sapien DNA. When activated, it disperses nanospores into atmosphere, which is then absorbed into the body tissue and blood stream allowing us to relay analysis of chromosomes in any life form encountered. Horaxians have six more chromosomes than humans."

"I'm sure there have been tens of thousands of humans sentenced to the Abyss," Zomo said. "How do we find errr...the major?"

"We have record of his DNA at time of his bestowment to our authorities," Hatshepsut said. "It is stored within device and we will be alerted once match found."

Since word broke of the Horde's approach, Ballistic had begun to pace around the room trying to keep control of his elevating foul mood. Without realizing, he ventured too close to the Horaxians. Kaya Maghan and Nanonramu rapidly covered their faces and stepped back.

"Filthy smelling human," Nanonramu said. "Mind your distance when I am not in full armor. Your germ microorganisms are deadly." Nanonramu felt the worst of the sensual barrage as his antennae were highly sensitive to smell.

"You think that's bad, then you should smell your breath," said Ballistic.

Atomu also had a look of repulsion on his face as he surveyed the humans. "We find collaborating with Homo sapiens a displeasure most grievous. It will mark my reputation strenuously earned. Scorned we shall be by our people. Let us not make this ordeal any more difficult than already defined."

"Sir, one question," Adcox addressed the colonel. "How do we even know if the major's still alive?"

"For the sake of all our worlds, we better pray to God he is. It's as simple as this, we don't find the Black Guard commander...we lose the war."

***

As a planet, Kemeta possessed many prerequisites for terraforming, including sufficient mass, gravity and water in frozen form. All it needed was atmosphere generation, planetary heating and atmospheric pressure. The world generators, the Horaxian's atmospheric processors, were built on Cunga Sigma and hauled in sections to Kemeta. These enormous facilities represented the pinnacle of an advance civilization, alongside superluminal travel. But they were incapable of completing this complex job on their own. Planetary engineers worked feverishly in hazardous conditions to break the surface ice into its component hydrogen and oxygen, then they created a sink for the hydrogen. This aided the generators in the formation of Kemeta's atmospheric pressure. Afterwards, as part of the ecopoiesis stage of the process, billions of microorganisms were released into the atmosphere well before the heating process was complete, since they were capable of surviving the icy conditions.

Kemeta was on course to one day be almost as green and rich in life as Earth, or at least before mankind ruined its natural beauty near the end of the twenty-first century. All of this promise and optimism existed until the Horde arrived.

The *Odysseus* advanced into the orbit of Kemeta and approached its artificially created atmosphere. Like most human vessels of these depressing times, its condition was far from pristine. It was covered with patched metal sections throughout its hull due to makeshift, rushed repairs. The vessel, with its aerodynamic design like a jet airplane, raced toward Kemeta's thermosphere with its tint of green. This peculiar hue was in fact a planet-wide aurora caused by its super powered geomagnetic field. The power harvested on this world totaled more than all the imperial worlds combined. It served this power to the other planets by hauling it in large astrotankers with accompanying convoys.

Both teams were now in the ship's second cargo bay, strapped in along the bay's sides at their chests in a standing position. Only two people were missing, Flying Officer Zomo and Tronics, who were on the bridge of the ship. Adcox as always analyzed the environment of the bay. He watched as Ballistic applied his black face paint while staring down Jei'Gun, with Jei'Gun staring back, both in complete silence. Kaya Maghan's attention drew to Lewalski's hideous scars. Adcox knew the Horaxian wondered if they were Horde inflicted.

From within the hangar bay, Tronics' voice came through crisp and loud on the human team's personal comms system.

"Yo, peeps, picking up an electrical storm system at our destination coordinates. Estimated at category five, approximately three thousand kilometers in diameter with some bad-arse winds. Please advise, over."

"We've got a hurricane situation," Bronze said aloud to the Horaxians. He held on tightly to the guard rails and body support systems keeping them all in place.

"It is the eternal Oloiboni winds," Hatshepsut said. "The year-round anticyclonic storm. It will not subside."

"Roger that!" said Bronze. "Zomo, punch us through, out."

On the bridge, Tronics pressed a few buttons on the overhead dashboard while Flying Officer Zomo steered the ship via the control yoke, keeping an eye on the color-weather radar display. Zomo and Tronics were seated in a separate section from the rest of the bridges' seats in the cockpit area. Here, resided the main instrument panel with eight identical interactive displays that increased pilot situational awareness. They watched the spectacle of the wide-spanning, grey-green rotating winds that swirled around a bowled-shaped dark eye.

"All right, babygirl. We're within the exosphere," said Tronics, assessing rainbow images of the storm on his radar display as the turbulence of atmospheric entry rocked the ship.

"Atmospheric-entry speeds: high-hypersonic, thirty-four Mach. Altitude: twelve hundred kilometers and descending."

"Better slow us down before we get chopped to pieces, Z."

At the lower altitude the air became dusty and grey, minimizing Zomo's visibility, but soon Tronics identified a gigantic structure towering in the distance. He nudged Zomo's shoulder. "Look starboard. A world generator."

"I never get tired of seeing them!" Her eyes opened wide in awe. "Beautiful!"

The enormous structure was both wide as it was tall, reaching high into the clouds, its zenith concealed by the thick grey-green mist.

"No world generators are manufactured any longer, so I heard," said Tronics as he used the ship's display to view a radar generated image of the structure's vast dimensions. "Their empire is in too much turmoil and anarchy now. The Horde's depleted their resources." His voice shook with the rocking of the ship.

"They've depleted ours too."

The weather worsened as they headed within the raging storm, furious winds jolting and destabilizing the ship. The young Private Akerele convulsed like he was going to throw up; Adcox spotted Nanonramu and Kaya Maghan sharing a concerned glance right after they observed Colonel Bronze.

"Steady my ship, Flying Officer!" Colonel Bronze yelled.

In the cockpit area of the bridge, Zomo could only shake her head. "The colonel doesn't appreciate the skill it takes to keep this rust-heap spaceborne." Both her hands held tightly on the throttle.

"You could lodge a complaint with Lewalski if you're that upset about it."

"Yeah right! Only Akerele's that dumb. Max the power to the ESM!" said Zomo.

"Electronic Stabilizing Mechanism now at maximum. We're still in for a rough ride though."

After much turbulence, the ship settled as it neared the surface and snaked the beautiful, yet treacherous frozen landscape of breathtaking grand mountain ranges. The *Odysseus* arrived at a canyon, far deeper than anything on Earth. On the other side, within the white, snow covered mountain was an off-white artificial structure, lodged in-between like hardened amber.

"We have arrived," said Hatshepsut, looking out of the cargo bay's transparent hull sections.

"The Jumbie Abyss of the cursed," Kaya Maghan commented in a shaken voice.

"I never thought I would be seeing this place," said Ballistic.

"Into the depths of Hades," Adcox said to himself, taking in the horrid sight and remembering the stories men had told about the Abyss for decades. It reminded him of the mythological underworld of old.

Alpha Atomu overheard the men speaking and felt the need to display his knowledge. "The Abyss was once shelter built hundreds of years past to protect the great people of Beloved Kemeta from an evil prophesied. One we now believed to be Homo sapiens. It is miles of underground chambers reinforced in metal and stone, by design an impregnable fortress. Then, in freak accident, one of the weapons stockpiled inside, a neutron bomb, was detonated from the inside. No one knows how it happened. But though the deed was prior to human contact most believe it was man's doing, as they did on lost paradise Adored Okavanga."

"Now you listen real good, hotshot," said Captain Lewalski. "We weren't the ones that bombed Hope. You better get that straight." The XO had fought to keep a poker face in response to the Horaxian's insults, but Atomu seemed to have struck a nerve.

"You listen, *Lewalski* Captain. My people had existed in peace for thousands of years. It was you, *humans*, who infected us with the virus, war. Yet we were defeating you despite your lengthy experience of conflict because *we* have more *conviction*. But well do I know your history. Three thousand years past on your pitiful Earth, your Hittite ancestors would sack a city, then they would sow poison weeds on ground so it could never be resettled again. Therefore, the tragedy of Adored Okavanga is what your kind would say...*your style!*"

Lewalski squinted his sole eye and his nostrils flared. "I was there, evacuating survivors left from the fallout, up to my chest plate with endless piles of dead bodies. I heard the screams. It was your military that pressed that button to start the war they always wanted..."

"Lies and conjecture, pompous Captain, but irrelevant." Atomu waved away Lewalski's words. "The Abyss' stored radioactive material, with it's half-life of two point five million years, meant abandonment of this most sacred refuge. But we found use for the void asylum, as prison for those most condemned. If we make it back out alive, we will be first to do so."

"Only the worst human and Horaxians were banished within its depth," said Kaya Maghan. "No one was ever released."

A thought sparked Ballistic's mind. "Wait, if this place is radioactive, then won't the guy be dead by now? And everybody else in there? This isn't a prison, it's an execution. Colonel, this old-ass Horaxian is taking us for a ride. This is a waste of our time, sir."

"Impudent human," said Atomu. "Even past prime I could carve name upon your chest."

"Human Sergeant," Hatshepsut began, with the calmest of voices. "The radioactive isotope was designed to radiate at highest levels for its first few hundred years, and then reduce output by eighty percent, enough for average being of young adult age to last an estimated maximum of eleven years exposure. Since our target is more than just a man, he may be gifted strength sufficient to survive longer."

Adcox pondered aloud. "The major must be important for our leaders to go through all of this trouble."

"I pray," said Kaya Maghan, "that the inmates would have torn the souwrak apart by now." He smiled at the notion.

Jei'Gun turned to Kaya Maghan. "Let our hope endure that it may be among living. Jei'Gun's blade yearns for human blood...too long it has been!" As customary for Anubianites, he referred to himself in third person.

"Our mission is to get him out alive, remember," Adcox said to Jei'Gun as diplomatically as he could.

"Jei'Gun's memory is not always so good, like who is enemy and who not."

"Sir," said Akerele. "What are the rules of engagement for the other inmates?"

Atomu answered before Bronze could, in an attempt to stamp his authority. "Even if alive, they are already dead. Kill any opposition."

"Alpha Atomu," said Colonel Bronze. "Do you have a map of the facility? With all those tunnels it would be pretty easy to get lost."

"We have acquired map, but I am not authorized to permit Homo sapiens access to sensitive Horaxian information."

"If you're not here to help, then stay out of our way alpha," Colonel Bronze said, staring his counterpart down.

"If you do not like my terms, then journey into the depths without map and no way of finding the cursed one. I am Alpha, you follow *my* lead."

"Sir, we still have that ultra-pulse device," Adcox said, "we could use that. Tronics, is that right? You receiving?" He remembered the device's capabilities, thanks to Tronics babbling on about every gadget he gets his hands on.

"Affirmative, sir," said Tronics over the radio. "The ultrasonic pulser will help you navigate. Yet another fantastic recommendation by our new LT, over." The transmission was appalling, chopping constantly due to the storm.

"Alpha," Jei'Gun called. "We should be joining our imperial forces to protect Kemeta our beloved. Yet instead, we risk life to find a demon banished. Its crimes despicable, but our silencing of the yearning to fight, almost equal in measure."

"Great warrior, prodigious killer of men," replied Atomu, "the scornful arms of defeat are already wrapped around Beloved Kemeta's precious neck. Defensive capabilities weakened by the humans, our Great Supreme King scrambles a mere splinter of fleet in desperation. A last stand for the males, females and young ones stranded on its dire surface. But Kemeta's soul will endure. Our people will endure."

Adcox watched in awe of the majestic landscape. "I wonder what its cities were like before the Polymorph? Before the wars?"

"It was paradise," said Hatshepsut strapped in opposite to him. "It is…it was, my home."

Adcox watched the tears swell up around her pink pupils as her eyes blinked horizontally. The pupils of Kaya Maghan also caught his attention. They refused to stray from Colonel Bronze. He had noticed Bronze's constant cough as it grew more frequent and whispered to Nanonramu. "We have had our human antivirus shots, yet it is best we venture not too close, in particular their leader."

The *Odysseus* dipped and weaved as it hovered to stabilize itself before it landed. Once it touched down on the surface, Zomo opened the cargo bay doors from the bridge. The wind howled like an alpha wolf as the teams removed their support rails and picked up their gear. Atomu ordered his pack to march and they bounced off the ship's metal ramp towards the prison leaving the humans behind.

"XO!" yelled Colonel Bronze. Nothing else needed be said. Lewalski's tongue functioned like a whip to slaves chained to oars on a colonial galley ship.

"Let's go, maggots!" were the last words he bawled in his husky voice.

Zomo entered the cargo bay and hustled to get her gear on to catch up with the group.

"Marines, would you rather go home?" Bronze yelled at Unit Forty Two.

"We rather die, sir!" Unit Forty Two responded in one loud voice.

"Let's move!" said Bronze, his body jerking to his cough.

In response, Hatshepsut, who had stayed behind, extended her right hand a meter from Bronze's face and revealed her black glove which came alive with sporadic lights and digital tones. "You have mild fever, human colonel. My analysis suggests you are suffering from the infectious disease human tuberculosis. Do you require vaccine?"

Adcox, in earshot, was sadden by the news though not surprised. He sensed the CO's failing health.

Bronze replied when his coughing finally ended. "I'm becoming drug resistant. Besides lass, I would have died years ago, just couldn't find the time." With that, the old man took off.

Ahead, Atomu quickly reached the colossal gates of the monumental structure. He signaled to the four armed guards upon the ledge and they opened the slow moving gates.

Colonel Bronze picked up Tronics' voice via the comms link. "Boss man, weather sensors have detected that the storm's eye has shifted and the worse of it is heading our way in approximately thirty minutes. Sir, I recommend the *Odysseus* relocates eight klicks east, away from its path, over," he said with a high level of background static muffling his common accent.

"Aye, copy!" Colonel Bronze had to shout in the whistling wind. "But I want you on remote communications for tactical operations. We may need your help locating the target. Out."

"Wilco, boss! Hey Adcox, don't forget the mobile transceiver towers, otherwise communications will be blocked once you're inside the walls, over."

"Got it, techno-tosser, just keep your nanotech-nickers on." Adcox shouted as he lifted up a black metal case in his right hand, the violent wind pushing his arm backwards.

"Wow watch yourself, superman," laughed Tronics. "Wish I was out there with you, bruv."

"I don't think Amanda and the kids would like the idea of that. Just watch my back."

"Wilco! Hey man, stay black."

Adcox laughed at his friend and comrade's words due to the obvious pale whiteness of his skin. "I'll see what I can do. Watch over us, wise *Odysseus*, so that we don't get lost on *our* journey."

Lieutenant Adcox then tried to catch up with the rest of the team heading inside the prison gates.

***

Darkness shrouded the inner walls of the facility only sparsely lit with the flames of torches hanging along the ornamental, gothic stone walls. The two teams marched with weapons and weapon gauntlets at their sides, except for Hatshepsut who only held the stainless steel box in her hand that stored the DNA tracking instrument. Ballistic, on the other hand, had a metal harness strapped to his armor's back and waist, extending down the length of his legs. The exoskeleton was called "the vertebrae' – an electrically powered system which supported the weight of a weapon vertically behind his right shoulder, a very large weapon much different to the human military standard issue solar 506 assault rifle: an 8-barrelled machine gun comparable to a minigun.

A fat, aged Horaxian led the group, holding a staff with an artificial light source at the top, which simulated fire and brightened the pathway. He addressed the Alpha.

"This once hallowed refuge has fallen from the bosom of grace, Atomu, Wise Axe That Cuts Deepest. It is already cursed, yet you bring more of the human disease here."

The staff lantern helped to support his exceptional weight. In twenty-first century Earth, he would be described as morbidly obese, a term rarely used in these dire times of food scarcity and war. "Perhaps brethren, we should smite these filthy humans right here, for old time's sake."

Ballistic snapped back. "Fat chance, warden! You fat son of a b…"

"Stow it, Sergeant!" Bronze interrupted.

The warden responded, sure of himself, despite obviously being past his prime. "Listen to your master, Homo sapien. My skill with an arm blade, legendary. In old age I could still kill you with the ease I wipe sweat off my brow." He laughed to himself, his massive midriff wobbling with each heavy step. Thanks to his gut, no one could walk beside the warden down the walkway.

"The only reason you yet live to be old and heavy Zotana," replied Alpha Atomu, "is because I saved your oversized rear from jaws of death in Battle of Neptune."

"And now I am warden of Jumbie Abyss. Life is truly a gift." Zotana sarcastically remarked. "Still, who could ever forget Neptune, when you and I led numerous mega-packs in victorious charge against our villainous Homo sapien foes. From the mines of Astonishing Rogue Basarwa to the floating sky lands of Consecrated Sha'hel, troops cheered our names. Honored we were in person by our unblemished Great Supreme King and Shando the Grand."

"We lost a third of our fleet at Neptune," said Lewalski.

"It was a good year," replied Atomu, nodding his head in delightful reminiscence.

They arrived at the end of the pathway to a sizable circular door. "We are here," said Zotana. "The platform behind blast door will take you down to the depths. You are on your own once inside."

"How many inmates are in there?" asked Captain Lewalski.

"Given average life expectancy, population is estimated at ninety thousand, but rations we provide are only enough to feed numbers lesser than half that whole. They say the sickness drives them insane. I hope you have brought enough ammunition," said Zotana.

"Well, we can see where all the rations went," said Akerele softly, spooked by the realization Zotana had overheard.

Zontana smiled at the young private. "You know, you humans think you are so special. You actually thought your Earth was center of entire universe." Zontana threw his head back and laughed, pleased with himself. "How...inexcusably idiotic. In the Abyss' depths you will witness truth, that you are celestially inconsequential, immaterial and insignificant. Your closest function is that of galactic plague; cosmic cockroaches regrettably difficult to step on and crush."

"Stuffing your fat-ass face isn't the only thing you do too much, chubby," said Ballistic, stepping ahead of them all. "Just open the damn door. Let's get this show on the road."

Nanonramu picked up a staff lantern similar to Zotana's but still unlit. While he did so, Zontana continued to speak. "One last thing which may be cause for concern. Two decades past, an Ariman was imprisoned in the Abyss."

"By the whites of the Great Supreme King's beard!" said Nanonramu, he twisted his head to look at the warden then his Alpha.

"Ariman?" Kaya Maghan said as he broke out in a pant. The warden's words hit Adcox, Akerele and Zomo hard as well as their bodies stuttered.

"This has just got a whole lot worse," said Akerele. "Aren't they extinct?"

"Sir," Adcox said to Bronze. "I don't think we have enough men or enough fire power to complete this mission."

Nanonramu was just as shaken up by Zontana's words. "The coward human may be right."

"There is no turning back now," replied Bronze, "we need to complete this mission before the Polymorph reach Kemeta."

"Let's just hope the Ariman's dead now after all these years," Zomo said.

"From what I've seen," said Lewalski, "they don't die so easily."

Zotana addressed his war-brethren one last time. "I would wish you good luck, old friend." He then turned to Unit Forty Two. "But ever since the stars crossed our once glorious path with humans...luck has forever abandoned us."

Chapter Four - The Abyss Gazes Also Into You

"We are ready, Zotana," said Atomu. "Open the gates." He then walked up to each member of his pack and stared them in the eyes. "Brethren...do you fear?"

"*No alpha!*" they responded loudly, except for Hatshepsut. The Horaxians activated their helmets. The protective metal automatically covered their cranium first, then the front of their faces, and then clicked in place around their collar bone latch. Atomu's helmet had additional decorations of blue encrusted stones sunk in gold, dedicated to him for his glories in battle.

"Activate your helmets, marines!" commanded Bronze. His team immediately complied.

The door's unlocking mechanism switched on, creating a loud bang that echoed in the distance. Then, the thick, heavy blast door opened into a small, scarcely lit, empty chamber which had another blast door at the other side. They walked in, and the first door closed with a thunderous bang. This protected the warden and the guards from the deadly atmosphere of the Abyss.

Once shut, darkness descended in the chamber. The marines activated their shoulder torchlights. Nanonramu switched on his staff lantern, which provided more than adequate luminosity. This merely a precautionary measure, as their Horaxian helmet visors required no external light for good visibility due to its heightened light sensitive sensors.

"Adcox, deploy an MTT!" ordered Bronze.

Adcox sat down the metallic case he carried and pulled out one of the devices Tronics reminded him about. Smooth and slim, it was roughly thirty centimeters in height with a tripod base. Once he'd rested it down and powered it up, four panel antennas extracted, each oriented in opposing directions. After pressing a switch, several green and blue LEDs activated.

"The high gain transceiver is online," Adcox said. "Sir, I'm getting a data message from *Odysseus* on my heads up display, its Tronics. He says interference is too high, adjust the active gain and output power to the highest setting. Complying now."

Adcox soon heard sounds of audio tuning and the hiss of radio static then eventually Tronics' vocal signal burst through.

"Unit Forty Two, this is Dogpatch. Are you receiving?" asked Tronics, his audio was full of heavy static.

"Five by five," replied Lewalski, "like sweet-old country music, gadget boy."

"All right guys, the walls are a lot thicker than I thought. Let's hope I can maintain surveillance from *Odysseus*. Out," said Tronics.

"Roger that!" said Bronze. "Bag and drag, marines. Let's ride out."

A circle of lights in the middle of the chamber floor came to life with a domino effect and both teams edged inside the ring. A moment passed and the circular ground beneath their feet transformed into a downward moving platform. The distance to the bottom must have been over five hundred meters, yet to Adcox it seemed endless. The platform soon accelerated its rate of descent, forcing most in the group to take a knee or lose their balance. Adcox glanced over and noticed Kaya Maghan closing his eyes and speaking in tongues, some strange method to maintain composure he thought to himself. Or was it the madness; there were claims that the increasing riots and vicious crimes within their empire were fueled by a contagious mental disorder, and the male was far from the most stable.

Bronze and Lewalski stood close to one another. "Here we are again, Bronzy," Lewalski said, inspecting his rifle. "Back to back, like the raid on Cunga Sigma."

"Aye! It's about to get heavy, don't check out just yet old friend."

"Me? Hell, I'm harder than a rhino's erection."

"Well, luck's on your side. The ugly don't die young," said Bronze as he completed his weapons check. "And what you've got a lot of is grey hairs, rotten teeth...and ugly."

Zomo appeared frightened as she looked up and saw the top of the Abyss getting farther away. Her eyes then spun around the group to see if anyone had noticed her fright. Ballistic hadn't, yawning while he awaited the completion of their descent. Zomo's fear was concerning, but only half as bad as Adcox's. He placed his rifle's butt on the ground and clutched its thick barrel as if trying to crush it to pieces as he began to mildly hyperventilate.

Atomu hissed at Adcox's behavior and called out to him. "Prepare yourself, young cub. Death should be like a long lost friend's embrace."

The alpha's words might have stirred fire in the belly of his pack, but only served as a hammer to the boy's glass confidence. He forced his head down in an attempt to control his shakes. Adcox soon felt a gentle touch on his shoulder, then a tingle coursed through him. The sensation created a soothing effect, stopping his shakes dead. He flicked his head up and saw who the hand belonged to, it was Hatshepsut. It puzzled him why he felt the sensation of her touch on his body, through both of their suits. His breathing returned to normal but then the young man looked on at the protective suit which covered her voluptuous frame and became bewildered. Again, imperceptibly, Doctor Hatshepsut appeared to be glowing.

"What's happening to you?" he said, stunned at her fluorescent greenish glow.

"Biophosphorescence!" said Hatshepsut, knowing what he must be referring to. "Kemetan bodies build up high static charge due to planet's atmosphere trapping light particles. We glow in dark."

He recalled rumors he had heard of the phenomenon, until Lewalski's voice broke his trance.

"Marines, check your infrared and night vision."

As the platform neared the prison floor only one remained standing tall, Jei'Gun. Unfazed, his chest protruded out, fortunate to be balanced by the weight of his bulky elite-shakan armor and natural tree trunk-like muscular legs.

The platform finally reached the ground and they all stepped off. The chamber they descended into was illuminated by their light, but beyond their location, only darkness greeted them. The laser targeting beam of the Horaxian arm-cannons projected strong blue lines of light through the dark. Nanonramu's staff lantern provided the brightest light of all.

"Adcox, drop another MTT," ordered Bronze.

The young junior officer obliged without hesitation, dropping down to deploy another radio transceiver. Back on the bridge of the *Odysseus*, Tronics sat in front of three large monitor screens. One was blank, but the other two instantly turned on upon the sound of an alert tone. On one of the active screens, live footage streamed from the helmet cams of each team member being fed back to the bridge along with their names underneath. The other active monitor screen had sensor information from the MTTs with its inbuilt motion detection and environmental detection sensors.

In the Abyss' depths, the team briefly waited for Tronics to establish a stable connection. Ballistic's weapon stationed behind his right shoulder automatically moved with a slow mechanical motor churn. It maneuvered out and around his right shoulder then turned clockwise on its y axis and stopped at his waist level. "Time to bring the pain," he said aloud, grabbing hold of the large weapon.

"Radio Access Network established guys," Tronics informed the team. "Long range sensors activated. Time to fire up the ultrasound, over."

"On the double, Akerele," ordered Bronze.

The young private pulled out a device that clung to the magnetized plate on the back of his armor, which they used as a personal weapons hold. The gun-shaped device had triple the width of a solar rifle and half its length. Akerele pressed a button which caused blue rectangle lights on the side to light up one by one.

"Charged!" the private called out. Upon the pressing of the trigger it released a violet rippling pulse of energy that faded into the depths, then all the device's activity switched off.

Atomu watched on with displeasure while he activated his digital glove, then switched his attention to the map of the facility it displayed.

On the *Odysseus*, Tronics monitored all textual and visual data that streamed in via the team's heads-up displays. The blank screen sprang to life and showed a three dimensional image of the tunnels as the ultrasonic pulse executed its function.

"And then there was light," Tronics pronounced. "Ok, the pulse is currently mapping, but the echo range is approximately three hundred meters. After that we'll have to fire another one. Out."

While Tronics spoke, Hatshepsut wasted no time. She placed her silver case down and opened it up, revealing a silver triangular device and it immediately levitated without any further action by her. Next, she touched the dorsal area of her digital glove, which caused the hovering device to split into three equal-sized equilateral triangles. A press of another touch screen button sent the floating pyramids at blinding speeds down the tunnel.

"The Bio-scanners will traverse chambers and relay biological signatures of all life forms detected," said Hatshepsut.

"Good. We march, this way!" Alpha Atomu commanded and the Horaxians obeyed. Jei'Gun, ahead of the rest, strode with sure footed steps. Nanonramu and Kaya Maghan however, treaded more cautiously.

Bronze issued his men orders. "Stay disciplined and remember your training. It's dark, so ID targets before you engage. Sergeant, I want you on point. Akerele, guard our six. It might get tight down here so watch your line of fire, marines."

Adcox observed that Hatshepsut ventured empty-handed except for her digital glove and thought how brave she must be, especially in such a place. "Hatshepsut, where is your weapon?" He asked.

"I have none. I am not soldier." Her gaze locked onto her glove's display. Every part of it—palm, fingers and back dorsal outputted readings. "The radiation levels are at five julla bars," she notified the teams.

Ballistic twisted his face upon hearing her words. He moved close to the colonel and whispered. "Sir, I don't know whose side these guys are on but it ain't ours. Permission to terminate these white-haired sons of bitches as soon as this goes south?"

Bronze paused for a moment and whispered back to his marine. "Affirmative!"

They carefully traversed through the chambers. Their suits, protecting them not only from the radiation but from the heat, the smell of rotting flesh, and the thick and unholy, rancid air. The ground of the Abyss remained indistinguishable. What should have been blue stone floor was only partially exposed, and what they encountered was a black muck, ankle high, the remains of corpses, feces, dead skin and other unknown substances.

Adcox struggled in vain to make out the pure blackness of the Horaxian's faces, with the exception of the doctor's glowing figure. "Helm: night vision!" he commanded his suit's visual systems. His visor image changed from normal view to a green and black display which enhanced the light given off by the group's light sources, but it resulted in poorer vision. "Helm: infrared!" the images now changed to hues of red and orange. But the group's bodies could just barely be made out over the prison's structured walls.

"Helm: normalize view. Guys, I can't see a thing down here," said Adcox.

"Having the same trouble," said Zomo. She struggled to deal with all the darkness and soon began to pant, staying close to Akerele for security.

"I've got your six, Zomo," said Akerele.

"We've got crap ambient light for the night vision," said Lewalski, although he had his visor set to night vision, as did Ballistic. "And there's too much heat down here for the infrared."

Kaya Maghan released a snigger. "The pups are scared of the dark."

Atomu also laughed.

"Unit Forty Two, this is Dogpatch," said Tronics, his voice digitized due to the Abyss's structure. "There's something in your environment that's screwing up the light sensitivity of your optic sensors. Also, I'm picking up high amounts of hydrogen sulfide and a bunch of methyl sulfides down there."

"It is being produce by feces," said Dr. Hatshepsut.

Back on the bridge, Tronics screwed his face up with repulsion at discovering the source of the gases. "Wow, you mans are in some deep...*deep*...'

"Stop hogging my goddamn comms link," yelled Bronze. "Unless you have vital intel for me, shut the hell up."

"I detect elevated levels of methane, mercaptans and butane," said Hatshepsut, inspecting the reading of her apparatus. "Gases given off by decomposing corpses. It may not be wise to fire explosive ammunition within Abyss."

"Five by five. You all heard the lady," said Lewalski.

***

Although his suit's visual sensors detected nothing, Adcox couldn't shake the eerie feeling that they were being watched. As he and the others advanced, they came by lifeless bodies and skeletal remains along their path and he tried in vain to avoid stepping over all the partial corpses and carrion creatures sprawling inside them. Zomo gagged as if close to throwing up when she viewed the blood and fragments of flesh lining the walls.

"Captain, look at that," Adcox said, looking at the shoulder region of one of the bodies, which had chunks missing from it. "What do you make of it?"

"Teeth marks," Lewalski replied. "They've been eating each other. Stay sharp kid."

Dr. Hatshepsut knelt to inspect another corpse. "It would appear that all human DNA matches have had heads and spinal cords removed. Not severed, but ripped away with brute force's aid."

"The Ariman!" replied Jei'gun.

"We should not have come here," said Nanonramu, analyzing the litter of bodies and seeing most were without limbs.

A spontaneous burst of static saturated the marine's comms links, followed by Tronics' voice. "Guys, I've picked up something. Movement, twelve o'clock, minus a hundred meters."

Zomo, now spooked, spun her head in the direction of the threat. Akerele stood next to her, also under pressure but coping a lot better.

"Stay focused!" Lewalski said, looking at Zomo's condition. He crept to the front of the team to meet Ballistic.

"I've got something on my infrared," said Ballistic. "The signature is faint." All of the group now observed a red and orange image on their HUD displays as they switched to infrared.

"Wait for it, Sergeant," said Lewalski. He knew Ballistic had a tendency to be gung-ho and overzealous with a weapon. "Any one of these inmates could be him. We need confirmation."

"What is it, Hatshepsut? Quickly!" Atomu asked, keeping his voice low.

It took her a moment to read her sensors, she had to be sure. "Human....but not the subject."

"Ready troopers!" said Atomu. The Horaxians pointed their arm-cannons.

Out of the darkness a figure appeared on Adcox's thermograph. The team aimed their lights and saw what should be a human male pacing towards them dragging one of his feet that barely remained attached by shreds of bone. His bare-chested flesh had whitened and rotted with large chunks missing, his jaw hung inhumanly. Lieutenant Adcox took tiny steps backwards, feeling that the mindless inmate's ghastly, disfigured face had its focus purely on him.

"This is Colonel Bronze of the United Earth stellar marines, I'm ordering you to hold your position and put your hands up." The hideously disfigured inmate opened his blackened mouth wide, revealing discolored, malnourished fragments of teeth and released what sounded like a high pitch roar. Then he dashed towards them. The thundering of multiple weapons fire tore the victim apart. Even when the marines stopped, due to Bronze ordering a cease fire, the Horaxians ignored him and continued to shoot.

"That felt good," Kaya Maghan said as he dropped his firing arm.

Hatshepsut carefully approached the surely dead carcass and inspected it. "His body has emaciated and his ears and genitals have been ripped off."

Jei'Gun stooped down next to Hatshepsut. He reached to the jaw of the human carcass and broke it off. Then, he pulled out the tongue with a sharp yank, placing it in a small compartment on his waist as a souvenir.

"You're disgusting," said Ballistic, his minigun still smoking.

"Was that your father that Jei'Gun just slaughtered baboon?" Jei'Gun said.

"That's it, you monkey ass..."

A sudden noise reverberated in the far distance and forced Ballistic to halt his movement. Continuous echoes of high pitched roars rapidly increased in volume. Both teams stood deathly still.

"Check your ammo," Bronze told his team.

On the *Odysseus*' bridge, Tronics bashed buttons on the console in disbelief of his monitoring screens. "Rarse!" he uttered as multiple dots lit up on the motion scanner display. "People, you've got company. Do you copy?"

"Aye! How many, Dogpatch?" asked Bronze.

Tronics paused as he saw the whole screen light up with dots. "All of them."

"Where are they?" Atomu asked.

"Omnidirectional contacts, and closing fast, I repeat you are surrounded Unit Forty Two," said Tronics.

"*Doctor*?" called Lewalski, looking to Hatshepsut for answers.

Doctor Hatshepsut inspected all of the specimen DNA concurrently. Adcox backed away behind Bronze as he witnessed his display light up red and orange.

"I'm about to let the big bad wolf loose," said Ballistic, itching for combat. "Better hurry up lady."

With his thermal sights now switched off, the paralyzed Adcox witnessed the multiple targets creeping towards the teams in all directions with inhuman postures, their heads and limbs twisted up and mangled. Some of them crawled along the muck on the ground. Zomo lifted her solar rifle to fire as they drew near.

"Remember people, no explosive rounds nor devices," said Bronze. "Tag then bag, on my order."

Atomu roared at all of them to form a tight circle as the mutated inmates maniacally darted towards both teams at more angles than they could count and released blood curling shrieks. Their lower body garments were torn up, some fell off their bodies by the frantic twitching and jerking of their skeleton-like legs.

"Hold, we need confirmation the Black Guard's not one of them," said Colonel Bronze, putting his hand up in a tight fist.

"I'm reading human and Horaxian...but none are him," said Hatshepsut, stepping back behind Jei'Gun.

Ballistic released a smile on Hatesheput's revelation. "Time to unleash the pain."

The tunnels of the once dark fortress now came alight by spontaneous muzzle flashes as bullets rained out from the Horaxian contingent, cutting down the mutants. Under fierce attack, the marines too were forced into action. No one had noticed in the pandemonium of gunfire that Adcox had barely fired a shot. He could afford not to, since the twin towers of Bronze and Lewalski laid down fire methodically beside him. Systemically covering each other as they reloaded their magazines, not missing a beat.

The teams cleared a path in the front and advanced, but hundreds more mutants flooded the rear.

"Watch your fire!" yelled Atomu.

Three of the crazed inmates jumped onto Jei'Gun and he threw them all off. He grabbed one by the neck and slammed its head into the wall so hard its skull exploded. Adcox, startled by the frenzy, slipped, falling on his rear end. A mutated Horaxian pounced on him, striking in psychotic rage with its malnourished arms. He struggled to defend against its ferocity, but Ballistic soon arrived and impaled the mutant with his blade. He grabbed Adcox and helped him to his feet.

"Got your back, LT," said Ballistic, placing his knife in his metal utility belt.

Lewalski made sure to keep an eye on the yellow-lit ammo count of his solar assault rifle as he unloaded indiscriminately, yet with careful aim. In the end, a pile of dead bodies remained. "Clear!" he shouted, confirming the elimination of all hostiles.

"We must keep moving." Atomu ordered, reloading his gauntlet. The thick metal casing covering his weapon systems made his forearm three times as wide. They all advanced farther down the tunnels, their metallic boots splashing in the shallow, murky waters.

Tronics watched the carnage unfolding from relative safety. Hooked on all the action, he only just became aware that the mapping pulse wave had ended its operation. "Akerele, I need another pulse, over."

The private complied by blasting another wave and the mapping system recommenced. The MTTs granted Tronics longer monitoring ranges than the sensors built into the marine's or even the Horaxian's armored suits.

"All right," said Tronics. "I see multiple hostiles all over the western tunnel. The east side's clear, over."

"Copy Dogpatch, keep tracking," said Lewalski.

They approached a T junction in the large chamber and huddled together.

"Split apart we must," said Atomu. "For otherwise days our search prolong."

"Agreed!" said the Colonel.

Atomu continued. "Greater efficiency will be achieved if mixed we are in resources. Nanonramu and Hatshepsut, come with me. Human alpha, I will take your weak-framed Adcox Lieutenant and your runt female, or male, whatever it is," said the Alpha looking at Zomo, unable to decipher her gender. Yet Bronze saw cunningness in his chess move. Atomu's selection may have been light on combat ability, but that was the gambit to fool them all. The old male didn't care about cooperation. Without the human contingent he would have been minus the useful aid of Tronics' wider range sensors and assistance. Then he had Nanonramu's undying loyalty, the doctor's ability to find the target and medical skill, and he could use the two frailest humans as pawns for the slaughter if necessary. Colonel Bronze's face stiffened, realizing he couldn't always be around to protect the weaker members of his team. It was time for his junior officer to step up to the plate and be a man.

"I will relay all my findings to you, Mr. Bronze," said Hatshepsut.

"Cheers lassie!" said the commanding officer. He then briefed his men. "Listen up marines, first sniff of trouble I want you to haul, and I mean *haul arse*, back to the exfiltration point. We'll set up rally points every five klicks deep. Are you feeling me?"

"Sir, yes, sir!" said all of the United Earth team.

Before they split, Hatshepsut whispered a plea to the alpha. "We should permit the smart human aboard their ship access to my bio-scanner's data to aid quest using vessel's monitoring syste..."

"Silence!" Atomu barked at her. "Your birth rights do not give you dominion over me, Caroo. Press me again and here you will be left for inmates to gnaw on your bones."

As the Horaxians chatted, the colonel, coughing his lungs out, came to Adcox. "Remember our wee talk back in my stateroom?"

"Unforgettable, Colonel. But maybe Ballistic should ..."

"Conserve your ammo," Colonel Bronze interrupted.

"Yes, sir! But colonel I think Alpha Atomu is trying to..."

"I know...just remember your training."

"Yes, sir!"

"Don't drop your guard like you did in the hangar bay. You think the Horaxians are our friends? They're not.

Neutralize them if necessary." His index finger struck hard on the concerned young officer's chest plate.

"Yes, sir!"

"I'm making you personally responsible for Zomo's life, you feeling me sonny?"

"Yes Colonel, I'm feeling you." The lieutenant gave a skittish nod of his head.

"Time to put a scar on that pretty face."

Bronze walked off to join the team of Jei'Gun, Kaya Maghan, Lewalski, Ballistic and Akerele.

***

Hours had passed, yet the situation still intensified as both teams searched the tunnels battling hundreds of mutated, crazed inmates of both races. Most of them were exhausted from fighting. Their attackers were vicious and consistent in their assault. Bronze's team had covered more ground thanks to the competitive combative spirit of Ballistic and Jei'Gun. The latter seemed to enjoy impaling his victims with his arm blade, which extracted from his suit's left forearm. He struck deep into a disfigured Horaxian inmate's rib cage, the resulting purple blood gushed down his arm.

"Are you tiring, weakling?" The elite-shakan warrior chuckled, seeing Ballistic slightly out of breath. Unlike the sergeant, the extra proteins inherent in all Anubianites had gifted Jei'Gun with incredible strength as well as endurance.

"I've got enough energy to kick your ass as soon as we're finished up here," said Ballistic, trying to control his breathing. Although fatigue had caught up with him he was enjoying himself, his minigun's automatic, machine churns drowned out all other noises in the depths.

"Slaying lesser foe spawns audacious words from tongues of cowards," said Jei'Gun.

Ballistic squared up to Jei'Gun. "Jei'Gun, first time I heard it I thought...such a cute name...so...*tender*."

Kaya Maghan watched as the Anubianite's forearm containing his blade raised with intent. "Not yet, Power Made Flesh," he pleaded of his brethren. "Soon...but not yet!"

Common sense reaffirmed its position in Jei'Gun's mind. "My blade will come to claim you soon. Jci'Gun keeps his words." He walked off to hack down another victim.

Kaya Maghan wanted their attackers to have as much human prey for their appetite as possible. Akerele and he found the savages little sport, constantly spooked by inmates ambushing them from the darkness of the wide tunnels. But it took a lot to phase Bronze and Lewalski. They'd seen it all and the aged veterans remained committed to purpose.

Meanwhile, Alpha Atomu's team made cautious progress through the darkness. Adcox felt bad for the other team yet thankful of his party's less hazardous route.

"Looks like the colonel's team drew the short straw," Adcox whispered to Zomo. They both listened to the endless gunfire on their radio transceiver.

"You don't know the half, mate," said Tronics amongst the radio static as he monitored both teams' progression. "It's pretty intense."

"We may never find him," said Zomo swinging her solar around to every noise, struggling to cope with the Abyss's conditions. "He could have died a long time ago."

Nanonramu overheard her. "They say no weapon forged can kill that which we hunt. No poison can conquer it. They say the Jumbie Abyss curses one's soul even in the afterlife. But the demon king has no soul. "

A notification sound pinging on the index finger of Hatshepsut's digital glove made her head shoot forward. "I have detected match, faint. It blipped upon screen then disappeared."

"Is it the demon king?" asked the Alpha, thoughts of the Black Guard commander flooded his veins with anxiousness.

"Eighty-nine percent probability," said Hatshepsut.

"It is upon us," said Nanonramu freaking out. He thought himself ready to bear witness to the living myth but he was wrong. His antennae stiffen outward, impeded by his helmet's glass. Adcox wondered if he might have made a run for it at any second.

"Finally," said Atomu. "Revenge on the one who claimed my five hundred will be mine."

"What the hell?" Adcox gawked as the old Horaxian revealed his true intentions. "Colonel Bronze, Colonel Bronze, this is Adcox, are you receiving? Over!" The speed of his words made them almost indistinguishable.

"Aye, Lieutenant!" replied Bronze on the radio.

"We may have located the target approximately..." Adcox looked to Dr. Hatshepsut.

"Two hundred meters south by south east along secondary corridor." Hatshepsut informed him, loud enough to be heard through his comms link.

"Please advise, over!" said Adcox.

"Location received, move in to confirm. We will rendezvous with you at the LZ in ten mikes. Out."

Then, immersed in darkness and silence, they heard a loud dull sound that created an echo, similar to a heavy object pounding onto a hard surface.

"What was that?" said Nanonramu in a high pitch voice.

A few seconds of dead silence passed, and again the sound echoed the chambers, a loud pounding sound followed shortly by more.

"They are footsteps, Nanonramu," said Alpha Atomu. "Large footsteps." The Alpha knew that only one thing could emanate such sounds. "Hatshepsut, can your lifeform detector pick up an Ariman?" As he calmly asked the sound persisted and became louder, causing the solid abyss walls to vibrate.

"No Atomu. The nanoprobes will not be able to penetrate its skin."

"Colonel, Colonel Bronze, sir," Adcox called in a state of panic. "I don't think we've got ten minutes."

"Adcox, watch out," said Tronics on the comms. "Something big just came up on the sensors heading your way, over."

Instantly, they heard a loud roar; a deafening, unearthly, soul destroying roar. The team were at a cross section, making the direction of the echoes impossible to determine.

"Where is it, Dogpatch? Tronics, talk to me!" pleaded Adcox.

"Ahh I don't know, LT. The ambient temperature is saturating the infrared and the radiation's screwing up everything else. Motion sensors might pick it up again though."

"Do not waste time," said Alpha Atomu, overhearing Adcox. "Arimans are too well thermally insulated. Plus it has already picked up our scent. There exists no escape now. Ready yourself, Nanonramu." The alpha braced himself with a monk's composure, ready to greet death. But the loud thuds induced fear into the very marrow of Adcox's and Zomo's bones.

"Unit Forty Two, come in. I repeat, come in," called Adcox in desperate whispers. "Guys, our situation just got real serious down here. We think the Ariman is tracking us."

Zomo stepped backwards as the footsteps got louder and Adcox swung his head to the tunnels on his right. He saw a blurry image in night vision mode. Detailed features were indistinguishable but what he did identify was the creature's incredible mass. Its height and width, far greater than the laws of human anatomy would permit.

The shadowy figure of the beast stomped towards them with thundering steps. Its eyes glowed bright yellow like a lion's in the surrounding darkness. Atomu, Nanonramu and Zomo unloaded shots at the creature but with no effect. Atomu, who led from the front, discharged an explosive round; it projected out the same nozzles as his standard bullets. Tremendous amounts of smoke from the round blanketed the entire area. Adcox stayed behind with the unarmed Hatshepsut and witnessed a large body silhouette through the smoke. The hulking monster rocketed Atomu's midsection with its enormous humanoid fist so hard he was propelled into the air and landed onto Nanonramu, injuring him as the rogue banged his head on the hard ground.

His alpha's body falling upon him caused Nanonramu to fire his weapon wildly and he unintentionally struck Zomo with two stray shots to her midriff. Zomo still stayed on her feet although injured and leaned against the tunnel wall. The slugs took the wind out of her but she regained her senses. As soon as she made an attempt to squeeze her trigger, her solar rifle was snatched away by the beast. Adcox heard the sound of bending metal in the darkness and moments later Zomo's stolen rifle rolled across the ground, balled up by inhuman, prodigious strength. Zomo screamed. Off balance by wrong footing, she tumbled to the ground.

The scene drove Nanonramu hysterical. His torso and weapon arm were pinned down by his superior's dead weight. His valor, broken by the threat of the beast. His anger, fueled by the sight of Adcox standing by Hatshepsut, weapon in hand doing absolutely nothing.

He bawled out to the lieutenant. "Quick fool, fire your weapon!" his words disjointed, disorientated by shock.

Unfortunately the situation overwhelmed the young officer's duty. He couldn't move a muscle.

"Stubborn mule! Shoot it before it kills us all," Nanonramu cried, but Adcox remained frozen. "Shoot, you coward, pale skin, souwrak, swine, shoot!"

The second group heard the trouble on the comms and ran towards their endangered comrades. Ballistic felt a sharp pain in his eardrums due to the distortion by Zomo's radio relayed screams. Lewalski and Bronze focused in on Nanonramu shouting at Adcox for help.

"Adcox, Zomo do you copy?" said the colonel but neither responded. "Adcox, lay down cover fire and fall back to rally point."

"I...I can't." He whispered, yet loud enough for Bronze to pick up on the radio link.

"We will not get there in time," said Jei'Gun.

"Dogpatch talk to me," ordered Bronze.

"Boss, your tunnel runs parallel on top of the lieutenant's team tunnel section approximately eighty meters ahead."

"Let's move! Akerele, we need a hole," said Colonel Bronze. They ran farther down the tunnel.

"But sir, the doctor said no explosives," screamed Akerele.

"He doesn't have Alzheimer's, Private. That was an order," yelled Lewalski.

"Hard copy, sir! I'll use the thermite." Akerele reached into his utility belt grabbing hold of a pyrotechnic composition pack and placed it on the ground, taking a little bit of time to set the charge. The young private's general knowledge often made him a subject of ridicule, but he was a genius with explosives.

"What's the delay, Private. Don't let me shoot through you," said Bronze.

"Apologies, sir, fire in the hole."

"We need to get way back, hurry," said Lewalski.

They all ran forty meters back to where the tunnel bent and ducked for cover. Moments later, the charge detonated.

Farther into the tunnels amongst the thick blanketing black smoke, the Ariman slowly paced towards Adcox and Hatshepsut. Its body was too large to be fully understood but its height was no shorter than eight feet. Its head remained covered completely by what resembled a large black conical hat that stretched the length of a man, concealing its face, and a black veil mysteriously surrounded its frame.

Adcox held his weapon tight against his shoulder, shaking and breathing uncontrollably.

"It would not stop it!" said Hatshepsut, placing her hand on his rifle which encouraged him to lower his weapon, surprisingly she seemed calmer than anyone else.

Bronze and the second group rushed to the scene, almost certain they wouldn't make it in time. Remembering Adcox's inability to follow his orders he tried once more to reach out to the young officer. "God damn it lieutenant, respond. I know you can hear me. Listen to me, you've got grenade rounds in your solar with a five meter kill radius. Let those doves fly marine *now, right now.*"

The Ariman came before Adcox and Dr. Hatshepsut. Huge black hands emerged larger than the size of a man's head. It curled its claws into almighty fists and raised them high in the air as if to finish them with one blow.

Then, through the obscuring blackness spoke a voice in an odd language. The voice stopped the creature from its intended action. They turned and saw the outline of a man stooped on the ground. He spoke in a language recognizable to the lieutenant. It was too dark to see the man's aspects, but Adcox vaguely made out his grey image from his HUD display. The man then made a strange jester with his arms. He lifted his left arm high in the air, tight fisted and slightly bent, placing his other fist at his left arm's elbow and across his chin as if to support the upheld arm. Upon witnessing this action the Ariman moved back, promptly disappearing into the darkness. Hatshepsut scrutinized her bio-scanner and saw that it had found an exact match.

They had located the Black Guard commander.

Turning to Adcox, she saw that his hyperventilation had become so intense he dropped on one knee. In the midst of the chaos the other team arrived to Adcox's relief.

"He is the one!" Hatshepsut called out pointing to the man in the shadows.

Jei'Gun glanced around and saw his fallen comrades on the ground and in a moment of rage he lifted his arm-cannon to shoot the Black Guard. Ballistic, reading what was about to happen, yelled as he jumped on Jei'Gun. But despite the sergeant's size and robotic enhancements, he proved no match for the elite-shakan. Jei'Gun threw the bald soldier hard to the murky ground.

Kaya Maghan pointed his arm-cannon towards Ballistic.

"Drop it!" said Bronze, with his solar rifle to the Horaxian trooper's head. Without breaking eye contact, he shouted for his executive officer. "Secure the target, Captain!"

Lewalski removed a sidearm from his waist and turned to shoot the Black Guard, but when he pointed his shoulder-light, shocked greeted him. The Black Guard's body lay on the ground, locked in an unnaturally stiff pose, shaking involuntarily. Both races now pointed their weapons at each other.

Hatshepsut called out. "Everybody please elevate your calm. We are on the same side. Please, let me examine him."

Reason won over the colonel. He signaled his men to drop their weapons.

"Go see to your pack," Bronze said to Jei'Gun.

The Horaxians soon followed suit and raced toward their fallen alpha, accept for Hatshepsut who accompanied Unit Forty Two to the target's body and checked his vital signs. The bearded face of the enigmatic individual they'd come all this way for was so blackened by dirt it camouflaged his features in the shadows of the Abyss.

"His body is displaying waxy flexibility, said Hatshepsut, "somehow he became catatonic." The darkness and muck made it impossible to clearly see the man's bare chested upper torso.

"XO, knock him out," said Bronze, ever vigilant of the Black Guard commander's capabilities.

"Wilco!" Lewalski responded. He shot him with a sedative and the target's body went limp.

"He is unconscious," Doctor Hatshepsut said, assessing the lifeless man.

Colonel Bronze stared at the black, rectangular piece of metal surgically lodged into his neck. "Black Guard!" He said to himself, identifying the Symbiotic Program Unit. Bronze was one of the few in the group who had seen the Black Guard first hand. When activated, they spent most of their deployment behind enemy lines. "Lock him down! Jei'Gun, prep your wounded, it's time to exfil," commanded the colonel, hearing the intense moans of pain coming from the injured Atomu.

Akerele saw to the injured Zomo, and Lewalski and Ballistic secured the target, preparing his body to be lifted.

Bronze shook his head at the sight of his junior officer cowering. "Sergeant, help me secure the perimeter," the colonel ordered Ballistic. He then walked to the rear of the group, ignoring Adcox's condition.

"Boss," said Tronics, "I don't think you need to worry about the inmates, at least not for now."

"Why's that Dogpatch?"

"They had you lot surrounded, keeping their distance. Then they all moved away."

Bronze took another look at the lifeless Black Guard, believing he knew the inmates' motive, and he didn't blame them.

Hatshepsut knelt down beside the young man and performed a common Horaxian ritual of kindness by placing her left palm on the left side of his helmet's visor and her right palm on the forehead area.

"It is all right. Breathe human lieutenant...breathe!" She said with a tranquilizing voice, powerful in its soothing effect. He felt the tingle again. Snapping out of his ordeal, his breathing returned to normal.

Chapter Five - Mythological Dissection

High in the thick, greyish-green Kemetan sky, the *Odysseus* floated amongst the masses of fleeing civilian Horaxian spaceships. On its bridge, the lone soldier Tronics franticly pressed buttons on a side computer terminal. He was shocked by electrical sparks as he opened a small component hatch to gain access to the bridge's engine management circuitry and inserted his probe. It almost took his eye out.

The bridge's double doors slid open and Colonel Bronze and Zomo rushed in.

"Why are we still here, Corporal Manning?" The colonel's armor matched Zomo's, covered in blood and black stains of filth.

"Good question...I don't know."

"What?" said Bronze, now wide-eyed. His nostrils flared like they were about to release steam.

"Boss man, we got serious problems. Somehow, and I don't know how, the circuitry of our string drive and a whole lot of other systems just went offline. I'm guessing it was the storm but our shielding should have held up. It almost took out the whole ship. I rerouted power to the levitation systems but we're dead in the water right now," said Tronics, sweating terribly.

"Jesus laddie, we have company coming our way of the worst kind. I need this ship out of Kemetan orbit ASAP."

"Wilco boss, but we're looking at two to three hours for me to bypass the damaged circuits and charge the secondary cells." Tronics assessed Zomo's condition. "How's your ribs, Zomo-san?"

"Solid! The armor caught the shell. The suit's nanofibers should self-repair in...'

"Are you her physiotherapist?" Bronze madly interrupted. "You think we have time for this? Zomo's job is now ship repairs. I need you down in the infirmary. All hell's breaking loose and the Horaxian doctor is about to perform an analysis on the Black Guard." As the colonel walked out of the bridge with Tronics, he spun around and shouted at Zomo. "Get my ship out of here, Flying Officer!"

"Roger that, Colonel."

***

Adcox welcomed the sight of Tronics and the colonel as they entered into the chaos of the infirmary. The grey of its walls were illuminated by the bright lights of medical monitoring screens. It contained four patient beds but only two were occupied and all present gathered around them. The Black Guard lay restrained and unconscious on a medical bed guarded by the stellar marines. But both teams' attention were drawn by the agonizing growls of pain projected from the other side of the infirmary. Atomu squirmed around on the thin, blood soaked mattress in unbearable pain.

Hatshepsut tried her best to treat him as he refused to keep still. "The pain releasers were not enough," she said to the humans. "Dangerous it may be, but I may require some of your human morphine and an internal anticoagulant."

"No! No human medicine." Atomu struggled to cry out as he choked on his own purple blood.

"Almost every bone that forms your rib cage has been shattered," said Hatshepsut, "your lungs have collapsed and you have severe internal hemorrhaging. Without their medicine you will..."

"No please, please..." Delusional from pain he pleaded, "It will poison my soul for eternity, please no..." Atomu cancelled his trail of words. He noticed the lack of emotion on the faces of Lewalski and Ballistic and it fueled his rage. "My cries entertain you, filthy humans? You mock my demise? I curse your forsaken kind. May your star's light scorch your flesh. May your atmosphere's oxygen poison your undeserved lungs." Atomu then reached for Jei'Gun in desperation, grabbing hold of his armor. "Jei'Gun...hon...honor me!" his words lingered in the air.

Jei'Gun maneuvered with no hesitation. "Jei'Gun's hands will do your will, Alpha!"

At that moment, Hatshepsut realized what was about to happen and cried out. "No, don't!"

In a flash, Jei'Gun grabbed his alpha's neck and broke it, honoring his superior's words as well as his warrior code.

"I could have saved him," Hatshepsut shouted.

"And risk being beheaded myself? This is our way, the warrior's way." Jei'Gun was drenched in more blood than any other soldier.

Nanonramu, Kaya Maghan and Jei'Gun all unsheathed their arm blades and lowered them to make them touch close to the ground. They bowed their heads and in a chorus of voices chanted. "Lost, The Wise Axe That Cuts Deepest. His title will forever ring in the hearts of warriors!"

"I now assume mantle of Alpha," said Jei'Gun.

The colonel used this cease in the commotion to address everyone. "Listen up people, we've got problems. Corporal, situation report."

Tronics came in middle of the group screwing his face up to the stench coming from the armored suits. "Basically, you know that special creek we've often spoken about? Well we're up it right now."

"To the point, soldier," said Bronze.

"All right! The geomagnetic storm measured several kilohertz in magnitude higher than our shielding could handle. Our primary electronics is offline. Electromagnetic hull polarization's is also fried so we've got no solar radiation protection."

"So what? Get us out of here fool," said Jei'Gun.

"Well, tough guy, that's the main problem. Somehow it must have knocked out the *Odysseus'* string engine so superluminal flight capability is not happening...period."

"Then fix it," said Ballistic getting in Tronics' face. "Aren't you supposed to be a genius? Next time you go on point with the big gun and maybe I'll push the buttons all day."

"With the main electronics offline, we can't land," said Lewalski.

"That's affirmative, capo," said Tronics. "Backup systems are maintaining our levitation, keeping us in the air and they should hold up. But we're floating over water right now and the storm is pushing us towards the capital city. We're eighteen kilometers away."

Ballistic swore out loud. "A lot of good floating around in this dump of a planet's going to do."

"There is a Horde swarm coming our way, man," Akerele said, his jaw rattling. "We need to leave now. That capital's going be a hot zone."

"Do you not have antimatter propulsion?" asked Hatshepsut.

"Yes, ma'am," said the tech expert. "But our gamma radiation stabilizer was fried too. That's a minor though. I can get that back online in no time."

Hatshepsut's eyes lit up. "We sit upon one of the largest natural deposits of antimatter. We can use Horaxian shuttle pods to collect some from capital's stores."

Captain Lewalski interjected. "Lady, it will take us five years to get to Horax Prime on antimatter. I'll have a stroke by then."

"But at the least," said the female, "we can clear immediate danger and then somehow secure assistance."

Akerele shook his head. "That will put us in deep space, but incapable of escaping or evading."

"Horde swarms will cut us down," added the captain.

"Flying Officer Zomo at present is trying to get the string drive online," informed Bronze. "Tronics will join her shortly but let's not take chances. Our plan B will be to get help from Horaxian authorities on the ground. They must be able to spare us a ship."

"General Baizan's commanding the *Sword of Damocles*," said Lewalski. "They're maintaining a presence at a forward listening post. Our last orders were to get the Black Guard to it and they will escort us to Horax Prime.

Unless you have any objections, elite-shakan?" Both senior officers looked to Jei'Gun for his thoughts.

"I have had no response from Kemetan planetary command. Threat of Horde has our people in disarray, and I cannot contact the Illustrious Horax Prime," Jei'Gun said.

"The Polymorph must be jamming long range signals," said Tronics.

"Look, I was there when the Horde obliterated Biosphere-12," ranted Ballistic, his natural eye looked as though it was on fire. "Three billion people wiped out just like that. Let's leave this dump, forget Horax Prime. We've got our own problems to deal with."

"Settle down, Sergeant!" ordered Bronze.

"Coward!" yelled Jei'Gun.

"Why don't you and your fellow scumbags go fight your own battles," Ballistic blasted back.

"I said that's enough, Hasselberg!" said Bronze.

"Alpha Jei'Gun," called Kaya Maghan, "forget words of these infidels and their demon curse. We must return to our pods and re-join our ranks in defense of Kemeta beloved."

Adcox had been silent with embarrassment since his return from the abyss. He analyzed the exchanges, and could practically hear the big male's warrior code's screams for him to abandon the mission and help his brethren impede the heinous flood that approached. The lieutenant knew he needed to do something to subdue his warrior call. As an imperial knight of the elite-shakan guard, Jei'Gun's code of honor was his answer.

"We need to focus our efforts on getting Major Hawke to Horax Prime," Adcox said. "Jei'Gun, you and your brethren swore to get him there. You can't abandon your word. Please help us."

Kaya Maghan was repulsed by Adcox's request, and even more repulsed by Adcox referencing the forbidden name. "Jei'Gun, ignore the foolish pup, we must..."

"Silence! Alpha speaks," said Jei'Gun. "We follow orders. We must deliver cursed one to the Divine Council." His usual harsh tone now diminished.

A burst of repetitive bleeps sprang from the medical systems monitoring the infirmary's other patient. It shifted the room's attention. They all turned to the lifeless body on the bed in the room's corner. Hatshepsut walked over to the Black Guard and everyone gathered around. Though Nanonramu and Kaya Maghan stayed back. Kaya Maghan's breathing accelerated at the sight of what he had only heard as a young one to be the demon overlord of death. His mind refused to believe the monster's body was real. The Black Guard were said to only exist in ghostly spiritual form, slaughtering civilians then vanishing into the darkness only to reappear continents away wreaking further havoc. Nanonramu fared no better, as with all Rogue Basarwans he had long heard the horror stories of the Black Guard and their demon knight commander. They were considered folklore, to the extent Rogues dared not to speak of them in fear of being cursed.

Adcox surveyed the body of the mysterious man held captive by metal straps around both his feet and arms. His dark-skinned, coarse face and streaks of grey in his beard placed him in his mid to late forties. The bright light of his operating bed illuminated his head's thick braided hair which extended down past and over his shoulder. Most of the jet black hair was canerow plaited in untied, medium sized rows; half was tied up at the back by the crown of his head, the other half of his long-length hair fell down his back in single braids.

While the universe's most feared man lay unconscious, Dr. Hatshepsut had already connected him to electronic probes and his vital statistics were displayed on a monitor screen. He lay there bare yet muscularly chested, clothed only with ripped, black strips of fabric, his bare feet blackened and bloodied with blisters. The leader of the Black Guard had severe scar tissues all over his body, indicating fourth degree burns by either fire or electrocution. On the monitor at the head of his bed, functional magnetic resonance imaging displayed a three dimensional image of his brain in red and orange; the red showed the areas of heightened activity.

Lewalski analyzed the long, massive scars across his torso which could only be the marks of a man that had been severely lashed by a whip. "What's his situation?"

"Not good!" Hatshepsut responded, accessing the readings while the medical alerts continued. "The subject's basic bodily functions are deteriorating. I cannot yet decipher how subject still lives. There are enzymes within body that repair DNA and can keep up with damage caused by radiation's poison if absorbed dosage is low enough. However, this dosage should have been fatal. What also aided subject is unusually high amounts of ultra-potassium iodide within his system."

"What the hell does all this science crap mean?" said Ballistic. "Is he going to live or what?"

"It helps to protect body from radiation," said Hatshepsut. The doctor paused for a moment in fascination then continued. "Incredible! Internally, subject's body is riddled with adhesions."

"Allegions?" asked Akerele.

"Adhesions, dumbass!" said Zomo on the comms link, silently listening in all the while.

"Hey piss off Zomo!" The private shouted into his radio.

"It means he's been cut open," said Bronze.

"Multiple times it would seem," said Hatshepsut. "Evidence of extensive surgery."

"No," objected Bronze, "he's been tortured." He knew first-hand what a soldier goes through as a Horaxian prisoner of war.

"If you think his front is jacked up, you should see his back," said Lewalski. "Like he was backstroking through electrified barbed wire."

"Look...its neck," said Nanonramu to Jei'Gun. He referred to the faded scars encircling the neck of the unconscious man.

"The marks of a prison collar," replied Jei'Gun. "Once installed removal was said to be impossible."

The doctor turned the Black Guard's head with her right hand while placing her other hand on his shoulder and she was instantly jolted backwards. At the same time, two of the monitor screens blacked out.

Adcox caught her. "Are you ok?" Now all the Horaxian troopers present aimed their targeting beams at the Black Guard's head.

"What just happened?" asked Bronze, looking toward the doctor.

"I received what felt like electrical discharge, but I am unharmed."

Tronics quickly whipped out his data-slab which started off as a cube but unfolded itself to form a flat screen. He ran the tablet along the Black Guard's body and a Magnetic Resonance Image displayed on screen. He called the colonel over to take a look. "Boss man, looks like the charge emanated from whatever this thing is implanted inside his neck. It extends into his trapezius."

"It's his SPU!" said the colonel, thinking back to the wars he fought involving the Black Guard.

"What is SPU?" asked Jei'Gun.

Lewalski answered. "At first, the Black Guard Knights often went rogue, executing missions and killing when they weren't even ordered to. They had to be constantly kept in battle or stasis due to their need to kill. As a control mechanism, each Black Guard Knight was then given an SPU."

"Symbiotic Program Unit," Tronics said picking up from here. "I've heard of it but I've never seen one before. It's an artificial intelligence program which is connected to the cerebral cortex. Its secondary function is in-field tactical assistance via data retrieval, software control mechanisms and a barrage of sensors. But their primary function was command and control, with a direct connection into their host's neuromuscular junctions and limbic systems to control their emotions and neuropatterns via nanoprobes. They are essentially a whole, meaning that..."

"That's enough, Corporal!" Lewalski stopped him short of revealing too much detail of their living weapon. Colonel Bronze gave an inconspicuous "Job well done" head-nod to his executive officer.

"Is it operational?" asked Nanonramu, technologically inept. He stepped close to see the data-slab with his black antennae protruding close to the corporal. Tronics covered his nose and mouth, squinting his eyes.

"Rarse! Bredren, you Horaxian's stank before but..."

Nanonramu gritted his teeth and extended his palms towards Tronics' throat.

"Stand down, trooper!" Bronze ordered. He turned to Tronics. "Add more silk to your words and answer the male's questions."

"All its sensors are operational," said Tronics. "No structural or electrical damage. Its power cells were designed to last three hundred years but theoretically indefinitely. But its offline, doctor, you activated some kind of auto defense mechanism. I should be able to shut that down now." After inputting commands on his slab, Tronics turned to the doctor. "It's all good now, girlfriend."

You could tell Hatshepsut was puzzled by what he called her. Ignoring it, she carefully turned the unconscious man's head and saw a rectangular metallic device protruding from the base of his neck. Dotted around the solid block of metal were what looked like black microchips embedded in his flesh.

Lewalski stared in amazement at the scarred body. "What kind of hell has this man been through?"

"Strangely," said Hatshepsut, "I would deduce that most of subject's scars appear to have been results of injuries inflicted at an earlier date than incarceration into the Jumbie Abyss." She identified further signs of explosion scarring and multiple bullet wounds.

"Will he live long enough for whatever he's needed for?" Adcox asked.

"I am at odds for complete comprehension of my analysis. The subject's body has absorbed too much radiation and punishment. Since the catatonic state in the Abyss, condition has rapidly deteriorated. It is unlikely subject will survive journey to Illustrious Horax Prime."

"So our brethren died for nothing?" said Kaya Maghan enraged.

"Maybe not," replied Hatshepsut. "As a last chance solution I have a highly experimental drug called Tabulrack that can absorb radiation in body's cells, and re-strengthen them at molecular level." She pulled out a vial and a syringe and placed both of them together then hesitated, staring at both Jei'Gun then Bronze with the upmost concern. "On human physiology this is a death sentence. The drug should only temporarily grant subject strength long enough to reach Illustrious Horax Prime, but then it will eventually terminate life."

"The Black Guard are as tough as they come, Colonel," said Captain Lewalski. "We've got little choice." Bronze rarely sided against his captain's council.

"There must be something else we can do?" asked Lieutenant Adcox. "That's going to kill him."

Hatshepsut commented again. "I am certain subject will die without the Tabulrack. Your warrior may yet still survive its effects, although if so, it will slowly lobotomize and subject will never recover."

"Let's proceed, Doctor!" Requested Bronze with no emotion.

"Mr. Bronze, sedate the patient. I cannot. The pain will be unbearable," she informed him.

"Acknowledged!" Bronze replied. "Everyone clear the infirmary. Give the doctor some space and let's get cleaned up." It was not that Bronze had a lack of care for the Black Guard's comfort, but he had become too familiar with pain and now developed a numbness to it.

"Human Colonel," Kaya Maghan called out. "A thing of importance you neglected. Let nothing dim your lights, at all times brightly they must shine."

"Wise words!" said Lewalski, before he left infirmary.

Adcox heard rumors that had spread across the Horaxians worlds. That the Black Guard preferred to attack in darkness, that the light weakened them, and almost like a reversal of photosynthesis, they became stronger in the dark. Until Captain Lewalski's response he thought it merely superstition. But he had little chance to contemplate further, most had vacated the infirmary and it presented him an opportunity to approach his commanding officer regarding his inactions. "Sir, I just wanted to say I'm sor..."

"Police Atomu's body," said Bronze cutting him off. "Then remain here in the infirmary, *guard detail*, and whatever you do, stay out of my frigging sight." He turned his back on the young man and made his way out the room.

Tronics came to Adcox's side. "If the old man treated you nice, it would mean he doesn't like you! He's just in one of his moods mate, don't worry."

"Yeah!" Adcox's eyes fell to the floor.

"I got to go sort out the string engine. I'm glad you made it." Tronics raised his fist and Adcox touched it using his own. In the fashion of an older brother, Tronics rubbed his hand in the saddened marine's low cut hair before leaving.

Adcox stood still, riddled with guilt. The thought of how he froze up in the abyss made him clench his fist in anger. His eye then caught the glimmer of light reflected by the long needled syringe held by Hatshepsut as she leaned toward the Black Guard and injected him in the chest.

"Now what?" asked Adcox.

"We wait to see if patient lives through it."

"He will. I know it." Adcox whispered.

After a few moments of silent inactivity, the mystifying man's body began violently convulsing, only the limb restraints held him to the bed. The doctor checked his vitals. "Patient's body temperature is sky rocketing. It's...his...blood must seem as though on fire."

The Black Guard released soul-chilling screams. His muscles tensed and his veins popped out as though about to burst, yet his eyes remained shut.

"Doctor, can't you help him?"

"I cannot. His will to survive is all he has now."

The screams were as continual as they were deafening. The man writhed, jolting, trying to break free of his wrist restraints and escape his agony. He gritted his teeth as his neck snapped from side to side. Hatshepsut placed her hand over her mouth as though perhaps to stop herself from crying.

"Have you seen anything like this before?" Adcox asked, watching on as the bed rocked and rattled.

"No! This is wrong. No longer can I allow patient to endure this. This is torture." she said, consumed with grief.

Hatshepsut moved toward the life support control that could end his pain while ending his life simultaneously.

"What are you doing?" asked Adcox.

"I am cause of his pain. He will most likely die and should not die like this."

"Wait, Hatshepsut," Adcox placed his arm on her shoulder and received another tingle from her body. This time it was an unpleasant sensation, more like a low current electric shock and he moved his hand away. He was stunned by how she appeared to be glowing even though they stood in the bright lights of the infirmary. "You can't. Earth Command and the Divine Council wouldn't have gone to these lengths if he wasn't important. We must do what we can to save him. It will be worth it, I know it. You said he would have died anyway."

Dr. Hatshepsut's shoulders dropped as she eased up from her tense state.

"He'll make it. I just know it," said Adcox, drowned out by the man's cries.

***

A few hours passed. The screams that seemed like they would never end had finally stopped. The blood and filth which recently stained the infirmary had now been cleaned. The Black Guard lay once again motionless with his eyes shut. Doctor Hatshepsut occupied herself by analyzing a sample of his blood using a microscope.

"How is he, Hatshepsut?" asked Adcox, standing over the restrained man's body. Hatshepsut finished her blood checks and investigated her patient.

"His condition appears...stable. All vital signs are at concerning levels but improving. All as you predicted Lieutenant Adcox."

"Please just call me Diomedes, you're not a soldier. It's my first name."

"You appear to have a connection with this man. Did you know him?"

"No, but when I was a kid he was like my...well, he was a hero. The Black Guard for me were like guardians who watched over us. Guardian Angels!"

"That is not sentiment Horaxians share." She stopped looking at the monitor screens and closed her eyes for a moment. "I try not to hold hate in my heart. But if I did, my feelings for him after genocide of our Precious Matelot-6 would consume me."

"I can understand."

"Diomedes, what caused you to seize in the Abyss? Do you suffer from a human phobia?" she probed, leaning her body toward the young man.

"I couldn't help it. I just panicked. I've always suffered from panic attacks."

"Perhaps, but I have seen similar episodes before from patients. Horaxian minds are not so dissimilar to Homo sapiens. What you experienced was a type of post traumatic reaction. Something happened to you, very early on in your existence that triggers your episodes."

"Well, I guess I was too young to remember," Adcox replied.

***

While they monitored the Black Guard's condition, tensions rose on the bridge of the *Odysseus*. Nanonramu and Kaya Maghan paced around in anxiousness. Ballistic rubbed his bald head, while gazing at the bridge's frontal viewing screen, witnessing great flashes from the distant city. A city that grew ever larger as they neared. The sight and sounds of the booms mesmerized the young Akerele.

Most of the explosions were courtesy of Horaxian warship and mega-sentry missile fire; the mega-sentries were similar to the medieval artillery that once lined colonial shorelines. But they attempted to stop a foe that could not be stopped.

Colonel Bronze, Captain Lewalski and Alpha Jei'Gun stood around a small desk at the rear of the bridge and a map of Kemeta capital displayed on the digitized desk top.

"Here are the capital's two main space stations," said the elite-shakan, pointing to two positions on the map.

"The closest is this one east of the city center," said Bronze. "That's where we'll head if we can't get the string drive back online."

"That's if there's any Interstellar birds even left," said the one-eyed Lewalski. "The Polymorph have probably wiped them out."

The group all stopped at the sound of a monstrous boom, and the sight of a mushroom cloud slowly rising up into the atmosphere.

"This is end of Beloved Kemeta," said Kaya Maghan.

Jei'Gun's shoulders sunk and his voice softened from its usual hardened form. "The first wave of Horde must have crashed against planetary central base of operations like a

Sanaga meteor storm. Cut off from the Illustrious Horax Prime, it is each pack for themselves now."

Tronics' voice appeared on the bridge's speakers and with immaculate timing. "Tronics to the bridge, are you receiving, over?"

Colonel Bronze moved to the bridge comm controls closest to him. "Corporal, Zomo, what the hell's going on?"

After a brief audio distortion, Zomo replied. "Good news, sir. Reenergizing the last four D-brane compression cells and then it's sayonara. ETA twenty minutes."

Tronics added. "On our current drift speed and trajectory we'll be at Kemeta capital within thirty minutes."

The bridge breathed a sigh of relief.

"It's about bloody time you proved yourself useful, Corporal. Bronze out."

"Thirty minutes is cutting it real close," said Private Akerele. "Let's hope we make it in that time."

***

As she moved about in the infirmary, the doctor continued to assess the Black Guard's vitals, while Adcox sat watching from the seated corner area in deep thought. It was the first time he had ever been alone with a Kemetan, let alone a female Kemetan. He then realized he'd never been alone with a Horaxian period. Were they all like her? She had a thickness to her physique, and he found himself at odds dealing with the unappreciated sensations her voluptuousness conjured. He watched her move with graceful strides, with the type of elegance ancient queens of Greece or Egypt would have displayed. The young man also pondered if the scent of cinnamon, sorrel and orchid fragrances were perfumes, or might it be her natural pheromones.

Any other day she would have solely captivated his mind but just four meters away lay the most dangerous man in the universe. That was what they used to call him, and already, the Black Guard's actions saved his life from the beast within the Abyss. Then, a puzzling thought entered his mind.

"Hatshepsut, I'm a bit confused. Back in the Abyss, what did the Black Guard say to the creature to stop it?"

"The Black Guard spoke to ancient one in an old Horaxian language, only used by Arimans, the people of the first nation. Few Horaxians now understand their tongue. They say it can take fifty to a hundred years to become fluent."

"One hundred years?"

"Speculated it has been, that Arimans can live for over eight hundred years. I have spent time among them whilst conducting genetic research but I cannot accurately translate language. It did sound as though he said 'our time has come.' But to answer question, it was not words uttered that halted the Ariman. He gave the ancient one equivalent of what you would describe as a salute. An Ariman sign of respect."

Adcox pondered the meaning behind the words "our time has come" until a third voice spoke, braking his concentration.

"Lieutenant Adcox," said a female voice in a smooth, soft tone with only a slight accent, close to Caribbean in dialect.

Adcox bolted out of his seat and knocked over a glass beaker alerting Hatshepsut. He had no idea what was going on, all he knew was that the voice came from the Black Guard's bed area. Backing up to the wall, he hailed his unit via his suit's comms link to come to the infirmary.

"Who was that?" Adcox asked, the hairs on the back of his neck stood erect.

"This is Symbiotic Program Unit Eve6676214, the SPU of Black Guard Squadron Officer Commander Major Hawke. Thank you for retrieving us from the Abyss, Lieutenant Adcox and Doctor Hatshepsut." The gentle female voice had an almost musical and singsong quality.

"You're welcome!" said Adcox, his best on the spot response. He noticed that when the voice spoke green lights flashed on Hawke's shoulder.

"We...are...welcomed!" said the voice.

"Is he ok now? Major Hawke?" he asked the SPU.

At that moment, the rest of the ship personnel returned to the room in such haste they bumped into each other. Captain Lewalski used his shoulder to muscle past Kaya Maghan, angering him in the process.

"His priority vitals are gradually restoring," said the voice emanating from the flashing metal construct on the Black Guard's neck.

Colonel Bronze stepped forward. "SPU, when will he regain consciousness?"

"Colonel Bronze, the major has been conscious since we boarded the ship."

With the exception of Adcox and Hatshepsut, everyone in the infirmary looked at each other then raised their weapons higher; they cautiously encircled his bed.

"Please stand down," said SPU Eve6676214. "We have no hostile intentions."

"Tell that to the *Ploiarion,*" said Ballistic.

After a brief moment, the major's eyes opened.

Hatshepsut crept closer and was first to greet him. "Are you all right?"

"We're alive!" He responded in a tired, gravelly voice.

Colonel stepped forward. "Hawke, you are on board..."

His words were intercepted by the restrained man.

"The *Odysseus*, United Earth vessel, K900 fighter class. We know where we are, Colonel. Why are we restrained while are our enemies walk freely amongst us?" His slow, husky voice lingered his words in the air as though he struggled to breathe.

Hawke's statement infuriated Jei'Gun. "Souwrak! I should part your head from its cursed frame!"

"Sir," said Adcox, "the Horaxians are no longer our enemy."

The Black Guard turned his head to the marine. "When standing in the way of our purpose, *all* are our enemy." As he spoke, he began to wheeze.

"What's wrong with him, Doctor?" asked Adcox.

"He is weak. His shortness of breath will improve gradually as his lungs battle effects of radiation's poison. But he is also suffering from muscle and bone atrophy. Little there is, that I can do to aid him. It is amazing that he yet lives. I am about to administer booster shot of human nutrients to combat his malnourishment."

"Careful, Doctor," said Kaya Maghan. He began to speak in tongues to himself again. Hawke's dark piercing eyes watched Hatshepsut's every movement and despite his restraints and a room full of soldiers, her hands trembled as they veered in close proximity to her patient to inject his medicine.

"Your presence is required at Horax Prime," Bronze informed him. "Where a committee has been established with Earth Command."

***

"Its restraints must stay on at all times." Nanonramu reminded the humans as he stood the farthest away from the bed.

The Black Guard looked directly in the eyes of Bronze. "So now we are the dogs that must answer its master's call?" He still struggled to speak as if he was clinging on to life.

Jei'Gun leaned over and came face to face with the broken man. "You, butcher of a billion, are nothing but a corpse. As soon as you are no longer needed, Jei'Gun will slit your throat, slowly and painfully." The big elite-shakan flexed his arm and shoulder to display his intent.

"Take your Rogue friend's advice," said the Black Guard. "Keep the restraints on, that goes for all of you. Especially you."

Zomo's elated voice burst onto the ship's comms system. "Guys, we are back online, preparing the string-drive for a jump ASAP."

"You won't make it to Horax Prime, Colonel," said the Black Guard.

"Why's that?" Bronze asked.

"Colonel Bronze," chirped his SPU Eve, "they are already here."

The infirmary's communication system came online in a sudden loud rasp. "Incoming Polymorph energy signature, brace for impact!" screamed Zomo.

An external explosion rocketed the ship, throwing everyone off their feet. The team slid across the floor as the vessel dived, tilting left, tossing everything not held down in a complete frenzy. The infirmary's aft wall ripped open. The tumbling Kaya Maghan was thrown out of the ship, falling out of the sky to his peril. The rest of the team of both races held on to anything they could for dear life as the wind and engine fumes forced them to activate their helmets before the colonel got the order out.

Bronze shouted disjointed words to Zomo, attempting to ask her to land the ship safely while Nanonramu nearly fell out of the peeled away hull. Jei'Gun grabbed hold of him.

Zomo's only focus fixated on the helm steering controls and trying desperately to guide them to safety. "Mayday, Mayday, Mayday! We're going to hit just outside of Kemeta central," she informed the crew while gripping the control stick with all the strength in her tiny arms. "This is going to be a hard landing!"

The ship spiraled out of control, into the built up metropolis. Most the buildings were rounded in shape and six stories high. The *Odysseus* swirled and fell at a tilted angle with two black trails jetting out from its engines. A

Horaxian stellar warship, an enormous vessel with quintuple rear engines glowing bright green floated in the sky, fired blasts of dark orange beams of energy at a target shrouded in dark clouds. Emanating from the clouds, streams of grey smoke rained down like miniature meteors breaking through the atmosphere. So did the *Odysseus*, as it crashed behind a row of buildings, followed by the bang of a horrific crash.

Chapter Six - Caught In A Horde Storm

Even while tainted by war, Kemeta's capital still retained a fraction of its beauty. The planet's extreme magnetic field reacted with the minerals in the composite material used to build its roads and building, and after a few years of exposure all of its infrastructure shined in bright white. With the intense magnetic field and decades of power generation, the Kemetans learned to enhance the effects of magnetism. All of their transportation systems used electromagnetic levitation as well as many of their architectural structures.

But the view of this exhilarating metropolis was ruined by blocks of damaged white buildings and pavement stretching for miles in Kemeta's majestic aurora, with its hues of blue, purple and green.

The wreckage of the ship littered the ground, which had been fragmented into rubble from battle. Surrounding the downed ship were bullet riddled buildings with shot-out windows; glass shards remaining lodged in the frames.

But mostly, dead bodies scattered the streets surrounding the *Odysseus*, in so great a number that the ground could barely be seen. All of them were Horaxian bodies and only few were undefiled. Torso's without limbs, heads minus the bodies and corpses missing a face, revealing the fleshy insides. Insects had already started to converge on the intestines and other exposed organs.

From the wreckage Private Akerele emerged, bruised and battered but in an otherwise good state. Then

Nanonramu rose up with his head gashed, his purple blood trickling. Tronics followed and dusted himself off. Zomo was unscathed, thanks to the bridge's reinforced bulkhead walls which had remained mostly intact.

Colonel Bronze woke up on the ground to see Captain Lewalski's limp body resting on him.

"Get off me, Mike, you lazy bastard." Bronze's face was blackened on his forehead and chin.

Lewalski came to, his left leg had a shard of metal that had pierced through his flesh and fractured his femur bone. An explosion blew apart a section of the *Odysseus*'s hull and rattled the team. Out of the smoke, the elite-shakan Jei'Gun emerged.

"Jei'Gun, look above." Nanonramu pointed upwards and both males laid eyes upon Kaya Maghan's lifeless body lying on top of a tall streetlight, impaled from the fall.

Jei'Gun and Nanonramu both unsheathed their arm blades and lowered them so that they touched one another's close to the ground. They then lowered their heads and in harmony chanted, "Lost, The Dark Star, his title will forever ring in the hearts of warriors!"

Simultaneously, their heads rose to witness the shining silver of a Horaxian fighter-craft falling from the sky and crashing into the street light, generating a loud explosion.

Colonel Bronze regained his sense of duty upon the thunderous sound. "Is everybody all right?"

Most of the stellar marines responded with words uttered in discomfort.

"Can you walk, Mike?" asked Bronze.

"Walk? Hell, I can run a marathon," said Lewalski, but then gritted his teeth as his injured leg struggled to hold his body weight. "Last time I checked."

"Zomo, Akerele, give the XO a hand," ordered Bronze and they both came by Lewalski's sides and placed his arms over their shoulders.

Lewalski, even though injured, watched in awe of the beautiful colors of the Kemetan skyline, the constant aurora caused by its intense magnetosphere.

"We must get to Kemeta ground base," said Nanonramu.

Bronze watched as a few Horaxian troopers ran straight past them in hysteria, so frightened they didn't stop or even acknowledge that they were human. Jei'Gun grabbed one of the Horaxian warriors in mid-sprint with one hand, hoisting him off the ground. The male, out of fright, wrestled against being restrained before the elite warrior's words halted him.

"Who is in charge now? Why are you running from direction of Kemeta's forward operation base? Why are you running at all, trooper?"

"H...h...Horde's first wave, it destroyed main defenses inclu...including our central base. Apex Ngolo Diarra is...is...'

"Is what?" bellowed Jei'Gun.

"He commands what is left of...of the forces at new temporary forward operating base..."

"Where?" Jei'Gun bawled.

"Ax..Axis...Axis 239!"

"Since you are so eager to depart world, coward, let Jei'Gun cast you upon journey."

"Elite-shakan, no..." The trooper wasn't given enough time to plead. Jei'Gun crushed his windpipe with his one hand.

After the Anubianite whipped his head from side to side, then spun around in three hundred and sixty degrees. "Where is the cursed one?"

"Sir!" said Private Akerele, hurrying to Bronze side. "I've looked around and I can't find the Black Guard. Adcox and Ballistic are missing too."

"Hatshepsut is also among missing," added Nanonramu. "Find them we must."

Tronics began to shout out the missing member's names and moments after he heard a response. Amongst the rubble, a heavy piece of broken-off hull section shifted and underneath lay Ballistic. He was tossed out of the falling vessel as it crash-landed and skidded across the street surface. The remnants of Unit Forty Two rushed to his side.

"Real soft landing, Zomo," Ballistic said.

"On your feet, soldier!" ordered Bronze. "We need to find the lieutenant and the Hawke."

Painfully, Ballistic rose and executed a quick weapons check on his minigun.

As the group combed the wreckage, more Horaxian troopers and civilians scurried around the city, screaming in utter disarray. Nanonramu saw something on the pavement's grey and white rubble that caught his attention. There were two aisles of disruption in the dirt, its undisturbed nature meant it had been freshly made.

"Something was dragged across here, two bodies," said Nanonramu. He then looked in the direction of the trail that bent around a giant statue of the Great Supreme King. "We must follow trail."

***

Adcox awakened from unconsciousness to feel himself being nudged. He opened his eyes to see the dirt-smeared face of Hatshepsut resting next to him. White dust covered their lower halves from being dragged.

"Are you ok?" he asked her.

"I believe so."

He sat up. "Can you stand?"

"Yes, Diomedes."

Adcox then scanned for his missing rifle. He noticed a fountain close by and saw that its water had turned purple with the blood of slayed Horaxians slumped inside. Shock consumed him as he witnessed the Black Guard commander, leaning over the fountain, freed from his restraints. The bearded warrior bowed low and scooped bloodied water with both hands and washed his face in the same nonchalant manner a traveler would on a tropical beach.

Hatshepsut also looked on in wonder at his unclothed muscular back mangled with keloids and hypertrophic scars. Never in her life as a medical doctor or biologist had she glimpsed such a sight. Adcox wondered if they were burns? Perhaps corrosive acid injuries or produced by some barbaric torture method?

Hatshepsut tapped the young marine and directed him with her head movement to something standing upright against the fountain right next to Hawke, the lieutenant's solar rifle. It was as if the major hadn't noticed they were conscious as he passed his wet hands over his dark face and long plaited hair. Adcox crept forward to retrieve his firearm.

"Not the best place to lose your weapon, soldier," said Major Hawke, his back still faced Adcox. He then reached for the rifle right beside him, too far away for Adcox to get there first.

"Drop the weapon or we'll drop you," shouted Ballistic.

Hawke turned to see the rest of the group had surrounded him with weapons levelled on him.

"We don't think that's possible, Sergeant," replied the mysterious man.

"We did in the Abyss," said Ballistic.

"Really?" Neither the Black Guard's face nor voice portrayed any emotion.

"Maybe it needs some convincing," said Jei'Gun.

Akerele and Zomo caught up with the team, the two helping to support the injured Captain Lewalski.

"Hey, back off Horaxians. He's ours," Akerele said.

"Silence you souwrak!" Said Jei'Gun in sharp dismissal.

"Just wait!" said Adcox, rising up to stand. He crept toward Major Hawke. "I don't want any trouble major, I just need my weapon back."

The major stared silently as the young lieutenant reached to nearly an arm's length away. "Interesting!" said Hawke, glancing over to Hatshepsut. "It's all yours, Lieutenant." He extended the weapon out to him and Adcox grabbed hold but didn't take his eyes off him. The legendary man's actions were confusing. His willingness to submit without fighting even more bewildering, he did not flee when he could have. Adcox found it peculiar for an escape expert to be so...unopportunistic.

"Jei'Gun, we need to get to the F.O.B," said Lewalski, "and get whoever's in charge to give us a ship." After he spoke, the captain pulled out the thin, jagged, metal fragment from the ship protruding out of his leg.

"Yes, but first we must cover it up," said Jei'Gun referring to the Black Guard, disgusted by the sight of the half-naked, disfigured body. "Knowledge of cursed one's presence here would decimate our ranks just as worse as any Horde attack."

At his words, Nanonramu bent down and pulled the black robe off the corpse of an aged male at his feet. He then looked at the Black Guard and froze in his tracks. His antennae rose high and stiffened. "Human female," he called out to Zomo. "Cover it!" What Rogue wanted to touch the body of a demon?

Ballistic marched up to Hawke and placed his hands in metal restraints he had removed from his utility belt.

"All right people," said Bronze, before coughing again. "Any sight of the Horde, use extreme prejudice. Corporal?"

"Tell me what you need, boss man," replied Tronics.

"See if you can find a satellite so we could track the Polymorph's movements."

"I'm already on it, there's one still orbital. Hacking in now."

***

They made their way through the city, watching the sight of sections of buildings falling out of the sky. Plumes of smoke streamed down from the clouds, concealing hidden objects that bombarded the capital. The hood of the black robe cloaked Major Hawke's face, yet he never flinched at the loud sounds of the bulky, sharp-tipped warship firing its big guns high above, nor the Horaxian screams and multiple weapons fire in the distance that caused the group to react with jittery movements. Adcox, Zomo and Nanonramu especially.

Nanonramu's antennae moved independently around like it floated in the wind, detecting all manner of sensory information. "I can smell death, countless death," he said with a nervous shutter.

Adcox had no words to describe the appalling scene of the endless Horaxian corpses, but words weren't necessary, his sunken face said it all. Most of the dead were half eaten. Their murderers had a habit of devouring the heads first then taking their time to return for the rest of the carcass. But some preferred to feed their bellies full. He raised his head to gaze at all the dilapidated buildings and wondered how much of its state was due to the current Polymorph assault and how much damage pre-existed courtesy of years of economic depression and anarchy. Those insignificant thoughts disappeared as he sighted the large creatures circling high in the sky. He couldn't make out any distinct features but he identified their flattened bodies that looked similar to flying manta rays. They filled the sky like a swarm of locusts, releasing bone chilling shrieks.

"Horde rays, hundreds of them!" Hatshepsut said, stopping close to him.

"They have air superiority, please stay close, Hatshepsut," said Adcox.

She gazed at him, no doubt surprised by his concern.

"It's just that you're not armed," he added.

She released a simple nod at him and continued to walk.

Hatshepsut and Zomo choked as they trekked past smoke plumes fueled by burnt out armored fighting vehicles and mutilated bodies. As they advanced, the streets became crowded with more troopers, alive ones, but mostly injured and in total disorder. Tronics had his data-slab in one hand and his hi-tech laser weapon in the other, which became the focus of Colonel Bronze's displeasing eyes.

"Thought I told you next time you're in the field I want to see something standard issue in your hands, Corporal?" Bronze said without bothering to face him.

"Just wanted to prove its effectivity against the Horde, boss."

"When we get back, laddie, there's going to be a reprimand. Are you feeling me?"

"I felt you, sir. Up and down, sir. In places you never even wanted to be felt."

The wind energized in a violent howl. Adcox saw that Hatshepsut had become quiet and withdrawn, her eyes downcast. He soon identified the source of her frown, amongst the countless dead bodies covered in purple blood, lay many young children.

She stopped by the body of a juvenile female. Both her legs had been torn off. Her tiny left arm still reached for her toy, which resembled an hour glass in the shape of a female doll. The toy was tinted, filled with a silver grainy substance. Hatshepsut reached and grabbed hold of the toy, her hands trembled by her sadness.

"The Polymorph take no prisoners," said Adcox at her side, feeling stifled by the stench of death. "They show no mercy."

Hatshepsut placed the toy in the dead youth's hand in an upright position. As she did so, the silver grains inside the hour glass began levitating from the object's lower half and defied gravity as it flowed into the upper section.

"Her time should not have ran out," she said, her eyes swelling with royal blue tears.

"What's up with all the static on the comms, Corporal," Captain Lewalski asked Tronics, still in deep discomfort. "Auto filters are not working."

"It's this atmosphere, sir. The super strong geomagnetic field is ballsing up everything. But I'm trying to manually correct it now."

Suddenly the SPU's voice emanated from the neck of The Black Guard. "Warning! Incoming projectile."

They all scattered as an explosion impacted with an immense detonation, killing some of the Horaxians that were scurrying around. The group however were unscathed due to Eve's warning, accept for Akerele whose left eardrum was blown out from the bang. A loud, unholy scream rang out. They turned to see a Horaxian impaled by a humanoid creature with overdeveloped shoulders and trapezius muscles, but no neck. Its pulsating, small and deformed head resided at the center of its chest and protruded outwards deflating and expanding.

It had three torso upper limbs, with the torso itself held upright by two large feet. Of the upper limbs, one had a clubbed shape, and the light brown of the creature's flesh revealed a yellow energy that circulated through the stub.

On its right arm was a porous, enlarged and deformed hand five times larger than a man's.

Its third upper limb stemmed from its back and wrapped around to its hideous front. This one had no hand, only three long blades hardened like a rhino's horn, and lined with fine razor sharp teeth. In short, it was an abomination, worse than even a grown man's worse nightmare. The monster's biological blade was what had impaled the hapless Horaxian. As green tinted saliva drooled from its mouth, its arm which bore its only hand now began to metamorphose into an elongated spear and struck the man's head, knocking it straight off his shoulders.

"Polymorph drone!" said Adcox.

"Watch the cursed one," Jei'Gun said to Zomo and Tronics, he and Nanonramu stepped forward.

Tronics accessed his digital city map. "It hasn't seen us. We can detour via axis 112."

They made attempt to move out of view of the creature's cyclopic eye which was twice as big as a football and lodged into its lumpy back. The Black Guard now chose to break his silence. "We have company!" They all braced themselves at the ready, eyes locked on the Horde drone. "Not that way!" he said. They all turned around but saw nothing. A sudden shadow descended upon them. In a flash, they looked above and saw two Horde rays swooping down, mouth and claws opened and ready to strike.

"Duck!" Bronze cried out.

The team jumped to the ground frantically firing to fend the creatures off. One of the rays grabbed Captain Lewalski, its sweeping wings blew blinding dust in their eyes. With its beefy, widespread talons it pierced Lewalski's armor and flew off with him. He bawled out in agony, his assault rifle spraying the area and Akerele had to push Zomo out of the way.

Bronze stared emotionlessly at the sight of his old friend being carried away. They rose back to their feet to the sound of a roar, accompanied by the hammering footsteps of the brutish Horde drone which had killed the trooper now charging straight at them.

The group unleashed a hail of bullets, yet the beast kept coming, their rounds absorbing into its flesh. From the drone's stubbed limb, yellow energy built up, expanding the appendage. It unleashed and impacted just wide of the group but close enough to throw Akerele and Tronics off their feet.

As most of the group moved backwards, one stepped forward, Ballistic, unshaken and determined. He squeezed hard on his trigger and his minigun tore through the creature's chest, bringing it down. After only a few seconds something happened to the body of the vile creature; it rapidly decomposed into a fleshy ooze and evaporated completely.

The Black Guard seemed unfazed by his surroundings but intrigued by the vanishing body. The creature left no trace, not even a spec of matter or residue remained.

"Quickly, push forward we must," said Jei'Gun.

Adcox only knew the captain for a brief moment but the sorrow of his loss got to him. The man was a rock, and he felt the mood of the team had changed irreparably.

They journeyed onwards until they reached a side street and Adcox noticed movement on the ground that captured his attention. Standing in the cross section, the lieutenant's blue eyes lit up at the identification of a man on the ground crawling towards him.

"Look, it's the captain," Adcox said, alerting everyone.

Impulsively, he dashed to help Lewalski who was missing a right leg and a left forearm. His head awash with blood, the captain crawled towards them over the white stone rubble that littered the streets.

"No, Lieutenant, stop!" yelled Bronze.

Adcox didn't listen, trying to get to the captain. A sudden shower of bullets riddled the body of Lewalski, when Adcox turned around he saw the weapon of Colonel Bronze raised and smoking. In front of the dead captain the ground spontaneously rumbled. A gigantic Horde ray emerged from the rubble causing numerous tiny stones to rain down on the terrified lieutenant.

Two more rays appeared out of dark window frames and surrounded them, shrieking as they swooped down from their ambush point. The group fired upon them. Jei'Gun discharge a grenade round and the two winged monsters from the windows flew away. The largest ray, its talons close to grabbing Adcox, succumbed to his team's combined fire.

"It was a trap," said Bronze. "He was already dead. Let's keep moving." Bronze lingered a moment at the sight of Lewalski's corpse; the rest of the group pushed forward, all accept Adcox who stayed beside him. "I'll be seeing you and Julia soon, old friend," said Bronze, he turned to Adcox. "A man once said that good, temporarily defeated, is stronger than evil triumphant."

"Martin Luther King Jr. I believe, sir."

"Keep it simple, son. One, check your line of fire. Two, shoot. That's all you need to remember."

"Yes, sir."

"And never, ever, take your eyes off the Black Guard commander." Bronze paused. "The man can become a shadow."

'What in the world is that supposed to mean?' The young lieutenant thought to himself.

***

As they ventured onwards Adcox spun around, fixated on the innumerable screams in all directions. His ears pinpointed the epicenter, the highest magnitude of chaos. It was in the direction they were headed. The crowd of Horaxian troopers increased in density as they neared the Forward Operating Base. Adcox watched as civilians hurried to safety and the lieutenant glanced up for a split second to take in the vista of sophisticated aerial train lines which perhaps until recently levitated trains throughout the metropolis. A foul odor was given off by the extreme amount of arm-cannon gun propellant that lingered in the air, creating its own haze. It also induced nausea in the human contingent.

More Polymorph creatures filled the streets, ripping apart Kemeta's population. They were unstoppable, even when one was downed, three more took its place and they swarmed the city like an army of ants engulfing every patch of pavement. The planetary defensive forces were far from an impregnable unit, nor a valiant one. Half of the troopers were so struck with fear they put up little fight. Others were killed by their foes while attempting to escape and evade. No males, females or children were spared. The Horde slaughtered all without amnesty, without taking prisoners, no rules of engagement or chivalry, and without a picosecond of hesitation. It was the soullessness of their savagery that had broken the spirit of the two races.

The human-Horaxian group were near the thick of it and the noise of battle became deafening. The Black Guard watched the fight closely, particularly the Polymorph. He saw a great beast with a shape close to a triceratops but twice larger in mass, and six thick, hefty legs. It had seven long horns on its head, three of them were the length of two cars placed together. Its armor was super thick, stronger than any human or Horaxian tank, lining and overlapping its body like sheets of rugged steel.

"*Mammoth!*" a trooper screamed once he laid eyes upon the creature. A form of energy built up within its throat, causing its fatty neck to illuminate and swell. It squeezed its neck muscles inwards and then jolted it outwards projecting a ball of energy from its mouth that flew a great distance, over four hundred meters and above the group's heads. It hit a mega-sentry defense cannon and annihilated it along with the immediate area, leaving a huge crater. The mammoth monster then smashed through the troopers, trampling them and pulverizing their armored vehicles. Concealed under his cloak, the convicted soldier identified something strange, another Horde drone, a replica of the first one. It started to violently convulse and numerous long crablike legs grew out of it. Within seconds it mutated and broke apart. What was once one beast became many smaller crablike creatures, each as big as German shepherds. They pounced on their Horaxian victims, stinging and biting them to death. One trooper who had been bitten began to spasm so hard Major Hawke heard the snapped of him breaking his own back.

"Neurotoxin!" Hawke whispered to himself.

The Black Guard took notice of multiple black, spherical objects in the distance close to six and a half feet in height with a slimy, thin outer shell. They were Polymorph cocoons. An incalculable amount scattered the city streets, raining down from the shrouded sky in their grey pillars of smoke. He watched as a few came to life with a burst of internal orange and yellow energy, creating cracks in its outer shell. From inside the oozing amniotic fluid more Horde drones emerged, like reptiles out of their egg. Yet the Horde were fully formed and ready to do what they were born to do...kill. All the fallen Polymorph seemed to disintegrate from flesh to an ooze-like substance, then finally into nothing.

Jei'Gun shoved Hawke with his gauntlet. "Move, souwrak!"

***

They made it to the city plaza, which functioned as a temporary Forward Operating Base; a mere stronghold of barricades, rows of encircling stone, armored vehicles and steel, guarded by troopers and artillery on the street. The last FOB was a highly fortified bunker, yet the Horde destroyed it as if it was built of straw. Fixed, secured strongholds became pointless...this was out and out war. Adcox took a moment to gaze at the bloodied defeated troopers; some wept inconsolably, some were disoriented, as though their minds were on another planet. He wished that he hadn't noticed their faces, recollecting Bronze's words to "never stare in the eyes of a broken man." These were once proud warriors, an army that was well on their way to defeating mankind.

A broad warrior with armor decorated in gold and colored gems captured Adcox's attention while he screamed commands in a gravelly voice. He was Apex Ngolo Diarra, an Apex, Horaxian equivalent to a general, and commander of the defense of the city.

"Protect the mega-sentries!" bellowed the Apex as he marched around the makeshift stockade. It formed an outer perimeter to the plaza's inner stone walls. "Hold the perimeter! Sub-alpha, reinforce the left flank!"

Jei'Gun approached Bronze. "Human Colonel, come with Jei'Gun. We must speak with the Apex."

"Aye! Ballistic you're with me, rest of you guard the Hawke. Engage the Horde only as a defensive measure but remember we are not here as combatants."

As they walked off amongst the congregation of troopers, Adcox and his team soon heard pounding footsteps, intermingled in the sounds of Horaxian battle-cries and arm-cannon rounds. A colossal figure treaded in bold strides towards them. Its long hanging, bright-white hair wrapped in thick individual dreadlocks equaled a man's height. Most of the locks were heavily matted, others, especially the ones at the front, were single plaited and slimmer. Even the largest of men would be dwarfed by the creature and its mood looked foul. Adcox and Tronics stared with their mouths' wide open.

"The last of the Arimans." Hatshepsut said as the beast moved closer, perpendicular to where they stood.

"Not just any Ariman," voiced the Black Guard, choosing a rare moment to speak. He appeared mesmerized by the view of the hulking creature. Its massive shoulders bounced back and forth and as it marched, troopers were quick to clear its path, its eight foot, two ton muscular mass gave them a good reason too. The oversized helmet and black armor it wore were comparable to medieval warriors of Earth, revealing black herculean skin on parts of its body unprotected by metal.

These huge brutes were their aboriginal ancestors, who once thrived on the first planet of the Horaxians. Walking mountains of pure muscle and skin almost as rock, they were over ten times stronger than any man or elite-shakan warrior. Their head hair was always long, forbidden by their laws to be cut.

What was also noticeable was a metal collar wrapped around its neck, pulsing periodically with a blue standby light. All of a sudden the beast halted in mid motion, sniffing the air in a somewhat confused state. The seemingly impossible happened, and the Ariman's face became even angrier than it was before. It released a sharp roar.

"Urk'Tark!" the massive ancient Horaxian yelled in a bellowing voice. "Where are you?" Its deep angry voice resonated in the air almost like it had been digitally synthesized with additional harmonics layered into it. The brute sniffed the air again, this time pinpointing the source of the scent and turned its body to none other than the Black Guard commander.

"Mighty Rey'Jax!" Major Hawke said.

The Ariman began stomping its way towards him. As it did, its collar begun to light up with brighter blue pulsating lights. Zomo raised her weapon at it.

"Unless you're planning to tickle him to death, put that away," said the major.

As the Horaxian goliath reached closer he raised his fisted hand to strike the Black Guard. Zomo and Tronics moved out of the way in fear.

"Please brother!" the major uttered, in a searching voice, a yearning voice but not one of fear. A trooper that had been escorting the giant slammed his finger down on his digital device. As Rey'Jax's arm extended, his collar released a flash of red light as it activated and stunned the Ariman. Electricity pulsed through his neck and his spine. The device was a prison collar, designed to enslave its wearer by tapping into their central nervous and peripheral nervous system and electrocuting their synapses when required. The Ariman's large canine teeth emerged, due to his excruciating pain but still he attempted to fight against the electricity's effect of involuntarily contracting his muscles, preventing him from moving closer to endanger the Black Guard. The giant fought on savagely against the debilitating effects while speaking words in Ariman tongue as his head reached merely inches away from Major Hawke's skull.

"Urk'Tark!" The Ariman said again.

The Black Guard, the only one unfazed by the giant, uttered a few words back in the Ariman tongue. He smelt the familiar scent of wax made from Ariman bear fat drenched in Rey'Jax's hair.

"Get back, beast!" a trooper shouted as he pressed another button on the control pad that increased the power of the prison collar and repelled Rey'Jax back as he began to suffer respiratory paralysis.

"Safe to say, he doesn't like you, Major," said Tronics, relieved the giant Horaxian had reached a safer distance.

"There were once thousands of Arimans before Battle of Cyclonis," Hatshepsut said addressing the group, "but they were killed for insurrection by the High Apex, Commander Cagn. I have not seen any in six years...until today."

Adcox may have been unaccustomed to Horaxians in general, but every human being knew the name of Cagn. He represented the symbol of Horaxian military might.

"Do you know what they were saying to each other?" Zomo asked Hatshepsut.

"I am unable to fully translate it, but he did call your Mr. Hawke...traitor."

"Seems like somebody can fully translate," said Adcox. "Question is, how does he know how to?"

A sad frown descended upon Hawke as he watched Rey'Jax being marched to the frontlines of the battleground surrounded by troopers.

***

As the rest of the team waited, Jei'Gun, Bronze and Ballistic made their way to the commander of the Kemetan defensive forces. Jei'Gun turned to the two humans. "Do not mention presence of cursed one, for our requests will be trounced by scornful ears. Jei'Gun alone shall engage the Apex in dialogue."

"Wilco!" said Bronze, nodding his head.

Jei'Gun then walked up to Apex Ngolo Diarra who wore a multitude of thick-linked blue and gold chains around his neck, his black cloak draped weightily across his back and right shoulder. "Honorable Apex, most humbly we request audience." Jei'Gun said, repressing his usual aggressive tone.

The Apex barely looked at him. "What is it, elite-shakan? Time is precious."

"Jei'Gun has been tasked mission of great importance with humans beside me. Report we must to the Divine Council on Illustrious Horax Prime."

"Very well, I will provide cover for you to evacuate. Speak with my sub-alpha!" said Ngolo Diarra, eager to continue with his affairs. The sound of automatic weapons fire intensified due to the onrush of Horde breaking through their lines.

"Apex, Great Warrior, our ship now destroyed, superluminal-flight capable vessel we now also require."

"That I cannot do. I need all vessels to defend planet. Horde first wave crushed most of our defenses."

An explosion nearby rocked the ground, spraying dust on the anxious colonel and Ballistic.

Jei'Gun pressed on. "Given us this charge directly from the Divine Council. We must deliver something of importance vital to our people..."

Ngolo Diarra interrupted. "And where is the Divine Council now, noble warrior? They have forsaken us. They have delivered me only one stellar warship to withstand Horde's might. Kemeta depends upon capital, if this mega metropolis falls so will entire planet."

The colonel felt he needed to speak out. "Kemeta *will* fall, Apex..."

"Jei'Gun commanded you to not break words, human," said Jei'Gun.

"Bollocks," said Bronze. Too late to fear anything now, he needed to get the message across. "It's inevitable, but billions can be saved if you can get us to Horax Prime."

Ngolo Diarra glanced at Bronze's rank insignia and flared his big, jewelry-pierced nostrils. "How dare you press me, *human colonel*! You desire ship? You will have to fight first. Then perhaps, grant I will your request. Until then, be gone from sight."

In an instant, the ground surrounding them shook violently, unbalancing everything and everyone within a seventy-five foot radius. Soon after, it broke apart and numerous large spiny tentacles reached out; wrapping around the Apex, Jei'Gun, Bronze and a few other troopers. One tentacle tried to grab hold of Ballistic but he shredded it with minigun rounds. But another tentacle lashed him, knocking him back. He had been spared a horrible fate. From what gripped the colonel and the others in its spiny tentacles, there was no escape.

Their end had come.

"Colonel!" Adcox yelled in a lingering cry some distance away. His desire to help was destroyed by Tronics' scream.

"*Horde charge!*"

All the marines and Horaxian troopers engaged in a firefight with the attacking Polymorphic crabs and drones. The Black Guard stooped down with both knees bent pointing upwards and analyzed the ferocious battle. He seemed uninterested in picking up any Horaxian weapons that lay by his feet and joining the fight. Neither did he seem to care about the danger of the Polymorph's presence. His sluggish body movement indicated an onset of fatigue but also that he was comfortable. Like an old man returning to his place of birth and tranquilized by nostalgia, war was all he had ever known, and in the chaos all around him, he found peace.

The Black Guard commander did, however, pay close attention to Adcox and Tronics as they tried to fend off the attack. Tronics' blasts from his laser sent out straight, intense streams of light with a ring of electricity arcing around the seemingly non-evanescence beams. It struck its Horde target and blew a whole straight through its flesh. Not stopping, the beam went farther on to hit another drone behind it, going straight through its body also. It seemed to kill the creatures before they had time to accept death, since they continued coming forward briefly before dropping to the ground. Tronics panned the beam horizontally and it sliced through three rows of multiple Horde drones, proving its effectiveness. He counted to himself, always conscious of the time that elapsed on each sustained beam.

Adcox mumbled to himself, "Check my line of fire. Shoot." Then applied the colonel's advice with shaky hands. His heart sank watching the scattering troopers. Their infamous discipline and solidarity in the human wars had been transformed by the Horde into cowardice.

In the distance, the Black Guard's eye caught the attention of another type of Polymorph who many regarded as the most dangerous of them all. They were fewer in number than the other Horde subspecies but far from mindless. Some questioned whether they understood spoken language but simply chose not to communicate. These unusual Polymorph were less restricted by reinforced biological armor like their drone counterparts, and capable of great speeds, faster than a tiger at full pace. Their tall, slender bodies gifted them the agility to leap great bounds. But their weapons conjured up the most fear in souls of men. It was a short scepter forged of bone and flesh; at its top, a fusion of black and purple energy emanated from an orb.

Major Hawke saw this one special Polymorph rip its scepter from the lateral side of its abdomen. The weapon and its body appeared biologically whole, and as the scepter pulled away from its side, vines of flesh burst from being overstretched. The creature had ten black tendrils on its head, five on each side, which moved around independently like eels in the air. It raised its right arm, extending its hand and stretched out its long, oozing, clawed fingers. As it did so, the tendrils all aligned upright and remained dead straight. The Black Guard commander witnessed extreme levels of fear descending on a group of troopers, so much so that they lowered their weapons and froze in their tracks, like animals too scared to even flee. To him, this behavior appeared unnatural.

The slender Polymorph then raised the scepter high with its left hand and it ignited. A surge of energy arced and connected with a hapless trooper, annihilating him and leaving no trace of his existence. It then waved the weapon and pointed it toward another male in the group of six. The scepter began to throb, once more it ignited and vaporized only one male, who went without a fight. The tall Polymorph, with a cranial structure formed naturally as a helmet, placed its scepter back on its rib cage area and repulsively, strands of skin and blood vessels grabbed hold of the object, fusing it with its body once more. It turned and walked away sparing the remaining troopers. The surrounding multitudes of Horde crabs were not so forgiving. They immediately pounced on the immobilized males.

"Eve!" called Major Hawke. "Execute a residual energy signature scan a hundred and ten meters north by northwest of our current position, highlighting atmospheric anomalies and mitigating Horaxian battle and civilian technology."

"Please state the energy properties you require scanning," said Eve as she activated her embedded spectrometer.

"Infrared!"

"The Polymorph's body insulation emit no heat signature."

"Cosmic energy, gamma rays."

"Scanning, none found."

"The whole electromagnetic spectrum."

Eve responded after a longer delay. "Scanning...none found."

"What are you looking for?" asked Adcox, eavesdropping all the while.

"Scan human and Horaxian extended periodic tables," said the veteran, ignoring Adcox's question. His speech increased in velocity. Whatever he was looking for, he was focused on finding it fast.

"Scanning...none found."

"What about gravity?" The major asked.

"Unusual residual localized gravitational forces detected."

"Trace signature and create a digital copy." Now he had finished his objective he looked toward the young marine. "Conservation of energy, Lieutenant. I've found breadcrumbs."

As Adcox tried to make sense of the Black Guard commander's plans, his colonel and sergeant were in dire straits. Bronze struggled bitterly to break free of the tentacles crushing his armored suit at the midsection, pressing upon his ribs to the breaking point. His wits were sharp enough to raise his helmet up before it was too late. As the rumbling ground broke apart in loud, echoing cracks, a body-mass bulged out of the rubble, revealing the face of what commanded the tendrils. For those that believe the Horde were evil incarnate, this face was their unholy affirmation. Never across a billion galaxies would one ever have imagined a creature formed so hideous, even more so than the drones.

A captured trooper was in such utter shock that he passed out, his body slumped in its tentacled coil. Two more troopers in close vicinity to the monstrosity fell lifeless to the pavement. A third followed. Part of what had stunned them all were the hundreds of encircling eyes scattered all around the creature's body and all moving independently. Tiny insectoids crawled in and out of its enormous circular mouth armed with five rows of long, sharp, shark-like, jagged teeth. All of this repulsiveness was contained within a massive pulsing head that periodically expanded close to twice its size and covered with ruptured blood vessels that flapped in the air.

Few had been known to survive once gripped by a Horde squid. It squeezed one trooper until his body broke in two, then it drew Apex Ngolo Diarra into its mouth.

"No!" He wailed in despair. "Help...help me! Somebody please! Please!" His cries were futile. The creature swallowed him almost whole, severing his knees off with its bite. Jei'Gun and Colonel Bronze paused and traded glances after this horrific event. Although they were from different worlds separated by endless stars both shared the same thought for this one brief moment, a thought which caused them to drop their arms and halt their resistance...complete dread.

With a simultaneous burst of energy, both experienced warriors struggled even more feverously than ever in their lives to break free. They were well aware to avoid gazing directly at the monster as they frantically struck its tentacles with little effect. Its dual repulsive image and smell was known to paralyze, which was the reason why Bronze raised his helmet to activate his suit's life support system.

"*No!* Jei'Gun is Power Made Flesh," said the Anubianite, trying to catch his breath, breathing as deeply as his embrace would allow. "Jei'Gun will not die this day."

The elite-shakan unsheathed his arm blade and hacked at the thick tentacle with all of his remaining endurance, finally cutting it off. Testament against those that devalued brute strength, he proved its worth and did the impossible. Falling, he rose back on his feet and sunk his mechanical mitts into the severed tentacle, still wrapped tightly round him, still biologically programmed to squeeze him to death. Using his gifted upper body, he tore it off his frame. Now ready for the fight he hacked at two more tentacles.

Bronze too refused to give up even though his fate looked doomed. He heard the sound of the tentacles crushing the midsection of his armor as if an aluminum can. As the ground squid reeled him into its mouth, he remembered the days his strength and endurance surpassed younger men and wished what he lost could return, if only for this one last favor.

Yelling from crushing pain, he punched the tentacles with his only arm that was free, not gifted with Anubianite bionic armor but still he fought until the bitter, unsavory end.

Ammunition ripped into the monster's tentacle and it severed off, dropping the colonel. The bullets were courtesy of Ballistic now back on his feet and he shot at another tentacle attempting to snatch him. As Bronze dropped, his battle experience told him to roll and this action unraveled the severed tendril from his body. He got up, and looked at Ballistic with great concern. The metal toothed man was firing so wildly at the Horde his bullets hit two Horaxian troopers. Bronze knew that Ballistic's hatred for Horaxians was so strong, that in his current enraged state they and the Horde were one. His man had gone haywire as he yelled all manner of insults to his dual foes, paying no attention to his surrounding, drunk off of his killing frenzy like sharks at the scent of blood. Bravery was what Bronze demanded of his men but recklessness was dangerous. He knew that if he didn't calm the big man down, he may lose the one thing cybernetic implants could never replace.

"Ballistic!" Bronze yelled, but his enraged soldier ignored him, the rotating barrels of his minigun shredded to pieces everything in its path. *"Sergeant Hasselberg!"* he screamed even louder.

"Yes, sir!" replied Ballistic, as if he wanted to rip his colonel's head off.

"Stay focused marine. Grenade!"

Ballistic reached into his utility belt and threw a grenade to his commanding officer. Bronze activated it and threw it into the ground squid's mouth; moments later it detonated and completely destroyed the creature, spraying orange slime on everything in a thirty meter radius. The squid's remains and its slimy residue then rapidly vaporized into nothingness.

"Took your sweet time, Sergeant," said Bronze in a foul mood.

"Apologies for my punctuality, sir." Ballistic came back to his senses, the immediate danger averted.

"Delay like that again and I'll kill you myself!"

"Sir, yes, sir!"

***

While Unit Forty Two and the surviving Horaxians fought in vain, one remained unaffected by the chaos. Though his head remained buried deep within his hooded cloak, the Black Guard was still fully aware of his surroundings and chose to tunnel his focus to significant points of interest. As his mind deconstructed the battlefield, for him time itself slowed down. A dead Horde drone Tronics had just downed drew his attention. Something intrigued him. He wondered if the corporal's laser beam shots were too clean. Normally, the Polymorph automatically disintegrated upon death yet this recently wounded drone was immobile, yet still alive. The tech expert's weapon incapacitated its victim while leaving so much of its vitals intact, its biology hadn't yet processed its death. But Hawke noticed something else. Shell casings from Horaxian munitions littered the ground and he detected that some were stuck to the squirming body of the creature. He moved closer to it, dangerously close.

"You monitoring this, Eve?" asked Major Hawke.

"Affirmative!"

"Orientation assessment, which way is north?"

"Ten degrees latitude by two hundred and thirty degrees longitude, according to the geographical maps of Kemeta in my database. However my magnetometer is unable to..."

"Acknowledged Eve!"

The Horde drone finally began to degrade and disappear. He glanced around at the ruined city as though he searched for something else, turning around in a complete circle inspecting the half broken buildings and bombed vehicles. He located two mega-sentry defense cannons, one destroyed, the other one intact and appeared functional, abandoned by its operators. The mega-sentries were the equivalent to stationary robots and carried four missile batteries on the rear of their rotating chassis. On its right and left were twin, multiple-barrel autocannons capable of offloading twenty thousand armor piercing shells per minute in synchronized rapid fire.

He then focused on the vast multitudes of rail lines that crisscrossed throughout every inch of the entire city. His eyes opened wide, his body language was obvious, he'd found what he was looking for. The Major fell to the ground breathing heavily, his broken body had yet to fully recover from its ordeal. He watched as the marines battled desperately.

"They need your help, Keegan!" Eve's exotic voice almost seemed sympathetic for a machine. Major Hawke's silence displayed no desire, and no ability to help. He looked up and made out the plumped body of Colonel Bronze through all the anarchy. Bronze seemed to be screaming something as he ran toward the team, something that couldn't be heard, drowned out by the explosions and gunfire. But reading his lips, Hawke deciphered the name that Bronze called out. The major turned his head lethargically toward the marines of Unit Forty Two and the man being called. Then in the sky, Hawke identified the colonel's cause of concern. Two bloodthirsty Horde rays were swooping down for the kill, and their prey was

Lieutenant Adcox. Unfortunately the young man was too preoccupied fighting off the Horde crabs, to his peril.

***

In another part of the city, a Horaxian engaged in battle all alone against an encircling multitude of the vile Polymorph, the only one with the might to do so, the Ariman Rey'Jax. His size surpassed most of them but his strength was the reason he could fight toe to toe, for it was far greater. He punched one drone and it flew meters away onto a battered vehicle, causing a small explosion that killed a few more. Another approached him and he hoisted it up high above his head then threw it like a military press onto two more Horde drones. It was as if god granted strength a body and created Rey'Jax. Like a bushman's cutlass slicing through tall, thick grass he bulldozed his way through a wall of drones. They attempted to rush him in numbers but he used his bulk almost like that of a merciless bully, throwing and slamming them around. Straight after, he retrieved two small metallic objects from his waist and slid one of them through his black oversized fingers; the other, which looked like a short metal stick, was gripped in his left hand. Both devices began to transform; the one on his left morphed into a long, white staff and then the top branched out into a double axe shape. The other expanded to form a reflective shield. As another Horde drone rushed in he sliced it in two with one great swing, his axe surpassing a grown man's height. You could almost feel sorry for the Horde as he continued cutting them down.

***

Meanwhile, Bronze hopped and hobbled over as quickly as he could to Adcox's aid. His armor crushed at the waist side from the ground squid's tentacles. Adcox, while in mid action looked up and saw the ray creature darting for him but shock paralyzed him. Bronze released explosive rounds with conviction, killing the creatures, but one preceded to spiral in a death fall toward Adcox.

At the last minute, Bronze jumped and knocked the young man out of the way of danger.

"It's not your time yet, sonny!" said the old soldier panting. The colonel rose back on his feet battle-ready, determined to go down fighting this day. Although his face twitched from the pain of his crushed-in armor stabbing into his abdomen. Suddenly he gasped for air, a Polymorph biological spear tore through his lung cavity and armored chest plate. Behind him stood a drone. The blood from his ruptured lung sprayed all over Adcox's face. Ballistic responded by letting rounds loose and downed the drone.

"*Colonel*!" Ballistic yelled, so enraged that he continued to fire at the beast even though it was already well dead. "ARHH!" he roared, refusing to release his trigger but then he was forced to fire at three more drones attempting an ambush.

Adcox caught his commanding officer as he fell. "*Hatshepsut!*" he screamed and she rushed to his injured colonel.

"Look!" said Zomo pointing in the far distance. The stellar warship that levitated in the Horde-filled sky all this time was engulfed with smoke and fire and had begun to rotate in free-fall, nose down.

"Oh no!" said Tronics, only focused on the crashing vessel's engine flames, which had now changed from green to a beaming rose-red.

"What's wrong?" said Akerele.

"The string core." Tronics and Jei'Gun shouted in unison. Tronics turned to the group. "Everybody get down! Activate your helmets." Instead of ducking for cover himself, his attention shifted to switching off his laser weapon and data-slab.

The titanic warship crashed in a loud thunder of ash, smoke and debris. The light emitted from its impact flashed as white as ignited magnesium, blinding all who looked on with naked eyes. The detonation of its string core engine created a fireball, flattening the surrounding buildings, and leaning the edifices farther away. Thousands of Horde drones and mammoths were incinerated in the spherical fire wall. Omnidirectional, overpressured air and dust moved at the speed of sound, lifting every Horaxian on the battlefield off the ground. It took less than thirty seconds for the shockwave to hit the team.

Everything quieted in the secluding dust-mist. Jei'Gun shook off his daze from the shockwave and rose to his feet. His first instinct was to find the Black Guard. He spotted him under the guard of Zomo and Akerele, but he could not locate Nanonramu. With his armor being similar to his surrounding kin's, he vanished in the dust covered crowd and commotion.

"By the hands of the Great Supreme King!" exclaimed Jei'Gun. "The warship explosion, it has obliterated most of the Horde army."

"Yeah," said Ballistic, dust covered, standing shoulder to shoulder, "but they'll be laying and catching more cocoons any minute. They'll have their numbers up in no time."

Tronics reactivated his electronic devices. He knew the electromagnetic pulse of the string engine detonation wouldn't have affected his armored suit, but it would have killed his contraptions. But his focus switched to his colonel. Rushing to his side, he left the rest of the team to fight off the few residual Horde.

"Just sit tight old man. I'm going to get you out of here, don't worry," said Tronics, overwhelmed by grief.

Adcox still held the colonel in his arms as Hatshepsut assessed his wound. It didn't take her long.

"His injuries are too severe. I am sorry," she said.

"Forget it, lassie! I'd rather die!" Bronze said with difficulty, spitting out blood with his teeth fully red. The hole and cracks in the colonel's suit sizzled like beef on a grill. Its nanofibers were at the end of their lifecycle and could no longer self-repair. Bronze gripped the metal collar of Tronics' combat suit and pulled him closer. "Pick up your piece of junk, you fool. Suppressing fire, give them hell."

"Wilco, sir!" Tronics said as tears swelled in his eyes. He looked at Adcox as if to say, "Take care of him," and returned to the fight, remaining close to his beloved colonel.

"Sir, I'm sorry," said Adcox. "That I couldn't, in the Abyss, I let you down and..."

The colonel responded, trembling with the mustering of fleeting strength. "You didn't, when commands are not followed, first it's the leader to blame." Bronze battled the pain on every word in a struggle to breathe. "I saw you needed help wh...when you transferred but I didn't spare time to pre...prepare you. I was blinded by...the loss of my wife. It's up to you now."

"I can't do..." Adcox wasn't allowed to get the words out.

"You've finally gotten yo...youur chance tooo...prove yourself. Complete the m...mmisssion. The Sword in the

Dark is the key. See it through to the end, that...is...an...ord..." Colonel Bronze never had the chance to complete his sentence.

"Doctor, quick, preserve his brain functions," ordered Ballistic. "If we can get him back to Earth, cybernetics might..."

"Warning!" said Eve, interrupting loudly. Her scanners were the first to detect the danger that Ballistic soon after realized. It was a long range bioblast from a Horde mammoth soaring towards them.

"Incoming!" Ballistic yelled.

Adcox saw the entire sky come alight as the ball of energy fell towards them. He heard the boom of the impact...then everything went black.

Chapter Seven - A Legend Awoken

From darkness, blurred images emerged, accompanied by opaque buildings and blotted movements. The dazed and disoriented Adcox sensed he was moving, and not by his own locomotion. His vision fully returned and he saw himself being dragged out of danger by Ballistic's sole natural arm. The rest of the team survived the blast and were all shaken and stunned. Hatshepsut treated Private Akerele for a head injury. They could hardly complain about their condition. Most of the surrounding troopers never survived the mammoth blast.

Without giving Hatshepsut enough time to properly treat him, Akerele came to greet Adcox, relieved he was alive. "Are you ok, sir?"

Adcox failed to respond. His head tremored, his body locked in its position. Tronics rushed to the aid of his good friend who was like a brother to him.

"Has he been hit? What's wrong with him?" Tronics asked Ballistic.

"Combat stress reaction," replied Ballistic.

"What?" asked Akerele.

"He's shell shocked, step aside." Ballistic punched Adcox without warning cleanly across the face. "Snap out of it, Lieutenant."

It was a kind gesture, the muscular sergeant's unrestrained upper body strength could have killed him but he measured his blow well and it seemed to have had the desired effect as Adcox reanimated. Gasping for air, the lieutenant clutched Ballistic's shoulder plating. "I can't...I can't..."

"I don't care!" said Ballistic. Adcox doubted he even knew what the distressed, inexperienced soldier needed to say.

"Akerele," Ballistic shouted. "Cover the left flank. Zomo, watch for aerial attacks."

A notification sound on Tronics' data-slab alerted him and he glanced at it. "Guys, hate to break this up but I'm reading multiple Polymorph signatures. There's got to be tens of thousands of them."

"We will drown in their swelling numbers," said Nanonramu, re-emerged through the chaos. "Once their forces regather, it will be the end."

"We're all going to die if we don't get out of here," said Adcox in a weary, hallucinating state.

"We are not going anywhere," Jei'Gun said as he approached. "No ships can be spared."

"Plus, Horde controls our skies," Nanonramu said.

"Then we fight!" said Ballistic, reloading his minigun.

Adcox sat on the rubbled street in a state of confusion and once again his body seized as it did in the Abyss. As he moved his shivering hands to place them on his face and saw his palm covered in Bronze's blood, it only served to exaggerate his panic attack. In his state of despair he noticed the Black Guard close by just sitting there, quiet, watching his every move. His mind sparked, halting his shakes. Surviving another Horde offensive was an impossibility and he realized only one salvation existed.

"Major Hawke, please sir, help us," Adcox asked breathing heavily.

Hawke said nothing. He just returned a blank stare.

"Please help us," repeated the young officer.

"We have!" Hawke whispered.

"What?"

"We have helped you."

"What do you mean?"

"I dragged you and the doctor out of harm's way from the collapsing debris when the ship crashed. I killed the Polymorph that tried to attack the crew, you were all unconscious. Who do you think caused the Horaxian warship to crash?

"Holy crap, that was you?" asked Tronics.

"It was overrun by Horde," said Major Hawke. "Eve disabled its levitation systems. The explosion it created wiped out most of their first wave assault force. What more do you want?"

"So now you're happy to die here?" asked Adcox.

Hawke smiled before he answered. "Fifteen years in a radiated tomb couldn't kill us. We don't fancy the Horde's chances."

"Enough of your lies," Nanonramu said. "It is just waiting to escape."

"We could use as much manpower as we can get," said Ballistic. "Especially a Black Guard."

Jei'Gun was quick to respond. "It was Black Guard. It is now aged and weakened, barely can it stand." He spat a brown substance on the ground close to Hawke's feet and it released smoke as it melted the surface. "Black Guard...even at its pinnacle it would be nothing to me. It is a warrior no longer."

Adcox's attention was disrupted by many out of sync voices. They originated from the Horaxian troopers in the near vicinity upon hearing the dreaded name Black Guard.

"It has returned," said one male as he backed away.

"They have brought the demon here," said another.

"The cursed one has brought Horde's wrath upon us," some whispered, some screamed aloud. Young males hadn't forgotten the stories they were told as children, about the Demon King and his unholy army of spirits that preyed on Horaxian living flesh and that were finally conquered by their great leader Cagn.

Akerele repeatedly shook his head at the dire mess of the situation, but Zomo and he were preoccupied looking out for any stray Horde.

Adcox pleaded with the warrior once more. "I can't imagine what you have been through, but I don't want to die here. They say there's nothing you can't do, so can you stop the Polymorph?" he asked, an ambitious request.

Hawke answered by giving a simple nod.

"That's all I need to know. Zomo, cut him loose," said Adcox.

Zomo walked over to free the Black Guard, but Jei'Gun knocked her down with a push, causing her rifle to fall out of her hands. "The demon king remains prisoner of war, forbidden to be freed." Jei'Gun raised his arm aiming his targeting beam at Adcox's head.

With the elite-shakan distracted, the cloaked man rose up and with a lightning wrist movement, miraculously undid his handcuffs. His speed was incredible. He whipped his body around and launched a kick that drove his blackened bare foot deep and hard into the Anubianite's waist area. The force made Jei'Gun's head and shoulders bend forward and he stumbled back as his abdomen plating absorbed the kinetic energy. With no breaking of motion, the major stooped then jumped, swinging his back leg around and performing a powerful spinning crescent kick. He struck the face plate of Jei'Gun's helmet, but the Anubianite was unfazed by the blow. As the man landed, he drove two hard punches to Jei'Gun's jaw plating. Still with blinding speed Hawke then grabbed Zomo's rifle that fell from Jei'Gun shove and struck the warrior's helmet with its butt. It knocked him backward with a more devastating effect as the butt clanged against his solid-metal helmet. Amazingly, the Black Guard's assault was executed so rapidly that no one could react. The major gripped the rifle, inches from pulling its trigger.

"No! Do not!" Hatshepsut pleaded. The rest of the group raised their weapons at him.

"Is that all you have left, demon? Pathetic!" said Jei'Gun. He appeared to be yet unharmed by Hawke's attacks, only furious.

"Stop," implored Adcox, "please Major, lower the weapon."

"Yes, sir!" said Hawke with heavy breaths as he lowered the rifle and threw it back to Zomo, with barely enough strength to do so, his body swayed with fatigue.

Jei'Gun had waited his whole life to battle with the Black Guard commander, much like the scribed knights of old Earth who dreamt of slaying dragons to test their courage and bring glory to their names. His duty to the empire to deliver the cursed one unharmed went out the window, diminished by his desire to claim the greatest of trophies. Jei'Gun unsheathed his arm blade and pulled his arm backward to strike down the butcher of a billion.

Hatshepsut's quick hands pressed on his chest plate and tranquilized him. "Please Jei'Gun, on this day enough blood has been spilled." Her natural soothing abilities did their job. The big male dropped his arm, retracting his blade.

"So what do we do now, genius?" Akerele said to Major Hawke.

"We give them what they want," the braided veteran replied.

"What's that?" asked Zomo.

"A war!" Hawke spoke with an aura of determination. "We must engage them directly, but win the battle indirectly."

"Cursed creature," Nanonramu said. "Horaxian forces are too few in numbers. The command line, broken. All our Apexes slaughtered."

Ballistic interjected. "And they've knocked out the planet's orbital and major ground defense systems. We have no adequate means to counteract their offensive."

"You've got us!" Hawke replied. "Eve, is the hyper rail grid still operational?"

"Scanning," she paused a moment. "The northern network has been destroyed by the warship explosion. The remaining grid is damaged but operational, although it is presently offline."

"Activate it." Next, Hawke shifted toward Tronics. "Corporal, we need power diverted from the global grid to the train lines throughout the city. Can you do it?"

"Yeah, sure, if I had a quantum mainframe hardwired into the network, a thousand exabyte processor, a genie's lamp and about an hour, I could hack in..."

"You've got thirteen minutes." While Hawke lay on the bed of the infirmary presumed to be unconscious, he was able to assess the corporal's genius and flair for exaggeration.

"Wow...wait! How much power do you need diverted?" asked Tronics.

"All of it!"

"The entire planet's?" asked Hatshepsut, her vocal pitch elevated.

"Then what," asked Akerele. "You're going to cause some kind of explosion?"

"Not exactly," said Hawke.

"Wait a sec." Tronics caught up with the major's thinking. "You're planning on turning the grid into a superpowered, superconducting electromagnet." Even the team's engineering specialist stood in disbelief.

"What?" said Ballistic and Akerele simultaneously.

"Foolish creature," Jei'Gun said, "what good would that do?"

"The Horde's armor is made of a bioorganic metal...and it's ferromagnetic," Hawke replied.

"How would you know, demon?" asked Nanonramu.

"The corporal's laser weapon charges their armor and it generates a temporal magnetic field. The power build up on the magnetic rails of the train grid will amplify the already electrostatically charged Kemetan atmosphere and recreate the same effect as his weapon...citywide."

Tronics could hardly pay attention, working away on this data-slab to make a head start on the major's request. "All right, I'm getting somewhere but we have a problem, sir. Here's a map of the city." Tronics used his slab to project a large holographic image of the city for everyone to see. It was a blue three dimensional map on a diagonal tilt; green sections highlighted areas of the city Tronics needed to discuss. "There are two failsafe valves; one's located here and another eleven blocks away here, which needs to be released. But it's purely mechanical, I can't activate it remotely. Someone needs to get to it. Err...somebody that's not me."

"Real hero, Tronics!" said Zomo.

"Heh, I've got two kids. Those valves will be behind Horde lines in any minute," said Tronics.

"Leave that to us," said Hawke in a stern, deepening voice. "Just drop anything metal you've got before I hit those valves."

"Never will your plans succeed, monster," said Nanonramu.

"This planet is one big power station," said Hawke. "It produces triple the annual power output of Earth and Kepler-Terra combined every month and we're going to concentrate it all right here on the rail grid. It will work."

Hatshepsut interrupted. "Wait, most of the city's construction is not metallic so your plan will not destroy our capital. But it will leave the entire planet without power. Defenseless, half of Kemeta will freeze to death."

"Doesn't look like we've got much of a choice," Ballistic said.

"We need everyone to do as we say," Hawke ordered.

"You are not in charge here," replied Jei'Gun.

"No we're not, he is!" in slow motion Hawke raised his fingers and pointed to Lieutenant Adcox, taking the young man by surprise.

Jei'Gun laughed. "The radiation has fried your brains, baboon. The scared pup?"

"We were assigned to collaborate with the humans," said Hatshepsut, "and Lieutenant Adcox is now the highest ranking officer after Captain Lewalski, excluding former Major Hawke."

"Have you lost mind?" Nanonramu said. "He is spineless, look at him."

Jei'Gun continued the insensitive trail blazed by his brethren. "This pretty one has no scars upon face. A frail seed incomplete of its germination, unfit for leading males in war."

Adcox's expression said it all. He too wanted to be rid of the responsibility.

Jei'Gun continued. "We take no orders from human scum, especially one whose ability is second to all!"

"You do now!" said Hawke.

"Let's do whatever the major says," said Adcox, the only command he could give at that moment that made sense.

Hawke laid down his orders while pointing out positions on Tronics' map. "Listen carefully, we need to hold them right here within the city center, where the train lines are most concentrated. The lake creates a natural barrier on the west of the city. We'll position all the still operational artillery, armored fighting vehicles, SAM sites, land batteries, portable anti-aircraft missiles and explosives all along the right flank forming a defensive perimeter. Lieutenant, we request that you coordinate what's left of the Horaxian troops to form a defense line right here from major axis 143 to 421. Get all remaining troopers to this LZ. We're going to funnel them in."

"The perfect killzone," said Ballistic, assessing Hawke's strategic brilliance.

Hawke looked Adcox dead in the eyes. "No extractions, no medevacs, no exemptions. I don't care if their legs are blown off, if they can breathe they hold the line."

Hatshepsut interrupted once again. "There are still civilians trapped within city. We must deliver them to safety."

"Man, woman and child," said Hawke, "if they can hold a weapon, they hold the line." He turned to Ballistic. "You ready for war, Sergeant?"

"Is that a joke?" said the big man as he twisted his neck with a mean face. "You're not the only hard bastard out here today, Major." He spun the eight barrels of his minigun.

"Good! The mega-sentry on the bridge is still operational. We need someone on that gun but whoever mans it will be a big target. They'll need to have serious balls."

"I'm on it!" said Ballistic and he began to remove the minigun from its harness. The heavy weapon would restrict his mobility and he needed to be quick. "Akerele, keep the big bad wolf safe for me."

"Copy, Sarge!" Akerele replied.

Hawke turned his head to Jei'Gun and Nanonramu. "We want you to round up a hundred of the strongest males you can find to defend that right flank. Rogue, help Adcox rally everyone here."

Jei'Gun and his brethren had no desire to follow the Black Guard's orders. The elite-shakan stared at Hawke and opened the mouth hatch of his helmet to spits a brown, liquid, substance that sizzled on the ground once again.

"Sir, I don't think we can pull this off," said the shaky voice of Adcox. "There aren't enough boots on the ground to hold the line."

"We have enough!" Hawke roared. He then turned to everyone in ear shot, which included wounded troopers on the ground bracing for their last moments. "It doesn't matter what you think. It doesn't matter how many men we have, and it doesn't matter if we die. It doesn't even matter if we live. But invincibility lies in defense and on my call *you will* defend. And all that will matter, all that history needs to remember, is that on this day, when things were at their darkest, and they needed you the most, those few humans and a handful of troopers...they held that line."

***

Jei'Gun listened with contempt, not with the demon among men, but with himself. Nanonramu stared at his superior awaiting his word if he was to act. He uttered to Nanonramu. "Rally the troopers. Jei'Gun marches to the right flank." His voice expressed a disgust with himself for agreeing with Hawke's logic.

A loud noise now blanketed the mega metropolis in the form of a slow wail. The Horaxian civil defense alert permeated throughout the capital, spreading panic through its indigenous population. They all knew the reason why it sounded. The Horde were making their next major charge.

Yet still, one was unshaken, Major Hawke, evidently in his element. He pulled out a syringe which had a green liquid inside and as he pulled it back, Hatshepsut noticed something that troubled her.

"That is antidoroxiline!" She placed her hand on her side pouch and opened it. Her fingers searched as though something was missing. "That belongs to me."

Hawke paid no attention to her as he injected the substance into his heart, pressing down on the plunger to empty the syringe.

"What's he doing?" Adcox wondered.

"He has taken a form of artificial adrenaline to combat his atrophy. His heart will go into overdrive, temporarily pumping high volumes of blood to his limbs and strengthening his muscles."

"Ok, that's good," said Adcox.

"Then it will kill him," she said.

"That's not so good."

Hawke forced in a deep breath as his body began to convulse as one would if they were having an epileptic seizure. He gritted his teeth and clenched his fist till his knuckles looked close to bursting, trying to counteract the shakes.

"Your body will overheat. You will die of hyperthermia," said Hatshepsut.

"We've got about fourteen minutes before we shutdown, longer if I can keep my heart rate low enough." Hawke's muscle contractions eased up and his breathing normalized. "Get on the horn, Lieutenant. Tell everyone to dig in."

"I think we should have just put Jei'Gun in charge, sir," said Adcox, "the Horaxians won't listen to me."

Hawke focused on the sight in the distance, a blackness engulfed the white city. That blackness constituted the uncountable Horde mass. Consuming land and air, this alien tsunami of extinction now gushed towards them.

Hawke stepped forward with his back to the group. "Well, perhaps they'll listen to her." He pointed to the doctor. "Lock this city down by any means necessary. Don't let the colonel die for nothing." Hawke sprinted off in the direction of the Polymorph legions.

"Don't you want a weapon, sir?" yelled Zomo, puzzled.

"We are a weapon!" said Hawke.

"What in the world..," said Akerele in disbelief at the sight. The major's actions seemed ludicrous, insane, the sight of one man advancing on a sea of vile creatures.

"He's crazy!" said Zomo as they stared in amazement.

Adcox gazed gobsmacked, but then broke his astonishment. "Tronics!" he yelled, wiping Bronze's remaining blood off his face and moved close to his friend. Hatshepsut followed him.

"What's popping?" said Tronics, feverishly pressing away at his data-slab to bypass Kemeta's energy grid software safety protocols to get all its power rerouted.

"I need you to work out a way for me to communicate to all the troops on the battlefield and ASAP." Adcox spurred out his words in desperation, peering in the direction of the slowly approaching yet still distant enemy.

"Bredren, what I'm doing ain't like tying your shoelaces."

"Arghh, come on Kev. I'm in over my head here." Adcox waved his arms in annoyance.

"All right mate, all right, I'm going to create cooperative diversity on every speaker and antenna in fifty klicks. Just a sec."

Adcox witnessed his friend's talents in telecommunications countless times, but in all their years he had never seen Tronics' hands move so fast as he inputted commands.

"All right, you're on the mic," said Tronics handing Adcox his tablet which he configured to project the lieutenant's voice throughout the city. As Adcox grabbed hold of the device, video footage of him relayed on multiple, large public display screens, holding every Horaxian's attention.

"Planetary defense troops," Adcox's jaw rattled to the high pitch microphone feedback which howled on the citywide speakers. "The Horde have ga...gathered their nnnumbers and...are, and are they are..." As the young lieutenant spoke, Tronics shook his head at his friend's terrible performance. "We...we...we must form a perimeter..."

In a knee-jerk reaction, Hatshepsut snatched the tablet. "People of Beloved Kemeta, I am Princess Hatshepsut. Swear your ears and will to my words. We must make a stand or all that we love will be lost this day. We can defeat Horde but you must not give in. Please, it is of extreme importance you remove and stay clear of any magnetic objects immediately. Troopers, listen to human Adcox Lieutenant, rally behind him. Form defensive line immediately from axis 143 to 421 and do not let them through. This is home. Fight for home."

Her words were moving. Injured troopers that lay broken spirited rose to their feet. Battered Horaxian warriors shook off their fears and regained their fortitude. Reinforcements poured in around them.

"Good job!" commended Adcox.

"Can't say the same to you," said Tronics.

***

Meanwhile, Hawke ran with a fast, consistent pace toward the swarm while bullets crackled passed his ears and explosions impacted the streets.

As the Horde's distance shortened to nearly two hundred meters, Hawke veered off to the left hand side of the street toward a stationary Horaxian bus which was powered by magnetic levitation. He shoulder-barged the back doors open and slid inside along the floor ten meters to the front where the control systems were. Jumping on the control seat, he pushed two touch-screen buttons on the dashboard. "Emergency override protocol: vector jalua, yulan, talaw." he voiced.

"Override code invalid!" replied a computerized voice.

"Technology does change in fifteen years," said Hawke.

Horde drones surrounded the vehicle, ramming it, moments away from tearing through. "Authorization circuitry has been overloaded," Eve said.

The bus levitated fifty centimeters off the ground. Hawke pressed the activation button and the vehicle took off at a high speed, crashing into the Horde drone ranks that were spread thick. Their sheer numbers, which caused the ground to tremor, far outweighed the Horaxian defense forces. Hawke used all the strength in the muscles left in his broken body to hold onto the steering touch-sensitive pad as the bus rocked and jolted from the endless drones it crushed, and also from bioblast explosions and bullets blazing from the Horaxian counter offensive.

***

The males defending Kemeta braced to respond to the onrush. Jei'Gun was in the thick of it on the right flank, leading the troops. "We hold them here, troopers. For the Great Supreme King!" he cried loud and confident, the speakers in his armor amplified and added an echoing effect.

His words fueled the males and they shouted back in a chorus of voices. "For the Supreme King!"

"Do...you...fear?" screamed Jei'Gun.

"No!" cried the battle-ready males.

"Weapons free!" Jei'Gun's last command, upon which his brethren unleashed the heavy artillery. Horaxian tank rounds devastated the Horde's assault, the SAM sites containing multiple missile batteries released high yield ordnance weighing in on the Horde's clusters. Jei'Gun held shoulder mounted rocket launchers that fired missiles from both shoulders, with three rocket tubes along each arm. He gripped the firing trigger in front of him that connected to the launcher via a metal harness.

Akerele, Tronics, Adcox and Zomo all battled hard, staying in a close group at the center of the fighting as the funneled Horde wave attempted to break upon them. Weapons fire rang out and drowned out all sounds, even the roars of endless Polymorph drones. Unfortunately Adcox's skill with his solar rifle was shoddy and lacked discipline, the most ineffective marksman in his team. He struggled to aim accurately due to the never-ending explosions. To him it was as if the ground never stopped shaking. But if solar rounds were an argument for death, the drones took an awful lot of convincing. Genetically durable, the alien foe each withstood a barrage of bullets before they were downed.

The marines of Unit Forty Two watched as two drones physically merged together in a biological fusion, then the dual body mutated and deformed. What were arms became flattened wings. What were two heads turned into one large, toothed skull. The metamorphosis was complete and what emerged was a Horde ray. It took to the sky, snatching two troopers manning a light infantry vehicle.

Hatshepsut lay low and close by, providing medical assistance to a wounded trooper. She looked up and saw some civilians hiding in a bus. "Apply pressure to wound and elevate the legs," she said to a young male helping her with the injured. She found Adcox. "Diomedes! Hidden are civilians in there, we must find safety for them." Her hand directed Adcox to the bus.

***

Hawke still traversed the treacherous streets. Unfortunately, the Black Guard's bravado had come at a price. A Horde crab had made its way inside the bus and pounced on him, seeking a chunk of his skull. He held it back for dear life trying to steer and made a sharp right, knocking over Polymorphs in the path. The centrifugal force exerted by the turn on the crab allowed him to push the creature back.

He turned the corner and encountered the whopping mass of a Horde mammoth. The beast charged and broke the bus in two down the middle. Hawke flew through the front windscreen at the moment of impact, rolling and landing on the ground. He rose unfazed. Trampling on the bus's metal chassis, the humongous beast turned to Hawke. It's accompanying five Horde drones also converged upon him. His fate looked sealed.

"Now, soldier!" said Hawke.

Two missiles rocketed the belly of the large beast and blew it away. Its guts sprayed the streets and its lifeless mass fell to the ground.

"Get down!" The unknown voice yelled at Hawke.

He complied, diving onto the pavement. The Horde drones were moments from pouncing on him until large caliber armor piercing ammunition from a mega-sentry's twin autocannons swept the drones off the streets like a hurricane.

"Good job, Sergeant!" Hawke said, wasting no time as he rose into a sprint.

The unknown voice belonged to Ballistic; they spoke via a radio link between Eve and his suit's radio transceiver. Ballistic sat on a mega-sentry cannon on top of a bridge. His warmongering deserved an award for gallantry, but unfortunately attracted the wrong attention. A score of

Polymorph drones ascended on his elevated location and he picked them off. Unbeknown to him, two rays also had him in their sights. They stiffened their tales and fired energy blasts from their bulb endings. Regrettably, fearlessness was Ballistic's blessing, not agility. He dismounted the mega-sentry but too slowly to evade the blasts. They destroyed part of the cannon which resulted in trapping his left arm, the one still natural, under the weight of the right-side autocannon as it deformed upon impact. He bawled in agony, the screams were heard by the remaining marines on the comms link.

"Ballistic!" Zomo shouted looking up at him from a distance.

"Arrghhhh! I'm stuck!" Ballistic said bellowing in intense pain.

"I'm coming Sarge, hang in there," said Akerele. "Zomo, stay here and cover Tronics."

"Go!" she said, without breaking from firing. She held up better in the Kemetan capital than in the Jumbie Abyss despite the adversity being greater. Yet the number of surrounding troopers that fought alongside her dwindled as the Horde's siege intensified.

***

The battle thickened across the city as Major Hawke arrived at the first safety valve, situated high above, underneath one of the many overhead maglev train lines. He climbed up the circular metal structure toward the lever fifteen meters above him. Opening the wire-mesh hatch that surrounded the large lever, he used all of his body weight to force the lever down as it screeched before locking into its lower position.

"Patch me through to Tronics."

"Communications link established," said Eve.

***

In the city center, the Polymorph were beginning to penetrate the defensive line. Tronics crouched next to Zomo and heard Hawke speaking on his comms system.

"I've just flipped the first valve, Corporal. Proceeding to the next one, over!"

"Copy, sir. I can see that on my screen, over!"

"The power diversion better be ready, marine!"

"Roger that, brother-man! All the power has been rerouted. As soon as you hit that second valve it's prepped to pump straight through the rail lines, over!"

"Acknowledged! Out!" replied Hawke.

***

As the battle raged, Hatshepsut and Adcox were with a group of seventeen civilians hiding inside the bus. Most were elderly males and females, along with a few cowering young children, all frightened stiff. Hatshepsut moved close to a shivering little girl and she placed her left palm on her left cheek and her right palm on the child's forehead, looking in her eyes. "We will keep you safe, little one," she said performing the Horaxian facial ritual to calm the youngster down. "It is not safe here." Hatshepsut said addressing the crowd. Adcox waited close by with two troopers on guard. "We will help you get to Dudus subterranean tunnel. It will take you outside of city. Prepare yourselves." She nodded to the little girl, who smiled.

While she comforted the crowd, Adcox checked in with his team. "Tronics, status report."

Tronics' ability to multitask was astonishing. He stopped firing his laser weapon to prevent it from overheating and then shouted, "Watch the flank!" to a troop of males. A split second after, he whipped out his hand gun, firing rapid and precise shots at Horde crabs while holding his slab in his right hand that had a digital map of the battlefield and indicators of Polymorph and troop presence. "Defenses aren't holding Diomedes, we're dropping like flies and the bastards keep coming. In fact, their numbers are growing. We won't last much longer, LT. Over!"

"Hang in there, bruv," said Adcox. "Akerele, come in. How's Ballistic doing, over?" he asked on the crackling radio link.

Akerele responded. "Not good, sir. His arm's trapped under the gun turret, and six men couldn't lift this."

"Damn it!" yelled the nervous lieutenant in frustration. If his breathing got any worse he'll hyperventilate again. "Ok, copy, ahh...just try to get him out of there. Find something to give you some leverage. I'll be with you soon as I can, out."

Hatshepsut touched his shoulder and nodded. She then signaled the group to start following them and they all took off. After only a few meters the two Horaxian warriors helping to provide an escort were blown away by the bioblast of Horde drones. Their remains sprayed all over Adcox. He shouted for the civilians to crouch against the wall as more and more drones closed upon them. Their situation looked dire, stranded out in the open.

Until he saw the drones' attention had shifted. An axe blade spliced through one of them like cake and straight through another in the same swing. It would have taken formidable power to accomplish such a feat, and it was formidable. It was Rey'Jax the Ariman.

He pulverized a crab with his fist, then extracted and expanded his shield from its handle again and charged at three drones. It was pure luck for the Polymorph that they seemingly did not possess emotions, otherwise they would have been stricken with fear of the mighty aboriginal Horaxian. His huge fist shattered the ranks of onrushing Horde like a battering ram would a rotten door. One drone that broke through the muscular barriers made of his arms tried to impale the brute with its arm-spear but like a ship colliding into a rocky shore, the biological blade shattered. The drones with vicious desperation fail to rip hold of his biceps due to their abnormal mass. His savage onslaught dwarfed anything seen by his foe. He walloped another drone with such a mighty blow that it would have landed a mile away.

The brute then lifted an abandon military vehicle and raised it high above his head. In an amazing feat of strength, he threw it on to the incoming Horde. His foot with its inhumanly gigantic size crushed the Horde crabs into a slimy ooze, cracking the pavement along with it as it crashed down. They attempted to blast him but every shot was blocked with his shield. But then the even larger Horde mammoth spat a tremendous ball of energy from its mouth. It impacted directly where Rey'Jax was fighting, throwing him into the air. His body hit the ground hard and slid. He lay dead. His left hand still clutching his battleaxe which soon retracted and reverted back to its original handle state. His shield fell from his grasp and reverted to its handle-only state, landing only meters away from Adcox. With their only threat now defeated, the Horde closed in on the lieutenant and the civilians.

***

The Black Guard commander sprinted through the streets of a city that now appeared to have more Polymorph than indigenous life. With more time and more troopers his plans would have been victorious, but the Horde storm was unconquerable.

Crabs filled the streets behind him, pursuing at speed. They caught up to him; two pounced on his shoulders and back. He threw his cloak off and they fell along with it. Hawke's eyes were keen. He picked up the ripped off upper torso of a dead trooper, losing little speed and hoisted it over his scarred, unclothed shoulders. He then grabbed the right arm which held every trooper's arm-cannon and activated it. Shooting at the Horde crabs only barely kept them at bay. It seemed as if every crab in the city was pursuing him. Thousands of them covered every square meter of the white pavement, toppling over one another and clipping at his heels. Each one itching to sink their fangs and claws in him.

"Your cardiac rate has elevated too high," alerted Eve.

"Acknowledged!" replied Hawke, still at full pace.

Horde rays fired down at him, creating explosions that even killed their fellow crabs. Hawke sweated like a storm now. His breathing intensified.

"We will not reach the second valve in time at your current speed, and whether you maintain your current speed or choose to accelerate your body will shut down before we arrive at our destination."

"Affirmative." Hawke said. He did not appear to be bothered by his SPU's analysis, but he did act upon it.

The major crashed through the glass entrance of a bright white building on his left shattering the glass. Hundreds of crabs poured in after him. A Horde ray circled close to the top of the edifice waiting for the Black Guard commander to emerge. Out of nowhere the sound of more breaking glass drew a ray's attention. The major leaped out of a high floor, soaring over seven meters through the air and onto the back of the ray and it flew away. Some crabs also leaped, too overeager to catch him. They fell to their peril. The flying beast soared at speed in attempt to shake him off. Zomo and Tronics looked up at the sight in amazement.

With violent persistence the ray attempted to use its bulbed tail to strike Hawke but he outmaneuvered it. Their combined movement resulted in an uncontrollable mid-air spin and the major struggled to hold on due to the stink, mucus slime that covered its body.

"By the Supreme King's crown," said Nanonramu, his Rogue Basarwan poor eyesight proved incapable of seeing the flying ray in the distance. But when a nearby trooper spoke of a human bound to its back, he knew it could only be the one.

"Are you seeing this guys?" said Zomo.

"Amazing," said Tronics. "His plan's working. He's almost at the second valve."

Hawke's difficulties were all but over in his airborne journey over the city's train line network. A drone spotted him. It charged its appendage weapon and fired in attempt to kill Hawke, with no regard for its species member's life.

"Incoming projectile," said the calm voice of Eve.

Hawke's reaction was lightning as he turned the creature into the blast. It free fell through the Horde ray-filled sky, also darkened with smoke, and Hawke released his grip. The creature crashed onto an apartment-size power transformer station and it ignited into flames. Hawke landed on top of an abandoned Horaxian civilian vehicle, mainly black in color with a smooth luxurious bodywork. It had no wheels, designed only to hover. Its flat chassis became much flatter when Hawke crushed it down with his body weight, its price for breaking his fall. As much as the ray attempted to snap his head off he was thankful to the winged monster for reluctantly bringing him close to his destination in half the time it would have taken by foot as he rolled off the car-top.

He tried to walk but dropped to one knee, clutching his chest due to severe heart palpitations. His lacerated, bruised back convulsed. He looked as if he was about to pass out. The Black Guard commander's body was no longer able to thermoregulate itself.

***

On the other side of the city, the situation grew equally dire. A sense of hopelessness soon cloaked Adcox as his rifle ran out of ammunition. He and the group of civilians were helpless, as the Horde approached, Adcox was left to fire the less-effective shots of his sidearm. Hatshepsut told a little child not to cry and to close her eyes.

The lieutenant saw a nearby drone's outgrowth blaster almost fully charged and about to be unleashed. He looked down at the shield handle previously held by the fallen male of the first Horaxian nation. With a burst of animation he dashed for it. Adcox grabbed hold of the shield handle and stood in front of the group who were huddled together. The drone fired and within fractions of a second the handle protracted out a white shield with an area larger than the man himself. The blast hit and rocked him. Way out of his depth, the unseasoned lieutenant held on with all his strength as his feet slid backwards. The shield steamed from the blast. His palms stung from the absorption of the force. Another drone fired, he turned to defend it and did but the impact knocked him over. His slim build was far from gifted with muscular Ariman bulk.

As the Horde drones converged upon them with their limbs morphing into a variety of killing shapes, they were rocked by an explosion, courtesy of grenades tossed by Tronics. "*Get down!*" he cried to Adcox and the group. He fired his laser, moving it along its horizontal axis. The unbroken beam cut across masses of the enemy and burnt a line through the wall behind, but above the heads of the civilians. A remarkable weapon against the Horde, solar rifle rounds could never do such an effective job.

They all felt the ground shake and turned to see a Horde mammoth stampeding towards them. All six of its gigantic legs trampled troopers in its path. The dwindling planetary force unloaded all they had but nothing could stop its advance.

Tronics stepped up to the plate, firing his laser. Unfortunately, the free-space-path-loss attributed to the distance the beam travelled reduced its effective power. Even as the monster neared the laser was only able to inflict minor damage due to its heavily armored body. To make matters worse, smoke began to radiate from the laser gun. The temperature of the handle rose high enough to badly burn his hands. He threw it down with a yell.

"Piece of junk!" said Tronics, he held the trigger for too long and overheated the circuitry.

More defense troopers laid down suppressing fire and the colossal beast stumbled in agony. Then a Horaxian tank rolled on to the street, close to twice as large as a twenty-first century Earth tank. Clutching the controls was Zomo. She fired a double round that exploded the beast into steaming chunks of flesh. Within seconds, the flesh dissolved into nothingness.

***

Close to his destination, Eve's voice called out to the Black Guard commander. "The second valve is twenty-five meters ahead, thirty meters up above."

Hawke gave no response, he could only gaze up at the lever. He had begun to hyperventilate as his respiration rate reached dangerous highs.

"Your body has begun to shut down. Organ failure is imminent."

Horde drones crept towards him. He was surrounded.

"I'm sorry I couldn't help more, Keegan. I'm so sorry." Her last words were spoken with a peculiar sadness for her artificial form.

"Eve, emit an infrasonic carrier signal, broadcast a message."

"What message?"

"The message is a name."

***

At the city center, Zomo still sat at the controls of the tank but panted heavily, her short cut hair drenched with sweat. "There are too many." She shouted in grief at the countless monstrosities advancing.

Tronics still fired shots with his sidearm. "Every time we kill one, three more appear."

At that moment, the great Ariman arose with a burst of energy. Back on his feet, he unleashed a ground-shaking roar that echoed throughout the battlefield. Even more miraculous was that the few cuts and gashes he bored were instantaneously resealing themselves. He turned, witnessing his shield extracted in the young lieutenant's hands and moved toward Adcox with his enlarged canines protruding. The young officer understandably stepped back.

The juggernaut said something in his native tongue. The words were untranslatable to anyone but his expression was still detectable, it had changed to one of shock. As Rey'Jax trod closer he halted himself, swinging his mass from side to side. He had detected something. Growling, he turned around and then leaped away in a huge bound. The Ariman ran at superhuman speeds then took two more great leaps until he could no longer been seen.

***

High above on the bridge, Akerele tried to lift the turret off Ballistic's bloodied arm but it was no use. The Horde had surrounded them. The private fended them off with solar assault rifle rounds but the enemy's numbers were too many. Shots then burst through the monsters. Jei'Gun, accompanied by four other troopers used arm-cannon fire to clear the bridge. Jei'Gun opened his palms and released the infamous Horaxian vault grenade in the air. As it hovered over the pulsating heads of a section of drones, it released a spotlight-shaped beam of superheated plasma killing multiples of the abominations. Akerele's wide-eyed expression of relief changed to despair. In the distance down below, a Horde mammoth had also spotted them. It prepared itself to fire its destructive ball of energy.

"Go!" said Ballistic. 'Get out of here, that's an order, private!" He looked to Jei'Gun as he approached, and the big male stared at Ballistic's trapped arm. "You too you grey-haired ape. Move it!"

The energy built up in the mammoth's compressed lungs ejected and they watched it arc in the sky. Jei'Gun snapped his helmet back to Ballistic and he unsheathed his arm blade. "Remember within Abyss souwrak...Jei'Gun keeps his word!"

Ballistic knew his death was at hand. He glared intensely in the area of elite-shakan's eyes, his actual eyes were covered from view, concealed by two hardened black visual receptors within his long red helmet. Yet Ballistic still sensed something, something which soon became apparent. "Do it!" he shouted.

With no more hesitation, the Anubianite warrior swung his blade downward like an axe kick with a force no mere man could ever muster. An ungodly scream lingered in the air. Akerele scurried away, supporting Ballistic whose crushed natural arm had now been severed by Jei'Gun; his cybernetic right arm was around his comrade's shoulder. The blast hit the mega-sentry's turret and ignited its explosive ordnance destroying the bridge. The men got to relative safety only just in time.

***

North of where the defense forces rallied around Adcox and Hatshepsut, Major Hawke rested on all fours. His lengthy black hair fell over his face. His attempts to soldier on were admirable but futile as Polymorph drones surrounded him, ensuring no chance for escape.

The Black Guard gazed at the approaching creatures, ready to meet certain death. One ran in for the kill but then it felt a large fist punching through its mangled fleshly abdomen from behind and it fell down dead.

Rey'Jax hammered another drone. Sending it crashing into its kin created a brief moment alone with his mortal enemy. With little hesitation he charged toward the weakened Black Guard.

"Rey'Jax, no!" the major yelled, rolling to avoid a blow from the hulking giant whose fist cracked the ground. The Ariman adjusted himself to strike again. "We can save them!" Hawke said in the ancient Ariman tongue, pointing up high at the release valve. "I can save them!" he said again.

The Ariman's brutish nature concealed his intellect. He understood perfectly but as the Polymorph masses converged upon them once more, an internal struggle dominated the beastlike male, hampering his feelings to ignore his conscience and embrace his desire to kill. With his sizable left hand he lifted Hawke and tossed him into the air like he was a small stone. In that same second, Polymorph drones pounced upon Rey'Jax and their compounded body mass consumed him from sight. It seemed unlikely he could have survived their onslaught even with his titanic strength.

Hawke shot through the air, hanging onto the protective mesh door which held the valve high above and his weight ripped the rusted metal off its hinges. With speed he grabbed onto the safety lever and pulled it down, locking it into its lowered position. "It's done, Corporal!" he said as he hung. "Shut down your systems, Eve."

***

As Tronics fired his sidearm, which ran low on ammo, the tall marine checked the beeping alert on his data-slab. The display read "failsafe disengaged."

"Hawke has done it," said Tronics. Spontaneously he reconnected to his makeshift citywide communication system. "Kemeta, drop all your metal now!"

Instantly electrical surges propagated throughout the entire city's superconductive train grid. Crackling and a high pitched hum echoed throughout the capital. Blue and white electrical current pulsed like an energized lightning storm. Bullet casings, weapons and similar small metallic objects started elevating toward the sky, attracted to the magnetic field of the train grid. Most of the lines were positioned high above the city streets, but tracks also ran along the ground. Larger objects followed including the Horde crabs, drones, mammoths and brains, littering the skies and clumping to the lines. Some buildings were ripped apart by their magnetic contents. Even Horaxian troopers who had failed to heed the warnings were hoisted into the air.

Akerele, Jei'Gun and ballistic were cut off from the rest by Horde drones bent on killing. The young private realized that they would never get to safety in time, and also, that they were all still wearing their metallic suits.

"Get to the wall!" screamed Akerele. They darted for shelter behind a white wall of an edifice.

Adcox, Zomo and Tronics ran for cover inside a building and ushered in the civilians, their feet crushing the glass of the blown out windows. Tronics commenced the shutdown of all his electrical gadgets once more.

The magnetic force claimed the two stellar marine's weapons and slammed them up to the ceiling. Tronics himself was hoisted upwards along with Adcox, pinned to the ceiling due to the magnetic properties of their combat suits. The civilians were safe from the pull, as well as Doctor Hatshepsut whose protected suit was unaffected. Zomo, who took the opportunity to remove her armored suit, also remained grounded.

"The power's going to reach critical," Tronics yelled, bending his neck to assess the global grid's output levels from his slab that remained stuck to the ceiling.

Ballistic, Akerele and Jei'Gun were nailed to the wall courtesy of their suits and weapons. It only added to Ballistic's overwhelming pain. His cybernetic legs and arm, the only one he had left, began to bleed at the joints and he heard the sound of his own metal bending as it stuck to the wall like glue. He bled from the mouth down his bearded chin as one by one, his metal teeth were yanked out. The two men and Jei'Gun were raised off the ground ten meters in the air as the superconductive electromagnetic force tried to claim them too. A civilian vehicle hurdled toward them and bulldozed into the lower part of the building inches below their boots.

All the Polymorphs that covered Rey'Jax had been pulled to their doom and his grand size once again emerged. He appeared bruised and fatigued but not badly injured. The Horde's efforts were fruitless in finding the means to penetrate his genetic strength and his bruises healed within seconds. But now he too was pulled by the ferocious attractive force due his metal armor. As it proceeded to drag him, the Ariman punched his fist deep into the ground and lodged it in, helping to anchor his body as his legs were pulled in the air. He roared against the force of swirling debris.

***

The powerful attractive force even pulled Horde rays down from the sky. Drones attempting to hold on to objects were ripped apart, their limbs still gripped on for a few moments before they disintegrated. A large generator floated through the darkened sky, polluted from metallic debris. It crashed into masses of trapped Horde bodies along a section of the train grid and exploded. This resultant chain reaction ignited the entire grid. Spectacular, deafening explosions produced shockwaves that damaged most of the buildings in the city left standing from the warship's detonation. The fires from the blast also killed multitudes of Polymorphs and troopers. At the center of the collapsed buildings where the generator had exploded, a five hundred meter crater had formed.

***

Hawke's lower body garment caught on fire from stray flames and he fell through the air, hitting the ground hard. He gathered all his remaining strength and stumbled towards the nearby city lake just meters away. The closer he dragged himself, the worse he deteriorated and he soon began to spasm. He drooled, unable to close his mouth. Arriving at the banks he fell in and submerged within the purple tinted water, lost in its depths.

The Polymorph army had been annihilated along with half of the city. Hawke's plan had succeeded with huge losses and collateral damage. With the attraction force ceasing, Tronics and Adcox fell to the floor. Everyone in the city appeared out of their hiding places and onto the now safe streets.

"Can't believe he did it," murmured Adcox.

Hatshepsut stepped out of the building and spun all around, taken aback by the total destruction. "Oh my!" she whispered.

After a brief moment of cautiousness the Horaxians began to cheer and celebrate their victory. But one remained silent. Adcox thought he would have been relieved it was over, but his mind fixated on the countless battles he had used his wits to avoid only for others to die horrible deaths like today's carnage, taking his place. He fell to his knees and threw up. Palms on the ground, he saw two scrawny legs approaching and stopped in front of him. The lieutenant raised his head and saw that they belonged to one of the civilians who were hiding in the bus. The ninety year old Horaxian male wore a maroon cloak, similar to the one Hawke wore, but torn and dirtied. He was tall but thin; his movement aided by a transparent, glass walking stick which he hunched over. His face had a bluish tone and his hair was dark blue, both effects of aging on Horaxian physiology.

He uttered words with breathing difficulties. "Human...long before you were born our people knew peace," he said with a tired voice. "I was a warrior courageous for many years. Fought many wars, killed many humans with these once unchallengeable hands. These hands, of strength faded, no longer able to save my people."

As the old male spoke, a young girl called out, "Oldfather!" and came to grab his hand. The aged male looked at her and continued. "But today they are safe. I thank you for saving us." He turned and walked off with the little girl. Hatshepsut smiled, something she hadn't done for a long time. But that relief faded as she glanced around again at the aftermath of the battle. The city was in ruins, the Horde had repaved the streets with the dead.

Akerele carried Ballistic towards the rest of the team and Zomo rushed to give them a hand. Ballistic was drenched in his own blood.

"Where is the cursed one?" demanded Jei'Gun.

"I don't know," Adcox said.

"You were in charge, boy." Jei'Gun grabbed Adcox by the neck and hoisted him into the air, suspending him with one hand. "If it escapes, your head will line walls of Jei'Gun's bed cambers in the demon's place."

Tronics thought about raising his weapon at Jei'Gun, but his sidearm was no match for him. Plus, they were surrounded by Horaxians, it wouldn't have been wise. As always his smart thinking came to the rescue. "Hey big man, he must still be close to the second valve. I know where it is, and I should be able to track him using the satellite. But if you want my help, rudeboy, you're going to have to put our lieutenant down right now."

"Nanonramu, is that tank still operational?" asked Jei'Gun, pointing at the military vehicle lodged sideways in a crumbled building. He still held Adcox high in the air, choking him.

"I believe so, Alpha. Its EMP shielding would have withstood battleship's string core explosion, hyper rail as well."

"Get it out. Organize troops into patrols, slaughter any stray Horde. Meanwhile, Jei'Gun will take the annoying human tinkerer and hunt down cursed one."

***

At the lake, Hawke lay underwater, holding his breath. With a direct neural connection to his brain, Eve spoke to him.

"Keegan, your body's CO_2 levels are rapidly increasing. You will drown unless you surface now." After a brief pause she spoke again. "And he has not left the banks."

Hawke resurfaced in the purple tinted water and saw the Ariman laying in wait for him. His giant fingers curled into fists, but then the Ariman noticed a tank approaching with speed and decided to flee the scene. The tank stopped abruptly, sliding along the rubble, the human and Horaxian team offloaded the vehicle. All accept Ballistic who remained inside due to his injuries.

"Get out of water now." Jei'Gun shouted as he raised his arm-cannon and activated its blue targeting beam. Hawke maintained his position as he treaded the water. His long, jet black, plaited hair floated on the surface.

"Go get it!" Jei'Gun ordered the group.

"No wait, leave him," said Hatshepsut.

"Have you lost your mind?" said Zomo.

Hatshepsut seemed to be analyzing something and coming to a conclusion in her mind. "The water is fifty kelaus, one degree Celsius, keeping his temperature down and keeping him alive. He must remain in lake while antidoroxiline within his system wears off."

"Very clever," said Adcox. He speculated that Hawke must have known the lake would aid in his thermoregulation.

Chapter Eight - The God Of War Before Me

Amongst a convoy of Horaxian battle-ready stellar warships, one vessel stood out, different in design to the rest. It was the space carrier called the *Sword of Damocles*. The powerful human ship was being escorted by their untrusting allies as it neared its destination. Along a grey, metal, corridor of one of the few ships left in the entire human fleet that still maintained a pristine condition, soldiers stood aligned on both sides at attention. All were armed and most had cybernetic limbs, though many were missing any form of a leg or an arm. These soldiers represented the worst in human beauty, scarred and covered with ill-performed skin grafts and prosthetic sections in their craniums. This recycling of soldiers was all the by-product of an ever shrinking armed force.

A mechanical door opened and out came Adcox, Tronics, Akerele and Zomo. Followed behind them was Major Hawke. He was trailed by Hatshepsut, Jei'Gun and Nanonramu. Hawke's ankles had shackles with an energy beam that connected both leg clamps together, restricting his movement. Once again he wore a black cloak, the hood covered his face only revealing his thick, black-bearded chin. Both his hands were in restraint-gloves, and a second energy beam projected downwards from his gloves and connected to the horizontal feet-beam. Farther behind them were six more Horaxian troopers guarding Hawke on the Divine Council's orders. The soldiers lining the corridor were in amazement. Word of the Black Guard's presence aboard the ship had spread. They watched on in disbelief as he walked past and afterwards fell out of line in whispering congregations.

Inside a spacious situation room, one man stared at a wide display screen relaying footage of the warship fleet that polluted his view of the stars. The bulkhead walls were dark brown but the ceiling and floors were a shining silver. The aged man, with a full head of grey hair, stood in front of a hexagonal desk assembly full of empty chairs. In the corner resided a separate smooth desk and large armchair.

The man was a four star general, the most senior general in all of United Earth, which included all extraterrestrial territories. Only the field marshal who governed United Earth held higher rank. James Baizan had as much authority as the generals that sat on Earth Command, however his role involved more direct engagement of the forces in the theatres of combat. Being outside of Command, his decision making powers were more limited than those of the elected generals. But he was far from weary of war, and preferred a position directly involving operations. As a result, his peers held lesser admiration than he did among the men at arms.

The situation room's brown painted doors opened and an armed guard walked in with an immediate salute. "General, they have arrived. Awaiting your orders, sir."

"Send them in!" replied Baizan. The golden complexion general was a Centaurian, the first generation to be born on Biosphere-9. Its citizens referred to themselves as Centaurians since the stationary space city lay close to Proxima Centauri, Earth's sun's closest neighbor at four point two-four light years away.

"Yes, sir!" said the guard and walked out the room. He soon returned, accompanied by the remaining members of

Unit Forty Two and the Horaxian team, along with Squadron Officer Commander Major Hawke. They stopped in the middle of the room and Unit Forty Two held themselves at attention while Adcox stopped in front of the general.

"General Baizan, package has been delivered as you've ordered, sir," he said while executing his salute.

"At ease, men! Where's Colonel Bronze?"

"Sir...he didn't make it." Adcox dropped his salute.

"Bronzy...he was one of our finest soldiers, but more than that he was a great friend," said Baizan, with a hint of a frown. But only a hint. He had seen it all. In these times few remained close to the horror of war and lived as long as he had. Those that did were immune to the physiological effects.

"Indeed he was, sir," said Adcox.

"It's always the best that die, because they shoulder the burden. And when they're gone they can never be replaced. Which is why we are here." Baizan's eyes locked onto Hawke. "Take his restrains off and leave, all of you."

Akerele moved to comply, but Hawke had already freed his hands from their bonds and soon after the energy beams deactivated themselves.

"How the..." Akerele murmured as Hawke gave the bonds to the dark skinned private.

Jei'Gun stepped forward when he witnessed Hawke's release, knowing he was out of place to do so. He understood that even though he was not required to submit to human military hierarchy he stood in the presence of a respected man. To question Baizan's orders was out of line, and he faced being reprimanded by his seniors. But his boldness edged him forward. "This is an outrage, human general. Our orders are that it is not to be freed."

Baizan responded in a strong voice. "He will be delivered as requested by your Divine Council, but while he's in my presence the chains come off. Do you have a problem with that, elite-shakan?"

Jei'Gun paused a while then stepped backwards, and right up to Hawke's face to deliver a chilling stare. "We will be close!"

"Right where you want your enemies," Hawke replied, stepping inches away from his helmet.

Annoyed, Jei'Gun marched off along with the Horaxian contingent, with Unit Forty Two following behind.

"Lieutenant!" Baizan called out. "What's your name, son?"

"Adcox, sir!" His face was marked with patches of black soot and blood.

With eyes full of scrutiny, the general inspected the young man up and down. "Good job, kid. Carry on."

"Sir, thank you, sir!" Adcox saluted the general, then turned to Hawke and they shared a glance. "It's been an honor, Major." He saluted Hawke then left.

The general waited for the room to empty, then hobbled up to the former convict with a bad limp. The two men stood opposing each other under a meter away, eye to eye, heads held high in an awkward silence.

"The most effective weapon is one that remains hidden," said Baizan.

"That strikes from the shadows, then disappears once again," replied Hawke in a tired voice.

Baizan's eyes analyzed the major's poor physical condition and then he did something much unexpected, reaching his arms out he hugged him and Hawke returned the embrace.

"Long time, old friend," said Baizan.

"Long time."

"I nearly gave up hope you would survive. How's Eve doing? Is she still with you?"

"Affirmative general, we are one. A pleasure seeing you again," said Eve almost cheerfully.

"The pleasure is mine."

"You look good, James," said Hawke with a smile.

"You look god awful!"

"You should see the other inmates. How's the knee?"

"How do you think? Do you know how much it hurts in this cold-ass space carrier air conditioning?"

"You could of had it replaced a long time ago?"

"Could have replaced my Johnson too, put that on hydraulics. But there's nothing like the real thing."

"We'll take your word for it," said Hawke with a smile.

"I'm afraid we've got little time for catching up. Keegan, you were our finest. When times were darkest we turned to the Black Guard and you never let us down. We sent you into every hell in this universe and you never refused no matter how great the odds. More than that, you always got the job done. Well, things are at their darkest again. We are desperately losing this war. We need your help."

"Years ago we made sacrifices to ensure peace. After all this time, things are worse than ever." For an unknown reason, Hawke's attention was drawn to the large armchair in the corner of the room.

"Understatements should be against the military code of conduct, Keegan. The Polymorphs' strength overwhelmed biosphere-12. Command ordered its destruction, killing three billion stranded men, women and children. Gliese-Eden is now Polymorph-occupied. We lost Gaia Major and Minor, another seven billion. The Polymorph are spreading and infesting the galaxy. Meanwhile, most of Earth has become a wasteland. They're about to start terraforming but it's going to take years. Do you know how it feels to wake up every day to a nightmare?"

"Yes!" Hawke replied, flames of passion ignited in his eyes. Baizan's words were ill-placed.

"The universe is not the same now as the one we were a part of," said Baizan. "Twenty years ago I would have had a thousand men like Bronze all willing to go through the fire for the cause. There's no one left now."

"There's us! Just tell us what's needed, James. We'll see that it's done. But, before we go any further, who is he?" Hawke's gaze pointed to the corner of the room with the desk and large armchair, the back of which faced the two men.

An unknown voice emanated from the chair. "I returned, and saw under the sun, that the race is not to the swift, nor the battle to the strong, neither yet bread to the wise, nor yet riches to men of understanding, but time and chance happeneth to them all."

The chair turned, revealing an old Horaxian male. It seemed impossible Hawke could have known the man was present as the chair completely concealed his tiny stature, which was not in armor nor military uniform but simple clothing—a mix between a lab coat and a suit similar to what was worn on Earth.

"Ecclesiastes," said Hawke, staring at the old male.

The Horaxian rose from the chair, threading painfully slow with aid of a glass walking stick. "Ahh hah! I see your arduous years of incarceration had not dulled your prolific senses, Mr. Hawke. But I must give pause to wonder, they say a bird that spends too long in a cage can lose its will to fly," said the aged male, waving his fingers about as he talked.

"Hawke, I want you to meet Dr. Henry, the most renowned physicist of the Horaxian Empire."

"We know who you are," said Hawke.

Dr. Henry interjected. "The most renowned of any empire, but not just physics, Mr. Hawke. I have mastery of all fields of the mind and body; biology, philosophy, phycology, anthropology, archaeology, geology...'

"We get it!" said Hawke.

"Theoretical physics however is my favorite past time. Why? Because it is law, not like government laws that can be changed. Not like medicine that is based on probabilities, but like mathematics, physics is exquisitely absolute." The small stature of the Horaxian elder treaded towards both men aided by his transparent cane. "You know who I am. But do you know who you are, Ares personified in flesh?"

"Hc's also a pompous, royal pain in the ass," said Baizan into Hawke's ear.

"Yet my pomposity gives way to a much greater truth. That my all-encompassing mastery of the mind is only matched by your incomprehensible mastery of war. Which catalyzes a query, Mr. Hawke. How would you solve this colossal conundrum? How would you win this...cataclysmic conflict which condemns two great races?"

The doctor and the general remained silent, intrigued to hear Hawke's possible answer.

"When up against a stronger opponent, you must not fight them directly. You study them, use the knowledge gained against them and weakened from within. To achieve victory you must know your enemy."

"Yes," Dr. Henry said as he moved around perpetually waving his fingers. "An axiom we both conclusively share and this is why you are here. But so far that single truth has proven quite, as one would say...difficult." The liquid stains and rips in the doctor's jacket revealed his disorganized nature, derived from his complete devotion to his work rather than his personal appearance.

Baizan preceded to unload what information he knew. "Polymorph technology, along with their bodies, self-destructs when damaged, instantaneously evaporating. It seems as if it can also happen at will, which has made it impossible to discover any significant weakness thus far. They don't have a spoken language or method of communication we can comprehend and eavesdrop on."

"They're telepathic," said Hawke.

"That was our deduction," said Doctor Henry. "Some kind of collective consciousness."

"So vital intel can't be extracted as they can't be interrogated," Baizan said.

"Well," said Dr. Henry, "they do not appear to be riveting conversationalists in either case." He chuckled to himself. His once bright white, lengthy beard and head hair had aged to a blue. "Plus, the Horde seem to have intimate knowledge of our capabilities. What were first random attacks now appear to be malignantly calculated."

Hawke broke from soaking up the information to ask Baizan what for him was his most puzzling question. "Henry?"

Dr. Henry smiled and answered himself. "Dr. Henreyotomborufulonjaro actually, as I'm sure you were aware. But I felt my abbreviated pseudonym was best suited while I work alongside my human allies."

"It's not," said Hawke. He tried hard to conceal his fatigue, unlike his annoyance of the old male. His weary body had suffered too much punishment over the years. The major struggled to stand, and struggled even more to make it go unnoticed.

No doubt sensing Hawke's agitated mood towards the frail Horaxian, Baizan continued on. "Keegan, no one knows where the Polymorph come from. They appear mostly unintellectual. They do not negotiate. They can't be bought. They can't be reasoned with. Unlike most tyrants they don't even want power."

"So what do they want?" asked Hawke.

"They are solely bent on infesting and destroying every living thing in the universe," Baizan replied. "And when your mission is search and destroy, all that matters is the body count."

Dr. Henry spoke, balancing his weight on his cane. "The anchoring roots of most scientific truths are seeded on a theory, and I too have a theory. I believe the reason we cannot detect Horde's origin, and the reason why they disintegrate spontaneously, is because their presence here is in violation of certain laws, laws of existence itself. They do not belong to our universe, but another, a dark universe. As you should already know, dark matter represents eighty five percent of space matter. The dark matter universe cannot be seen, nor penetrated by punching a hole through space like one would in standard superluminous space travel."

The doctor continued to pace around while talking, but he no longer fixated on the two men and was now in his own world. "One needs to interact with dark matter first before one can utilize it or possibly go through it. Some see dark matter as a cosmic web, a support structure which allows matter to clump together. But in effect, it is the actual universe and we, in what we *perceive* as *normal* space, exist only in a subuniverse outside of the dark cosmos. The only thing dark matter projects onto our luminous universe is gravity."

"Well," Hawke said. "That's all a real pretty story, doctor."

"Indeed, Mr. Hawke, and you are the protagonist of this idealistically auspicious tale."

General Baizan added again to the exchange of words. "Only one piece of Polymorph technology had ever been recovered that did not disintegrate—the artifact you were discovered in floating through space fifteen years ago. After studying it for years, however we know little about it. Hell, we haven't even been able to get it open, but from what we can tell it outdates human and Horaxian technology."

"Some proposed it may originate from a different alien race all together," Dr. Henry said. "When Homo sapiens first located the unassailable artifact with you inside heading towards your Earth, they were certain it was a Horaxian weapon. In fear, they fired high yield missiles at it, twenty megatons...it did not make a scratch. Upon investigation, the artifact appeared to have the same hieroglyphic markings and indestructible properties as the MK1 and therefore perhaps just as powerful. It is this indestructible nature which was what allowed you to survive the destruction of our Precious Matelot-6 lunar colony, while all else was obliterated...as you should more than well know."

"What is MK1?" Hawke asked.

"We believe it to be the leader of the Polymorph army, but we'll get to that later," said Baizan urgently. "We need to know what happened on your last mission Keegan. What happened to the rest of the Black Guards...and most importantly, where did you find the artifact?"

"My squadron was being heavily pursued by an armada of Cagn's ships after our attack on his deep space battlestation. They damaged our ship and we were..."

Henry interjected, "You entered into the event horizon of a black hole?" his vocal pitch rose high in intrigue.

"Affirmative! In the Asatorin sector of space."

"I had deduced this before I had been officially informed. I believe the Asatorin quaternary star system just began collapsing. But you were sucked into a black hole yet you survived? This is very interesting."

"We can't explain how. The next thing we can remember was crashing on a planetoid in an unknown region of space."

"And your Nephilim squadron?" Baizan asked. "You told me before that they never made it."

"Affirmative! The planetoid was hazardous. They all died, one by one."

"But not you, my prodigal friend," said Dr. Henry releasing a subtle laugh. "Whose survival instinct surpasses the zenith of most forms of life. Mr. Hawke, nature shows us only the tail of the lion. But there is no doubt in my mind that the lion belongs with it even if he cannot reveal himself to the eye all at once because of his huge dimension. This artifact you discovered, it too belongs to a part of something, something perhaps too grand to be comprehended."

"Where did you discover the artifact?" asked Baizan.

"We too were dying, slowly. I wandered endlessly and eventually found what we believed to be an alien ship buried underground. In there was the pod, what you call the artifact. Eve was able to activate it. I was barely alive at that point but the pod somehow rejuvenated me. Using it, we were able to punch through to normal space. After that, the rest is history."

The doctor now rubbed his bluish beard with intrigued. "Think carefully, what did you see inside this ship? What did it look like? Its architecture, its contents?"

Hawke paused trying to recollect things his mind had buried deep for over a decade. "We did see something, an image, illuminating to a size larger than this room. Its individual elements were foreign to us, and so to were the alien inscriptions."

"Sometimes the whole is greater than the sum of its parts," Baizan said sensing a significance of this imaged guided by his years of experience. "The individual elements were indistinguishable but what did you sense when you looked at it, as a whole?"

"It was a map," said Hawke.

"An alien territorial map," said Eve.

Dr. Henry stopped in his tracks, placing a hand over his mouth as if to contain his excitement. "This is key to ending the war. This celestial vessel is perhaps just as powerful as the pod and could provide us the means to traverse dark matter space and exponentially increase our scientific development."

"Not to mention," said Baizan, "a strategic map of Polymorph's worlds and potentially, the weaponry to stop them. With this we can strike back."

"Does your Symbiotic Program Unit still have the ability to activate the pod?" asked Dr. Henry.

"Affirmative, doctor," Eve replied. "I should be able to reestablish a connection."

"Then we need you to go back to the dark universe, Mr. Hawke," said Dr. Henry. "We need you to retrieve this mothership."

Hawke for the first time did the impossible. After contemplating the doctor's request, he laughed. "You think your people are going to send us on a vacation to dark matter space? We're a problem, Eve and I...a serious problem. They'll never cut me loose, not if they're smart anyway."

"Well, if they are indeed smart, they will have to." Dr. Henry's long, blue, sharp ended moustache flapped as he talked. "You see, despite a decade of attempts, no one knows how to operate or activate the pod. It is somehow able to shield itself from our most advance probes. Your seemingly semi-sentient Symbiotic Program Unit is the only thing which has been able to successfully make a connection to the alien artifact, and as I have heard you and your SPU, like the immortal Pan and trusty Tinker Bell, are somewhat of a double act. Plus, if the planet is as treacherous as you claim, your skills will be needed."

"The doctor foresaw the significance of the connection of the pod, you and winning the war," stated General Baizan. "On Horax Prime, a special joint committee between Earth Command and the Divine Council has been established where the doctor and I will plead a case of the importance that your presence has for this mission. If we're lucky, a pardon can be on the cards upon successful completion of the mission."

Dr. Henry's old yet keen eyes detected a slight shake of the major's body. "Are you sure you are fit for this task?" He glanced at Baizan who had also noticed it.

"We're combat effective," said Hawke. "But we have only two questions. One. James, do you still have my...possession?"

"That's affirmative."

"And your second enquiry?" asked Dr. Henry.

"Where...is Cagn?" he said with a disdain.

"The High Apex?" Henry said stroking his beard some more and seemed to go into his own world once again. "Hmm...yes...one must pause to postulate the peculiar precedents of existence. It would never permit the presence of positive protons without their equal and opposite, negative electrons, to diametrically oppose. But who does the universe deem proton...and who electron?" He ended his self-indulged ramble and answered the man. "Commander Cagn's vilifying voice of condemnation of your release is why we could not get this committee sanctioned, having tried for the last three years. He almost succeeded in getting me quarantined for madness. It is only now with our dual extinction eminent that my words found audience and the Great Supreme King himself ruled in favor. But there is strong belief that Commander Cagn will convince the council to abandon the mission, and you will be sent back to prison."

"Cagn's rise in status has been meteoric," General Baizan said. "He is now the High Apex and the second most powerful man after the Great Supreme King. He controls the imperial guard. Most of the Horaxian military and his troopers worship him like a god."

"A false god!" said Hawke.

Henry noticed the resentment Hawke had in his voice. "Whatever past contentions you two have had, I ask that you set them aside. Do not jeopardize this vital mission."

"Will he be present?" asked Hawke.

"We're not sure," replied Baizan. "The High Apex has rarely been seen in person for years. He spends most of his time in his underground fortress on Anubia, so we believe."

"My grievances with Cagn are in the past," said Hawke. "I left that behind in the Abyss." He turned to the general with an ominous gaze. "General, we need to have a look at the pod as soon as possible, and there's something else we need of you."

***

Unit Forty Two took the opportunity to unwind in the ship's main lounge deck. It was filled with both ship personnel and marines. Some wore uniform and some were casually dressed, only a few were in full combat armor. Huddled together in a corner of the lounge deck were also the Horaxian troopers sent to guard Hawke, including Jei'Gun, Nanonramu and Hatshepsut. The Horaxian's presence generated a high level of tension in the air. At the other side of the lounge, the team all had drinks in their hands as they talked amongst themselves.

"That was pretty intense back there on Kemeta," said Zomo. "I thought that might have been the end of us."

"I'm just happy to be far away from those Horaxians," said Akerele, "and even happier to be away from that Black Guard. He's as creepy as they get."

Tronics sighed. "I still can't believe Colonel Bronze is gone, and Lewalski."

Akerele spoke as he sipped his drink. "The colonel was like a father to me, man. I'm going to miss him."

"To me too," said Tronics. "The old man was the balls busting grandmaster but he broke his back for us."

Adcox, moved by his friend's words, raised his cup. "Guys, a toast. To the captain and colonel, the greatest, and undisputedly the toughest men I ever knew." They all raised their cups.

"Argh!" cried Tronics as he gripped his cup handle and kissed his teeth straight after. "Damn laser overheated on me. I need to go make a few adjustments to it in a minute."

"You seriously molested the Horde when you pulled your thing out," said Akerele, his Nigerian mixed with Gaia Major accent coming through strong.

"You got to be careful how you phrase that, Ack." Tronics said as they all shared a laugh. "Hey, did you see that Horde mammoth coming for me?"

"Here we go again," said Zomo rolling her eyes.

"Tronics," said Adcox, "they don't just target you, it was aiming for all of us."

"Nah G, fourth time now, trust me. Those mammoths keep targeting me."

Adcox was alerted to another group of soldiers and their displeasing comments.

"Why don't they go back to their stinking planet," one man said.

He knew the insults were aimed towards the Horaxian group.

"Looks like things are pretty tense around here too," said Zomo overhearing the men.

In the dim lighting of the lounge deck, Adcox noticed Jei'Gun was facing directly at him. He was the sole elite-shakan warrior present, and the only one in the group who continually stared in his direction, with what must be an all too familiar look of disgust under his helmet.

"Sir," Akerele said to Adcox. "A bit of advice, don't walk down a dark ship deck while he's around."

"Mate," said Tronics, "that dude's got issues like a holographic comic."

Adcox frowned. "We just helped them save their planet, why does he have so much discontent towards us? To think, once we called ourselves long lost brothers from across the stars. It's surprising how quickly love can turn to hate."

"Hey," said Akerele. "One of the deck crew at the bar was saying that a human space carrier was fired upon by Horaxian warships."

Zomo shook her head at the news. "Sometimes I wonder if we're at war with two alien races. Every year relations get worst. We're still in a cold war with the Horaxians. If they were true allies they'd cooperate with us more. They're just waiting for us to get weaker."

"Well, I'm tired of all this fighting," said Adcox, "I thought I'll let you all know, I'm putting in a request to be reassigned."

"Reassigned to where, LT?" Zomo asked, stopping the consumption of her beverage. "The back line's no better than the front."

"Anywhere's better than special ops," replied Lieutenant Adcox.

"You want to go back home?" asked Akerele. "To end up like my people on Gaia? Those that weren't slaughtered by the Polymorph are being herded into filth-infested refugee camps. There's no hiding from the Horde."

"Every day we grow weaker," said Zomo, "and the Polymorph become stronger. With Colonel Bronze gone, we need you with us, LT."

"Diomedes is just a lil' shelled shocked," said Tronics to his friend's rescue. "All he needs is some R & R to clear his head."

"Look who's headed our way," said Akerele, pointing with his head.

Adcox turned and saw Hatshepsut approaching them.

"What is she doing?" Zomo said, knowing her presence will more than raise eyebrows.

"Hello!" said Hatshepsut, stopping in front of Adcox and Tronics. Her aurora went unnoticeable in the light of the lounge deck but her full lips and curvaceous figure were more than apparent.

"Hey!" Adcox replied.

"What's popping?" said Tronics.

"I wanted to ask how Mr. Hasselberg was doing?" Her extra-long hair now ran down the front of her left shoulder.

Adcox pretended to not notice the disapproving glares and increasing negative comments from the soldiers in the lounge. "He was critical at one point but doctors say Ballistic should make a full recovery. He's already put in a request for another cybernetic arm."

"They're going to turn the sarge into a robot in a minute," joked Tronics, bringing a smile to the group's faces and eased the tension.

"Well the biomechanics division are in short supply," said Adcox, "and he's had more than his quota. It could be months before he gets an implant."

"I have friends on Illustrious Horax Prime. I will arrange for one to be supplied."

Adcox chose to manage her expectation knowing full well Ballistic would never accept anything Horaxian made. "From what I heard, the sergeant's pride makes it difficult for him to accept gifts but we'll let him decide. Thanks, Hatshepsut!"

"Yeah," said Tronics, "Bless for that! Good looking out."

"And what of Mr. Hawke? Hatshepsut asked, changing the subject. "Your general seems to trust the Black Guard, but to unchain one so resourceful is unwise."

"Is that why you're really here?" Zomo asked supplying sting to her words. "They sent you over to gather intel?"

"I'm guessing they go way back," said Adcox, gesturing Zomo to calm down with a shake of his head.

"Where way back have they gone?" Hatshepsut said confused.

Adcox smiled. "Sorry, I mean they might be friends, I don't know. Besides, I don't think chains work on this guy too well anyway."

"He has knowledge of many things for a soldier," said Hatshepsut. "Such as biochemistry..."

"Physics too," added Tronics, "and a lot about Kemeta's infrastructure."

"Making him a very effective killer," said Adcox.

"He will not be so effective soon," said Hatshepsut. "The Tabulrack drug I treated him with is slowly drains his life, and there is no cure. He will meet death within day."

The lieutenant was only given a few seconds to contemplate the gravity of Hatshepsut's words before being alarmed by the circle of soldiers that had formed around him. One glanced at Adcox's rank insignia and addressed him.

"Lieutenant! Why are you talking to this Horaxian gash?" said a large man with a beige, prosthetic lower jaw that included his lower row of teeth. He turned to Dr. Hatshepsut. "Why don't you get back in your corner before you get hurt."

Adcox looked at the insignia on the arm of the soldier and addressed him passively rather than pulling rank on him. "Please sergeant, we're discussing details regarding a mission that's all, there's no problem here."

Another severely disfigured soldier with only one arm interrupted. "Oh there's a problem. Humans aren't allowed on Horaxian worlds, so they're not welcome here. Get her out of here."

"Hey, handsome," Tronics called out, smiling at the aggressive soldier, "you forget you're talking to an officer. Drinks aren't the only thing that could be handed to you in this lounge deck."

Another muscular, disfigured soldier missing a nose and standing behind the prosthetic jawed man raised his voice. "Why don't you and pretty boy go take a hike so we can deal with this alien trash?"

"Why don't you kiss my baby-smooth black arse?" said Tronics.

The Horaxian warrior-pack of eight moved in towards their female comrade, enraged by the insults they'd overheard. It was not just the disrespect towards one of their own, nor the fact she was female. She was a Caroo, her bloodline was royal.

"Impudent blasphemer," a Horaxian trooper shouted. "How dare you even address her. I should cut out your tongue, *boy*."

"Don't come any closer!" said the prosthetic jaw soldier. Adcox noticed that the boldness the men showed towards Hatshepsut had now diminished in face of the pack of males. The soldiers all took half a step backwards.

The lieutenant moved in between the two races and placed his hands out facing the both aggressors. "Stop! Stand down, all of you stand down, that's an order." The lack of confidence in Adcox's voice showed.

"Just get back on your ship, leave us alone." The soldier missing a nose yelled out with a shakiness in his words.

Suddenly, Jei'Gun crashed through his comrades and punched the man with the artificial jaw in his chest with such ferocity that he flew into the scattered file of soldiers behind him, knocking down three of them. Another man punched the elite-shakan in the helmet but it had no effect, and he screamed from the pain. Jei'Gun lifted him up with one hand by his neck and choke slammed him hard on the ground. Fighting broke out, it was a losing battle for the vast gathering of humans despite the Horaxian warriors being few in number. Adcox and Tronics tried to break up the fight, feeling a sense of responsibility due to their association to Jei'Gun, Nanonramu and Hatshepsut. But in stepping in they were attacked themselves.

Chapter Nine - A Tribunal Beyond Good and Evil

Five light years away from the doomed Kemeta rested the bastion of the Horaxian people, the symbol of their imperial might. The awe-inspiring Horax Prime. Every resource left in the empire was gathered to maintain its splendor. Within the most fortified region of the planet was the citadel, the command headquarters for the Horaxian rulers.

Deep within the walls of the citadel's gothic architecture, protected by hovering warships, mega sentry cannons and an army on guard, a group of elder males congregated, seated in a semicircle. Their faces were radiated by the bright plasma of electronic staff lanterns held by statues of past kings lining the gold and black mosaic walls.

Six living kings were present. Each represented the remaining worlds of the Horaxian Empire, and in the middle a large throne seated the empire's ruler, the Great Supreme King San Khomani. Across from the elders levitated a gigantic digital screen that took up the entire opposing wall. On the display was Earth Command, consisting of mankind's most senior generals: the Americas, EU, Africa, Russia and Asia. The EU general currently held the position of field marshal and effectively, with humanity under military rule, he was the leader of mankind. The additional five generals present governed the human extra-terrestrial colonies and also formed part of Earth command.

The closest, Earth's moon, officially named Lunar 1, had been transformed into a hospitable living environment in

2099. Lunar 1 was divided up as a reflection of Earth. Every country of every continent had their representative region, proportionate to its size on Earth, and classified as an interstellar territory of each nation. As the surface of the moon was only seven point four percent of Earth's, extensive subterranean terraforming was required to create space for the once overpopulated human race. The leading general of Lunar 1 was General Summers, a spectacled, greyed haired iron maiden who sat to the left of the field marshal. She had a hard time biting her tongue as they endured the endless list of demands imposed by the Horaxian elders. Their empire had shortages of food and water but the Horaxians would never trust humans for any form of sustenance, no matter how many levels of screening and testing they could perform. They also refused human material resources as well due to their perceived inferior quality.

Gen. Maharaj could only sit and soak up the Horaxians ordering of Earth Command's military resources to guard either dangerous or unimportant positions of the Horaxian battle maps. He headed Biosphere-9, the space city 6,276 km² in size floating stationery in outer space, four times as large as the European city of greater London, with six hundred million civilians. The number were fewer than half that, until the Polymorph appeared and destroyed Biosphere-12. Twelve was its newer replica city, similar to Canada in size.

The headstrong General Burns tried to voice some objections, all of which were shot down by the opposition. Burns controlled Kepler-Terra, originally called Kepler-62f, the next human stronghold after Biosphere-9 and one of five planets in the Kepler-62 star system. Kepler-Terra's close neighbor, Kepler-62e, was reserved for the animal and plant life of Earth to avoid their extinction, as the majority of Earth's wildlife no longer existed. Rather than being structured based on Earth's geographical and national composition like Lunar 1, each region of the exoplanet Kepler-Terra was sectioned for every major race of Earth. The Asiatic occupied the largest surface area, Caucasia represented the third largest territory, then the Indus. The second largest region was a cosmopolitan area where all races cohabited. Before population growth urged mankind to colonize Kepler-Terra, they first colonized the exoplanet Gliese 667cc. Renaming it Gliese-Eden, Geden its most frequent reference, it once thrived, until the Polymorph annihilated all human life on the planet.

After a temporary cease-firing of their demands, a Horaxian elder addressed the Earth Command generals about their situation. Just as with all the Horaxian kings present, an assortment of chains crisscrossed his face and neck, laced with precious stones. "Famed Nok – overran, infested. Unconquerable Enkush – overran, infested. Prodigious Cunga Sigma – overran, nuclear bombed, still, infested. Ten billion lives we have lost in infernal human wars. But now due to savage abomination that is Horde, extermination pounds on our very walls. In last fifteen years the souls of over thirty billion males, females and young ones have been reaved. Our current population now merely nine billion and dropping exponentially."

"Human population is down to just four billion," said the general of the Gaias, Gen. Tulu. "What it was in Earth year 1974. Most of our twenty-one billion lost were in the last five years of Polymorph attacks. Not to mention food scarcity, drought and disease. We're struggling to find asylum for the evacuated populations of Gaia Major, Gliese-Eden and Biosphere-12."

The Gaias were the two most extragalactic planets colonized by mankind. Laying ten billion light years away, Gaia Major, the isolated world, was given to all the indigenous people and small-island nations of Earth due to their loud cries of persecution, disenfranchisement and underrepresentation. The largest geographical area, Bantun, had been dedicated to all those of African ethnicity. Half of Bantun was liquid water, so vast submarine cities were constructed and once colonized, the population exponentially increased into billions. But no nation of Gaia Major exercised racial exclusivity. These largely tribal societies inter-traded, mixed and even intermarried due to an appreciation of each other's difficult and burdened history. Before the emergence of the Polymorph, this was a peaceful planet in comparison to Earth. The descendants of humanity's oldest people did not only choose to follow the ways of their ancestors much to the surprise of Earthlings. Difficulties attributed to being isolated so far away from Earth's assistance and with the military influence of Gaia Minor, the Gaians revolutionized space technology. Many further breakthroughs in science came from Gaia Major.

Gaia Minor, the smaller sister planet, was established as a military base and at one time had the largest build-up of weapons of war in the cosmos. But it wasn't enough. The Polymorph overran and infested both planets. Billions died defending the Gaias to the end.

Another elder spoke, he was King Yaser Selo, Kemeta's ruling monarch. "To sour matters already dire in definition, suffered we have now catastrophic losses on Beloved Kemeta. It is likely the planet will fall upon next attack. Shando the Grand leads evacuation of most of the inhabitants. Of course, many refuse to leave."

"We're sorry for your losses, King Yaser Selo," said the Asia general. "Perhaps we could have helped if you had not fired upon our space carrier, the *Lord Kitchener*, that was positioned close to your sector, killing some of its crew."

The Horaxian elder Amedo'dani shot up from his seat. "Firstly, your assistance was disdainfully unwanted, nor requested, nor required. Second, your renegade vessel fired upon our ship first. We grow tired of human lies. Lies that have persisted since you destroyed Adored Okavanga, ruining our initial coalition," He thumped the semi-circular table. As always, it was only a matter of time before the Horaxians brought up either Hope or Matelot-6. Things usually took a turn for the worse from then on.

"Your majesty, this is not true," said the Biosphere-9 General Maharaj. "Why sign a peace treaty and still constantly display hostility? This is supposed to be an alliance."

"Alliance?" said King Yaser Selo. "Fools, we were to ally with a race who so abundantly lack *conviction*."

The Great Supreme King had been sitting attentively listening to the exchanges. He raised his left hand and halted Yaser Selo's next words. "Senior council males, generals. We have many lingering problems and should make arrangements necessary to properly address matters. But assembled we have today for another agenda pressing. Tell our guests to enter."

From the edge of the Horaxian leaders' seating area a glass panel rose with a hum. Afterwards, the hall hissed with dispelled gas.

A guardsmen bowed and addressed the Great Supreme King. "Anti-human bacterial contamination systems have been activated, my lord."

Two elite-shakan imperial guardsmen, using their double-muscled strength, pulled each side of the giant doors by their golden, large-linked chains. In walked Dr. Henry and General Baizan, both hoping that their compounded respect, wisdom and reputations would sway the minds of two races. Both shared an inability to walk fluidly. Dr. Henry used his transparent, electronic cane; Baizan had a bad limp stemming from his right leg.

The Great Supreme King welcomed them. "Dr. Henreyotomborufulonjaro and Baizan, General. Two males who need no introduction to Homo sapiens and Horaxians alike."

"Thank you, Your Eminence," said Henry.

"And what of the Black Guard?" said Lunar 1's General Summers.

The name casted an eerie reception amongst the old males in the chamber and the hall quieted.

"Behold!" said Supreme King San Khomani.

From the center of the floor a flat, circular, silver metal levitated. Directly underneath stood Major Hawke on another identical circular platform. A blue energy encircled him, constantly vanishing and reappearing, though it never veered outside the circumference of the two circular metals. Instead of his Horaxian cloak, he wore a plain black uniform made of acrylic fibers. The major had no visible restraints, yet sensed his confinement. When he stuck his hands out, they were met with resistance. His palms highlighted blue as it imprinted on the invisible force field wall and he felt the coldness of the energy field throughout his body. As the cylinder rose to a stop, five guards surrounded it, but from a distance, pointing their arm-cannons high.

"The demon king!" cried a Horaxian elder in a shaky voice.

The aging North American general placed his glasses on, disbelieving his failing sight. "The Hawke!" he whispered.

"Its presence a bad omen, Your Eminence," said King Amedo'dani sat closest to the Supreme leader in a fearful voice. "We should not have brought it here."

"Excuse us, council members," said Field Marshall Montgomery. "But from what we hear of the Abyss, it doesn't seem possible one could survive. I know General Baizan's DNA check matched, but we'd like to reconfirm identification for the record. If you don't mind, Your Majesty?"

"Very well, proceed," said King San Khomani.

"Sir, please identify yourself?" asked the Field Marshall.

"Name: Keegan Hawke. Rank: Major. Number: 6676214, sir."

"Former Major, Mr. Hawke," said Field Marshall Montgomery, making everyone aware Hawke had been dishonorably discharged. "What was your designation?"

"Squadron officer commander of the Nephilim Knights."

"Place of origin?" asked Montgomery.

Hawke paused. "Arima, sir."

The Divine Council, as well as Earth Command, murmured in confusion.

"Ancient Arima?" said the Great Supreme King. "That is impossible. Humans are not permitted on our worlds, let alone birthed there."

"I was born in one of your human concentration camps."

"Is this true?" the Field Marshall asked his generals, himself in shock.

"I can confirm this is the truth, sir," said Baizan.

San Khomani glanced from left to right at his council males who nodded reluctantly in agreement.

"ID confirmed. Welcome back, Hawke," said Field Marshall Montgomery. "Your condition?"

"Combat effective, sir!"

Another Horaxian elder spoke out. "We have an incoming transmission from Commander Cagn. He wishes to join in the discussions via holocast."

Much remained unknown about the High Apex's origins. Most believe him to be born on Anubia, due to his strong and endearing physique. Plus, he headed the imperial guard, which consisted purely of warrior elite-shakan, the most formidable fighting force of the empire. Cagn's figure appeared in the sacred chambers in the form of a holographic projection at the center of the hall. As he stood, hands held behind him, an elite-shakan in full armor more splendid than the citadel's Anubianite guardsmen waited beside him. From the moment his holocast appeared, Hawke's dark eyes focused upon him alone.

Cagn addressed the committee. "And I looked, and behold a pale horse, and his name that sat on him was Death, and Hell followed with him. And power was given unto them...to kill with sword." Cagn gesturing firmly with his hands, his red cloak blew gently.

"High Apex, an honor it is for you to join us," said San Khomani.

"The demon knight should not have been freed," replied Cagn. "It is harbinger of death."

"I believe your words breathe unnerving truth," San Khomani replied. "But our very own and renowned Dr. Henreyotomborufulonjaro has fought for this audience, we owe him that much. However, I cannot see much good reason for cursed one to not return to fate of incarceration."

"Leaders of humanity," said Baizan, stepping forward with his good leg first, the only human pair of legs given the privilege of treading foot on their prime world in decades. "Great Supreme King San Khomani and rulers of the Horaxian Empire. You know why we are here. The doctor and I are confident that the Horde originate from dark matter space, unreachable by both our technologies. However, former Major Hawke was able to cross into the dark universe before, and while there he discovered an alien ship. That ship, we believe, has the same properties as MK1. With this mothership we can advance our technology, discover and or develop new weaponry with the same indestructible power as MK1 itself. We will be able to traverse dark space and lay siege to the Horde home world, possibly ending this war. But we need Hawke's help to accomplish this. We request he be released into our custody in order to carry out this mission. With the possibility of a full pardon upon successful completion of the mission and recognizing his years of conviction already served."

Cagn busted out in laughter. "We need *its* help you say?" his face now turned dead serious. "Like it helped on Kemeta? You heretic, there is no power left to run planetary defenses, nuclear waste and antimatter containment, or its thermal world generators. Billions will be smited by frozen death due to demon's actions and his bipedal ape accomplices. Kemeta capital lays in ruin, the abomination handed our planet to Horde upon platter."

Baizan's clenched his fist to the High Apex's voice. "Kemeta was being overrun. If it wasn't for Hawke's actions the planet would have been infested. The power can be restored. Hawke just bought Kemeta time, and in that time we need to act."

Rogue Basarwa's ruling King waived his hand signaling he intended to interrupt. "So, how was the cursed one able to reach dark space? That which has never been done."

Dr. Henry, still in his crumpled up attire, began to pace the room as he was fond of doing and answered. "He...it...was able to punch through to the dark matter universe because in the Asatorin region of space a quinary star system collapsed." As Henry spoke, he pressed a blue nob on his walking stick. His stick then projected a three dimensional presentation of four orbital stars. The stars soon then collided into each other as they swirled around.

The doctor continued on. "Their combined celestial force created a supermassive blackhole of over a hundred billion solar masses. The biggest on Horaxian record, its gravitational power so immense, as it curved space-time it temporarily fused dark space and normal space together. For that single moment in time they became one, in supernal unity. People view space as nothing, but space is actually a fabric. A fabric which can be twisted and torn."

"So what need have we of the demon?" asked Rogue Basarwa's King. "Can we not simply repeat act again ourselves?"

"Unfortunately…no, your highness," said Dr. Henry. "It is incomprehensible how one could traverse through a black hole and survive. Speculate I would, that circumstances exceptionally unique existed pertaining to this celestial anomaly, and it was strength of supermassive blackhole upon its birth that provided power necessary to breach dark matter space. That force would have been the closest thing to strength of Prime Spark, the big bang in Homo sapien terms. If we attempt to traverse it again, even a thousand times, the outcome most likely is that the singularity would crush any object into nothingness at every attempt. But there is a way, the unknown artifact discovered with the one named Hawke inside. It brought the cursed one back from dark matter space fifteen years past. The cursed one's companion supervisory apparatus, termed an *SPU*, possesses the capability to reactivate artifact. An ability that still eludes even myself. This pod, this artifact, can recreate a disruption in space's fabric great enough for a small ship to pass through.

But even if we simply request the cursed one to reactivate the artifact and left the demon behind. Once the barriers of dark space are crossed where would we go? How would we find Horde home world? Over five times more vast than normal space is the dark realm. And without the cursed one's SPU to activate mothership and access maps of the dark universe, we may not find Horde in a lifetime."

"Excuse me, Doctor," said the Russian general. "So you're saying his SPU unit is all we need?"

Yaser Selo's eyes widened to their fullest at the general's apparent proposal. "I am sure we can remove its contraption and assemble our own pack. The demonic Knight can return to the cursed Jumbie Abyss where it belongs."

"Negative!" said Baizan. "The SPU is surgically hardwired to his cerebral cortex and nervous system."

"Then I will rip it out!" Cagn's voice raised in a fury.

Baizan responded. "The SPU cannot remain activated or be reactivated if removed from their symbiotic host. Hawke has been there before, we need his experience and his skills to traverse the hazardous terrain of the planetoid where the ship was located. As I said, we need him."

"We need solutions." Cagn retaliated with conviction. "Real solutions not farfetched hope and pray strategies."

"As much as I hate to agree with the High Apex, he could be right," said General Burns. Even the poker-faced Baizan struggled to hold back his frustration with the Kepla-Terran general's words. Baizan then looked toward the North American general and wondered if he might speak out. The wrinkly American was known for his wisdom and often agreed with Baizan, but he also rarely spoke at all.

Doctor Henry voiced words to aid their quest. "All my research suggests Horde are multiplying almost geometrically. By my calculations factoring in frequency of attack, death rates, population levels, scarcity of resources and time required to build weaponry, and adding Shando the Grand's principles on requisites of war, then in three months to come we will lose our empire's two most outward planets and the Homo sapiens will be overwhelmed on most of their colonies, only Earth and their Lunar 1 colony will remain. In five months, all Homo sapien and Horaxian worlds will be Horde occupied. Our races may survive but they will be scattered across the stars like debris in the cosmic ocean."

"Outrageous!" cried Cagn. "You merely state obvious in pitiful attempt to misdirect truth. This Black Guard monster cannot be trusted. It is a living weapon. Its sole purpose, the destruction of life. I know its dark secrets concealed. It assumes form of man only in light, but in shadows murky its human skin casts off, revealing demonic wings, hoofs and claws. My own eyes have bared witness. Only I here have been burnt by its venom." He pointed to the blue scarring running to the top of his head that disrupted his hair growth. The center of his forehead had another blue scar. His echoing voice aided his vilification of Hawke.

General Baizan continued to defend the major. "This is all fictitious superstitious nonsense, Cagn." Baizan turned to the world leaders, taking a bit of effort to balance himself due to his bad leg. "His comments are spawned from his hatred for our fallen hero and his attempts on Cagn's life. Let I remind you, members of this hearing, that I have waged war on every moon, planet, space station, outpost and galaxy intelligent life has ever stepped on from the Milky Way to Pectocron. I have seen it all from microwave plasma pulse rifles to highly lethal biological weaponry. In short, I'm as seasoned as it gets and I'm telling you, Keegan Hawke is the most formidable, unstoppable force mankind has ever had. He and his Black Guard squadron had a near one hundred percent mission success rate. Most of our finest warriors in the field of combat have fallen through decades of war, including the rest of the Black Guard knights. Hawke is one of the last masters of warfare in the field. He is the best at what he does, people."

"And what exactly is that?" queried the Great Supreme King San Khomani. "I'd like to hear the cursed one answer."

Hawke took his time before addressing them. "Infiltration, completion of mission objectives, annihilation of any opposition. Survival...optimal but optional."

"An option thankfully he chooses not to ignore," said Doctor Henry with a smile.

"I too share the same concerns as some members of this hearing," said Field Marshal Montgomery who had been listening with diligence. "I do have a slight reluctance towards redeploying a Black Guard Knight into the field of combat again. Today's events on Kemeta are symptomatic of the problem. What was created to be the sharpest of swords turned into a highly effective yet blunt instrument. The word 'overkill' could never fully describe it. Deploying Black Guards was like nuking a whole town to kill one man. Orders were frequently ignored. Some say they went mad from the killing."

General Baizan knew the field marshal's opinions carried the most weight so he had to argue his case or lose it all right here. "Field Marshal, sir, but we did nuke a town, in Earth year 1944, and if that blunt instrument could have been dropped at the beginning of the war then perhaps millions would have been saved."

"The fact is, Baizan," replied the field marshal, "that it has been simultaneously glorious and tragic that Mr. Hawke has adopted 'by any means necessary' to be his only mantra in life."

"That is true, sir, however...we need that mantra right now," said Baizan.

"I agree," said the Lunar 1's General Summers. "Members of the hearing, there's been reports of heightened activity in the Polaris sigma system. MK1 may be breaking free."

Her news generated whispers around the hall.

Yaser Selo spoke with trembling hands. "If the Wings of Death should break its celestial bonds, then five months is too burdening of hope. We will be lucky if five days we endure. So it seems we have depleted most precious resource of all...time."

"If the cursed one was permitted upon journey," said Great Supreme King San Khomani. "Could we not place incarceration collar upon neck?" The news of MK1 warmed him to Hawke's involvement.

"It has been tried, Your Grace," said the Kemetan King. "Long before its banishment to the Jumbie Abyss, when we captured it before. The demon lord escaped collar, the only one ever to do so. How, we still do not know."

"Have we all forgotten the demon's sins?" yelled Cagn, infuriated with the Supreme King's question. "Have years of Horde swarms silenced screams of a billion Horaxian innocents slaughtered on once Precious Matelot-6 by its hands venomous. Have they?" he shouted more emphatically. "It has destroyed two whole worlds now even quicker than Horde itself." With each word uttered the High Apex Commander extinguished the aspirations of Henry and Baizan.

Cagn pointed at Dr. Henry. "You, heretic human sympathizer, you said this creature vile was found inside artifact? Did Horde not first attack within year of the demon's genocide of Precious Matelot-6? Council Elders, *it* brought Horde with it from dark space. *It* is in collusion with Horde...*It, is, Horde.*" He bellowed, hands high and stretched out with his fingers curled.

An uproar ignited the chamber. Most of the Horaxian elders rose with shouts for Hawke's return to the depths of the Abyss.

But Cagn was yet to finish with his prosecution. "How can we ponder making deals with such an evil? We have shamed ourselves and cursed these sacred halls by bringing it here. And we have cursed our race by allying with universal plague that is humanity."

Talks had now completely broken down as Horaxian shouts echoed the halls. Yaser Selo rose up in condemnation demanding Hawke's removal from the chambers.

Doctor Henry walked back to Baizan's side. "I envisaged a more fruitful conclusion to our momentous conclave," said the scientist.

"It's bad enough having to state one and one makes two," said the pissed off Baizan, "but having to argue why it does and lose is just disgraceful."

In this moment of pandemonium Hawke decided it was time for him to act. "Permission to speak?" His unforeseen request silenced the noise.

"Go ahead, Hawke," said Adens, the North American general, which surprised all the humans present. The old four star general was known to only speak when he had something important to say.

"I've killed many Horaxians, and before I die I'm sure I'll kill a few more," said the imprisoned man. The council members all murmured in complete disgust and shock.

Dr Henry whispered to Baizan. "By the whites of the Great Supreme King's hair, what in this woe-some world is this wavering, weakened, warlord *doing*?"

Hawke continued. "But right now I am not the enemy. When humans and Horaxians fought it was based on differences in ideologies, of culture. It was based on fear, and it was based upon breaking each other's ability to fight:

destroying warships, supply lines, and securing resources. We've just watched an attack on a civilian population. We're being exterminated. Why? Because we are not united. As we speak nations of both worlds are in conflict and turmoil. This is the fundamentals of war...divide and conquer, and we are being conquered. There's nothing random about the Horde's attacks. First, they watched us from the shadows as both races weakened each other through decades of warfare. The axiom of war is to avoid what is strong, attack what is weak, and too many years of battle have weakened your resolve. They've crushed your will to fight, now you sit quietly hoping they show mercy. But power concedes nothing without demand. It never did, and it never will. The limits of tyrants are only prescribed by the endurance of those whom they oppress.

I know what you're feeling, you're all scared. The greatest weapon which they wield is fear itself. You see, they knew if they attacked us in one blow they couldn't defeat us, but fear is most powerful when given time to fester and corrupt the soul. This was their plan all along. To conceal their form, keep us afraid and in the dark...but some things thrive in the dark.

We need to regain the will to fight with indomitable, immovable, insuppressible courage. To surgically implant fear in an enemy created unburdened with the concept. The object of defense is purely preservation but possibility of victory can only come from attack. Whether I stay or go we must bring the fight to them and this alien ship gives us the means."

Hawke paused and spun around to look everyone in the eye. Then he ended his speech in a low yet serious tone. "All they've seen is our ability to defend ourselves. Now they must know what it's like to feel the advancing sharp end of the sword."

A long silence descended in the hall. Dr. Henry looked on nervously, General Baizan's expression edged towards unimpressed. He was a man unfamiliar with being kept waiting.

"Committee members, your verdict," said Baizan, unapologetic for his tone, believing he knew their decision.

After a moment of deliberation amongst themselves the North American General Adens cleared his throat then spoke. "Eighteen years ago, Earth calendar 2179, in battle with the Horaxians orbiting planet Nortona, the string engine of my ship was hit. I was a sitting duck with four enemy ships surrounding me. Does this event ring a bell to you former major?"

"Sir, we only recorded it as mission one-six-two. But affirmative general, we remember."

"One-six-two huh?" General Adens chuckled to himself. "Well I recorded it a little more miraculously than that. I was being hauled back to Horax Prime. Then I saw the most...unbelievable sight. You and your Black Guard Nephilim squadron running on the planet's orbital rings of ice, raining fire down on the fighter-crafts and dragging a thirteen ton engine core." The general smiled and shook his head from side to side still in disbelief after so many years. "It was incredible, the sight of someone running in space. You stormed on board, killed every hostile that moved, installed your string core and got us the hell out of dodge. I've never seen anything like it in my life."

The North American general looked at the field marshal with a nod and the field marshal reciprocated. He continued. "I don't know how you're able to do the things you do Hawke, and I have serious doubts this mission will be successful. But what I am sure of, is that if there's anyone that can do it, it's you, and once again I thank you. Earth Command approves."

Field Marshal Montgomery now took over proceedings. "We will assemble a team to operate with the former major and as the artifact is in our possession, we would like permission for the mission to be human commanded. If you would grant us the honor Great Supreme King. However, for the acts committed on the ark ship *Ploiarion* and Matelot-6, we cannot formerly reinstate Mr. Hawke into the service. I guess now it comes down to you, Your Eminence."

"You stand before us, most hated of all humans," said San Khomani, looking at Hawke. "We do not truly know what you are but our people see you as curse. I think it is time we unleash that curse upon our enemies. I, Great Supreme King of the Horaxian Empire, approves of mission. Nevertheless, my council does not agree to your pardon, upon completion of mission you will return to prison. Although, if assistance proves fruitful then perhaps not one as inhospitable as the Abyss. Also, we will have Horaxian presence accompanying you. Do you accept these terms?"

"We accept," agreed Hawke. "But we have one request, Rey'Jax, the Ariman also comes along. Or the deal's off."

After a short discussion inaudible to all but Horaxian elders, the Supreme King responded. "You will have your wish."

The Council members rose up and dispersed. Cagn's holocast disappeared and then reappeared right in front of Hawke's invisible confinement cell. Alongside him stood the elite-shakan, Apex Kibu'Kan, the highest ranking knight of the imperial guard.

Hawke moved near to the confinement wall to come as close to Cagn as he could. The High Apex's eyes had no pupils or irises, just a milky white sclera with tiny, blue blood vessels sprawling within. His face looked like one of a middle aged Horaxian male but without blemish, sharp and flawless.

"The Sword in the Dark," Cagn said with a grin. "The King of Darkness himself. Look Kibu'Kan, we stand before an unvanquished yet fallen god." Cagn and his companion laughed.

Hawke's voice soon broke their humor. "And thus you clothe your naked villainy...

"...and seem a saint when most I play the devil," said Cagn. "Well, am I versed in your kind."

"You've done a great job confusing the masses and tarnishing my name, Cagn."

The High Apex laughed again with pure delight. "Even your own people curse you. But I should not take all credit, you made it too easy."

"You're afraid to show yourself in public and come here in person?"

"Afraid of what? You, Black Guard commander? You do not fool me with your innocuous threats. You can barely even stand."

"But we're still alive!"

"Yes, strange, that the radiation of the Abyss had not killed you."

"As luck would have it, the blue tar from my Cungan cigars contained Ultra-Potassium Iodide. It diffused into my blood stream, protecting against radiation poisoning. Who would have thought? And we were just starting to enjoy the sunshine and fresh air."

"And now free, perhaps you will try again to do what you dismally failed? To claim my life? Oh tormented Sisyphus."

"Master," said Kibu'Kan, his voice distorted by his enlarged elite-shakan warrior helmet. "The Jumbie Abyss was punishment undeserved. Give Kibu'Kan the honor of killing our greatest adversary." Kibu'Kan referred to himself in the third person as like all Anubianites.

Hawke then eyeballed Kibu'Kan. "You must be disappointed Cagn, your girlfriend hasn't gotten any prettier."

The big elite-shakan threw his fist with a forceful rage at Hawke's face, forgetting his presence was merely a holographic projection. His virtual hand passed unimpeded through the force-field prison chamber. "Soon your skull will make the finest addition to our trophy hall," said Kibu'Kan. "Right next to your father's and mother's."

Hawke placed his hands against his confinement field and as it illuminated his palms he felt its coldness once more. "Time has been my ally, Cagn. We'll be coming for you real soon. So sit tight, because there's no moon, no nebula, no clandestine rock in the endlessness of space where we couldn't find you."

Chapter Ten - I Deceive The Sky To Cross The Ocean

Ever the bone chilling sight for the crew of the *Sword of Damocles*, was the armada of Horaxian battleships that surrounded the great Horax Prime in defensive formation. Adding to their chills were the turrets of the guardian gun, a menacing weapon platform the size of a small town. The grey, rotating dodecahedron with weapons that could destroy a target light years away was stationary but its weapons tracked the space carrier's every movement as they journeyed outwards from their supposed ally's home world. As if the colossal weapon wasn't enough, so cautious the Horaxians were of their prime world that three mega-class warships followed the carrier until it reached the outer limits of the Horaxian star system.

From inside the *Sword of Damocles'* docking bay, the hanger doors opened and a small transport ship landed with a smooth thud. Shortly after its doors opened and out stepped Hawke, Baizan and Henry along with a four-man, armed security detail assigned to accompany Hawke on Command's orders. They walked toward the internal docking bay airlock doors, with Hawke matching the elder gentlemen's slow pace though not by choice.

"I've notified what's left of Unit Forty Two to prep for the mission as you requested," Baizan said to Hawke. "Some of them were pretty banged up, you sure it wouldn't be wiser to assign a new special ops team?"

"They'll do, sir," said Hawke.

"For the last time, could you cut the sir crap out. The Horaxians are also sending the elite-shakan and the trooper that brought you back from the Abyss. It seems like they had trouble finding anyone that would go on a mission they deemed to be a lost cause, especially with the cursed one."

"Our forces are not what they used to be," said Doctor Henry, staring at Hawke with a grin. "Just like many other things."

"What about the young doctor?" asked Hawke. "We're going to need her too."

"She's a civilian," replied Baizan. The busying deck crew saluted him as he limped passed. "No one has authority over her. Saying that, she elected to come before she was even asked."

"You know these scientist types," said Hawke.

"I caught your remark," said the doctor. "I still wonder, can an old bird still fly?"

"Reinforced by purpose, even the impossible can be accomplished," said Hawke.

"So what is your purpose?" asked Henry.

"You're already aware," replied Hawke slightly agitated.

"I am aware. Everything in the unconscious seeks outward manifestation, according to your Mr. Jung. Even things that thrive in darkness must eventually come into the light."

"Doctor, give us a moment," asked Baizan. Words like "please" were retired from his vocabulary. Baizan also gestured using an open palm for the guardsmen to keep their distance.

The scientist strolled off, humming, with his walking stick tapping the floor. Being friends for a long time, Baizan sensed Hawke's mood, not that Hawke ever gave anything away. "That feeling of wanting to strangle him soon passes," said the general.

"We fear...not soon enough. Do you trust him?"

"There's only one man I ever trusted and I'm standing in front of him."

"James, it's only fair we let you know that whichever way this turns out, Eve and I, we're not going back in a hole."

General Baizan gestured with a little nod of his head. "I owe you more than I can ever repay. Pulled every string I could to stop your execution, it even cost me a star. But I fear the abyss was worse."

"You kept us alive. Now we're going to finish what we've started."

"Be the Sword in the Dark again," said Baizan.

"General Baizan, Major Hawke!" called a familiar voice.

It was Adcox holding a salute. Baizan told him to stand at ease.

"I wanted to report that the *Copernicus* has arrived and at this moment is docked in hangar bay seven. We'll have the final checks completed in approximately ten hours, sir," said Adcox.

"Make that a hard ten," Baizan requested. "Are you and your team ready for this mission?"

"Sir, we will be, sir."

"All right. That'll be all...Captain."

"Captain?" replied Adcox, stunned.

"That's affirmative. Accounts of your courage, ingenuity and valor on Kemeta have exalted your status amongst humans and Horaxians alike. We'll be counting on your leadership. You will be in charge of this mission."

"Thank you, General, for the honor. But I was only recently made a lieutenant..."

"Well just don't let the Horde know that."

Adcox tried to persist in his opposition. "General, I can't..."

"You giving me an order, son?" snapped Baizan with sternness.

"No...not at..."

"Because only the glorious Field Marshal Montgomery, God almighty the beneficent, the merciful and my wife can wield such power."

"No sir, not at all, sir. I.."

"You're dismissed! Don't let us down, son!"

"Sir, no, sir!" said Adcox and he then looked to Hawke for a moment sensing his role in his promotion before walking away bewildered.

"Earth Command wanted to send a major from Unit Twelve to head the mission," said Baizan watching the young man depart. "I convinced them with you in an advisory role it won't be necessary."

"We appreciate the favor, James. If the Ariman agrees, then we'll have all we need."

"Well that's the other strange request I don't gct. But this kid Adcox, I'm going to give it to you like an arrow,

Keegan. Our new young captain is as green as the Neo-Amazon on Lunar 1. The boy's moist, he'll crack."

"He's holding up a lot better than Earth Command and everyone else from what I've seen."

"What are you getting at?" Baizan tried to maintain a low volume to not be overheard by the guard detail.

"Horaxians fire on the Lord Kitchener, taking lives and there are no repercussions?"

"Our forces are so crippled now we cannot survive a war against the Horaxians. They've caught up and surpassed us technologically. They have superior numbers, and most importantly their will to fight is greater. We're now little brother. We don't tell big brother what to do."

"What the...has mankind completely lost their balls?"

"We both saw this happening since the Horaxian wars. Humanity's...we've changed. It's like something's been removed from our spirit. Perhaps you might be able to help us find what we've lost."

"To do that, I'm going to need that kid's help. Trust me, the future of both races is going to depend upon him."

***

Later on, the team made their final preparations before they left for their journey. Tronics sat in front of a screen used by enlisted men for personal transmissions. Although he spoke to a woman on screen, his attention centered on repairs he conducted on his particle accelerator laser.

"I had to scramble this transmission. It's a top secret mission so I shouldn't be telling you anything. Keep it to yourself this time, Amanda." He said, wearing a plain black vest and matching bandana. His electronic probe arced electrical discharges on his laser with a welding buzz.

"You know I always do!" said his wife on the flickering screen with a West Indian accent.

"Yeah, right!"

"I cah believe you rescued this Black Guard man. He's nothing but trouble. Shelly-Ann's husband's cousin had a friend on that ark he destroyed. He deserves to stay in prison."

"Shelly-Ann's husband's cousin's friend, huh?" Tronics released a light snigger. "I don't know, babes. I mean he's not that bad. He saved our lives on Kemeta."

"He saved he-self more like it. That's your problem Kevin, all dem computers you does be playing with scramble-egg yuh brain. Boy, you shoulda been a colonel by now or at the least a major. But you too busy playing with toys."

"Yeah yeah yeah!" said Tronics, brushing her off. "Hey, D just got made a captain!"

"What, Diomedes? How? Lord Father Jesus that boy have more chicken in him than a farm."

"Come on," laughed Tronics. "He's doing great, they're thinking of giving him a medal for his defense of Kemeta."

"Really!" said Amanda exaggerating the word. "I've seen dem girls roasting marshmallows that started off harder than that boy."

"He said hi!"

"Tell him I said…give you the job."

Tronics laughed louder. "I'll put in a recommendation." He was more than used to his wife's melodramatic impulses.

"Hey, where my girls at?"

"*Girls,* your fadda wants to talk to you."

From his screen, Tronics' heard the sound of small hurrying footsteps.

"Dad's on the line," said a little girl in the background.

Popping on to the screen's view were two young girls. One was Tylah who was fourteen and the other, Carla, was ten and Tronics' youngest daughter.

"Hey dad!" almost in harmony, both in timing and excitement.

"How's my girls doing? Your mum told me you were giving her trouble."

"Oh my god, no we wasn't," said Tylah.

"Dad," said Carla, "we thought you were going to win the war already, what's taking you so long?"

"He can't win the war all by himself silly."

"Hey Tylah," said Tronics, "be nice to your sister. I'm trying babygirl, almost there."

"Dad, you need to step up the intensity of your training," said Tylah.

"Yeah!" shouted Carla overexcited. "Systro-mato-cally destroy the enemy."

"And lead mankind to victory," said Tylah repeating the words her father told her before he left.

Tronics and his wife couldn't help themselves from laughing.

"Girls you know I'm the man, right?" Tronics sucked his teeth to affirm is boast. "You shoulda seen me on Kemeta yuh nah, me and uncle Diomedes had it on lock."

Out of the blue, Adcox's voice came through on the speaker system interrupting their moment.

"Tronics, I need you down at briefing room three ASAP."

"Acknowledged!" Tronics said into his slab which he had already illegally wirelessly connected to the ship's intercom. He turned back to his family onscreen. "All right, I got to go pretty ladies!"

As he rose up his wife said her last words.

"Tell Diomedes we're all praying for him. And tell him to bring mah husband back safely too. That's an order."

"Affirmative!" said Tronics.

***

In a dark room with a computer screen in front of him sat Adcox. The screen displayed a login page with the title "Personnel Database" along with the Earth Command emblem. The doors slid opened and Tronics entered, raising a strong salute to Adcox.

"Captain of the forces, great leader of men," said the lanky corporal with a serious face.

"Mate, knock it off."

"Yes boss, whatever you say, boss man."

"Shut up! I already got enough of that from Akerele."

Tronics laughed. "He's going to start badgering you for a bonus now we've been assigned on this mission."

"Brother, dude's already been on at me about hazard pay. Why're they sending us anyway? I mean we're still pretty messed up from what we've just been through."

"Who else are they going to send? Our ranks are thin as it is. Plus we've seen what Major Hawke can do first hand."

"Yeah well he's the reason why I hollered at you. I was trying to find out some more about him but all files on the Black Guard are locked down."

"What exactly are you looking for?" asked Tronics.

"I don't know. But I want to find out as much as possible about him and the major comes across as someone that only tells you what he wants you to know, and not what you should know."

"All right step aside, bruv! I'm about to hack into Earth Command's secured files. We'll have about two minutes before the connection is terminated." The corporal soon raised an eyebrow as he typed away. "This is strange. A lot of top secret missions don't even have encryption levels this high. Most generals wouldn't have the authority to access these files." The soft tones, resembling multiple water droplets, continued as he pressed the touchscreen keys. "Boom! We're in. Now let's see, the Black Guard Initiative," reading the print onscreen.

Adcox's intrigue peaked in view of the screen's details. "This is a list of Black Guard missions. Go to Major Hawke's personal information."

"Arrr captain rrrrr!" said Tronics in a pirate accent. "Says here Keegan Hawke was born and raised on...Arima?" Tronics said turning to Adcox.

"That must be how the Ariman seemed to know him. His parents were a part of a crew on a science vessel that were attacked and placed into concentration camps." Both marines looked at the list of Hawke's decorations that automatically scrolled on screen.

"Rarse!" said Tronics in disbelief looking at Hawke's accolades. "This guy's decorated like a Christmas tree: three Victoria Crosses, five Earth Medals Of Honor, four Purple Hearts, a Lunar Cross and one Human Knighthood Order."

"HKO? I thought you had to be dead to get that," said Adcox. "Look Tron, it gets deeper. Specialties listed include: infiltration, assassination, asymmetrical warfare, insurgency and counter insurgence, guerrilla warfare, escapology, terrorism, antiterrorism, sabotage…"

"Sabotage?"

"There's something about the major. I have this feeling that I've met him before, don't know why."

"Check it out," Tronics pointed at the screen. "Dude studied almost every discipline of science; with a specialty in applied sciences, electronics, psychology and toxicology. He knows everything, about…"

"Everything! He's a Renaissance man." Adcox froze in deep thought.

"What's that?" Tronics asked.

"In the fourteenth to seventeenth century Renaissance men began a movement based on the rediscovery of classical Greek philosophy. That man is the measure of all things. They became experts on a significant number of different subject areas, and therefore were able to draw on multiple bodies of knowledge to solve the most complex problems. Tron, it's pretty clear to me now that we're dealing with a man that we could never truly understand."

"Something's up here. There's a file here called project Nephilim that has a higher layer of encryption than everything else. In fact, it's the highest encryption I've seen. I'm trying to hack it now."

As soon as the tech marine selected the file the computer responded with "Access denied. Unauthorized session has been remotely terminated."

***

Along the corridor of the space carrier, lit brightly with rows of pure white light, marched Akerele and Zomo, moving with a purpose.

"This is ridiculous," said Akerele. "This is the second time now we've been sent on a suicide mission Zomo, *suicide*."

"Every mission these days are suicide missions. Just pipe down, Private. You don't know what it's like to constantly hear your voice."

"Yeah, you and your Kamikaze people know all about suicide."

"Why don't you go back to the bush and chuck a spear or something, Ack."

"Hey, I don't give a damn about how dangerous it is. If you paid me enough I'd even risk my life and try some of your mama san's sushi. What I'm pissed about is, we should be getting thoroughly compensated. P.A.I.D!" He shouted, punching the ship's bulkhead as he walked.

"You're something else, Akerele." She shook her head. "You'll just gamble it all away again anyway."

"With Adcox in charge, now I can finally get what I'm owed."

"Well, I doubt he'll knock you out like Lewalski did when you asked the old man." Zomo laughed. "Don't worry, they'll sort everything out after we get back."

"What's wrong with you, you foolish girl? You don't ask for more money *after* you've done a job."

Upon his last words they arrived at the end of the ship's port side corridor in front of a double door. As Akerele pressed the keypad button to open the door, the marching of multiple boots distracted him. He spun around and was startled by the presence of Major Hawke accompanied by four armed men. Zomo and Akerele saluted him out of respect.

"Major!" said Zomo.

***

Hawke responded with a nod then waited for them to enter first. Inside the room sat the remaining group from Kemeta. Dr. Henry was present, along with two guards posted at the door that had just been opened. A large part of the left-side hull of the ship was a viewing screen relaying images of the stars. Nanonramu showed an unusual amount of composure being in an enclosed environment with Hawke compared to their first meeting. Still he never took his eyes off him. Jei'Gun periodically glanced at the major but he was preoccupied with performing a systems check of his armor by accessing the control circuitry within his right hand gauntlet. His weighty left and right shoulder guard rested on the table but as always his helmet remained on.

"Ah the Hawke," said Dr. Henry. "So happy that you accepted my invitation for this informal debriefing."

Zomo came to the old, hunched Horaxian. "General Baizan requested you be given a copy of our flight path for your analysis." Zomo handed him a digital tablet. She then took a seat next to Adcox whose left cheek was bruised red from the lounge-deck fight. His and Tronics' sentiment for the Horaxian warriors in the room who had come out better off in the skirmish had bittered.

"Arigato, my dear," said Henry. "It is astonishing. I have perfected three thousand two hundred and fifteen of your seven thousand Earth supposed languages. Your heterogeneous communication, so...counterintuitive. A harrowing price for your illegitimate Babelic towel. But please stay, sit, join us. We were just discussing particulars about our Horde adversaries. It would be good for you all to get up to speed with what we are up against."

Hawke took a seat and the doctor continued. "Horde biology is somewhat remarkable. We believe their skeleton consists of large quantities of a type of bioorganic steel. Their body's magnetic properties, combined with unusually hot and volatile internal fluids, are what enables them to generate an explosive-corrosive energy build-up which they then can discharge, with devastating effect. They have a unique toxicology making them immune to most chemical weapons and enables them to survive even radiation. Which is not a difficult task for some *seasoned* members of our audience."

"Those Horaxian geniuses," said Akerele, "they should have found that out before they nuked Cunga Sigma trying to stop the Polymorph."

Doctor Hatshepsut stepped in with her extensive background in exobiology. "The creatures are metamorphic. Given the right amount of their numbers for genetic material they can transform into any one of their subspecies types at will. From cocoons, which appear to contain a form of highly energized amniotic fluid, they emerge in their base neonatal form, that which we named drones. Also, analysis shows them to be sexual monomorphic and do not appear to have reproductive systems."

Adcox expressed his intrigue. "Which then raises a question. How exactly do they arrive at the cocoon stage?"

Activated by his cane, Dr. Henry displayed all the different forms of the Horde to the team on the viewing screen. Adcox saw a few other forms he had never seen before.

"What are their weaknesses?" asked Hawke.

"There are none, really," replied Dr. Henry. "They can survive more extreme ranges of temperatures than we can, almost on par with Arimans. They can even survive in the vacuum of space. Horde have regenerative limbs similar to reptilians, yet they are not cold blooded, and appear to be a unique blend between mammals and invertebrates. We suspect they are heterotrophs, and require sustenance form the consumption of other organisms."

"In other words...they eat people," said Tronics looking at Hawke. "Just in case that wasn't clear. Which well, it wasn't."

"You see," continued Dr. Henry as he paced in front of the group using his walking stick which now contained blue luminescent particles circulating throughout. "Plants photosynthesize and get energy from the sun. But it is not as efficient as eating the leaves of a plant. Which is also not as efficient as eating the animals that eat the leaves, and at the top of the food chain are us. Human and Horaxian biologies are like machines, capable in moments of producing over two thousand wattages of power. Some however, do not produce as much power as they once did."

"E=MC²!" said Hawke, choosing to ignore Henry's subliminal digs.

"Ahh, you are a clever one, Mr. Hawke," replied Dr. Henry. "Quite right, but it goes beyond your exalted Einstein's revolutionary equation. It is also Horde's ability to rapidly release this energy from food they consume and no doubt the effects of dark matter which is what seems to give them immense power."

"What about their technology?" asked Hawke.

Hatshepsut answered. "Living matter seems to be basis of their biological and even technological structure. Even their vessels are biotic."

"Their spacecraft are alive," said Nanonramu.

"What is also remarkable are their senses," said Hatshepsut. "All Horde species have six senses which includes telepathy. The drones and their whale spacecraft have poor vision. But what they do have is a seventh sense, electroreception. They can detect electrical energy, even the faint ones generated by every living creature. But the brain Horde and most probably the whales also have an eighth sense. They have a vertical line."

"What is...vertical line?" Nanonramu.

Hatshepsut explained. "They can detect prey by vibrations in surroundings, just like Earth's sharks' lateral lines, or the vertical line of Arimans."

"Brain Hordes..." said Hawke. "Would that be the tall ones, slimmer in build than the rest?"

"Indeed! To put it into perspective, my Black Guard friend," Dr. Henry stroked his long grey pointed beard. "If you were in a room behind an obstacle such as a large chair...for example. Unable to be seen or heard. Then even without its other senses a brain Horde could detect you were there because of the difference in air pressure caused by your presence." Henry squinted his eyes, staring at Hawke after yet another subliminal dig at him on how he was capable of detecting the doctor's presence in the room on their first encounter. Yet the Black Guard commander retained his poker face.

"So you cannot run or hide, coward," said Jei'Gun.

"Hai, Hawke san," informed Zomo. "They are the most dangerous."

"We saw one of them," said Hawke. "With what looked like a weapon in its hand."

"Yes, indeed," said Doctor Henry. "The scepter they wield appears to emanate a pulse of energy at a living target and completely vaporizes it. The brains display an extremely high amount of intelligence and form the head of the Horde command structure."

"And notoriously difficult to kill," added Akerele. "Crazy fast, I've see one dodge a full magazine."

"The one I saw, it had a strange effect on the troopers," said Hawke.

"Bites and wounds inflicted by Horde carry neurotoxins," replied Dr. Hatshepsut, "and can result in paralysis, muscle weakness, nausea, vomiting and death with symptoms manifesting themselves within four hours."

"No it's not that. It was fear. They were paralyzed with fear," he replied in his deep, breathy voice.

"Immaculately conceived, Mr. Hawke," said Dr. Henry. "It is my belief, also shared by some Homo sapien scientists, that the brain Horde use the sensation of fear to hypnotically cripple their victims much like a snake's poison. The ground squids have a similar ability but it is induced by the shock of sight and the scent of secreted pheromones. The brains are exceptionally different. We have conducted studies and there does not appear to be any biological delivery mechanisms. My empirical evidence suggest that they have the ability to psychogenically generate, project and induce fear."

"Before you go into any more intel, we need to know one thing," asked Hawke. "What is MK1?"

He sensed a rise in tension. The question caused a brief silence in the room.

Chapter Eleven - Galactic Bonds

"MK...Man...Killer!" Jei'Gun spoke as he extracted his arm blade with a snapping sound. His diagnostic checks ensured it was still fully functional after their battle.

"When it first appeared," said Henry, "it destroyed an entire human fleet. It went on to decimate half of the human defenses, base stations and outposts, hence the name. The Mankiller, from what we gathered, was the leader of Horde armies but yet it was different to the Horde. Its formed appeared robotic. It was also invulnerable to any form of attack. From what we have seen it cannot be destroyed."

"A killing machine," said Nanonramu.

"Just like you, Mr. Hawke," Henry said.

"So where is it now?" asked Hawke.

Adcox answered the major. "Eventually it launched an attack on the Horaxians, but they had time to prepare."

"Our esteemed Shando the Grand laid a trap," said Doctor Henry.

"Good old Shando," said Hawke. His mood upon hearing the Horaxian's name almost sounded like one of fondness. "But it doesn't quite add up, everything about the Polymorph is organic. Yet they're commanded by a robotic, artificial lifeform?"

"And an extremely ancient, sentient lifeform at that," replied Henry. "The Horde mothership you found on the planetoid of dark matter space may belong to the Mankiller. If so, who knows, it might be as much alien to Horde as they are to us. We managed to trap MK1 on a Magnetar, the strongest type of neutron star. We designated it as MK1 since we could not believe at first one machine could withstand all of our most advanced weapons, that it must have been another each time it appeared. But since its imprisonment there have been no others. There is a Horaxian warship in near orbit of the neutron star should it break free. An Earth destroyer is also on its way to support it."

"There are rumors from Divine Council," said Jei'Gun. "That the souwrak brought Horde's wrath upon us by stealing their technology. It deserves death for transgressions."

Adcox pondered if Jei'Gun's words were true. Was Hawke the reason for the Polymorph invasion? Could they simply just want their artifact back?

"But a neutron star's gravity is the closest thing to a blackhole," said Tronics. "We're talking over two hundred billion times stronger than Earth's gravity, but only twenty kilometers across. Is it really capable of breaking free?"

"The average neutron star's escape velocity is ten thousand times that of your Earth's," replied Henry. "However, the star is not stationary but hurling through space at stupendous speed. Soon it will come in close proximity to another star with two orbiting gas giants. It is speculated their combined gravitational pull could interact and disrupt each other. The disruptions may be only slight, but enough to allow MK1 to break free."

"Whether it breaks free or not, we are doomed either way," said Zomo.

Thoughts of MK1's unleashed was too traumatic for Adcox to handle, so he switched the focus back onto the mission. "Major, could you give us any info on this planetoid you crash landed on fifteen years ago? What's the atmosphere like?"

"Breathable."

"Is there any gravity?" said Adcox searching for more.

"Affirmative." Hawke conserved words as he did energy.

"Ground terrain, surface conditions?" asked Tronics.

"Hostile." Hawke looked noticeably uncomfortable when speaking about the planetoid. Like his mind had journeyed somewhere else, somewhere it didn't want to be.

"What is that supposed to mean?" said Jei'Gun in response to the major's answers. He stood alert now, as though ready to launch an attack.

"It's as hazardous as you can get," Hawke blasted out. "Nothing stays the same. The terrain constantly changes within the blink of an eye. I don't know if it's science or supernatural. It makes you hallucinate, and you can get lost for eternity. It's an endless, unforgiving darkness."

Adcox tried to ascertain what could have caused a man like Hawke, the Black Guard commander himself, such discomposure. In the face of the Polymorph on Kemeta the man was unflinching. But he couldn't decipher whether Jei'Gun's eagerness to engage in combat with him had a part to play, or was it purely the subject matter of the planetoid.

Doctor Henry spoke while waving his electronic cane. "Ah this could be an unforeseen effect of dark matter. You see ordinary matter; solids, liquids, gas and ions, they change state with temperature and pressure. So too can dark matter change but not just its state. Possibly, it can completely change what it is. This is most intriguing."

"No. It's not," replied Hawke in a stern, abrupt voice. He rose to leave the room and the guards readied themselves to follow. Hawke stopped before pressing the door control panel. "One thing's for certain. We won't all be coming back."

***

Adcox headed toward the crew quarters after what had come to be the most stressful period the young man had ever experience. As he strolled past the ship's crew who infrequently walked by he saw Hatshepsut standing ahead of him, alone, gazing out at the stars. He sensed that she had lost herself in deep thought. Her forearms rested against the white railing as she glanced out into the depths of space with a look of sorrow. Adcox beheld how her hair reached almost to the back of her knees and he seized the moment to admire the golden bands that bonded her bright white strands into a single length. He viewed her red tribal markings running down her back before they became hidden by her silver bodysuit.

"Hi, Hatshepsut," said Captain Adcox as he approached her, not quite sure of himself. "May I interrupt or would you prefer to be alone?"

"No, please. You are welcomed in joining me."

"Are you ok?"

"My thoughts are with my people on Kemeta. My family have influence, safe they are already on Illustrious Horax Prime. But many will not survive cold and will perish when Horde next lay assault." She turned to look at him. "Do you have family, Diomedes?"

"Yeah, Tronics' parents took me in and raised me so they're my family. I was told my mother died of cancer when I was young. No brothers or sisters."

"And your father?"

"He was in the forces. He died in service. It was secret ops so I was never told much about it."

"Do you remember him?"

"Bits and pieces, yeah. I have memories of being on ships with him. I was eight, maybe nine at the time. Strangely, I can't remember anything aside from that. I'm sorry for the loss of your people on Kemeta, Hatshepsut."

"Sorry for the loss of yours."

Hatshepsut noticed that Adcox had a bruise on the right side of his neck from the recent battle. "Please, allow me honor of treating your wound." She began reaching into her side pouch and pulled out a small device.

"No, it's just a scratch, don't worry."

"We will be in alien environment. You will be susceptible to potentially deadly pathogens. Hold still."

As Hatshepsut gently held his face in order to hold her wound-cleaning laser with precision, Adcox's felt a bliss that was on par with a deep massage.

"You give off something every time you touch me. Are you aware of this?" he said, feeling euphoric.

"I am aware. All Kemetans do. Our atmosphere makes our touch more sensual. We transfer energy upon contact." She was almost finished cleansing the injured area.

"It feels...nice...I mean it feels kind of pretty good." He snapped out his daze once he saw the fool he was making of himself.

"To cure your injury requires greater means than to create it. Do not follow in path of warmongering, as Mr. Hawke and Alpha Atomu. Their focus is confined by destroying and not enough on preserving."

Adcox felt mesmerized, not just by her touch but by her warmth of character. "You're a beautiful mind trapped in an ugly struggle, Hatshepsut."

"Thank you. I but merely play part to make difference, to make what is ugly beautiful again. I only wish I can do more. As we speak, millions are dying of sickness on our worlds." Hatshepsut completed the disinfecting of the wound and applied a transparent gel which acted as a sealant from the elements.

"I share your feelings. I just want peace. I'm not a warmonger. In fact, I think being a soldier isn't the role I should play."

"And maybe being simply a biologist should not be my role either, but something must be done." The Horaxian female stood right in front of Adcox, they were now almost cheek to cheek and his pale, white, skin contrasted against her black face. "This Horaxian year, there have already been one hundred and thirty-five thousand murders on our prime world. Before we made first contact with Homo sapiens do you know what murder count was?"

"I get the feeling it was a lot less."

"Since inception of official records, there were none."

"Unbelievable! I understand now why Horaxians believe humans passed on a virus to them."

"The Horaxian belief that life is a precious gift, and our unshakeable honor, shielded us from murder. Now hundreds are quarantined each day to prevent spread of madness. The murder and madness, both are but by-products of this war. War is destroying our people." Hatshepsut's thick Horaxian lips were dangerously close and he could practically taste what smelt like her sorrel and cinnamon aroma. The newly made captain lost himself in her bright pink eyes as they blinked horizontally. Slowly, he brought his mouth towards hers.

"To secure peace is to prepare for war," said a voice from behind them, which made them both jump. They turned around toward the source only to be greeted with the darkness of the corridor. A blue light formed, lifting the veil of darkness that concealed the obscure voice. Major Hawke emerged smoking his electronic cigar. "I have need of your skills, Doctor."

Adcox still tried to figure out how he managed to slip his armed guards.

"Can you not haunt some other corridors, Mr. Hawke," said Hatshepsut.

"We need you to conduct an analysis to find a connection between all the Horaxians vaporized by the brain Polymorph."

"Captain Adcox," said the major's SPU. "Could you assist the doctor by accessing Earth's bioinformatics database to compile a list of human victims, then transfer them to Dr. Hatshepsut also?" Each one of Eve's vocal responses generated green flashing lights barely visible on Hawke's lower neck.

"Eve, we don't have authorization to transfer data into Horaxian hands."

"Then don't get it authorized," said Hawke. "Ask your friend Corporal Manning to hack in like he did to help you access our files."

Hawke's knowledge of the event made the youthful captain gasp.

"What are you hoping to find?" asked Hatshepsut.

"A pattern," replied Eve.

"Why are you so sure there is one?" asked Adcox.

"The brains are choosing who they vaporize, we think there's a biological connection," said Hawke.

Hatshepsut stepped closer to Hawke with intensity in her eyes. "And what might the results provide you with? You should search for your own missing biological connection, Mr. Hawke. You cared nothing for lives in which you only consequentially saved on my planet. Was one billion people insufficient a number? You have now condemned billions more on Kemeta to a frozen death."

"Aren't we emotional today," said Hawke.

"It's all right, Hatshepsut." Adcox provided comforting words seeing how emotional indeed the young female became. Placing his hand on her shoulder to cool her temper, he felt the sting of an electrostatic discharge.

"Why fight at all when life has little meaning to you?" Hatshepsut asked. Seeing Hawke staring at her and realizing he had no intention of responding she walked off, leaving the two men alone.

"Quite the ladies' man," said Adcox only when she was no longer in hearing range.

"We were going to say the same about you," replied Hawke.

"I figured I should let you know, since I get the feeling you played a hand in making me a captain. I'm requesting that a more experienced officer command the mission and to be reassigned."

"But you've done an excellent job so far, leading us to victory on Kemeta."

"Ah come on!" shouted Adcox. "Sir, who are we really kidding here? You saved us on Kemeta."

Eve interjected. "It was your voice they heard throughout the city, and your face on all the screens."

"Eve, Hawke, everyone knows I'm not cut out for this. I just need to stop embarrassing myself."

"That's disappointing to hear, but we know how you feel," said Hawke, puffing out blue smoke. "This planetoid in dark space, I don't want to go back myself. I'd rather rot in the Abyss."

"So if it's that bad, why are you going?"

Upon Adcox's last words he noticed blood trickling down from Hawke's left nostril and a near undetectable buckle of the major's right leg. Hawke eventually realized and wiped it almost clean with the back of his hand.

"Hey, you going to be all right? You don't look too sturdy. Hatshepsut said the drug you took...it's, it's slowly going to..."

"We're combat effective."

Continuing the matter was pointless. He already deciphered that Hawke knew what he was going to say. "So if you're so combat effective, why don't you just take command of the team?"

"Negative! That is not our mission," replied Hawke. "To answer your question, we're going because despite my feelings someone who believes in us asked for our help, and we must answer the call."

"Baizan?" asked Adcox.

"Affirmative."

Adcox lowered his head and shook it as he struggled to deal with the gravity of Hawke's words. "Sir, I can't do the things you do. I'm not a Black Guard. I'm just not ready for this. I'm sorry."

"A long time ago I was imprisoned in a concentration camp on Arima, as you are now aware. Among the prisoners was a boy. He had to be no more than eight, nine years old. We were all being systematically tortured; physically, psychologically. Then from my cell I saw an elite-shakan warrior. He had come to eviscerate the boy just like all the others. What happened next before my eyes was unexpected. The boy killed the elite-shakan."

"Sorry to interrupt, sir, but it sounds a little farfetched that a kid can kill an elite-shakan warrior. How?" asked Adcox.

"He turned his strength against him. Over the years he was imprisoned, he learned how to disable and reconfigure the gripping mechanism of the elite-shakan's gauntlet. The boy managed to rewire the hydraulics in the gauntlet, crushing all the bones in the Horaxian's hand. From there it was a simple matter of removing his helmet and finding the heaviest object he could pick up with his scrawny arms and bashing the elite-shakan's skull in. After he killed him, he freed us all. Do you think he was ready to kill an elite-shakan? Few unarmed men can achieve that. He had to make a choice he wasn't ready for but he acted and he saved us. You have been called upon and you must act. The two young teammates that look up to you, the doctor and your friend who believes in you, they're all counting on you. Whatever decision you make is going to stick with you for the rest of your life."

The young soldier stared out into space, much like how he found Hatshepsut moments before. He questioned who he was, and who he wanted to be. "What happened to them? The boy and the people he saved?"

"They were hunted down and cornered. There was no escape off the planet anyway, so they killed themselves. Better than the slow painful death that was in store. I managed to escape."

"Sir, there is something I must ask. What went wrong with the Black Guard? They...you, were supposed to be a source for good?"

Hawke, bowed his head. "There is no hunting like the hunting of man, and those who have hunted armed men long enough and liked it never care for anything else thereafter."

"Hemingway!" said Adcox.

"Affirmative. All the killing, it changes you, corrupts you. A man can lose his way."

Although the major's face revealed no emotion, Adcox believed he sensed Hawke's deep resentment for his past deeds. "You know, you can make a difference here, people will follow you," said the young captain.

"They did once, now my name stirs hatred. We can't be that kind of symbol anymore. In life people worry about losing so many things. You should be more concerned of losing yourself. Because once lost you may never get yourself back."

"At least you had a purpose. I feel lost without even knowing mine."

"With problems comes wisdom. With adversity comes strength."

"Oh yeah, and what gives one courage?"

"The presence of danger," Hawke sternly replied.

"Ironic, because that's what I was afraid of."

"You're able to keep a level head while everyone else is losing theirs. People need someone they can trust. That's the only way we can win this war. Someone who has a heart that evil can never corrupt."

"Someone, like you, Captain Adcox," said Eve.

"We need you, Captain Adcox," said Eve.

Adcox had something to say to Hawke that had been at the tip of his tongue all this time. He couldn't explain why he had been afraid to ask. The question was a simple one, but not the answer he felt. "Have we ever met before, Maj..." Surprise greeted the marine as he looked up. Hawke had disappeared, vanishing into the darkness. He had stood merely two meters away.

***

"Attention people!" General Baizan's voice silenced the large situation room where Hawke was first brought before him. The team was in their full battle armor but without their rifles, only their sidearms. The Horaxian contingent was present along with Dr. Henry as well as Hawke's security escort. "As you should all be aware, your mission is to travel to the Asatorin region of space using the Human spacecraft, the *Copernicus*, transporting the alien pod first discovered by Major Hawke. The good doctor Henry has equipped the *Copernicus* with the most advanced shielding Horaxianly possible. Now, when you arrive at the LZ, Major Hawke will activate the pod, which will open a gateway to dark matter space. Once there, you will locate the exoplanet, planetoid Delta, and retrieve an ancient alien vessel and bring it in orbit of Lunar 1."

As Baizan relayed the mission particulars, Major Hawke rarely took his eyes off a strange metallic statue of a bird in the right hand corner of the room.

Baizan continued. "The mission's time to launch is approximately three hours so be ready to board the *Copernicus* by then. Major Hawke will function only in an advisory role and provide assistance with recovering the ship along with local knowledge of the terrain. But this mission will be headed by Captain Adcox.

"What? The pup?" Jei'Gun said in outrage, turning to glance at Adcox's underdeveloped arms in an appalled demeanor.

"Affirmative. You got a problem, elite-shakan?" replied Baizan, matching his contempt.

"Yes! He is a coward. The fabric he is cut from should be ripped to shreds and burnt in intense heat."

"Is there anything else?" asked Baizan, as he looked to everyone else in the room.

"Yes," said Jei'Gun. "The child's skill with weapon: poor. His knowledge of battle strategy: diabolical, a mockery. Not to mention this Black Guard souwrak! Even your own people shun it, sending their guardsmen here. This is all ridiculous, even by the disgracefully low standards of humans."

"If you've got a problem with the way we do things down here in Baizan's world, you can take it up with your superiors and you'll be reassigned. Is that understood?"

Anticipating his outburst, Hatshepsut intervened. "Abundantly happy we are to assist under your captain." She nodded at the elite-shakan, a gesture for him to accept her response. Jei'Gun remained silent and backed down.

"Fantastic!" replied the general, exaggerating the word. He couldn't be upset at the elite'shakan, since deep down he agreed with him. "Questions anyone...else?"

After the shortest of waiting times, he called out to the captain. "If you or any member of your team wants to back out, now's the time to say the word."

Hawke and Tronics cast their eyes at Adcox. His opposition on being a part of the mission was on everyone's mind.

"Permission to speak freely, sir?" Adcox requested, his voice cagey.

"You're on the operations deck of the *Sword of Damocles* not the Amistad. Go ahead son," said Baizan. As he spoke, the unusually quiet Doctor Henry held his cane to his ear. Something had taken his attention.

"General." Adcox collected himself. "Recent experiences have given me a lot to think about. I believe I speak for the team. In honor of the colonel, we will follow his last orders, and they were to see things through to the end."

Tronics and Zomo both released a smile of relief.

"Apologies for the rude disruption, my revered General," said Dr. Henry placing his cane back down. "I have just received word that another swarm has been detected. Our intel suggests they may be headed towards our Illustrious Horax Prime."

"What?" said Jei'Gun. "They would dare attempt final blow and strike at heart of imperial throne?"

"Notification," alerted Eve with her beautiful melodic voice. "I am monitoring Horaxian communication channels and the deep space swarm has deviated from a direct trajectory to Horax Prime. Shifted to an eight degree angle of incidence. We are now seventy five million miles from the Horaxian home world. It is safe to speculate..."

"That they are headed for this space carrier," said Dr. Henry. "Inexplicably, they are tracking us."

Tronics kissed his teeth while shaking his head. "Arghh, Mate! Just great, monster homing pigeons. If Amanda finds out how bad this mission really is, I'm in serious trouble."

Henry placed his cane to his head again. "Wait!" The room silenced as he listened. "Oh Prodigious Cunga!" His arm, weakened by what he had received, dropped limp.

"What is it, Henry?" asked Baizan. Due to his shock, the doctor failed respond and Baizan's impatience circumvented him. "Eve, talk to me."

"I have intercepted the doctor's transmission. The Horde infestation on Cunga Sigma has amassed a mega-swarm and they are on the move."

"To where?" asked the general.

"Horaxian projections indicate the highest probable location is their colonized rogue planet."

"Astonishing Rogue Basarwa?" uttered Nanonramu, his desperate eyes and antennae reached for Dr. Henry.

"Frightful indeed!" replied Henry. "Intel states that it is the largest swarm ever recorded."

"It's an invasion," said Adcox. Saying what the poor-sighted warrior knew but dreaded.

Nanonramu's antennae had lowered. Then it sprang up with his thought. "The army of my world stands a billion strong. Our defensive fortifications, five times the greater than Famed Nok when it fell. Horde cannot defeat us." He smiled, then walked to the back of the meeting room and plopped himself down in silence.

"That will be all from me," said Baizan, breaking the dire atmosphere. "Dr. Henry wanted to say a few words. Hawke!" Upon saying his name, the major ventured towards Baizan, who moved close to the entrance door and away from prying ears.

"Do you have it?" Hawke asked the general, as if he could wait no longer.

"Kept it safe all these years." He handed Hawke something wrapped in black cloth. The fabric had the Black Guard emblem embroidered on it, the white sword, as well as an inscription. Hawke unwrapped the cloth and revealed the concealed item. The handle of his sword's magnificently shaped guard and pommel still shimmered.

"It's been a long time," said Hawke, looking down at the hilt.

"Sometimes," said Baizan, folding the cloth back up, "it's the things which have been around the longest that prove the most useful."

"Thank you, old friend."

"Your suit's just arrived. I'll have it loaded onto the *Copernicus*. I have to go speak with command about the incoming swarm to debate our strategy. We'll have to talk later.

"That's the problem James, due process, the chain of command. Slows down our ability to act."

"It's called laws and military protocol. Unfortunately, some of us are still sworn to abide by them."

"Perhaps there can be *some* that don't need to. *Some* that can operate independently of rigid structure and feeble minded, short sighted politicians posing as soldiers. That *some* can be more devastating to the enemy than a whole army."

"Earth Command would never approve," said Baizan in an angered whisper, knowing where Hawke was going.

"Command is the problem. You've seen it yourself. They've lost it. If the Polymorph would've accepted mankind's surrender they would have thrown in the towel a long time ago. The Horaxians are right about us, we *do* lack conviction. That's why their warriors like the elite-shakan over there hate us. The command chain is compromised, there's a systemic virus that's been destroying mankind's soul for a long time. But if we could keep something in isolation, away from the body whole, it could remain uninfected.

"This is bordering on treason, Keegan. Your ideals would be seen as a threat. We tried this once before, remember?"

"Yes but this time it would be different. Because we're not talking about living weapons, we're talking about living symbols."

"Damn it, Major!" Baizan, looked up to check if his outburst was overheard. "The very mentioning of this would bring down the alliance. Just let this one go. Times may have changed but people still fear what they don't understand. I need to speak with Command. Time for you to go and do what you do."

Giving up, Hawke positioned his hand to salute the General.

"The hell with that crap," said Baizan, and he extended his hand out, which was soon meet with Hawke's in a strong handshake.

***

As Dr. Henry provided more information to the team, Adcox broke his concentration to see Baizan leaving the room.

"Once inside dark matter space, we will not be able to communicate with you," said Henry. "You may be alone but not without aid. Let me present to you some tools that may prove useful. First, allow me to introduce the most advance robotic unmanned aerial support drone ever created. I call it the Bird of Prey. Come here, Bird of Prey!" Henry gestured with his hands toward what had been assumed to be a large statue of a metal bird in the corner of the room with its wings half spread. Upon Henry's last words, the metallic statue animated, flapped its wide-span wings and flew to a hover over the center table before landing. Tronics and Zomo jumped.

Dr. Henry continued. "The Bird of Prey has advanced AI, precision-guided munitions, reconnaissance abilities, ultrafaron shielding, self-flight capabilities and a wide range of sensors. Plus voice command and control as well as a default auto action mode."

"*All right*! This is music to my ears, baby." Tronics moved closer to inspect the robotic drone, followed by Hatshepsut, Adcox, Akerele and Zomo. It turned its head around with a slow robotic movement to glance at all of them. The body of the artificial creature measured roughly a meter in height, but with a much wider wing span. Of its four wings; the two lower wings were shorter than the upper and held most of its explosive ordnance. Hatshepsut reached out and stroked the robot as if it was a real bird.

"You and I are going to be spending a lot of time together," said Tronics with a massive smile. Akerele and Zomo laughed with a lack of surprise at their comrade's enthusiasm.

"Acknowledged, Corporal Manning," replied the robotic bird, steadily spreading its main wings.

"Did I mention," said Henry, "it has state of the art visual and speech recognition, plus knowledge of everyone assigned to this mission within its database."

"It should provide perfect close air support," said Adcox.

"Mr. Manning!" said Dr. Henry.

"What's popping?" replied Tronics, his sole focus still on the robot.

"Ah yes, urban vernacular, ah hemm...would you mind helping me open this case and retrieving the device inside? Aging has a far more degenerative effect on Horaxian bones."

Tronics reached into his metal case on the ground and pulled out a device, shaped like two guns merged together, though it had separate parallel handles and sections of its barrels were also separated. Its red and black metal shined in the light.

"My next little item is what I've undoubtedly named the gravity disruptor." Henry tried to cover up his excitement as he presented it to the group. "It can release a blast that on impact creates an impulse gravitational force the equivalent of a low-mass star, at an object's center, instantly imploding it."

Tronics wasted no time inspecting every inch of the weapon as he passed his hand over its barrel with the delicacy one would a priceless heirloom. The barrel had similarities to a hand-gun, but elongated like a shotgun and far broader.

Dr. Henry continued. "I have tried to keep it lightweight but a drawback to its design means it must recharge after every discharge. Its center cubic magnetic rings rotates while it's activated and only stopped once the charge cycle is complete. Be mindful, it has an effective range of seventy meters and ermm...*well*...an *ever* so slight kick back."

"Doc, now this is dope," said Tronics in his element. "What's its beamwidth adding its effective Fresnel zones together?

"Approximately five to six meters."

"Nice. Hey!" said Tronics with enthusiasm. "What about the possibility of reversing the g-force polarity outwards as opposed to inwards. That could be equally devastating?"

"Yes indeed, excellent idea. I pondered that application myself. By reversing the polarity of the mass generator you could transmit a beam that would rapidly accelerate an object."

As the team chatted among themselves Dr. Henry noticed Hawke standing alone in the corner. Delicately, the major passed his hand over his sword hilt whispering undetectable words. Upon his vocalization the black patterns on the hilt responded by altering in form. Dr. Henry walked over to him. "Aren't you a little old to be playing with toys, Mr. Hawke?"

"Aren't you a little presumptuous to think we would believe you wouldn't know exactly what this is?"

"Why of course I do!" snapped Dr. Henry, his forehead wrinkled in a displeased frown. "Only the fountains deep within the sacred refuge of the first nation could create such a wonder. Why it is in *your improper* possession, in your...contemptible hands is the real mystery."

"Really?" said Hawke. "Your disguise of ignorance is as unimpressive as it is ridiculous."

"That statement holds weight coming from the unanimous master of disguise." Henry's frown began to fade. "Let me tell you something, Mr. Hawke."

"Something about myself, right?"

"Correct!"

"I'm pretty knowledgeable on that subject. Thanks anyway, Doctor."

"Well, since you know you cannot see yourself, so well as by reflection, I, your glass, will modestly discover to yourself, that of yourself which you yet know not of."

"Arghh God! Where's a straitjacket when you need one. Or a torture rack. We'd rather endure a Horde charge than your consult."

"Ironic that you should mention Horde. Some would say the Black Guard and Horde have a fearful symmetry. I have been granted the unfortunate honor to have witnessed one of your notorious Nephilim's assaults. Just as brutal as any drone. They were relentless, merciless and could not be reasoned with. After which, they disappeared just like Horde, into the dark."

"We were merely instruments of war ordered to get a job done, and we got the job done."

"Yes, your phlegmatic demeanor is shocking yet abhorrently expected. Mr. Hawke, it is believed all life is eventually doomed. If not by the galactic infection that is Horde or our racial hatred, then inevitably by the force of the universe itself—dark energy. It represents seventy three percent of the universe, causing it to ever expand away from itself. Eventually, after eons, all life will freeze to death. Perhaps our personal existence is somewhat in parallel. A man's heart can become colder if he is pushed farther away from humanity."

Their chat was halted by Zomo's raised voice. "Oh my God!" she yelled when she saw the room's door opening to an unbelievable sight. "It's Ballistic!" delight poured out from her.

The rest of Unit Forty Two rushed out to greet him. His arm was the main attraction, now only a short stub bandaged around his shoulder.

"Yo Killer B!' Said Tronics. "So they brought you out of the scrapheap huh?"

The ecstatic Zomo punched the sergeant on his chest and then grabbed him by the side of his neck.

"They realized I needed a mechanic and not a doctor," replied Ballistic.

"So what's the plan, Sarge?" asked Zomo.

"Well, I would say Flying Officer Zomo but you know me, I'm a little shy."

"Yeah, like a Biosphere-9 hooker," laughed Tronics.

"But since you asked. First; I'm going to get me some of that fine Keplar-Terran brandy. Then, grab hold of enough ammo to make the god of war himself cringe, let the big bad wolf loose and kill me some Horde."

"Woo!" they cried out in adulation.

"All right, the sarge is back in business," said Akerele.

"What's the mission?" asked Ballistic.

"It's the most dangerous one yet," said Akerele.

"Perfect!" Only Ballistic would be excited by that statement.

Adcox stepped out and the bald, bulky man raised a salute to him.

"At ease, Sergeant. Good to see you."

"I came for the debriefing. Ready to bring the pain, captain."

Adcox smiled uncomfortably as he laid eyes upon his amputated comrade. "Guys, may I have a word with Ballistic?"

Tronics, Zomo and Akerele touched fists with their crippled comrade's metal knuckles and they headed down the corridor.

"Look, Hasselberg, it doesn't look like you're quite fit for combat."

"I've been through worse, sir. It's only a scratch."

"This mission is more difficult than the others."

"That's why you're going to need me on board, sir."

"You're going to have to sit this one out."

"Negative, you can't do that, Adcox," said the sergeant, overcome by emotion. He realized his insubordination and regained control of himself. "Sir, I need to be out in the field. Biomechanics won't have another arm ready for me for weeks."

"And we'll be here when they do, the war's not going to be over. Take some time out to..."

"...I'd rather die. I'd rather die, sir." Ballistic bared the few metal teeth he had left trying to contain himself.

"Come on Ballistic. Take this opportunity, get some R & R, go see your family."

"I don't have any family, this is all the family I've got," His voice stayed strong as he battled his emotions. "I can't do anything else, sir, fighting is all I'm good at. Everybody's *crying* about the Horde, I'm glad they're here. That's right, I'm glad. They define me. Thanks to them I know what I am, I'm a soldier. Horde, Horaxian, it don't matter to me pal. I ain't running from nothing. They can find me. Once I'm through with the Horde those stinking Horaxians are next. I'll kill 'em all."

His crazed outburst solidified the young captain's belief that there was something psychologically wrong with the sergeant. "Ballistic..." The pain of Ballistic's robotic palm's desperate grab of his deltoid prevented Adcox from finishing his sentence.

"Please Adcox. Who's going to watch your back?"

"Sergeant, tell me something I need to know. The truth. How did you come to have metal teeth? Everyone says you never mention it."

Ballistic released Adcox's shoulder and his anxiety along with that. His body went limp, his mouth closed, his breathing quickly calmed. It was as though all emotion had been sucked out of him. "I tried to blow my brains out."

Adcox's suspicion was confirmed. Did the colonel simply turn a blind eye to the fact that Ballistic was most likely clinically insane? His mouth opened but he struggled to find the words. "I'm sorry, sergeant." The young man walked off, leaving Ballistic frozen still, broken spirited.

As the Sergeant looked up with sadness he saw Major Hawke standing at a distance, still within the room. He had witnessed the entire exchange. After a pause he raised his hand to salute Ballistic and the amputated soldier saluted back. After his gesture Hawke also walked pass him, escorted by his four guards, enabling another to be seen standing even farther back. It was Jei'Gun. The elite-shakan warrior and the sergeant gave each other an unbroken stare. Both held their heads high as they could giving the other a mean look, unsure of what to say or make of one another and abandoning the concept of speech.

***

"Captain Adcox!" Hawke called down the vessel's corridor. He caught up to the commanding officer. "Your assistance is required in the brig."

"What's going on?"

Eve responded. "The Ariman has just awoken. He is in a detention cell."

"Bring his shield," said Hawke. His words puzzled Adcox as Hawke was nowhere near him on Kemeta when he had picked it up.

Moments later both men were in a carrier-lift that transported them to the detention cells. Hawke's guard detail were squeezed tightly in.

"I don't think it's a good idea, asking me to do this," said Adcox as they waited for the lift to stop. "I saw how much he hates you so I know why you can't do it. But why not General Baizan?"

"Because he won't listen to Baizan, or any Horaxian. But we're certain he'll listen to you."

"Why? I think there's an equally likely chance he'll just kill us. I took his shield-thing and he had more desire to kill you than the Polymorph."

"Rey'Jax is bound by his code of honor. He will not harm you. But yes, he may kill me."

They stepped out of the carrier-lift and eventually came to the broad, reinforced gate of the detention cells. A guard saluted the men and activated the door which then electronically swung open, releasing an eerie sound of bending metal. It was impossible to tell how many inmates were in the population. The cells looked empty, but ahead of the two men were close to a dozen guards in front of one cell in particular. Adcox spoke out to the guards.

"We have permission to release the prisoner."

"Your authorization has already been confirmed, sir," said the sergeant of the guards saluting him. All the guards then held their weapons with a tight grip in preparation. The sergeant of the guard entered a code in the cell door panel and a light which previously shone red then turned green. "It's unlocked, sir! The Horaxian authorities have informed us his prison collar was reprogrammed to prevent him from endangering Horaxians and now also human life."

"You must convince him to help us," Hawke said to Adcox.

"Err...I'll try!"

"Good luck with that, sir," one guard uttered.

"Urk'Tark," said a bellowing voice. "I know there you stand. Behind walls effortlessly breakable. Your smell disgusting perverts my senses." The Ariman owned the deepest of voices which echoed against the solid flat cell walls and had a soul destroying effect on the guards.

"You sure this is a good idea, Major?" asked Adcox.

"Just remember, he is a prince amongst his people."

A guard grabbed the wide, circular handle lodged at the center of the thick weighty door and turned it clockwise deactivating the release mechanism. With most of his strength he pulled back the handle and the door opened. His fellow guardsmen all raised their rifles.

Cautiously, Captain Adcox and Major Hawke stepped into the spacious cell and observed the giant shadow of Rey'Jax sitting down in the poorly lit confinement. His skin mirrored the carving of an ancient sculptor. A mountain of muscle upon muscle ripped with definition yet marked with incalculable battle wounds. With his head-guard off, the Ariman's thick matted dreadlocks was fully visible and his scarred face struck fear in all the guards. Hawke told the guards to close the cell doors, much to Adcox's concern. The newly made captain then noticed the Ariman's helmet on the ground, it could probably fit an elephant's head.

Hawke greeted Rey'Jax with an Ariman salute. Left fist raised high in the air supported at the elbow with the fist of his right arm. "Thank you for helping us, brother."

Rey'Jax growled then spoke. "Brother you are *not*, can *never* be fitting that title when betrayer fits." As he called Hawke once again by an ancient Horaxian word for traitor, Adcox remained trapped by the spell Rey'Jax's voice casted with its magnitude of overtones. "This...immovable collar detested bounds me here," said Rey'Jax gripping the metal contraption around his neck. "But no help from me be received traitor. In fact..." The giant unhurriedly rose to his feet into the light. His height made the two men look like small children and Adcox took a step back. "Your mind is one too corrupt yet blessed with powers of precognition. Such power in evil's hands cannot be allowed existence."

"Warning," said the voice of Eve. "High voltage electrical build up detected."

"Uh-oh!" said Adcox.

The giant made an echoing step toward them, forced to bend his head due to his height.

"Forsaken you your strength, that force of legend, along with honor. I would have your head now."

Chapter Twelve - Unabsolvable Sins

As Rey'Jax's distance to Hawke shrank, his intent grew, activating the red warning status lights on his collar. He made one more unhurried, thunderous step and to Adcox it felt like the whole room shook as the sound bounced off the empty cell's solid walls.

"Calm yourself, oh great one," implored Hawke. "The collar has been reprogrammed to respond to humans as well. It will fuse your synapses and shut down two or at least one of your nervous systems."

"Perceiver of all, you of all, know I fear not...*all,* and death above all. Especially for good cause." The Ariman followed with another heavy step towards them, partially stunned by the electricity beginning to surge through him.

"Mighty Rey'Jax!" cried out Adcox. Unsure of what came over him, only having an urge to act. "Great Prince of all Arimans. We have been tasked with a perilous mission upon which the fate of humans and Horaxians both depends on. We need your help."

Rey'Jax turned his attention to Captain Adcox. The boy's words seemed to have calmed him down as the blue, electrical activity around the Ariman's neck deceased. "I am last of my kind, boy. My people, to live forever those the gods chose, have all fallen mournfully, dishonorably. Little do I care for fate of impetuous humans, nor their equal in transgressions my Horaxian descendants, who turned on us." His speech was unusually slowed.

"I understand! But is there nothing else of value to you? I've heard many stories of your people being a brave an honorable race. Isn't that honor and the memory of your people worth fighting for?"

"Lost are both in eternity's cruel grasp. This prison without walls marks shame everlasting. A race once worshiped devotedly, since time immemorial to man, now languished prey to unceremonious an end." The inhumanly deep voice replied.

"Perhaps, they are lost!" replied Adcox feeling a sense of sorrow for the big male. "If I had the power to bring them back I would. If I had the power to release you from your prison collar, believe me I would. The only power I have is the power to prevent you from coming on this mission. Just say the word and I will request your return if that's your wish. But this mission, we can save many lives from the Horde. So no one would ever have to feel what your heart feels right now, the loss of all they hold dear. They imprisoned you to strip away the one thing you had left, your integrity. They would force you by means of your collar...but I would merely ask. I didn't want this task, but I realized that I couldn't refuse and keep hold of my integrity, and honor. Could you great one? Isn't a quest to preserve these purest of all virtues and end countless suffering a worthy one?"

The Horaxian beastlike male turned his back to the men, leaving Adcox to marvel at his lengthy, matted hair that flowed down his back. He spoke out, still with his back turned.

"You stand in my presence armed with weapons wisdom and truth. Few humans wield such power, and few so young. Unless it is true..." Rey'Jax swung his head towards Hawke, squinting his eyes, then swung his gaze between both men repeatedly. He turned his whole body back to face them. "I agree to aid you. But there be one condition. In return for my help, upon service completed, I will end the king of the Black Guard's life."

"We agree to your terms," confirmed Hawke in a rush.

"No wait!" uttered Adcox. "We can't do that. Mighty Rey'Jax, your price is too high. There must be something else we can offer? I can bargain your release."

"By cursed blood must pure blood be repaid," said the Ariman.

"The fate of two worlds depends on this mission, but you're asking me to sacrifice one man's life for it."

Rey'Jax's multi-harmonic voice replied. "To object offer means you would rather risk two worlds' fate, for one man."

"Yeah, but, to condemn his life stains all that we're fighting to protect. How can a man profit, if he shall gain the whole world, but lose his own soul?"

"Too late, Captain," said Hawke intervening. "The offer has already been accepted. This is the Ariman's way. Rey'Jax is the prince of his people, so he's bound to uphold their ideals regardless of how you perceive them."

"So it is agreed. Young one, step forward," Rey'Jax analyzed how cautious the captain advanced and instantly frowned. The Ariman raised his jet black palm. "No, you must do so *boldly*, and state your name, but do so *proudly*. Or neither at all. Great deeds demand dignity."

Adcox heeded his words and stepped forward more daring. Rey'Jax knelt down on one knee and held an Ariman salute.

"Captain Diomedes Adcox," said the stellar marine, comfortable now.

"I swear by my father the last Omukama, great Lugalbanda and all the Arima nation, an oath to you captain, Adcox Diomedes. That Rey'Jax's axe, his loving companion, will wage wars against your enemies. And to protect your ideals I loan my virtuous might."

"Thank you, great prince," said Adcox. "In turn, I will do everything in my power to have your collar removed."

"It can never be removed," said Hawke, "not without killing him."

"I'm sure you would like that, Urk'Tark." Rey'Jax once again rediscovered his anger at the sound of Hawke's voice and reactivated the warning lights on the collar. "Like you, I am hard to kill. You should remember, you have tried. Wise maneuver bringing the carijan with you. Always the clever one." The Ariman's turned to Adcox to warn him. "Do not trust this Black Guard king young one. His words, falsely sincere, captivate and inspire. But he will destroy you."

Adcox looked at Hawke, puzzled and confused by Rey'Jax's words, and for the first time, a bit concerned of Hawke's intentions. He wanted to ask what "carijan" meant but suddenly he remembered something. "Oh, one more thing. I have something that belongs to you, Rey'Jax."

The young captain pulled out the handle of Rey'Jax's shield and stuck his hand out to give it to him. The handle's presence shook the Ariman, something took over him. He reached for it but then stopped himself. "Isih-lango!" he uttered under his breath, the word lingered in the air. Desire and excitement on his face turned to the saddest frown. Adcox felt as though he could see the formation of tears in the giant's reflective eyes. Also, for the first time he noticed the black, decorative markings enlaced in the handle's white metal altering in shape, forming new patterns.

"Keep it, young Captain. You did not find it, it found you. Chosen another it deemed more worthy. More worthy than the mightiest of all."

***

Inside hangar bay seven of the *Sword of Damocles*, multiple carrier personnel were engaged in vessel maintenance activities of the *Copernicus*. A forklift truck lifted cargo into the ship's hatch as the team comprising of Unit Forty Two and the Horaxian contingent entered the hanger and walked towards the opened ramp doors of the *Copernicus,* with Dr. Henry, Major Hawke and General Baizan all staggering behind.

A maintenance crewman stopped before Captain Adcox. "The pod will be loaded into cargo bay two in fifteen minutes, sir." He had to shout due to the *Copernicus*'s engines being powered on to standby mode.

"Yo Zomo," shouted Tronics. "Let's go run a quick diagnostic. Then do a dry run on the string engine and get it fired up."

"Roger that!" said Flying Officer Zomo. They both entered within the vessel's reinforced bulkheads followed by Akerele holding his rifle over his shoulder.

"Any further news on the swarm, General?" asked Adcox.

Dr. Henry jumped in. "As you may be aware, Mr. Adcox, Horde swarms open gateways through space to traverse immense distances but they must rest before each jump. I have developed a way to calculate when and where the next rest point will be along their trajectory..."

"...and when he does we'll be waiting for them," said Baizan.

Nanonramu entered the hangar with an eagerness in his footsteps to speak with the general. "Baizan General, what word from my planet? After orbital defenses engaged great swarm, unable I have been to make further contact."

"According to intel, the fighting has been fierce. Basarwa's orbital defenses have been completely shattered. With the battle now atmospheric, reports are sketchy."

The Rogue was speechless for a moment. But then he smiled. "Our warriors are over two billion strong. In space neither side has advantage but our terrain, unfamiliar to the abomination, will be there demise. Horde cannot defeat us."

Adcox was certain the Rogue had stated previously that their planetary army were one billion in strength, not two. But he put the Horaxian's mistake down to Nanonramu's masking of what must be grave concern for his people. Rogues were known to be emotionally complex.

"Let us worry about the swarm, my comrades," said Henry, "herd your thoughts to the mission ahead."

After saluting Baizan, Adcox walked off. Jei'Gun entered and walked side by side with Nanonramu. But soon they were halted in their tracks by the sound of baseful footsteps. Rey'Jax strode through, for once he didn't have to duck his head as the hangar bay doors were taller than him. Anubianites historically had always held a deep admiration for their aboriginal relatives and Jei'Gun was a statue in his armor as he surveyed the giant.

"Ariman strength is indeed valuable gift for journey," said Jei'Gun as Rey'Jax was about to walk past them. Jei'Gun then bowed his head slightly when Rey'Jax turned to acknowledge him.

"Just as fighting ability renowned of elite-shakan, never does it yield nor waver," replied Rey'Jax pausing his strides only briefly before walking on.

Nanonramu whispered to Jei'Gun in the softest of voices. "The Arimans rebelled against our High Apex, they cannot be trusted."

"Be *quiet* fool!" barked Jei'Gun, trying to keep his voice down. He moved his helmet to touch upon Nanonramu's ear. "Or see both our still-cherished heads parted from necks."

Hawke was last to enter the hangar.

"God speed, old friend," said Baizan to Hawke. "Take care of him, Eve."

"Will do, General," replied Eve.

Hawke nodded as he walked off. No surprise, he ignored Henry's presence.

"Oh, Mr. Hawke! I took the liberty of supplying some cigars to the vessel's cargo bay. Premium Prodigious *Cunga Sigma*, your favorite I believe, and not to worry I've added a few of your *usual* ingredients for flavor."

Hawke intended to ignore him again. But he then noticed Henry held a dusty book in his small, frail left arm and he identified the word "Principia" on the front cover.

"We thought you'd be reading something a little more up to date than Isaac Newton, Henreyotomborufulonjaro?"

"Our warships and your carriers swing around planets today based on the laws within this classic literature. I guess sometimes old things can still prove useful. Do you not agree, Mr. Hawke?"

Hawke looked at Baizan and shook his head. He walked off without bothering to answer.

"Time to fly, Mr. Hawke."

"Go to hell!" replied Hawke. Baizan released a half smile, so did Dr. Henry.

Hawke boarded the *Copernicus* and addressed Adcox. "Request permission to get some R&R and be notified as soon as the pod arrives?"

"Sure Hawke."

Adcox and Hatshepsut analyzed the way Hawke struggled as he continued down the walkway, pressing upon the bulkhead to prop himself up.

"His condition is deteriorating rapidly," said Hatshepsut.

***

Somewhere in the Polaris Sigma system, a neutron star hurled through space at extraordinary speeds. At a minimum safe distance from the stars' gravitational pull waited the Horaxian warship *The Virtuous Sword* in stellar orbit. On board the suspended titanic, the vessel's Apex gazed out toward the neutron star with a burning intensity in his eyes. Without facing his crew he ended his silence to utter the words they had long dreaded.

"Send word to Divine Council, stellar-planetary alignment is almost complete. Within next twelve hours gravitational disruption will reach zenith. If Death should break free, we shall stand in its path condemned with hopes of glory. Even if price paid be our lives."

His voice relayed ship wide and roars of "for the Great Supreme King!" echoed in every deck of the vessel.

***

The neutron star, with a city-sized celestial mass of only thirty miles in diameter, spiraled in view of *The Virtuous Sword*.

Deep inside its inhospitable atmosphere, an object swirled amidst the superheated vapors. The levitation effects of the super magnetic field combined with the object's own repulsion power, allowed it to hang in mid-air over the smooth surface of the star composed of degenerated gases.

The obscuring atmosphere thinned, revealing a humanoid shape to the object. Yet its body was not whole, only a wireframe outline encompassed by swirling metal fragments. To deal with the extreme gravity the entity had moleculerized most of its mass into microscopic fragments, though some pieces remained visible. But all still clung to its body by what appeared to be a thin, wire-like, silver substance. Only its eyes were clearly detectable through the debris, completely blue without pupils, a glowing blue. It was the Mankiller, and it struggled for dear life. The super intensity of the magnetar's gravitational might sporadically impounded its frame. A force so strong, a grain of sand dropped from its skies would hit the ground with the power of thousands of hydrogen bombs. A gravity great enough to crush atoms...yet it had survived.

***

At the other side of the universe, the *Copernicus* travelled across the stars to its destination, the Asatorin blackhole.

Adcox lay in his quarters, eyes focused on the walls, but his mind drifted elsewhere. The pressures of the mission would have plagued his mind if one thought had not distracted him. *Is she doing the same thing right now? Thinking of me? If I told her how I felt will she be disgusted? Could it ever work? Feelings were man's gift but it becomes a curse if the one who captivates your heart cannot receive them.*

"Alert! Captain Adcox," said Eve's voice on the stateroom's comms link.

"Yes, Eve?" He jumped out of bed.

"Keegan needs your help. Come to our stateroom, come quickly. Please!"

Adcox darted for the Hawke's quarters with Eve's puzzling voice echoing in his thoughts. How oddly human she sounded. Could artificial intelligence truly synthesize concern for a human the way her voice had.

The doors of Hawke's quarter's opened before he could press the entry button. Adcox was taken aback by the sight of the living legend barely conscious on the ground. Hawke's battle to fight off the drugs he had taken, had now been lost.

"Major, sir, are you all right?"

"His respiratory systems began to fail," said Eve.

"Let me call Hatshepsut."

"Negative," Hawke's trembling voice replied. "Just get us to cargo bay two."

Adcox placed Hawke's arm over his shoulder hoisting him up and opened the stateroom door. They made their way to the cargo area.

"I was unconscious," said Hawke. "How long did we leave the *Sword of Damocles*?"

"It's been a few hours," Adcox replied.

"I told you to inform me when the pod was loaded."

"I know, but you looked like you needed rest. I didn't see the sense in waking you just to give you a minor update."

"Does my condition look minor to you, sir?" said Hawke as he firmed the pain.

Adcox's mind had just connected the dots. "The Horde artifact, it can help you in some way?" The major chose not to respond, and he was not surprised. "All right! Perhaps you wouldn't mind explaining something else that puzzles me. I know SPUs have advance AI but just now, Eve sounded...different."

"...The superconducting electromagnetic explosion on Kemeta disrupted her vocal frequency harmonics."

"And somehow, made her more emotional?"

"We don't know what you mean."

"I think you do, sir!"

After a silence to contemplate, Hawke's dark and weary face turned to Adcox. "When Eve connected with the mothership in dark matter space fifteen years ago, her programming was altered."

"Are you saying it gave her consciousness?"

"We're not sure."

"I would say yes, Captain," Eve answered.

"Let's just say it did more good than bad," said Hawke.

Adcox half grinned. "More good than bad, interesting concept, Major. I studied ancient history and mythology in academics before officer training. Not much practical use, of course. They said Zeus had two jars from which he dispensed good and bad to mortals. One jar having good and the other the bad, and he portioned each for every man. I'd be very interested to know how he portioned you, sir."

Hawke's wheezing deep voice responded. "In the best of us there is some evil and in the worst of us there is some good. However, there are exceptions on each side."

Eve spoke more freely now that her secret was revealed. "We're guessing your love for mythology must stem from your name?" Diomedes was a Greek mythological hero. One day you will follow in the footsteps of your namesake and become a legend."

"Oh I seriously doubt that, Eve. The thing is, most of the Greek heroes of mythology achieved what they did due to their extraordinary strength. They were demi gods, or directly helped by gods."

"And you are different?" asked Eve.

"Errr...yeah! Real life's different, we're just men. Well, except for you, Major. You Black Guards are like demigods having been cloned and augmented and all."

"The Black Guard Nephilim were not clones," said Eve.

"Oh, so they *were* cyborgs. That's why they showed no mercy when they killed."

"Negative!" said Eve. "They were not machines, nor is Major Hawke cloned or part machine. Aside from the genetic variation inherent in all men, he is no different to any man."

"Just a man? But what about the Nephilim? Why was their file locked away so deeply? What were they? And are they really all gone?"

Eve began to respond but Hawke cut her off."

"That's enough, Eve," demanded Hawke. "Captain, there are some things in this universe it's best not having any knowledge of."

They arrived at the cargo bay doors and Adcox felt his suspicion of the weakened man swell. Hawke was a human puzzle, one with too many missing pieces. His concealment of information could make the most trusting individual paranoid. "How is it you're able to do the things you do, Hawke? And what do you intend to do with the pod? I don't know what you're up to but I can't allow you to jeopardize this mission. Too much is at stake."

"Trust us," said Hawke.

"That's not the easiest thing to do, according to your Ariman friend. Especially when you don't trust me."

"First of all, Rey'Jax is not my friend. Second, for what it's worth, we do trust you, and we do believe in you, Captain. With belief one man alone can defeat a hundred. That's the only source of our power."

Hawke pressed the access pad and the black cargo bay double doors slid open. "We'll take it from here." He carefully stepped into the cargo bay unaided, weak, but strong enough to stable himself. "One more thing. Don't make your feelings for the female so obvious?"

"Who, Zomo?" replied Adcox.

Hawke turned to face him, unimpressed.

"Crap! Is it that noticeable?" The young man glanced down both ends of the corridor to check if they were alone.

"We didn't realize that much has changed in fifteen years. Humans and Horaxians have relationships now?"

"They don't! There was a rumor of one account of it happening. They'd imprison you for it, Horaxians would be executed. I just can't help how I feel, she's so...gentle and..."

"Son...we are not interested," said Hawke. He pressed the door control closing the door right in Adcox's face.

"Damn it!" said the worried Adcox as he walked back down the corridor to contemplate his feelings.

***

"Lock it down, Eve!" said Hawke.

"It is done. Cargo hold has been locked down."

"Please open up the pod and set the Lazarus cycle for thirty minutes." Hawke dragged his legs over to a man-sized cargo container. He unlocked it and pulled out sections of his Black Guard armor.

"Will comply, however it is not enough time to complete a full cycle."

"Acknowledged," said Hawke as he threw on pieces of his armor, beginning with the legs and waist section. As he dressed, the pod came to life with flashes of green lights and Eve activated its doors.

"Eve, slowly start decompressing the cargo bay's oxygen levels down to sixty five percent."

"Keegan, the pressure will be so low air will have difficulty entering your vascular systems and could result in hypoxia."

"I hear you darling, it's ok."

***

Thirty minutes passed. The pod doors jetted out gas and opened. Hawke stepped out now in full Black Guard uniform minus the helmet. The body armor still shined black, tight-fitted with an oversized white sword as an emblem on his right shoulder plate extending down to the bicep area. The United Earth military insignia was etched on the left chest plate.

He looked rejuvenated as he rolled his head to stretch his neck, yet the reduced pressure caused him to breathe heavily. He dropped on one knee resting one hand on the ground. From his kneeling position he then fell to the floor and began doing press ups. His plaited hair hung with each repetition.

"Eve!"

"Yes Keegan?"

"Increase the gravity force to two G's."

"Gravity has been increased."

Hawke forced himself to his feet and staggered as a man would if all of his limbs were heavily weighted down. He began to jog around the cargo bay exerting tremendous effort. Much like a weightlifter's pectoralis major adapting to cast iron, with more rapidity his body adapted to the g-force and he gained speed transforming his movement into a relative sprint.

After his sprint he began to punch the cargo container that held his armor, delayed at first, then faster and stronger denting the reinforced material. Whatever doubt in his abilities that crept in from wasting away in the Jumbie Abyss had been vanquished now, his strength had found him again.

"Eve, increase gravity to three G's."

"I will initiate gravity amplification in approximately five seconds but I am monitoring your vitals."

Hawke gasped in agony as he fought to stay on his feet. Gritting his teeth, he lifted what originally were two fourteen-kilogram cargo boxes off a mechanical loading arm and onto his shoulders and he began to squat. As he rose up, his legs trembled as though close to collapsing but he made it up. He went down again with an agonizing yell and performed countless repetitions.

***

On the bridge of the *Copernicus*, Akerele burst through the sliding doors where Zomo, Tronics and Adcox were executing standard ship operational checks and going over the mission as they journeyed toward the Asatorin star system.

"We may have problems guys," said the spooked Akerele. "The Ariman's loose and he looked like he was searching the ship for something."

Tronics rushed to a display panel on his left. He accessed the internal hull security cameras and managed to find Rey'Jax.

"Looks like he's heading toward the cargo bay," said Akerele tiptoeing over Tronics's shoulder.

"Oh no!" Uttered Adcox. "He's going for Hawke, come on lets go. Zomo, stay on the helm."

They dashed off, hoping to prevent any altercation. The marines found Rey'Jax, staring inside cargo bay two via the glass viewing pane. His heightened vision locked on to Hawke's Black Guard battle-suit, which was more ergonomic and slender compared to standard issue marine battle armor. It made his blood boil, the man he knew was the man before the armor. The white sword emblem on his shoulder, to him and to all Horaxians, was a mark parallel to a pentagram or the swastika.

Adcox, Tronics and Akerele crept toward him without making a sound.

"Humans, what be your desires?" said Rey'Jax in a foul mood.

"We mean no offense Mr. Ariman…sir," replied Akerele as the marines treaded closer. "Just wanted to see if everything was, copasetic, if you know what I mean."

"When Urk'Tark asked my help I sensed something, now seeing him train proves suspicions."

"This guy's got a lot of names," said Tronics under his breath.

"He is afraid," said Rey'Jax.

***

Hawke continued his training. He pulled out his sword handle extracting its white blade. With the movement and posture of an expert martial artist he began to practice striking movements with force yet with grace. For the first time he felt his agility returning even though every movement required the mustering of a great deal of strength.

From outside the cargo bay Akerele tried to make sense of Rey'Jax's words. "What can scare a man that's spent a lifetime in the darkest whole imaginable?"

"His dread is of perils witnessed, beyond our stars."

"The planetoid where the ship lies?" Adcox asked.

"Yes! Urk'Tark is so hated by all, even death scorns him and chooses not to claim its most worthy prize."

"Mighty Rey'Jax," called Adcox. "Why do you called the major...Urk'Tark?"

"Arimans believe not in degrading concepts of entitlement. For us, one is born with no name, and one receives no name nor anything else until rightfully earned."

Adcox tried to make sense of Rey'Jax's words, the first nation must have given Hawke another name after he proved himself somehow. "So it's true the major lived on Arima for some time. Did you know him well?"

"Yes. A truth so shameful I affirm. He was raised and trained in ways of Arimans by Uru, the late Kalinda grand master, who was eventually killed by heresy's endorser the High Apex. The only human to be bestowed so sweet an honor unparalleled, undeserved. An honor lost when he and his...Black Guard most heinous killed Arimans numerous in Battle of Cyclonis."

"Please, if you don't mind, I'd like to know more about Cyclonis," said the captain.

"In the battle to control the strategic star system, ten to one the Horaxians outnumbered Homo sapiens. But then the dreaded Black Guard arrived and turned tides. Cut off they did, the troopers from their ships with a will unholy, and ferocity unimaginable. Unfortunately, the demons took no prisoners, they also did not simply kill. Disembowelments, decapitations...they were ripping the trooper's hearts out of chest with their hands. We Arimans were forced into the fight and mobilized to Cyclonis. Laws of nature demanded that titans must clash, and there he stood, one man...amongst giants."

"What happened?" Akerele asked.

"With our God-like strength and endurance, battle waged on seemingly endless. No other human nor Horaxian forces dared intervene. A stalemate would be its conclusion, lives claimed on both sides."

"But it sounds like you were close once, to the major?" queried Adcox. "Perhaps before Cyclonis?"

Rey'Jax for the first time looked at the members of Unit Forty Two. "When you gaze upon him you see a man. I see one who was once brother, a brother that turned on his own brothers...and vengeance will be mine."

Rey'Jax then turned and with little hurry stomped away, his heavy steps vibrating the hull. Soon as Rey'Jax disappeared, the marines peered into the cargo bay.

"Let's go see what the major's up to," said Akerele. He tried to open the doors but the keypad was unresponsive. "It won't open."

"He must have locked it down. Tronics can you open it?" asked Adcox.

"Gimme a sec." Tronics popped out his trusty data-slab cube and it unfolded. He quickly executed commands. "It's done, we're in."

The doors opened and the marines crept in. As they entered the pod doors opened, Hawke front flipped out of the pod with flawless form landing without a thud.

His acrobatic display was witnessed by Hatshepsut, Nanonramu and Jei'Gun who also arrived at the cargo bay. All Jei'Gun's helmet optical sensors could do was zero in on the Black Guard's armor, the brilliant whiteness of the sword emblem created a chain reaction of hatred. This was the demon form he knew, the one that murdered thousands of his clansmen.

"You look unexpectedly well, Mr. Hawke," said Hatshepsut. "So the pod has ability to also heal?"

"Was there something you came here to tell us doctor?" asked Hawke.

Nanonramu came forward. "We have been informed. The shining light that was astonishing Rogue Basarwa is no more." His antennae drooped as though it had lost all rigidity.

"Are you sure?" asked Adcox. Only Nanonramu was under the illusion the Basarwans could win. But it was the speed of their defeat what shocked everyone.

"It has been confirmed by the splinter of survivors."

Adcox came to him. "I'm sorry, Nanonramu. Please accept my sympathies."

"Your sympathies human are, acceptable. We were certain our underground fortresses would shelter us. Masses of giant Horde squids tore through. They were massacred."

"Let me know if there's anything we can do for you," said the captain.

"Thank you, Adcox Captain. I look to future. Through togetherness, may we be victorious so I may one day avenge my fallen."

Hawke addressed Hatshepsut again, as if he never heard a word of Nanonramu's announcement. "I believe there is something else you came here to tell me, doctor?"

Adcox wondered how he was so certain of what he had asked.

"I have completed your requested analysis," said Hatshepsut.

"What analysis?" asked Akerele.

"Mr. Hawke requested I analyzed data on the victims who were attacked by brain Hordes."

"Jei'Gun demands to know why," said the Anubianite.

"He wanted to discover if there were any connections," said Adcox.

Jei'Gun growled. "Why were you wasting her time with this folly?"

"Have you found something?" Adcox asked Hatshepsut.

"No, from what I can tell there does not appear to be any genetic, biological, pathological, neurological or any other similarities among the Horaxian or human victims."

"Good job, Doctor. We appreciate your efforts," said Hawke as a he ventured towards the cargo bay doors.

"Mr. Hawke," called Hatshepsut, "I sense you are hiding something."

Jei'Gun chest began convulsing with rage. "End your riddles, reveal truth, right now!"

Hatshepsut placed her hand on Jei'Gun to pacify him but sensed for the first time it had no effect. His rage had locked onto the emblem on Hawke's shoulder. "Please share your thoughts," said Hatshepsut. "It is least you can do in return for my research."

Hawke paused in the surrounding silence. "Your analysis does identify a link. That there is none."

"I don't understand," said Adcox.

"Please elaborate!" asked Dr. Hatshepsut.

"Biochemically, all humans are ninety nine percent similar to each other, the same for Horaxians. But we're guessing each of the victims of the Brain Horde's scepter blasts were as genetically different as possible. The Polymorph have an interest in the genetic variation in all forms of organic life."

Hatshepsut's lips parted in reaction to his words. "They are gene harvesting, collecting selected DNA from individuals."

"So possibly," added Tronics drawing conclusions of his own. "The brain Horde's scepter spontaneously moleculerizes organic matter and collects it somehow."

"But, why would they do this?" asked Adcox.

"That is the question," said Hawke. "People think the Polymorph are just brainless animals attacking us for food and land. But they have a purpose, a motive."

"And what is that?" asked Jei'gun.

"All is not always as it appears to be. That's all we can say," said Hawke.

"You, frail one," said Jei'Gun pointing at Adcox. "You stand there and allow the demon king to conceal truths and tells us more lies."

"Just chill out," said Tronics.

"Silence, Baboon! Your captain's cowardice infects mission."

"Please Jei'Gun, give him a chance," said Hatshepsut.

"You would defend pup, my lady? When your life laid in his hands within the abyss, he crumbled. And you, souwrak," he said turning to Major Hawke, "it's time to finish our matters."

"Listen to the lady, elite-shakan. I don't want to kill you, not yet anyway."

"You are shadow of myth you once were, Black Guard. We elite-shakan knights do not respect past glories, only strength. Yours has abandoned you."

Akerele scurried out of harm's way as the elite-shakan charged forward. The big male threw two punches and while looking down at the ground, Hawke was still able to evade them.

"Stop, that's an order!" said Adcox. He was without his weapon. Exercising caution, he removed the Ariman shield handle but then struggled to find a lever, button, or other means to activate it.

The Anubianite threw three more punches in quick succession but Hawke dodged them effortlessly and still had yet to look at his foe. It was as if he had a sixth sense, his agility was astonishing, he appeared to shift his position out of harm's way at a snail's pace despite the great speed of Jei'Gun's attacked. His composure was like a martial arts master of the highest dan. Jei'Gun's third punch crashed into the bulkhead wall indenting it with his power. Infuriated further, the elite-shakan knight extracted his forearm blade.

Nanonramu was himself frozen by his superior's actions. "Alpha please, elevate your calm. The humans are no longer enemy." His words went ignored.

Swipe after swipe, Jei'Gun lashed out but nothing could land. The Black Guard hadn't looked threatened the entire time. His breathing—calm, his form, flawless. Hawke whipped out his sword handle but it fell out of his hand, landing downwards-facing on the ground. His only error since the fight began. He then moved back as the Horaxian knight charged forward and this time it looked as if he was about to land a strike. Suddenly, the sword's blade extracted, propelling the hilt upwards and it rocketed Jei'Gun's chin, he balled out from the pain. The Black Guard's trapped had sprung and he pounced on the dazed warrior. Grabbing his gauntlet, Hawke removed its small access panel and with lightning speed cross wired the circuitry. A crushing pain took hold of Jei'Gun's hand as his bionic armor's gripping power inversed.

Jei'Gun made one more desperate attempt and lashed out again but Hawke rolled out of the way and his arm blade became lodged in the wall leaving him exposed to attack. Hawke rose up, sword handle in hand.

Adcox watched in disbelief like the others, overwhelmed by the major's new found agility, and the familiarity of his skill in disabling Jei'Gun's gauntlet. But principally it was the Black Guard's eyes, void of its usual calmness and composure, now filled fury and desire to kill.

"We could let you live," said Major Hawke. "But then we'd have to always watch our back. Perhaps it's best we put you out of your misery."

"Do it demon, for I will kill you, my rage never ending," screamed Jei'Gun in agony, his hand still being crushed.

Hawke raised his sword handle toward Jei'Gun's face. All he had left to do was extract the blade.

"Major, don't do it!" ordered Adcox, as he observed Hawke's breathing intensify and his sword hand trembling. "What's wrong with him?" uttered Adcox.

"Death is like a long lost friend's embrace," the major said, his decision, a death blow.

"Enough Urk'Tark!" the deep harmonic voice bellowed, echoing around the room. "The elite-shakan is not your enemy. He has further role to play on path ahead, as do you. Drop weapon, or face my wrath."

"As you wish, your majesty." Hawke lowered his hand. "Lucky we made sure you kept the hand." He then walked out of the cargo bay and back down the corridor. Adcox and Hatshepsut chased after him while Nanonramu rushed to Jei'Gun's aid.

"Hawke, wait!" Adcox shouted but he continued his pace. Adcox looked at Hawke's hand and saw his fist were still balled up. "I need everyone focused, you're the last person I thought would be losing their cool. What happened back there?"

"I saw your eyes, Mr. Hawke," said Hatshepsut. "For but a moment, you lost control. You were going to kill Jei'Gun, as you were on Kemeta. Like a marauding lion that has tasted Horaxian blood...you enjoy killing."

Hawke continued to walk towards his quarters, still refusing to respond.

Hatshepsut caught up to him. "I have read historic counts of Black Guard attacks, extreme violence consisted with all. Fifteen years ago, the genocide of Matelot-6, what happened? Did you lose control then also? I must know."

"Some will see it that way."

"I need to be to able trust you if we've going to get through this," Adcox said. "You're going to have to start telling us the truth."

"Acknowledged, Captain," Hawke replied trying to flee the conversation.

Adcox placed his hand gently on his shoulder. "Major, I know it must be difficult for you. But just this one time, please, tell us what happened on the ark?

Swayed by the compassion of the young man, he developed a sense of obligation and finally halted.

Chapter Thirteen - Perihelion of Darkness

The squadron officer commander of the Black Guard was back on the Ark vessel, fifteen years in the past, close to the Matelot system. On the screen in the briefing room given to him by the Ark's Captain Mensah stood Baizan. Here he was still a major-general, two ranks below his future rank as general. Major-General Adens also stood present. This was the DNA encrypted message sent to the *Ploiarion*, an intelligent program, a recording with the ability to interact with the viewer as though it was a live feed.

"It's good to see you, Major. You look terrible," said Baizan on screen.

"We're alive, sir," said Hawke through the half-crushed black helmet.

"What you're viewing is an adaptive response prerecording of a message sent three days ago. We picked up Eve's trans-spatial SOS beacon. You're fortunate, you always are. You could have been drifting in space for centuries before detection. Where's the rest of your Nephilim Squadron, Hawke?"

"K.I.A., all of them. They're gone, sir."

"Gone?" Baizan looked at Adens as if he was punched in the stomach. "Hawke, we both know that's not possible."

"It's true, sir."

"This is not good. Major, our intel suggests the Horaxians are building some kind of advanced weapon on Matelot-6. We don't know what exactly it is but there's a lot of speculation. Some say it might be capable of destroying Earth's sun by spontaneously converting all of its matter and transforming it into a red giant."

"If it's true, it will engulf Earth and all of the inner planets."

"We don't know what to think."

"We're soldiers, major-general. We're not here to think, we're here to act."

"That's why we need you, Officer Commander Hawke," said Adens. "We were counting on your entire Black Guard knights. Intel suggests whatever this weapon is, it's about to be deployed. Hawke, Cagn is behind this."

"We already knew that, and we know what must be done. Eve, retrieve the coordinates of the lunar colony."

"Query, Generals," said Eve, illuminating his neck with flashing lights. "How is Major Hawke supposed to stop the weapon from being deployed?"

"They want us to take over the ark, Eve."

"Hawke," said Major-General Adens, "you've been gone for some time. "Millions of Horaxians have been relocated and now reside on that moon. A lot of civilian lives could be lost if you do this."

"Acknowledged," said Hawke.

Baizan spoke once more. "Not all members of Earth Command have sanctioned this mission. The joint leaders are still deliberating. There are those that believe mankind will eventually lose the war so the arks are of vital importance to our existence. But there are others that think what we have is worth saving."

"And you, sir?" asked Hawke.

Baizan frowned, his forehead wrinkled. "You know I was there when they bombed Hope, Hawke. I lost two sons from the fallout. I swore an oath to protect our home worlds from *all* threats. I can't let this happen, we won't lose another paradise on my watch." Baizan's emotional words hit home to both men. "We can't mobilize a counterattack in time. We've only got one chance and that's you."

"If Cagn is behind this," said Hawke, "then this is Armageddon."

The North American general came closer to the screen. "Ark vessels aren't military. The crew have their own specific mandate. They won't allow you to take over the ship, not willingly. We cannot order you to agree to this. It's a suicide mission and not one you'll want to survive from anyway. To destroy an ark for any reason…not even Baizan can save you from the hangman."

"Victory can only be attained through sacrifices," Hawke replied.

"Also," added Baizan. "I think I should warn you. Ark vessels aren't designed for combat. They have limited offensive capability."

"It has me," said Hawke.

"I would have liked to be in the field with you again, old friend," Baizan said. "It's been an honor serving with you."

After a farewell salute by the generals, the screen went blank.

Major Hawke ended his story, and witnessed Hatshepsut's body shaking trying to contain the fury within.

"You monster! How could one commit such atrocities?"

"We gave them a chance. We told them to abandon ship, I merely incapacitated anyone who opposed me. If they had listened immediately they would have survived. But by the time they eventually did, their shuttles were too close to Matelot-6. No one could have known the blast radius would stretch so far. It shouldn't have, Cagn was..."

"Murderer!" Hatshepsut cried out. "You did not know for sure there was weapon on lunar colony. Horaxian authorities stated the facility was a world generator actively terraforming."

"That's what Cagn told everyone. Did you see this atmospheric processor yourself?"

"Stop trying to deflect. You need proof before you hold lives at risk."

Adcox struggled with what to think of their exchange but he found himself developing resentment for a man he once admired. "What exactly was this weapon supposed to be?"

"We don't know, but an atmospheric reactor detonation isn't supposed to reduce an entire moon to subatomic particles and annihilate escape shuttles way out of blast radius. And if we hadn't stopped him, either way billions would've died."

"But since it was predominately Horaxian lives, it mattered little?" asked Hatshepsut. "Are we so hideous to you that our lives are not sacrosanct? Do you have to hate us so much?"

Both men noticed her long hair rising miraculously above her head and her aura reappeared.

Hawke responded to her questions. "When you've been beaten and tortured to the brink of death, then nursed back to good health only to be tortured to near death over and over again for years, you'll automatically know the answer to that question."

"I had loved ones on Matelot-6. My birth mother was there." Hatshepsut panted ferociously unable to close her mouth or control her actions as she rapidly punched Hawke in his chest. "You killed her. I have lost so much because of you."

Adcox was stunned by a sight he had never witnessed. Hatshepsut's body was suspended five inches off the ground and she glowed even brighter. She released a green, electrostatic build-up as she struck Hawke's chest and the resultant shock jolted his body.

Hawke's voice sank. "You're not the only one to lose your whole world, Hatshepsut."

"We are sorry," said Eve.

"You do not value life," said Hatshepsut, "all life is precious. Though you are but one man, your existence threatens us all. Please, end your endless fighting."

Adcox placed his hand on Hatshepsut's upper arm to calm her down, but then drew her into his embrace. As she descended she buried her head in his chest, sobbing her blue tears.

"She is right you know," said Adcox. Hawke was like a hero to him, and no kid wanted to see their hero revealed to be so terribly flawed, only forever exalted in their eyes. "Sir, you can't see that there are some things more important than the mission."

Hawke's blank stare fixated on the both of them in each other's arms and Adcox understood why. For although fifteen years had passed since his incarceration began, no human and Horaxian had ever been in each other's embrace. Hawke spoke out.

"It is in mankind's nature to fight, just as it is in our nature to love. They are opposites yet both are needed to make us whole. Either one unused or misused is foolish. But to deny that what is hardcoded within our DNA, the necessity to fight, the will to fight, is a crime against one's own soul. Hate and fear corrupts absolutely but the will to fight for what you believe in is a sacred virtue. You devalue what you love if you lack the heart to battle all adversaries to protect it. Evil triumphs when good people do nothing. You both claim life is precious yet you don't want to fight and die for what you cherish, and for that...perhaps we care more than the both of you."

Major Hawke departed, but stop himself after only a few steps. "This killing that you despise so much, it will never end. Not until we complete our mission. There's nothing more important than that."

Adcox responded, addressing a concern he had long felt the need to express. "This assignment is to recover the Horde mothership. Our mission doesn't have anything to do with High Apex Commander Cagn, Hawke."

"Maybe yours doesn't!"

As the sound of the major's departing footsteps dampened, Hatshepsut lifted her head up to stare into Adcox's blue eyes.

"Will it ever stop?"

"What?" asked Adcox.

"The killing! The Horaxian Empire expanded and merged bringing forth peace. But since mankind's dawn your history has been a cycle consistent of the opposite. Increasing your numbers, dividing your population and then both divides wage war upon each other. Some of your conflicts lasted centuries. Are our fates now intertwined? Will we now wage war against Horde for a lifetime? And if we succeed will our differences not rekindle an endless war?"

"I don't know. I hope not. Sometimes, differences can help to form stronger bonds." Adcox stared into her majestic pink pupils as he spoke. "Great things can emerge when opposites unite."

"Well, you and I have a difference which divides us."

"That I'm human?" asked Adcox in a lowered tone.

"No."

"No?"

"I mean yes, but no."

Adcox had managed to confuse the young female.

"I was referring to Mr. Hawke," she replied.

"Oh, oh yeah, right," said the embarrassed officer.

"You put too must trust in your Black Guard friend. Clearly his actions serve only himself. He has his own agenda, one which he is yet to disclose."

"I still want to believe there's good in him. He was a great leader once, he can be one again."

"But what purpose deems that necessary? Already do we have a great leader." Her stare caused his face to turn red.

"Thanks!" Adcox smiled warmly, "but you saw yourself, I'm no leader. Jei'Gun only seems to respect you and that's the only thing keeping him in check. But still he and Nanonramu are within some measure of control. The Ariman, and the major is something else entirely."

"It is not I whom Jei'Gun respects. He upholds laws of our people and has sworn oath as elite-shakan knight. As I am a Caroo, from noble house, he respects and honors my nobility."

"Well, I'm an orphan, Hatshepsut. I have no house, no renowned title."

"The worth of a man is measured by much more than his riches or what his title may be."

Hatshepsut rested her left palm on Adcox's left cheek and her right palm on his forehead and stared in his eyes. The young man's skin perspired as anxiety and desire consumed him. She spoke softly. "You will earn respect and admiration of your team by content of your heart, as you have earned mine."

The impulsive strength of his desire overcame his fears and he moved closer to her lips. As his proximity neared he reflexively closed his eyes and tried to steady his pounding heart to embrace the imminent historic event.

Hatshepsut's white, single-plaited hair rose up above her head once again due to a static build up caused by the nearing of the young captain's lips.

"Diomedes!" she shouted.

Adcox opened his eyes and saw that the Ariman metal shield had activated itself from the handle he still held on his fist. It formed a semi-circular shape greater than their combined bodies, its white shined so brilliant he felt as though it radiated its own light. After a moment the shield retracted automatically and in doing so revealed the hulking body behind it.

"Trouble I sensed," said Rey'Jax, forced to bend his head as it scraped the upper hull. "Thought you required help with the Black Guard."

"No, it's all right," said Adcox.

"Well do I know him. If you desire, I can break *one* of his legs. He will still be combat effective, trust in me."

"No, no we're fine, thanks," Adcox replied to the persistent Ariman. "Rey'Jax, the shield, did you activate it?"

"I did not, Captain." His deep, super-harmonic voice reverberating throughout the corridor.

Hatshepsut stepped in front of Rey'Jax to address him. "How did it…"

She discontinued as she saw the Ariman pulling back his torso and raising his left hand over his face as if to shield his eyes from a bright light.

"Please do not venture directly into my vision's field." Rey'Jax blasted the words out as quickly as possible, coming across both angry and concerned. Adcox and the doctor were bewildered but she dared not disobey him and stepped back. With an odd cautiousness his hand shook as he lowered it. "Your Biophosphorescence…its radiance invisible to mere mortals, is blinding." He spoke without looking at her.

He must be referring to ultraviolet light, Adcox thought, but the captain wanted to solve a more baffling mystery. "Please can you show me how to operate this shield if I'm to use it?"

"It responds to the name Isih-lango, an ancient Ariman wonder formed in the sacred Shari fountain. It acts via the heart of its wielder. I cannot help you with what you seek." Rey'Jax uttered a few final words as he walked off. "But remember this. It is not your slave!"

**

Hawke found himself back in cargo bay two performing an unusual form of martial arts kata, wearing his legendary Black Guard armor. His entire body alternated fluidly in choreographed patterns of movements as he performed the Ariman ancient art.

"Everything is coming together as you predicted," said Eve in her sweet, creole accent. "The mission being approved, Rey'Jax being present and astonishingly, Captain Adcox and Dr. Hatshepsut are forming an emotional connection. Emotions are fascinating. I'm still getting used to the sensation."

"Overrated...and redundant," Hawke said punching the air, constantly re-posturing his body. "What about operation Bird of Prey, status assessment?" Hawke stepped, turned and kicked all the while maintaining perfect form.

"It has taken approximately fifteen years to slowly create an override code for the core system using the data from the mothership. Nevertheless, with the help of alien technology it is proofing difficult. I'm still only seventy two point three percent complete."

"Not good! Could you complete it in time?"

A silence lingered as Eve assessed the correct answer. "No, Keegan. As there are millions of yottabits of data, a theoretical maximum of eight-four point seven percent completion can be achieved within the next ten hours. But I must shutdown most of my primary systems to achieve the processing power necessary to reach that percentage in time. Once I have activated the pod I am afraid I will be limited in my capacity to help you for the remainder of your mission."

"Do whatever's necessary. I'll manage."

"We still have two major threats to our mission. One is MK1. The stellar alignment is nearing completion and it will be freed soon. The second is the identification of the traitor."

"Leave that to me."

"Keegan, you are aware that most, if not all the humans and Horaxians accompanying us on our journey will not survive."

"I am aware. Not all, only the one's whose deaths are necessary."

"I do not understand. You have the power to prevent their deaths. Yet you will choose not to?"

"As your conscience grows, you'll realize that power doesn't define anything. It's only a tool, without the wisdom to control that tool, the power itself is worthless. Whatever happens must be allowed to happen. To whatever end."

Zomo's voice came onto the ship's communication system interrupting his exercise. "Attention, we're approaching the dark matter space entry point, everyone suit up and report to the bridge."

On Zomo's words Hawke took in deep breaths remaining still in contemplation.

"I detect heightened neurological activity in your brain's amygdala area. I believe what you're experiencing is...panic."

"I always knew I'll be back there, I just never wanted to be."

"We suffered much there, you lost your nephilim, and I lost the closest thing to sisters along with them."

"Eve, thank you for everything. For being there with me all through the darkness."

"We are one!"

"Major Hawke!" said Tronics' over the comms link. "The captain requested you prep the pod for the dark matter space jump."

***

Everyone hustled on the Copernicus' bridge. Tronics hectically hit buttons on the helm console to rectify an engine power output minor alarm and Flying Officer Zomo gripped the flight stick yoke. The team had already strapped into the personnel area behind the cockpit with Adcox sat in the captain's seat at the center of the bridge. The ship shook badly due to space conditions, and on the viewing screen debris streamed past at high speeds. The only ones on their feet were Tronics, just barely, and also Rey'Jax who waited at the back of the bridge in front of the main entry doors.

"People, we've just entered the Asatorin system. Everybody buckle up," said Zomo.

"Activate your helmets and your suit's life support systems," said Hatshepsut. "Our bodies cannot endure over sixty g-force unprotected."

"We're approaching minimum safe distance of the quaternary star system," reported Zomo. "It's dead ahead, sir."

They looked on in wonder as the black hole created a spectacle of light and power as it fed on other hapless celestial bodies that lay as far as trillions of miles away. Out of the top and bottom of the spherical hole shot a burst of green energy.

"Incredible!" uttered Hatshepsut astounded.

"Look at the gamma ray bursts," said Tronics, pointing his finger with excitement at the polar beams of extreme bright light. "The readings are off the chart. We're staring at the most powerful energy event in the universe that we know of."

"Let's wait for the major to give us the green light before we get any closer," said Adcox.

"Roger, Captain!" said Zomo.

"Yo...Big R, you secured?" asked Tronics, addressing the giant.

"I am prepared, Corporal," replied Rey'Jax.

Rey'Jax's manner was unflinching, on his feet much like a mountain in the path of the most destructive hurricane. Adcox wanted to advise him to strap himself in for safety but Rey'Jax's mass would never fit a chair, nor a pressurized suit. The captain knew about the extreme conditions Arimans could endure, some rumored that they could survive the void of space. But it seemed impossible the ancient prince could withstand the jump with only the protection of the ship's life support systems.

"I can detect a sound," said Rey'Jax. "Low frequency, pulsing."

Tronics' gasped as he read the instrumentation. "Rarse! Something's not right here. Gravimetric levels are way too high for our current coordinates. Rey'Jax somehow must have heard the distortions on the hull caused by the gravimetric pressure before our sensors picked them up."

"Zomo, what's going on?" asked Adcox.

"I don't know, something's wrong, a system malfunction or something." Her eyes darted around at all her display alerts.

"*Fool!*" Jei'Gun yelled. "Too close you have drifted to the supermassive black hole. It claims us."

Zomo's face blushed red. "I'm sorry, Captain. The gravity caused a malfunction in our instruments."

"We have to give Hawke more time," replied Adcox. "Zomo, make some space between us and the black hole."

"Five by five, pushing all thrusters in full reverse." Zomo pulled back hard on the ship's steering yoke but her immense struggle was obvious. "It's not working, we don't have the power."

"Imbeciles!" yelled Nanonramu. "We will be crushed into nothingness by the singularity."

"We got a chance," said Tronics. "A smaller black hole would have stretched our bodies into infinity once we crossed the event horizon but with a supermassive black hole, the tidal forces are much weaker, spaghettification might not occur. Not immediately anyway."

They all began to feel the scorching heat radiating from the matter crushed by the interstellar monster. The light given off by the accretion disk of debris engulfed the *Copernicus*, forcing the team to cover their eyes.

"Quick," Adcox said. "Adjust your visors to the light. Major Hawke, how long before the artifact is activated?"

"Six minutes. I hope. Can't be sure. Eve and I are working on it. Sit tight, out," said Hawke's voice on the radio channel.

"Ohhh, we'll be sitting real tight in a minute," Akerele said squinting his eyes from the brightness.

"What is that?" asked Jei'Gun, upon hearing the sounds of a constant pounding.

"That's the power of gravity impacting our hull and the superheating of metal," said Tronics. He analyzed the ship's systems monitor. "Hull integrity decreasing rapidly. Now at seventy percent."

"We have disturbed the beast while it feeds," said Rey'Jax. His armor began to steam as the hull temperature surpassed scolding levels.

"There's got to be a way we can buy more time. Think!" said Adcox.

Tronics' eyes lit up. "Centripetal force, Captain!"

"We...spin around it?" queried Adcox.

"Affirmative, boss! If it was Earth's sun we could gain enough escape velocity to break free. But this g-force is too strong."

"Least it should give us some time," replied Adcox. "Let's do it, Zomo!"

"Attempting to change trajectory into an orbital spin," said Zomo, "Hold on to your hats people. By my estimates we're about to hit at least five thousand Gs. That's approximately forty nine hundred meters per second squared."

Nanonramu hyperventilated has he yelled out. "The ship will break apart. The gravity is too strong. Our suits will not protect us."

"I'm shutting down the ship's artificial gravity." Tronics informed the crew. "We don't need the extra pressure."

"Give Jei'Gun the flight controls, pale skin runt," Jei'Gun commanded Zomo. "The extreme g-forces will render you unconscious. Human females are too frail to endure such conditions. Your numbers must be truly dwindling if they put you upon frontlines."

"Back off, tough guy," shouted Akerele. "She knows what she's doing."

"Like she knew what she was doing on Kemeta when she crashed ship?" Jei'Gun turned to Adcox. "Make the right decision, *noble leader*. Give Jei'Gun the con."

"The Anubianite has a point captain," said Major Hawke's voice on the bridge's loud speaker. "His bionic armor would shield him from the g-forces better than her suit. If she passes out, we're all dead."

"But I'm a much better pilot, Captain, and there's a lot of debris out here. I can do this."

Though Adcox sensed her nervousness, he also felt the conviction of her belief. Forced to make a tough call, he paused for a minute glancing back and forth from Zomo to the elite-shakan knight. Briefly, he closed his eyes in contemplation and called it. "Give her a chance. The con's yours, Zomo."

"So this be the type of leader you are?" said Jei'Gun. "Making childish sentimental choice."

"All right, let's go baby," said Tronics. "Circumstellar!" He shoved Zomo on her shoulder to psych her up.

The ship began its orbit and within moments its stellar curve exerted extra pressure on all of their bodies.

"Will our inertia negation system hold up, Tron?" asked Zomo, her voice shaky from the motion.

"Err...unlikely. In fact it's failing. Down to fifty percent."

"We will be knocked unconscious," shouted Nanonramu's unsteady voice.

"Hull integrity twenty percent. The aft section is breaking apart," informed Tronics. They all look up as the bridge's upper hull begun to bend inwards.

"*The ship will implode*!" cried Nanonramu at the top of his lungs.

"We just hit seven hundred and twenty G's," shouted Zomo. The only thing shakier than her words was the ship itself.

"Distance from the event horizon," informed Tronics. "Two point five AUs and rapidly decreasing." He then stared in wonder of the swirling illuminating particles that consumed them. "It's tearing apart space itself."

"Useful information only, Tronics. Stay focused," ordered Adcox.

Akerele bawled from the discomfort. Every time he breathed out, he gritted his teeth trying to maintain consciousness. *"I, can't, breathe!"* all of the crew experienced equivalent difficulty. Expelling air was barely manageable, but inhaling took a tremendous effort.

"Three...thousand...Gs...people.We're...well...within... gravity well." Informed Zomo, straining to speak, only able to glance at her monitor screen to see the simulation of their ship within the black hole's photon sphere and ergosphere. Inches away from the projected boundaries of the point of no return...the event horizon.

Even the mighty Rey'Jax's strength now began to buckle under the celestial force. He dropped on one knee, placing one hand on the ship's hull floor. Forced to endure the worst suffering, as his body mass was larger, the effects of gravity wreaked the worst havoc upon him. The great prince soon fell lifelessly on the bridge floor.

Using all of her skills, Zomo maneuvered through the debris but then a loud explosion jolted the ship. Her HUDs display registered their number two engine had taken a direct hit, the ship was breaking apart.

Struggling to breathe, struggling to even speak, Tronics continued to monitor the ship's systems. *"Life support...down. Inertia negation...fifteen percent and failing...Multiple...hull...fract...'* Before he could finish Tronics passed out. The effect of the gravitational force's magnitude on his brain pulled his blood down and away from his head and his heart was unable to pump hard enough to keep the flow going.

"Tronics, wake up!" hollered Adcox as forcefully as his lungs could allow him. Hatshepsut soon passed out too, followed by Nanonramu.

Akerele, and Adcox waned but held on as their suits steamed. Adcox was spooked when he turned to see the private's pupils starting to roll back into his head. Young Akerele shook his head trying to get a hold of himself, he spat out some blood. Jei'Gun's helmet masked his feelings but his breathing was much more controlled from the look of his composed body. Zomo also fared better than the others though not as well as the elite-shakan. Her experience as a pilot had helped her to endure the extreme G conditions. She witnessed great clouds of space debris being sucked into the black hole.

Soon a voice rung out on the bridge's speaker system, it was Eve. "The pod is now fully activated. Prepare for Dark matter tunneling. Rupture in the dark space fabric commencing. Flying officer Zomo, please change course and head directly towards the singularity."

In the cargo bay, Hawke lay inside the pod which shielded him from the gravitational force. The alien pod now emanated a dark purple glow and it surrounded the cuboid.

Zomo witnessed a dark purple glow envelope the ship and couldn't tell whether it had something to do with the space conditions or Eve activating the pod. She had no choice but to follow Eve's request. Zomo steered the ship deep into the belly of the collapsed star.

Suddenly darkness and silence consumed them.

Chapter Fourteen - Incalculable Intentions

The *Copernicus* entered through the dark matter space rift, and as it did, the purple and black energy field generated by the alien pod dissipated. What was revealed around them was empty space, and directly ahead, a planetoid body. So close to the planetoid was the ship, the Copernicus will be considered to be in near orbit. The ship, mangled and broken, streamed through the horizon inverted and on fire.

Zomo turned the ship right side up, though its inversion assisted Akerele's and Adcox's blood flow, yet they were still in shock from the gravitational pressure exerted upon them. Their mouths remained wide open and both their heads rolled with the turbulence as though their necks had no muscle strength left. Akerele's arms flopped at his sides. As a result of Zomo shutting off the gravity, small objects floated throughout the bridge including solar rifles and Tronics' data-slab.

"Sir, we have a system-wide electronic failure," Zomo said to her captain. Receiving no response she called out for him again. "Captain!"

Zomo's cries for help and his sense of responsibility pulled him back from the brink to full consciousness. "I'm with you. Barely." Adcox looked out of the viewing screen and spotted the blackened planetary landscape. "That looks like the planetoid Hawke mentioned.

"Affirmative! But the problem is it has atmosphere. In a minute we're going to burn up and break apart."

"Akerele, wake up Tronics," ordered Adcox, still disoriented, still bewildered. But his corporal's ingenuity and sharp mind in difficult situations was what he needed most right now.

Akerele attempted to disengage his safety harness but then vomited. In his condition, reaching Tronics was impossible.

Adcox shook his head trying to snap out of his dizziness. "Talk to me, Zomo!"

"Sir, we're about as aerodynamic as a tank right now. I can't keep the *Copernicus* airborne. I have to touch her down ASAP."

"Negative, flying officer!" said Hawke's voice on the comms. He attempted to get to the bridge but the turbulence and zero gravity combined bounced him between the ship's walls suspending him in mid-air. "Eve has uploaded a surface map of the planetoid. Land on grid coordinates 193885."

On Zomo's dashboard, the three dimensional map appeared. It had contours and cross sectional grid lines, as well as distance numbering. Grid 193885 highlighted in blue on the map.

"Major that grid is over thirty klicks away. We're flying on half an engine which is on fire. We need to land right now, sir."

"All right, set us down Zomo," said Adcox.

"Belay that flying officer. Head to the grid. I repeat, do not land," ordered Hawke.

"Sir, if we don't land, we could free fall and crash at any moment," replied Zomo.

"Then we crash!" said Hawke.

"What?" Adcox jaw dropped.

"I told you, the souwrak has lost mind," said Jei'Gun, conscious the entire time but silent until now. "It has contracted madness from the inmates within Abyss' depths."

"He could be right," said Akerele regaining his full senses. "Maybe that Horde pod has driven him skitso."

"Losing power to vertical control. Altitude dropping," Zomo informed the crew.

"Look Major, we need to land now," Adcox said.

"Don't do it!" said Hawke, spinning weightlessly around the ship's corridor.

"I'm in charge here, Hawke. Set the bird down, Zomo."

"Rey'Jax, stop them!" cried Hawke.

Adcox and Akerele turned and saw the Ariman unconscious, or perhaps dead, his giant fingers had torn holes through the floor.

All the floating objects dropped due to the effects of the planetoid's gravity pulling them back down as the ship fell through its skies.

Zomo steered the *Copernicus* towards the surface, but with a non-functional Instrument Landing System, the battered ship spiraled and hit the ground hard, breaking apart as it slid across the jagged landscape. The planetoid surface consisted of black rock and soil, with only a tint of blue across its uneven terrain. Aside from the hills, canyons and cliff walls, nothing existed.

Adcox opened his eyes and saw simply blackness. But then movement occurred, Rey'Jax revealed his colossal body, he had shielded Adcox from injury.

"Thank you," said Adcox. "Are you all right?" as he glanced at Rey'Jax's smoldering flesh.

"Yes!" The Ariman's voice was breathy, almost hoarse. "I require but moment to heal." He dropped down sluggishly, placing his hands on the ground.

Amongst the bridge's ruptured hull that still remained largely intact, Adcox saw Zomo rising in discomfort, surrounded by her smashed display and damaged interfaces, with a red bruise on her forehead. His mind then switched to the rest of the group.

"Akerele!" shouted Adcox, "see to Tronics."

His private dusted off the bits of debris that covered him and rushed to the electronics expert, nudging the corporal to get him conscious. Nanonramu came to on his own. Meanwhile, Adcox leaped to the lifeless body of Hatshepsut who lay on the ground still strapped to the chair which had broken off in the crash. He called out her name removing her from her harness. There were no signs of life no matter how hard he shook her.

"She's not responding. I don't think she's breathing," said Adcox.

"We must manually preserve her brain functions," said Nanonramu. "Quickly, move pale skin."

"CPR!" uttered Adcox. Remembering Hawke stating that the planetoid had breathable atmosphere, he retracted his helmet along with hers and began mouth to mouth, his pale white cheeks opposing her black skin marked by red tribal paint. His execution was methodical initially, breathing into her lungs via her big lips. But soon into the procedure his body language altered. He released his hand from Hatshepsut's nose and his dramatic start to the procedure now became...subtle. For him, the sensation was overwhelming. He felt like he was floating off of the euphoria. After a prolonged moment, Hatshepsut opened her eyes and he stared into her bright pink pupils, losing himself in the moment. The team looked on, confused by the event. They would had probably been more suspicious if not for the traumatic ordeal of the crash, coupled by being mesmerized by their new surroundings, visible through the wrecked bridge. Not to mention the fact it was unimaginable that human and Horaxian mouths would make contact for any reason other than necessity, and that was unlikely even still.

Tronics came to his feet at last and he joined in staring at the pair while rubbing his sore neck. "So Horaxians don't need chest compressions?" he pondered aloud looking bewildered. He turned around and saw Private Akerele's mouth and chin all bloodied and formed a look of disgust by his recollection of being woken up by him. "Aww, please don't tell me you gave me mouth to mouth, Akerele?"

Akerele spat out more blood. "No, I just ate a mouthful of your wife's curry goat and rice."

"Lucky you're still alive brother."

Nanonramu helped Hatshepsut back to her feet. "I advise an extra dose of inoculations should be administered, Doctor. Human germs are deadly."

They all exited what was left of the ship via the sizable rupture in the bridge hull.

"Where is the cursed one?" asked Nanonramu.

"Over there," Jei'Gun said as he pointed. Hawke stooped on a ridge two hundred meters away with his back towards the team.

"Damn good, flying soldier!" Adcox said with a smile.

"Thank you, sir!"

"Arigato, man!" said Akerele. "Good thing those kamikaze instincts didn't kick in, half pint." He used his forearm to push her in a playful way. She shoved him back even harder like a little sister would a big brother, showing that she was made of tough fiber.

Jei'Gun growled. "The female runt crashed our ship again, yet you congratulate her?"

"Request to salvage the tech, sir?" asked Tronics, being wise to Adcox's lack of leadership. I'd like to get the drone airborne."

"Ah yeah, good idea," said Adcox rubbing his armored gloves through his short black hair. "Zomo, as a contingency, could we get this ship operational?"

"Unless we find Merlin's magic wand down here that's a hard negative, Captain. All engines are fried."

"Great, just great," said Akerele. "So we don't go home unless we find this stinking mothership."

"Yes," snapped Jei'Gun, "hideous human, so stop your babbling and let us proceed."

Zomo surveyed her surroundings then looked up in the sky. "Notice something guys? Space here seems very dark."

Hatshepsut also looked to the sky. "There are no moons, no planets, no stars."

"No, they are there," said Hawke. Moments ago he was over two hundred meters away, now mysteriously he appeared right next to Adcox. "Our eyes just can't see them. Everything's different here." The young captain noticed that Hawke's eyes centered on Flying Officer Zomo. She had also realized, and tried to maintain her composure, but found it uncomfortable and she turned away.

"Hey what's wrong with you, man?" said Akerele at Hawke. "There was no way we could've made it to your grid. You trying to get us killed?"

"Most of you are better off dead now anyway, because we won't all make it to the grid," Hawke replied.

"Nonsense!" said Jei'Gun.

Adcox interjected. "Wait, hold up. The coordinates you gave to Zomo mustn't be more than twenty kilometers southeast from here. Now that's a march and a half on this uneven terrain but we can do it."

"Have you checked your compasses?" Hawke asked.

Adcox activated his helmet and it extracted over his head, which enabled him to check his navigation display on his HUD. He saw that the north needle of his compass spun wildly counter clockwise. "My magnetometer's gone insane!"

Tronics assessed the same effects on his data-slab. "The planetoid's surface must be composed of metals or magnetic properties."

Adcox deactivated his helmet. "All right, so I guess we're down to basic land navigation skills. Unless Eve might be able to help?"

"Eve is offline, Captain," Hawke said.

"Why is your ghost offline Urk'Tark?" asked Rey'Jax as he stumbled out of the Copernicus' hull in slow motion, suspicious as always of Hawke's behavior.

"Dark space entry caused a system overload. We've got other problems, Captain. Grid ID 193885 may no longer be where we must go by the time we get there."

"What do you mean, Mr. Hawke?" asked Hatshepsut.

"It means it has forgotten where it is," said Jei'Gun.

"As we said before, on this planetoid the geography constantly changes. At first we thought I was hallucinating. I wondered every inch of this place going insane. The target LZ will periodically change coordinates. 193885 was the grid ID Eve last positively detected the ship before her systems went down."

"So that's why you wanted us to stay in the air?" said Zomo.

"This is ridiculous!" Jei'Gun uttered as he walked away to assess the terrain himself.

"So how do we find Horde ship?" Nanonramu asked. He was comfortable with the darkness, the echolocation generated by his antennae extended his perception of his surroundings where his poor eyesight failed.

"I can still get us there. But we'll have to keep a steady, fast pace."

"So how do *we* locate it?" said Jei'Gun. "Just in case you have *unfortunate*...accident out here?"

"We're sure you'll be our hero Jei'Gun. No harm will come to us."

Akerele stepped toward Adcox, "Sir, I better recover what I can of the rations and munitions, especially the RPG. Workout what gear we have left and get it prepped."

"Right! Good idea."

"Sir!" They all turned and saw Tronics returning from inside the ship. "The UAV is still fully operational. I'm about to deploy her now." He lifted the gravity disruption weapon and placed it carefully on his back-hold.

"Better do it quickly, we need to move," ordered Adcox.

"Bird of Prey: online. Activate voice command," said Tronics.

"Status: online, voice command already activated," replied the monotone, computerized voice of the bird on his suit's transceiver. The eagle-robot was still out of sight within the ship's cargo bay.

"Bird of Prey: full system initialization!" commanded Tronics.

"Inertial navigation system, flight, weapons systems, sensors and surveillance systems: all activated. What are your orders, Corporal Manning?"

"Aerial reconnaissance," commanded Tronics.

"Acknowledged, activating flight mode."

"All right. Let's go baby. Initialize!"

"Initializing," said the drone. It broke through the hull wreckage in sight of the team, and flapping its quad-wings twice, took off into the air. The bird soon activated two bright spotlights which circled the area of the group.

"We don't want to hang around here too long, sir, trust me," said Hawke. "We're going to have company soon."

"What the hell do you mean?" asked the alarmed Zomo. "Is there something out here?"

"No, I think he means the swarm." Adcox said. "The Horde weren't coming for the space carrier, they were coming for us."

"Affirmative!" said Hawke.

"All right everyone, let's roll out," Adcox commanded. "Do you need a weapon Major?"

"Negative!" Hawke marched ahead.

"That's a relief," said Zomo as she came up close to Adcox.

***

In the vastness of luminous space, the *Sword of Damocles* waited at battle stations. They knew what was coming. On the bridge was General Baizan and Dr. Henry along with the ten bridge crew, all on high alert. Commodore Hussein stood next to Baizan, he was the most senior naval ranking officer of the space carrier. Although the flagship was officially under the commodore's command, Baizan commanded all operations while on board. Dr. Henry sat by himself, playing with a Horaxian rubix cube device, but it was spherical and shone green when he locked its moving parts into position.

"General Baizan, commodore, we're picking up the Polymorph swarm approaching our bow," Commander Xiao informed. He was the commodore's first officer.

"Go to red alert," ordered Baizan. "Arm all weapons, prepare to engage the enemy and put me on the comms, all hands."

"Aye aye, sir. You're on the comms."

"Crew of the *Sword of Damocles*, this is General James Baizan. A swarm is approaching. I want all crew members at battle stations." He turned to the senior naval officer. "I want those stellar-birds in the air, Commodore."

"We're launching the jets now, General," said commodore Hussein.

Commander Xiao interrupted. "Sir, the swarm has arrived."

A small, encircling purple energy materialized in space, and the spiraling iris swelled larger than the space carrier itself. Out emerged the Horde swarm. Two gigantic creatures appeared which were formed less like a ship built by a civilized race but bearing more resemblance to a Dunkleosteus or Megalodon, and other prehistoric fish. The enormous Horde whales matched the size of the space carrier as they glided through the ocean of space like interstellar sperm whales, with millions of organic material swirling around them of various sizes. The organic fragments were rock-shaped, but soft and malleable, and had a multitude of long vines coated with a slimy substance, some stretching over a hundred meters.

Within the whales' thick layer of skin contained hundreds of thousands of cocoons and an army of drones and brain Hordes. Surrounding the great beasts was a convoy of star rays in their thousands. The whales travelled short interstellar distances by propelling themselves using exhausted superheated gas. But this means of travel was only momentary while they reenergized themselves for their space jumps, made possible by their wielding of dark matter.

"Target the whales, fire missiles," ordered Baizan, balling his fist up. He'd rather be out here than surrounded in luxury and comfort. If only armed with a can opener he would charge the Horde front anyway, to the very last man.

"Firing missiles from battery one, sir," replied the commander. Eight long projectiles launched but as the missiles neared the whales the vine-rocks seemed to intentional move into their path. The warheads detonated upon contact with the encircling debris.

Baizan thumped the console. "Order fighter squadron alpha to clear a path through the swarm for missile bombardment. Get bravo squadron to concentrate their fire on the rays."

Eleven fighter spacecraft scrambled from the flight deck and headed straight for the swarm. A wide hull-gate opened from the ship's port side and nine more fighters scrambled out of hangar deck four.

Bravo squadron engaged the rays, killing vast numbers. Their assault provided adequate distraction for alpha squadron, who then concentrated their efforts on the dark green rock-like debris of protective boulders. Their missiles blasted a path through the debris-shield.

Both squadrons' action brought them under the attack of rays and while the fighter's weaponry were formidable, the rays vastly outnumbered them. The winged Horde had the ability to adapt to outer space conditions. In the absence of air for lift, they propelled themselves by the energy contained within their bulbed tails. The shrieking monsters swamped the fighter jets, destroying them all.

Still focusing on his puzzle device, Dr. Henry raised his hand. "Oh General?"

"Not now, Henry."

"Perhaps you should take note of their trajectory."

Commodore Hussein squinted his wrinkled eyelids. "They're coming straight for us. They're going to ram us."

"Yes," said Baizan, "and then probably try to infest the ship."

"Their moving fast," start the commodore. "We should maneuver..."

"We're not going anywhere. Commander, where are my AMBs?"

"We have four antimatter bombs ready to fire, General," replied Commander Xiao.

"Proceed."

"All four, general?" said the concerned Xiao.

"Affirmative!"

The four missiles shot out of the ship's rocket launchers; two detonated by smashing into the rocky debris, one was intercepted by sacrificial Horde rays. The remaining missile's obstacle avoidance system swirled it into a direct path with one of the giant whales. The shockwave from multiple megaton warhead detonations shifted the carrier's heading and rolled the *Sword of Damocles* along its longitudinal axis until its reaction control system kicked in. Its EMP shielding held, yet the lighting on its bridge and the display instrumentations flickered. Their viewing screens went black.

"Talk to me, people," said Commodore Hussein, as he and Baizan returned to their feet.

"Primary sensors are fried," informed the stocky commander, "it will take a moment for them to self-repair. The secondary sensors are coming online now."

They all watched the view screen flicker on, and larger than they had hoped to behold, the two whales emerged. Their reinforced skin resisted the bombardment, acting like the reactive armor of a tank to anti-tank missiles. Both of their sets of three blinking of eyes, each almost the size of a football pitch, haunted the bystanders as they neared collision.

As the whales drew closer they changed their angle upwards and soared straight above the *Sword of Damocles*.

"They're not attacking?" said Baizan.

"Looks like they are en route to somewhere else," calmly said Henry. "For *someone* else."

General Baizan's eyebrows rose once he realized what the doctor meant. "Hawke! They're headed for the mothership. If we can't stop them, least let's try to cripple them." He saw that one whales' fin was missing and its skin was severely damaged. Chunks of its flesh were blown off from the Antimatter bombs. "Commodore, I want all ship's weapons to target on that nearest whale and get charlie squadron to lay assault."

"Acknowledged, General!"

The space carrier's guns tracked the escaping swarm and out of hangar bay three another six jets flew off to attack the closest whale.

"Fire everything we've got," yelled Baizan. "Except for the AMBs and thermonukes. At this range, if the blast doesn't kill us the radiation would."

Clouds of smoke surrounded the gun batteries as they fired their ordinance and the compounded barrage devastated one of the whales. Eventually, it rolled over on its belly and fell past the ship's stern, succumbing to the onslaught.

The other whale shortly after began to glow purple. A narrow beam of energy emanated from its head and projected out into a near point in space. The focal point grew larger with each passing second, creating a rupture in the space fabric. As soon as the swarm entered into the rupture it closed and the energy dissipated.

***

In the unknown regions of dark matter space, the team marched on through arduous, uneven terrain, full of sharp-edged rocks and large crystallized spikes. A light mist formed as far as the eye could see no higher than at knee level and became a serious problem for most of the group.

Zomo panted, her eyes scanned all directions as she squeezed her rifle. Hatshepsut wondered how the team's unassisted breathing was possible on a floating rock with little atmosphere and supposedly no life. She scanned for biological readings. "I am detecting atmospheric readings that I just do not understand. Life form sensors are all saturated."

Nanonramu used his antennae to sense his surroundings. "This rock is completely barren, no water, no trees or grass, no life at all."

The blanketing white mist now rose to chest level. "The fog's getting thicker," Akerele said.

"Corporal," Adcox turned back to find Tronics. "Could you set the UAV to keep track of us?"

"Good idea. Bird of Prey: activate your geomapping and FLIR cameras and setup a thirty meter squared alert zone based on our heat signatures."

The bird of prey responded with its computerized voice from high above. "Initiating! Command complete, alert zone established. Tracking!"

"Good boy!" said Tronics.

In minutes, the mist consumed them entirely. Adcox's breathing increased and his muscles tensed up. He was having a mild panic attack and tried desperately to keep it concealed. The marines all raised their helmets to activate their HUDs Forward Looking Infrared surveillance but Tronics left his down and used FLIR sensors on his electronic slab instead. He turned to see the distress on the face of his friend and attempted to comfort him.

"Easy superman. Don't forget what I always tell you."

Adcox's panic eased and his despair transformed into a smile. "Yeah, stay black, I'm still working on that." Tronics had always had a tranquilizing effect on him since they were kids. Akerele and Zomo overheard them on the comms link and laughed.

"Well, I'd hurry up if I was you," said Tronic keeping a straight face.

Adcox felt a hand on his armor's shoulder and spun his head to see it belonged to Hatshepsut.

"Just in case I get lost in mist," she said to him.

To the captain's left, the elite-shakan watched Rey'Jax far behind the group threading at the slowest pace. He shouted out to him. "Mighty Ariman, do not stray too far behind. This mist treacherous vanishes even your prodigious stature, to fatal lost."

"Worry not knight, I can see clearly through the fog, and I can still track your scent if my vision grossly impaired." Even through the mist Rey'Jax's retina picked up blue florescent glows emitted by the team's bodies invisible to all but him. His eyes were covered by a thick membrane, reflective to any glimmer of light in the darkness much like the big cats of Kepler-62f, Gaia Major and Earth before them when animals once roamed wild. "I can hear something. A low frequency," said the Ariman.

"I think I hear it too. Some kind of tremor," said Zomo.

Before long they all heard the loud smashing sound of boulders falling from a height and moments after the ground shook.

"Damn this fog!" said Zomo, she turned in every direction, weapon high, searching, her heart palpitated.

"I'm not getting paid enough for this," Akerele murmured as he shook his head.

As he spoke, Tronics discovered something on his digital device. "I'm picking up serious seismographic activity. There's some kind of geological event happening right now."

The mist thinned to a minimum amount of opacity and revealed a miraculous sight. The geography had changed completely. A mountain stood in front of them, stretching miles across in either direction.

"How did this get here?" said Nanonramu. "We would have seen it before," glancing up at the formidable mountain.

"This is ridiculous," Private Akerele aimed his comments at Hawke. "How are we ever going to find this ship if mountains keep appearing out of nowhere?"

"Pipe down, Private, that's an order," said Zomo, growing tired of his constant complaining. It only served to make her ordeal more difficult.

"I don't get paid enough to pipe down, dwarf."

"Is there any way around, Major?" asked Tronics.

"Negative!"

"Akerele, let's get out the umbilical," said Adcox.

Akerele pulled out a thin extractable cable from his metal backpack and attached it to his utility belt, then proceeded to connect it to each person's belt. When he attempted to attach it to Jei'Gun he was pushed back almost off his feet.

"Be gone!" said the elite-shakan. Utilizing his superior upper body strength, he started climbing, stabbing his arm blade into the rock to support himself.

As Jei'Gun led the way, Hawke then followed using more skill than brute strength, also unattached to the rest of the group. After linking the climbing cord to everyone, Akerele then looked at Rey'Jax.

"Halt!" The Ariman raised his hand up. "Do not...tiny man, for if I fall survive I will but my weight will drag you all down to your doom."

"Yeah, that's...that's not a good look," said Akerele.

Adcox prepped himself for the climb, he pulled out the Ariman shield handle and decided to place it on his fist in case of the unexpected.

"All right," said Zomo "Oluseun Akerele, time you put those climbing skills you learned in the jungle to good use."

"Just get out the way and don't stare at my ass."

"Keep dreaming!" she shot back.

Akerele began his climb and the rest followed, placing their weapons on their magnetized back-hold. The human team all had small boot spikes which they activated via their forearm controls, allowing them to better grip the mountain edge. For the unskilled rock climbers in combat armor it was a punishing task, further complicated by the rock face's peculiar and inexplicable tendency to deform its shape at their arm and foot holds.

As the team reached their half-way point, the mountain shook. First to sense the danger, Hawke reacted, stabbing his sword into the mountain face. The quaking elevation fractured, breaking away chunks of black rock. It took Jei'Gun off guard as he reached for a protruding crimp and he fell. But he was caught by none other than Adcox. The young captain's suit built-in hydraulics systems which reduced the effect of his armor's weight, blew its arm valves taking the brunt of Jei'Gun's heavy mass. But it wasn't enough. Adcox felt as those his shoulder had dislocated. He cried out, his other hand gripping the mountain face with slipping fingertips.

"Somebody help!" Adcox gasped, his biceps near bursting from the unsustainable strain.

Tronics watched his friend and the elite-shakan swaying in the icy, howling wind and raced to assist them. The Anubianite warrior was certain the human would drop him at any minute due to his constant insults, yet the same scrawny, undeveloped arms that disgusted him not so long ago held on. Its armored joints leaking hydraulic fluid.

Smaller stones and debris fell from the top of the mountain down on them as the tremors worsened. Akerele, higher than the rest, was hit by the falling rock. Losing his grip, he fell. The climbing piton helping to support the team's weight was then also struck by falling debris. It dislodged, and the addition of Akerele's body weight caused Adcox lose his only grip and fall, followed by Tronics, carrying Jei'Gun along with them.

Zomo, who was underneath, had no time to place her spike firmly into the rock and she was also pulled down, followed by Hatshepsut and Nanonramu, all to their doom. But luckily the Ariman's humongous arm extend outwards and grabbed Private Akerele saving them all from death. He told Akerele to wrap the cabling around his waist which he did and then Rey'Jax began climbing, pulling the whole team up. Hawke himself fought to hang onto the tremoring mountain face.

"Look out!" Hatshepsut screamed.

A large boulder fell towards them at a speed too great to dodge, but as it neared Rey'Jax swatted it away as if it was an Ariman blood fly. The impact of his hand against the rock released a lingering cackle against the mountain's hard surface. The Aboriginal male now reached level with Hawke and squinted his eyes at him as both their long hair swung with the wind. The major looked away from his scornful gaze. Rey'Jax glanced down at the rest of the team hanging on and dependent on him, then he continued his ascent hauling them all with him. With the exception of Hawke who made his own way up. All the while the Bird of Prey circled around the team.

Rey'Jax arrived at the mountain top and pulled the team up over its edge. Hawke, the last to make the climb.

Adcox surveyed the desolate landscape and felt the wind pick up with an eerie whistle. He knew it was a sign of trouble ahead. They marched onward on the blackened, cracked, parched field of rumble and craters, pieces of dry ground blew into the air. Adcox had to administer a pain releaser for his busted shoulder, but his armor's nanotech would repair his damaged arm motors and valves with a little time.

"People, I'm picking up some wind speed here," said Tronics monitoring the anemometer embedded in his device. "Looks like its increasing."

At that moment Hawke stopped dead, staring into the distance. Adcox could sense something had rattled him but he refused to speak. So they all waited with increasing tension.

"Everyone get down and hold on to something, now!" demanded Hawke.

The team looked up ahead and saw a wall of wind and dust heading towards them. But the barren land provided little to shield themselves with.

"Get behind me, quickly!" shouted Rey'Jax.

"Bird of Prey: climb to high altitude," commanded Adcox, bracing for the ferocious dust storm. Hundred and twenty miles per hour wind roared and swept all the team off their feet. Rey'Jax and Jei'Gun were the only ones strong enough to withstand the wind force. Yet the elite-shakan warrior could hardly move forward. But the two tons of Ariman muscle and bone anchored him, allowing him to advance. The remaining team formed a chain of bodies suspended in mid-air holding onto each other just before Rey'Jax stood in front to shield them. Even Jei'Gun and Hawke were forced to seek cover behind him. Despite his strength, the aboriginal Horaxian had to make sure footings on each stride as his long locks and plaited beard blew wildly. After a while, the others were able to regain their footing but they still had to stand within the Ariman's wake.

Eventually the wind calmed. As it did, the team realized that the terrain had changed once again. Now the ground became soft and their feet sank into the black mud up to most of their shins.

"Better keep your helmets retracted," said Adcox. "Conserve your air supply."

"Human Corporal," Nanonramu called out to Tronics. "Have you attempted using metal bird to scan for mothership?"

"Don't waste your time," said Hawke.

"Who asked you, demon?" said Jei'Gun. Rey'Jax watched Hawke suspiciously, even Adcox who saw sense in the Rogue's comment found the major's statement peculiar.

"You, tinkerer!" Jei'Gun pointing to Tronics. "Use robot, now."

Tronics' composure rendered him incapable of being offended by the inappropriate manner of Jei'Gun's request. He used his device to connect wirelessly to the UAV's optical sensors and relayed imagery. "I've already sent the bird out to survey the terrain but so far I've got zero on geophysics. Nothing on magnetotellurics or thermographics. I can't create any kind of tomography of this rock. But I'm no geologist."

"Dark matter has no emissivity," said Hawke. "It's cloaking the ship."

As they continued their march the muddy wasteland worsened and the shorter team members, Akerele and Zomo, were over waste deep. Rey'Jax however had an easy time and he picked up the five foot two Zomo throwing her over his shoulder without asking, noticing her difficulties.

"Thank you, mighty Rey'Jax," she said.

The rest of the team had to suffer the ordeal of wading in the thickening mud.

"Major," called Adcox. "Was it this bad before when you were here?" The ever thickening mud was taking its toll and he keep his weapon high as he could.

"It was much worse. It's going to keep changing and keep getting worse. This is just the beginning."

"Just as Dr. Henry said," Hatshepsut spoke out. "I think that dark matter is a transmutable substance once energy is induced into it."

"You mean it can somehow speak?" questioned Akerele.

"Brother," said Tronics laughing, "that there, that was pretty dumb. I can't lie."

Zomo shook her head at him and Private Akerele shrugged his shoulders as to say "what did I do?"

Hatshepsut continued. "Matter changes state with temperature and pressure, both which are forms of energy. Dr. Henry said dark matter also changes but not just its state. It can completely change what it is."

Adcox theorized. "So the geography is changing because...well, essentially energy is being applied to it?"

"We believe the ship might be pumping energy into the dark matter and creating all the conditions we're are experiencing."

"It would make sense as to why we are able to breathe," said Hatshepsut. "Perhaps there is water or liquid nitrogen somewhere on planetoid and the ship is pumping electricity into it, producing gaseous oxygen and nitrogen."

"Still," Tronics said, battling with the mud. "That doesn't explain the sea level atmospheric pressure and the gravity, unless the dark matter is creating that too."

"Perhaps the geography transformations are some kind of defensive mechanism," said Adcox.

"Whatever you do," warned Hawke, "don't fall asleep or pass out here. The psychological effect of falling unconscious on an open plain and waking up buried fifteen feet under solid rock is soul destroying. Trust me." His words terrified Zomo who had been quiet for most of the journey.

As Adcox treaded through the black muck he noticed that he'd stepped on something which had a different property than that of the natural ground. He reached to the ground trying to feel his way through.

"Guys, I've just stepped on something," said the captain.

He handed his rifle to Tronics then sank both arms into the black liquid which now flowed with a viscosity close to water, but his muscles hadn't the strength to hoist the object out. Nanonramu came to his assistance still yet their strength combined couldn't lift it fully out of the liquid. It was a metal plate forged into a smoothed curved shape.

"What the hell's that?" asked Akerele.

Rey'Jax lowered his eyebrows which formed wrinkles in the skin of his forehead. His eyes narrowed and straighten, tension traversed through his lips and mouth. All triggered by the sight of the object. "It is what remains of combat armor."

They all turned to Hawke, who himself seemed to be having trouble dealing with the sight of the discovered armor, refusing to look at it. Jei'Gun was stuck in suspended animation within the dark waters as he identified the broken fabricated metal.

"Combat armor of what?" asked Zomo.

"Nephilim," said the Ariman prince. "The Black Guard."

Hatshepsut's eyes inspected it. "By the size of chest plating it must have been giant. There are huge lacerations on the left scapula and humerus area as well as evidence of blunt force trauma."

Akerele became jumpy at the site. Nanonramu in a flash released his grip and the metal sank back into the liquid.

"It was ripped apart!" said Rey'Jax angrily.

"Friends of yours?" Jei'Gun said to Major Hawke.

"Perhaps you can explain, Major?" said Adcox.

Hawke paused in reluctance before he decided to open his mouth. "When our squadron crashed here, all their Symbiotic Program Units malfunctioned upon dark space entry, just as Eve did and the *Copernicus'* electronics. The Nephilim's sole purpose was to kill. Their SPUs kept them in check, once they malfunctioned..."

"They became relentless killing machines but with nothing to kill," said Hatshepsut.

"So you turned on each other?" asked Adcox.

Rey'Jax with his huge fist struck a tall rock and smashed it, jolting Zomo sideward on his shoulder. The top half of the rock split and slid down to the other side of the base. His prison collar activated. Three status lights turned on with high pitched clicks. "Not the first time you murdered your own brothers." Rey'Jax said in disgust. Hawke turned his head away from him.

"It's all right, big guy," said Zomo, gripping on to the oversized forehead area of his battle helmet.

The Ariman calmed and the collar's lights turned off.

"We should keep moving," said Hawke.

As the former Black Guard commander took off, the group shared the same thoughts; how could the cursed one survive in battle against what once wore that giant armor? Its size must have been close to the mightiest one, Rey'Jax, and its strength not far off, and not just one, but an entire squadron of perhaps over thirty Black Guard Nephilim? This one being?

Nanonramu ventured close to Jei'Gun so his words would go undetected. "The demonic Black Guard's SPU contraptions were shut down. The Hawke's ghost is now also offline. His mind may have become corrupted just like the others. Craven for blood."

Jei'Gun opened his mouth guard to spit out a brown substance, his usual custom. The substance reacted with the soil and the ground bubbled then sank. He still felt the pain in his crushed hand making his anger swell. "Be on the ready to kill it. Jei'Gun will not die by its hands." As the elite-shakan spoke he turned to Rey'Jax as though concerned.

They marched on, and with the disappearance of the mud, Rey'Jax took Zomo off his shoulders. Once again the geography changed. Everywhere around them crystal rock formed, some were small; others grew before their eyes as large as hills. The temperature dropped suddenly making most of them shiver. Except for Jei'Gun, and the Ariman who benefited from the first nation's inhospitable environment. His skin, super resilient, combined with his mass, kept him well insulated.

Fatigue came upon the group after the hard trek through the muggy liquid. They now found themselves in a field of tree-like structures made of brittle crystals which rose eleven feet in the air. The trees behaved more like vines intertwining and obscuring their path. Jei'Gun, Nanonramu and Hawke used their blades to cut through the crystal vines but their progress wasn't quick enough for Zomo, whose head spun around constantly. The vines created a feeling of entrapment.

Adcox took the opportunity to catch up with Hawke who led the way meters ahead.

"If I were you, Captain, I'd watch out for your flying officer."

"How did you know it was me coming up on you?" said the puzzled Adcox since Hawke had detected his presence without needing to turn around.

"Lucky guess."

"So what's wrong with Zomo?"

"She's got Nyctophobia."

Chapter Fifteen - In Comes The Tide In The Affairs Of Men

"What the hell's Nyctophobia?" asked the bewildered Adcox.

"The doctor will tell you." Without turning around, he also somehow was able to identify Hatshepsut coming up behind them. Yet the former Black Guard commander appeared focused on whatever lay ahead.

"Hey Hatshepsut, what is Nyctophobia?"

"It is an acute fear of darkness."

The youthful commanding officer was disappointed in himself that he hadn't recognized this before. He now realized why she outwardly objected to going into the Abyss to the colonel. It must have been torture for her yet she held it all in.

"I'm going to go and check on her."

As Adcox left for his young comrade, he turned back noticing Hatshepsut and Hawke talking. Although they were out of hearing range, judging by Hatsheput's body language, their conversation was not a light-hearted one.

"How you holding up, Zomo san?" Adcox asked. She attempted to lie but her increased distress levels forced her head down. The crystal jungle was too much for her.

"Sir...I'm...I'm struggling here. In the air I'm fine but...well...' Akerele arrived next to her and her eyes swelled with tears. "We always had the colonel and Lewalski before. I mean I know it's selfish but I just wish Ballistic was here on point. They all kind of took the edge off, you know? We never had to worry."

"I know how you feel." Adcox smiled.

"Yeah I thought I was the only one," said Akerele.

Zomo raised back up her rifle as she sniffled and clear her throat. "But we got you now, Captain."

"Roger that, you've got me."

"Thanks for sticking with us," she said sniffling.

"Yeah, we won't let you down, sir," said Akerele.

"Hey," said Adcox in an uncharacteristically authoritative voice. "You'll never need to worry about letting me down. If we fail, as commanding officer I'm responsible. But we're not going to fail."

The poor girl. Despite her amazing abilities, she was merely seventeen years old. Adcox had only now begun to realize how much these young marines depended on him.

"Let's go ladies," said Akerele mimicking their former Captain Lewalski's raspy voice. "Don't be flattered, Zomo. Your face is like a Cungan's back." Zomo tried to punch him in the face but missed. "Hairy, with white spots." He laughed his head off.

Ahead of his fellow marines, Tronics tried to keep a visual track of the Bird of Prey through the overhead crystal mesh. Not watching where he stepped he bumped into the back of Jei'Gun.

"Watch it, souwrak!" The Anubianite warrior lifted his blade inches from Tronics' face. After pausing to let his temper simmer down Jei'Gun continued forward.

Tronics was accustomed to daily threats by Bronze and Lewalski, as well as his wife even before that. So he never feared the elite-shakan warrior unlike the rest, more due to foolishness than bravery. "Mate, you need to lighten up you know that," he said, with his usual composed East London dialect.

"Disgusting creature. Jei'Gun has no desire to mate with you, and Jei'Gun is as *light* as genetically possible, pale skin. Keep your distance."

"Pale skin? I think the atmospherics is messing with your visual sensors."

"Compared to the absoluteness of Horaxian skin, *all* humans are pale."

Tronics saw his point. His blackness was more of a dark brown. But Horaxians were void of any color, of any shade, their skin had a richness to it like smooth black marble. The tech soldier noticed Jei'Gun's attention centered on Rey'Jax as he watched the Ariman use his chest to break through the crystals branches.

"Rey'Jax is pretty tough, huh?" said the engineer.

"Yes, he is. The ultimate warrior."

"Did you mans ever used to hang out before?"

Jei'Gun turned to him, agitated by the ridiculous manner in which the corporal addressed him but he struggled to get mad by his sincere approach. It was the first time a human had ever asked him something unrelated to a necessity. "The Arima nation rebelled against High Apex, against imperial crown, we could never...*hang out*." Jei'Gun paused. "But long before their insurrection, Anubianites worshiped people of first nation as living gods. To stand with royal bloodline that spawned our race is most rarest of privilege indeed."

"I hear you, brother."

"Jei'Gun is not your brethren!" yelled the Horaxian, halting his movement. After staring down the corporal he continued his march.

"Well, I'm just glad we have his strength on our side."

"Strength and glory upon battlefield are what we of Unyielding Anubia value above all. But he has something else Jei'Gun has longed for but never truly possessed. He has honor, that is something a warrior, a true warrior must die not without."

"If you value honor so much, you should give my boy Adcox a break..."

"Arghh! A child in man's armor is still but a child. Only your half metal human sergeant had any heart infused within him."

"Adcox has got heart. Well I mean he hasn't got heart but, he cares about everyone, even you. He's the most honorable man I know."

Jei'Gun wanted to object to Tronics' words but then remembered how Adcox saved his life by refusing to let go of him on the cliff edge. His voice then softened. "That, maybe the only thing your friend holds of worth. The only reason why Jei'Gun has not sliced his un-aged throat...yet."

Tronics ignored Jei'Gun's last words, since he had finally laid eyes on the Bird of Prey through an opening.

"All right, son. Whatever you say," said the marine distracted by the Bird.

Jei'Gun halted. Once more he extracted his arm blade and turned slowly to the engineer. "What, did, you, call me *baboon*?" His yell was loud enough to catch everyone's attention.

Tronics promptly move away from Jei'Gun seeing his limited allowance had been breached.

Moments later Adcox caught back up with Hawke and Hatshepsut who led the expedition meters ahead far enough away from the group that words can go unheard. "Major Hawke! Thanks for the heads up about Zomo. Also, I'm sorry I went against you back on the ship. You know I got a lot of respect for you and..."

"Save it, sir. We understand, you were protecting your team. It's your unit."

"It's not easy, being a leader, making the right call."

"You're our commanding officer. Every call you make is the right call." Hawke paused for a moment. "But perhaps...you should have brought the sergeant along."

"Ballistic? Come on, he was injured."

"He looked fine to us, slight scratch on his arm..."

"The guy's arm was severed off by chuckles back there."

"That's no big deal!"

"No big deal?" repeated Adcox flabbergasted. "We're not Black Guard Nephilim expendable killing machines that can just be thrown into the fi...'" Realizing the harshness of his words, he stopped himself. "I'm sorry. I didn't mean that."

"It's all right, Captain."

"I know the loss of your brothers at arms must have been difficult."

"You focus too much on ability and not enough on the strength of will. Ballistic's presence would have boosted your squad's morale."

"Sir, I don't think Ballistic was well, and I...I don't just mean physically."

"Perhaps. But perhaps *he is* well and it's everybody else that's sick. He was willing to sacrifice and endure pain to protect his team. We won't win this war without men of conviction. As for the Nephilim, they were my men, and in a twisted sense I considered them like my children. But to me they were never brothers. The Arimans were the only real kin I ever had."

"Sir, what made you turn against them, may I ask?"

Hawke paused a while, deciding whether to answer. "I felt all alone in the concentration camp, my mother died being dissected like a fish, my father, tortured to death then lobotomized. They made me watch them throw his body to Ariman lions, but the chemicals used to torture him were so abominable the beasts wouldn't go near his rotting corpse. Little did I know it wouldn't be the last prison I'd escape from."

"You were the boy that killed the elite-shakan." Adcox didn't need Hawke to confirm it.

"The Ariman Kalinda grand master found me and adopted me. The Arima nation kept themselves isolated from their Horaxian descendants. They held no ill will against mankind and opposed the war. Rey'Jax and I lived as brothers. One day I was told by my mentor to return to humanity, against my desires, may I add. But I never felt I belonged amongst mankind. Hell, I've still never even been to Earth. There's only one place I see as home. You must wonder how I can fight and kill Horaxians when only they have ever shown me love in its purest form?" Hawke paused a moment then continued. "The fog of war impairs the vision. Cagn wanted to neutralize the Black Guard threat, but also, he was afraid of the Arima Nation. In an ingenious move to eliminate both threats, he launched a strike on Arima and blamed it on the Black Guard. We didn't know the Arimans were coming to battle us on Cyclonis but when they arrived, my Nephilim attacked. I was caught in the middle and as a soldier I had to act. But to answer your question, it was evil personified and made flesh that forced our hand against my own. Cagn."

Hatshepsut, baring witness to the entire conversation, felt sorrow for Hawke. Although she could never agree with his killer instinct, she understood that he was a product of a cruel fate no man should ever have to endure. The branches of his life, poisoned inescapably by their infected roots.

"So what happened after that?" asked Adcox.

"We managed to convince my brothers of Cagn's lies and they launched an insurrection. But with their ranks decimated after Cyclonis, Cagn moved against them with the might of his clandestine elite-shakan guard and launched surgical strikes catching them unawares. Most were killed. Rey'Jax as prince of his people was enslaved to dishonor him and as a symbol of Cagn's power."

"Such terrible fate!" said Hatshepsut sadden by Hawke's words, a solitary tear rolled down her cheek. "And now Prince Rey'Jax vows to end your life, so I have heard?"

"Because of his code, Rey'Jax won't make attempt on our lives until everything is over. That's one of the reasons why we brought him. He is the only person we knew we could trust. One more thing you should know. Arimans have heightened senses. Even far away he can hear everything we say."

Adcox checked behind him and saw Rey'Jax staring at Hawke, as he'd done for every second they've been on the planetoid, at a distance he thought impossible for their conversation to be heard. Only now his enlarged face, partially concealed by his giant helmet, had become one of sorrow. The captain was humbled by the Hawke's sacrifice to condemn his life to Rey'Jax in return for desperately needed help. He admired the major's courage to make the ultimate sacrifice, first back on the ark, his bravery on Kemeta, now here and perhaps countless times before for whatever he believed in.

Yet the young marine wondered if an end to such a turmoiled existence was exactly what Hawke desired and who better than his noble brother still esteemed in his eyes. Adcox looked at the dark skinned, braided haired man and could tell that his eyes had seen too much but yet were still determined to see the end goal fulfilled. The Black Guard commander was every bit of the legend he thought, and he now found himself beginning to draw strength vicariously through this legendary source. "Colonel Bronze was right, the Sword in the Dark is the key." He whispered to himself.

***

The team had made it past the crystal jungle and arrived to crater-filled open plains.

"Alert, alert!" said the robotic voice of the Bird of Prey soaring low through the pure black sky. "Aperture radar has detected non-human and non-Horaxian spacecraft."

"It has discovered mothership?" Hatshepsut said.

Rey'Jax stared behind them up into the sky with intense focus, his telescopic vision like a sniper scope. "No...Horde, they are here!"

"Readings confirmed," said the Bird of Prey. "Spacecraft has been identified, Horde ship is on an intercept course."

Tronics vented. "Well merrily merrily, life is such a dream out here. Ain't no mountain high enough for these guys."

***

Miles away from the team, the animal-like ship hovered high in the air. The hardened outer-skin layer over its mouth opened revealing a fleshy membrane and out of the moist, mucus secreting sublayer shot out thousands of cocoons. As they hit the ground, out hatched fully formed Horde drones.

A wave of panic swept in amongst the expedition team, they raised their weapons preparing for war.

"This is just what we needed," commented Adcox. "Tronics, how much time we got?"

"The whale has stopped advancing. It's stationary, four klicks east. I'd say we've got twenty minutes before this becomes a bad neighborhood."

"Okay, okay...ahh," blabbered Adcox. "Dig in and take up defensive positions."

Hatshepsut intervened. "Captain, we cannot withstand Horde wave. We must get to the mothership before it shifts position again, otherwise doomed we will be." Hatshepsut, though unskilled in the art of war saw the futility in the commanding officer's orders.

"What do you suggest?" Nanonramu asked, turning to Hawke. He remembered the Black Guard's strategic genius on Kemeta and warmed to him now in this time of need. Jei'Gun turned his helmet to Nanonramu with no doubt a bewildered look on the face underneath it.

"Sir, I recommend a Parthian shot," said Hawke, "retreat and keep moving while we lay down suppressing fire to impede their advance. We should be able to get to the ship before their numbers swell."

"This is absurd," said Private Akerele. "We're never going to find this magical ship now. The Horde's going to cut us down. Now the major crashed here fifteen years ago right? Right?"

"So what's your plan, brother man?" asked Tronics.

"It might be easier to find the wreckage of his ship instead."

"That's not a bad idea, Akerele," replied Adcox. "Its flight recorder should still be operational. Tronics and Zomo can then use the spare parts to repair the *Copernicus*."

"...and we can get the hell out of here," said Akerele.

"What are our chances of finding this mothership, Hawke?" asked Adcox.

"We can find it, I guarantee you."

"Our mission will be incomplete if we stray from chosen path," said the Ariman, a rare moment of siding with Hawke. "For now, Urk'Tark's words we should follow. Horde's evil will soon blanket us. Prepare yourselves." Rey'Jax stood in front of the team and loudly addressed them. "These dark stones have served as our tormentors. Now may they serve as our enemies' unmarked graves.

Bleach them with their blood, and break them with echoes of your battle cries."

"I have theory," said Hatshepsut, she had spent a long time in silent contemplation. "I think the mothership is reacting to our presence just like antibodies in our physiology."

"We are like...virus?" Nanonramu asked.

"Correct," said the exobiologist. "Dr. Henry said the mothership predated Horde. It might see Horde as hostile foreign body also."

"We haven't got time for this," said Akerele.

"Wait, Ack. So what, Doc?" asked Zomo, wanting to see where the doctor was going with this.

"So we have just brought more viruses to the host..."

Captain Adcox interjected. "If that's true, the planet's geophysical reactions are going to start getting a lot more severe."

"If ship acts as would organism," said Rey'Jax, "then that would make it sentient."

"It's possible," Adcox replied, "however it could just be an auto defensive measure. If the ship is alien to the Horde, then at least we've got one advantage. Hawke is the only one familiar with it and perhaps this terrain, amongst us and the Horde."

"Bird of Prey, change of orders," Tronics said via radio communication link to the UAV. "Horde counter-offensive mode."

"Command acknowledged, counter offensive mode engaged."

"Take care of yourself my friend," said Hatshepsut watching the bird circle wide.

The team doubled their pace, as they did, more seismic events occurred. To them, it felt like the planetoid was breaking apart as the flat ground they journeyed on spontaneously transformed, rotating from hills and valleys. Jei'Gun and Nanonramu moved away from prying ears as they traverse the difficult terrain, all accept Rey'Jax's for obvious reasons. "Oh great one!" Jei'Gun called out addressing the even bigger Horaxian male. "You perceive all, but even if Jei'Gun could, Jei'Gun does not hide his words."

"Then breach them, Anubianite. You have my audience."

"Your hatred for the cursed one runs deep but shallows compared with my own, and yet Jei'Gun ponders, how does one locate something that moves constantly? The souwrak thinks us fools. Jei'Gun does not believe it knows where we are going."

"What deeply concerns me, esteemed knight of Unyielding Anubia, even more so than Horde's wrath...is that he knows exactly where he leads us."

***

The *Sword of Damocles* drifted in the depths of space, systematically exterminating the remnants of the Horde. It was easy for Baizan to pick off the strays which he tried to accomplish without delay as no one knew if the amount of rays left over were enough biological material to transform into another more destructive Horde species.

As General Baizan stood with the commodore deeply engaged in battle planning, Commander Xiao interrupted their conversation.

"General Baizan, we've just been hailed by United Earth destroyer C. L. R. James which is approaching Polaris Sigma, sir."

"Put them onscreen!" replied Baizan, the four stars on his shoulders gleaming in the bridge's light. He rose up from his seat with wide opened eyes and a menacing stare. The entire crew of the bridge froze with anxiety, every living creature with a conscious had feared the location known as Polaris Sigma and any reference to it, for it had the star which bound death incarnate.

"Aye aye, sir!" said Commander Xiao.

An image of the C. L. R. James' bridge came onto the viewing screen. The commanding officer, Rear Admiral Hall, stood center screen, his face covered with distress. He saluted General Baizan with the only arm he possessed before speaking.

"General Baizan, moments ago we lost contact with the Horaxian warship The Virtuous Sword that was stationed in orbit of the neutron star. We just pulled images off a probe in the Polaris Sigma system. Sir, take a look at what we found at the warship's last known coordinates."

The screen flickered to an image of The Virtuous Sword, more accurately, the wreckage that remained. Drifting large fragments of bulkhead walls, blown off multiple-barrel rotary cannons and worst of all, hundreds of floating bodies of dead Horaxian warriors.

Dr. Henry stopped playing with his contraption to take a closer look. "Judging by the fragmentation the ship was completely disintegrated by an immense force."

The Rear Admiral returned on screen. "General, we've lost track of MK1."

If Baizan had multiple serious levels his highest setting had just been activated. The closest human world to Polaris Sigma was Biosphere-9, his home, and the Centaurian in him yelled out deep inside like medieval warriors in a phalanx.

"Threat level code Avalon," Baizan blasted out. "Rear Admiral, maintain high alert and fall back to an orbit around Biosphere-9. The *Sword of Damocles* will rendezvous with you there and once we get there, be prepared to fight to the last man." Before he could move into action the general overheard an officer on the bridge of the C. L. R. James.

"Rear Admiral Hall, sir, sensors have just picked up an unidentified object heading our way with speed," said Hall's executive officer.

MK1 finally emerged, soaring through space. No longer were sections of its body torn away and broken into swirling metal fragments. It had reformed and solidified into a silver, metal body. On its back were wing-like metal structures which moved as it flew yet without flapping, resembling more a bat's wings than a birds. It joined its arms and fist together in a forward position and as it held them there, a blue energy build-up occurred beginning at the robot's center and travelled up via its shoulders to the forearms. The intense energy beam was unleashed, hitting the ship and obliterating it.

On the bridge of the *Sword of Damocles*, a bright blue light and accompanying screams engulfed the viewing screen before it all went black and silent. Not one soul on Baizan's ship moved.

"Its power is incredible," said Henry, who seemed more excited than concerned.

"Whatever," replied Baizan, the only man unfazed, his mood had gone foul. "I want that thing tracked, now."

"Telemetry from deep space probe *Rigon* has just detected an unidentified object approaching us fast," said a Lieutenant. "Analysis confirms its MK1, sir."

"Perhaps," said Dr. Henry, "when the Hawke reactivated the pod it sent out some type of beacon. In which case MK1 is also headed for the mothership."

"Not if I can help it," said General Baizan, his tone reflecting his determination. "Commander Xiao, put us on an intercept course."

The broad first officer delayed the general's request and glanced at his commodore who knew exactly what he was thinking. Then he responded to the general. "Sir, that thing just took out two warships. What in the world are we supposed to do?"

"I didn't stutter son. I don't repeat myself either," Baizan said.

***

Back in dark matter space, the team were on the move and quickened their pace.

"Here they come," shouted Jei'Gun. "Let it begin."

They halted upon sight of the large flock of the Horde ray vanguard and braced themselves for an imminent assault.

Adcox told Hatshepsut to stay close to him and they shared a glance for a moment. She seemed more nervous now than she did on Kemeta. He badly wanted to comfort her, desiring to hold her only for a brief moment. This could be the last time they saw each other. But he stopped himself in fear of prying eyes. He couldn't. Just as their races were unprepared for the Horde, they were even less ready for what the young man longed for in his heart.

"Good luck, Diomedes!" she uttered.

Jei'Gun looked at their exchange, sensing more meaning to their closeness than purely protection. It was his duty as an imperial knight to protect the crown and all of the great supreme king's monarchical family. He knew of little reason why the female, who was eighth in line for the crown, would choose to seek protection from one other than himself, who represented an order which had guarded her ancestors since ancient times.

Adcox felt his panic attacks returning to haunt him. As he watched his rifle shaking due to his nervous hands, it served to hasten his breathing and worsen his distress. Rey'Jax positioned himself by Adcox's side to ensure his safety. He noticed sweat dripping onto the stellar marine's chest plate and the big male stooped to speak to him softly so no one could hear. "Why fear inevitability, young one? Arimans are forged to endure time, but when your Earth gods molded your kind to their image, never did they share their immortality. Your weapon arm is weak through lack of adversity. Its trembles can only be sturdied by purpose, and only great peril can unite purpose with strength."

"Incoming!" screamed Akerele looking at the rays diving into weapons range.

The team fired on the winged monstrosities. Weapons fire lit up the battlefield. The creatures released cringe-inducing shrieks as they fell from the sky. Nanonramu fired recklessly. Jei'Gun must have only wished he had two arm-cannons instead of one, his marksmanship exemplary. One ray swooped down at him and he pulled his arm back in waiting. As it drew in for its kill he unsheathed his blade and sliced through the ray severing it in two with a furious roaring swing. After a quick reload Akerele gave the ray flock all he had. Zomo covered the other one hundred and eighty degrees of sky behind him.

"Get down Zomo!" yelled Akerele, pushing her out of the way of a blast from a ray's tail, it impacted nearby covering them with tiny pieces of rubble.

The Bird of Prey used its superior firepower and speed to counteract the rays' naturally gifted aerial maneuverability. It peppered them with multiple rounds from its miniature winged gun turrets, which it withdrew from inside its wing frame.

Tronics had difficulty targeting the flying creatures with his laser beam. Their agility got the better of him and their loud shrieks frustrated him even more. Close by, another ray fired a blast at Adcox and Hatshepsut. Rey'Jax jumped in the way and shielded them with his body. Adcox saw the smoke coming off his back, the blast blew a hole in his protective armor plating but his burnt skin tissue instantly began to heal itself. The mighty one was unshaken, in fact, he was mad. The same Horde ray swooped down with speed to attack Adcox but Rey'Jax leaped, grabbing it in mid-air.

He slammed it to the ground then brutishly stomped on it to insure the kill.

Adcox took a quick glance all around and noticed that there was one man on the team that was not fighting, Major Hawke. Low he stooped, facing in the direction of their journey, away from the battle and without a care in the world.

After a while Akerele yelled, "clear!"

It was over, all the rays were dead. Adcox and Hatshepsut's eyes examined the fallen winged abominations and notice something. The simultaneous realization caused them to turn to each other in disbelief.

"Everybody look," said Hatshepsut. "The carcasses of the dead rays, they are not disintegrating."

"It must be because we're in dark matter space," Adcox said.

"Dr. Hatshepsut, quickly," stressed Hawke. "Retrieve DNA from one of those rays."

"We do not have time for this, souwrak," said Jei'Gun. "This was merely their vanguard, their main assault force will soon break upon us like Sanaga tidal wave."

"The data will aid us. It will only take a moment," said Hatshepsut. She activated her digital glove and pressed near to her thumb knuckle. After which, she injected a cauterized carcass with a probe.

Nanonramu sniffed the air right above one of the carcasses while the doctor conducted her work. "Their smell, it is unusually aromatic, soothing."

"I don't know what you're on about, rubeboy," said Tronics baffled. "They stink." He twisted his face up at suffering the smell.

"Try having heightened senses," added Rey'Jax, covering his nose because of the seared flesh's bombardment.

"You could have helped us back there, Major," said Adcox revealing his agitation.

"That is not our mission."

Rei'jax turned his head sharply at an angle. "Horde ground force approaches."

Tronics assessed the multiple icons moving towards their location on his slab. "Big R's ears are impressive."

"What do you see, bruv?" asked Adcox.

"The bird's detected a large assault force headed directly for us. The drones are over five thousand strong and more cocoons are hatching."

"Distance?" asked Akerele.

"Errr...under five kilometers. They're going to be on our arses like fourth degree piles any minute." Tronics reached for his back-hold. Demagnetizing it he grabbed the gravity disruptor and turned it on, witnessing the central magnetic cubic rings begin to rotate around the dual barrels in a spark of light and constant humming. Unsure of when it would complete its charging, he placed it back on his back-hold.

They all begin to hear what great Rei'jax detected moments before, a rumbling, this time it wasn't the planetoid that generated the sound but the Polymorph war machine in the march. The distant sound rattled Private Akerele, Zomo and Tronics.

"This is crazy," said Akerele. "We're not going to find this stupid ship. We're going to die out here."

"*Private!*" Adcox yelled and got his attention. "Hand me the RPG."

"What's the point, Captain?" Akerele insubordinately replied.

"*Hand me the RPG.*"

Akerele grabbed the strap hanging over his shoulder and removed the rocket launcher, handing it to Adcox.

"How much rounds we got?" Adcox asked him.

"I couldn't locate the extra warheads. The four in the tank are all we got."

Nanonramu saw something that made his jaw drop. "Look, the mothership? Up there!" They all turned around with excitement but discovered that it was nothing but a monolith, oddly shaped by the planetoid's geophysics. "Can your eyes not see?"

Hatshepsut placed her hand on the Rogue Basarwan's cheek. "Nanonramu, the effects of the planetoid are causing you to hallucinate."

"There *is* no ship," yelled Akerele. "The major doesn't know where he's going."

"Pull yourself together, Private," said Adcox grabbing Akerele by his armor's neck collar. "Scorched Earth, I need you to lay down some mines. Do what you do best and do it fast. Give him a hand, Zomo." Adcox then looked to his corporal. "Tron, help me out on that ridge."

Zomo and Akerele ran toward the direction of the oncoming Horde and began laying down four columns of mines equally spaced apart, moving backwards toward the team.

Adcox led the way up onto a ridge east of the team's location with Tronics following behind. The young leader's adrenaline began to conquer his fears as the ridge altered growing taller and wider. He noticed Hawke's eyes locked on him as he climbed but the major's blank stares were rarely accompanied with words. Still, he felt himself growing annoyed with the Black Guard's inaction. Once at the summit they looked over the edge and saw a frightening sight: thousands upon thousands of Horde swarming towards them.

"Rarr!" Said Tronics. "Nah bruv, we're not going to make it." He lowered his weapon in disbelief of the numbers and dropped to his knees.

"We've come this far." Adcox unfolded the rocket propelled grenade launcher, it snapped into place and locked. He then out-folded the laser targeting apparatus on the top of the RPG and activated the targeting beam. "I need you to keep a lookout for me. Stay sharp Kev."

Tronics shook his head. "Nah G, I'm just an engineer. Why the hell did I come here?"

Adcox knew he had to reverse Tronics' unset of dread before it entrenched itself. "You've held out fine all this time."

"Bruv you don't understand, I normally just provide support for the team. Support! We're in balls deep here. I saw you were all cool and you're normally falling apart so I was just putting on a brave face."

"Kev, we can do this."

"I promised Amanda I'll make it back."

Adcox came in close. "Look, you've got three beautiful women in your life and they mean just as much to me. I don't want to break their hearts either. We don't have much time. I'm ordering you to cover me, Corporal. Are you feeling me soldier?"

Tronics smiled. "All right superman, let's do this."

Adcox hoisted the RPG over his right shoulder. The four warheads inside made up most of the eighty centimeter weapon's weight. "Target locked. Fire!" said Adcox.

A rocket propelled from the weapon and a plume of smoke vented out the rear, but no recoil. The smart missile whizzed through the air intelligently navigating over the terrain. It exploded in the hub of Polymorph army, creating a massive blast wave owing to its high yield thermobaric warheads. Adcox fired another rocket. A direct hit in the high density Horde swarm. A ray spotted them high on the ridge and soared in for the kill. Tronics used his laser to saw it in half. Then, from a far distance he saw that a mammoth had projected a large ball of energy that volleyed high in the air.

"Yo! *We gotta go now*!" yelled Tronics. Adcox fired one more rocket but they both fled the scene without witnessing its impact. As they made their descent, the energy blast hit the ridge and it blew apart. Out from the rubble Adcox emerged and he dragged out his friend who was coughing and looked disoriented.

Both marines rejoined the team.

"Captain, the mines have been laid," informed Akerele.

"We need to keep heading east, Captain," said Hawke.

"Ok, let's move people."

As they dashed off, Tronics watched the view of the Horde wave from the eyes of the Bird of Prey via his electronic slab. "Bird of Prey: deploy your highest yield air-to-surface missiles," he commanded the winged robot.

"Command received, executing offensive." The Bird of Prey unleashed its missiles upon the Horde, but it did little to impede their advance, so vast were their numbers.

The tiring group endured more seismic activity as the terrain ahead altered once again, flattening, with sporadic deposits of jagged rocks. A mixture from elephant and antelope sized boulders levitating at head height in the air. Most were motionless, but some drifted, knocking into each other.

"Young Captain," said Rey'Jax. "Our position is elevated and rock field provides cover adequate for skirmish. With our ranks tiring, we should maintain defensive perimeter here while your warriors rest momentarily."

"Sure! Akerele, Zomo, defend the right of our position."

"Roger that, sir!" said Akerele.

"Jei'Gun, could you and Nanonramu guard our left flank?" asked Adcox. Nanonramu as always waited for Jei'Gun's decision. The elite-shakan gestured left with his head and they both reposition themselves.

"Tronics, stay tracking the Horde's movement. We don't want any surprises."

"Affirmative, boss man!"

"We should leave Urk'Tark where he is," suggested Rey'Jax. Looking at Hawke ahead of the group. Adcox had no argument.

Despite the imminent Horde attack, Hatshepsut gave into her intrigue to analyze the DNA collected on her glove.

"Is this some kind of localized microgravity, Tron?" Zomo asked the corporal, alarmed by the suspended rocks.

"Nah, it must be something about the rocks because we're not floating. No unusual gravity readings on my scanners. I am picking up a lot of subterranean electrical charge. My guess is this is some kind of superconductive effect."

"This place is getting stranger by the minute," said Akerele.

"Attention everyone!" said Hatshepsut to the team. Her lips parted in absolute shock and for an unknown reason she stared only at Hawke. "I have just ran DNA trace. Horde DNA has genetic material matching mammals, plants, invertebrates, reptiles, insects and amphibians of both Human and Horaxian planetary origin. Plus other unknown DNA."

"That is impossible!" said Nanonramu.

"No, it's true," said Hawke. "That's not the only genetic material they have. Tell them, Doctor."

"It's not just animal and botanical life, its largest DNA constitution is Horaxian and Homo Sapien."

"So they're us? I don't understand," said Zomo, equally astonished by the revelations as everyone.

"Maybe they take our DNA when they eat us?" Akerele said.

As always, Zomo shook her head at him. "Do you grow horns when you eat buffalo, moron?"

"Girl these things aren't exactly us. Who knows how they operate."

"No...this is xenogenesis," said Major Hawke.

"What?" asked Jei'Gun.

Hatshepsut replied. "The creation of offspring which are different from either parent."

"Are you saying they evolved from us?" questioned Tronics.

"Negative, Corporal," said Hawke. "Not abiogenesis. Somebody, somewhere, is playing god."

"More like Dr. Frankenstein," said Adcox.

"And you have had knowledge of this the entire time?" Rey'Jax said to Major Hawke. They all cast their distrustful eyes on him.

"Look there," Hawke said. "That's where the ship's located." He pointed to a black, cavernous mountain landform miles away on slanting terrain. "We're almost there."

Suddenly, the ground shook from multiple detonations. The tremors caused Hatshepsut to stumble and Tronics had to take a knee. The group paused to watch the Horde ranks being decimated by Akerele's exploding mines. But the mines were not enough. The planetoid surface peeled away around the group, rising up just like black ash in the reverse direction.

"Everybody get down!" commanded Adcox and he pulled Hatshepsut into a ditch for cover.

Most of the team dropped down, as the floating rocks that were gently drifting now shot through the air, crashing into each other and breaking into smaller pieces.

***

"*Attack!*" Jei'Gun cried and bullets ripped through the Horde army, but they remained undeterred. Neither was the elite-shakan warrior, while everyone else had dropped low, he remained standing at the sight of Rey'Jax also on his feet. He felt the need to prove himself to the warrior of Anubianite legend. A tall order, as Rey'Jax ran towards the onrushing flood of drones. He jumped high in the air over a vile herd and fell to the ground so hard it broke apart, toppling six of them. One had the misfortune of its chest being caved inward due to the momentum generated by the Ariman's speed times his mass.

Although the human-Horaxian team was fighting fiercely, it proved impossible to beat back the Polymorph. The creatures slowly began to envelop them.

"Don't let them surround us," cried Adcox in vain.

Fortunately many of the Horde were hit by the speeding boulders. Tronics crouched, cutting columns of Horde down with light blue, unbroken beams of his electric laser. But to make his ordeal more distressing, his makeshift weapon had overheated.

"Bloody hell, not again." Tronics said to himself. "Piece of junk."

He placed his laser back onto his weapon hold, then reached for his sidearm still in its holster. At that moment he witnessed five drones coming together and merging into one repulsive mass. The mass grew at an accelerated rate and formed six massive legs and a head. As its flexible skin morphed and hardened, a Horde mammoth emerged. The behemoth Horde charged through with such ferocity it trampled a drone and some crabs. Rather than go around a tall rock pile it crashed through with its seven unbreakable horns heading straight for Tronics.

"No no no! Why do they always come for me?" Tronics looked down at his sidearm with despair. Despite its high impact ammunition it was no match for a mammoth's armor. "Bumbaclot!" he uttered.

Chapter Sixteen - The Sum Of Their Fears

On the *Sword of Damocles*, the anxiety levels were at their highest as the crew dashed around the bridge in pandemonium. "General," said the commodore. "MK1 is moving faster than we predicted. It's going to be coming up on us any minute."

"What? We should have had hours before it arrived. How the hell could anything move that fast? Battle stations!"

"There it is, approaching our starboard!" said the commodore.

"Fire everything we've got commodore and I mean everything."

MK1's speed was so fast on its intercept trajectory to the ship that it disrupted space around it. The carrier's turrets and missile batteries release a steady cloud of munitions at the incoming enemy. The majority hit on target, creating multiple immeasurable explosions. Out of the fire the invulnerable robot emerged with no slowing down.

"Brace for impact!" General Baizan ordered.

The Mankiller flew straight through the side of the ship and out the other side. Its space-bending wake blew a massive hole in the ship and the bridge rocked violently.

"Keep firing!" Baizan shouted at his officers having to hold onto a desk to keep his balance.

"Sir, MK1 is gone. We're unable to lock onto the target," said the commander.

"Damage report!" commanded Baizan.

Commander Xiao assessed the carrier's monitoring systems. "Hangar bay six to nine and decks twelve to sixteen have been completely destroyed."

"Evacuate the crew from the damaged sections and mobilize a repair crew. Get Command on the line," said Baizan, he then looked at Dr. Henry, "I wish we could have bought Hawke and the team more time."

Dr. Henry still played with his puzzle contraption throughout the commotion twisting it into different configurations, undisturbed by the events. "The unstoppable force, the immovable object. We will see which of the two are truly invincible."

The thinning white haired commodore spoke to Henry. "The Hawke's the best at what he does but I don't think anything can stop the Mankiller. He's just a man, Doctor. He barely survived the abyss."

"Ahh, but yet he did survive, he survived Matelot-6, Cagn's execution squads and the battle of Beloved Kemeta too," said Dr. Henry. He didn't look at the commodore or Baizan, purely fixated on his intellectual apparatus. "Do not let his demeanor fool you, my dear commodore, he is more than just a man. In fact, I think Mr. Hawke wanted to be in the abyss, and also on the battleground of Kemeta. Flies do not see a spider's web until it is too late. But, do you know what can also detect a spider's web, comrades?" Henry finally looked up at the men. "Another spider!"

***

On the planetoid in dark matter space, Tronics faced imminent danger from a stampeding Horde mammoth. The rest were preoccupied dealing with the numerous drones to assist him. In the depths of his dismay, he heard someone calling out to him.

"Corporal! The gravity disruptor, use it now!"

Expeditiously, he pressed a button on his armor's forearm control panel. One second later, the weapons-hold on his back was demagnetized. Dr. Henry's gravity disruptor released from his back plating. He grabbed hold of it. Its magnetic coils were aligned and stationary. The length of the barrel glowed blue. He fired at the oncoming mammoth.

The gun blasted out a colorless surge of energy at half the velocity of a bullet, only detectable by the distortion it caused in the air, warping it as if to tear apart the localized atmosphere itself. Upon impact, it rocked the beast. Crushing it inwards instantaneously like a hydraulic press crushes an old car. The mammoth imploded splattering its bodily remains. The Horde drones within the blast radius were annihilated. Their orange fleshy innards sprayed everywhere.

The recoil of the advanced weapon sent Tronics flying backwards past Nanonramu hitting the ground and toppling over multiple times. It knocked Corporal Manning so fast it took him a while to regain his senses. "Slight kickback, eh?" Tronics said aloud remembering Dr. Henry's words, then he turned to Major Hawke. "I owe you one, Major!"

Tronics inspected the weapon and saw its magnetic rings rotating once more indicating it needed time to recharge. "Don't worry babygirls, daddy's coming home." He said to himself.

In the heat of the battle Hatshepsut saw one of the hovering large boulders heading towards her at speed. But she was unable to move out of the way in time. Out of nowhere Rey'Jax arrived and grabbed it. His feet sliding along the uneven ground. Using some of the rock's own momentum he dashed it at a file of drones.

"Zomo, stay focused. Take out the crabs," screamed Adcox. She obeyed and started picking off the nearby nine-legged creatures.

The captain himself ran out of ammo from the heavy fighting. From his position lying down flat he looked backwards to reach for another magazine and when he looked up again a Horde drone ambushed him. Frantically he tried to fend the monster off but it was futile, the drone was over five times his weight. Its third arm transformed into a hundred thin tendrils which wrapped around the marine hoisting him in the air. Secreted green saliva dripped all over Adcox's helmet visor which he just had time to extract. Out of one of its three upper limbs, its oversized hand transformed into a spear to end the captain.

Akerele hadn't noticed his commanding officer's peril as he fought to beat the Polymorph back. At the corner of his right eye the private spotted one of the flying boulders heading towards him. He whipped around to fire a grenade round, obliterating it. Turning back again the private ripped apart drones with more explosive rounds.

Jei'Gun threw Horaxian vault grenades in the air. As they flew over their onrushing crab targets, they released their spotlight-shaped beams of superheated plasma killing scores. The elite-shakan knight turned to his left and noticed five drones rush into each other and biologically merging. Through his helmet he witnessed the whole become greater than the sum of its parts; their combine mass expanded and began to mutate. He knew the danger that lay ahead once it completed its transformation.

Adcox struggled as desperately as Colonel Bronze once did wrapped in Horde tendrils. The drone lunged its spear forward to impale the captain but it was halted by a stabbed through its head, which lay at the middle of its muscular chest. The orange blood drench Adcox's suit. Hawke had saved his life and with another swipe of his sword he severed Adcox's binding tendrils. The dead drone's body fell on the captain as he landed on the ground, crushing down on his slim frame. He had to use a great deal of strength to push it off to his right. With one hand Hawke helped him up. He rose only to see the conjoined drones-mass completing their transformation into another Horde mammoth. It wasted no time charging through the boulder filled plains. Adcox and Zomo's combine firepower couldn't bring it down in time as it turned at a slight angle aiming for one marine in particular.

"You may have been right, Tronics," said Adcox. "Think you better run."

"Arghh, mate! This is ridiculous!" Tronics cried. He blitzed towards the rear of the team.

Rey'Jax appeared and rammed into the mammoth from its side then delivered a mighty blow to its stomach. The Ariman and the behemoth, which was far greater than his size, battled viciously toppling over each other like two Kepler-62e grizzly bears fighting over territory. The mammoth's massive bulk prove too difficult for the Ariman to deal with. They both tumbled over a nearby newly formed cliff edge, out of sight.

"Guys, we're not going to make it," wearily yelled Tronics assessing their dismal survival odds. "There's too many of them." He continuously fired his sidearm while waiting for the gravity gun to recharge.

But Jei'Gun was now in his element. Ready to embrace death, he extended his arm blade and back-slashed the first approaching drone across its midsection. Even with his bionic armor the well-built drones made a difficult kill. Forgetting his projectile weapon, he lost himself hacking his way from drone to drone. A distant beast charged its bioblaster. By the time he realized it was too late. A grenade round then blew the drone away before it could fire. He saw that Adcox had been covering his rear.

Zomo's fears had now been cured by the medicine of battle. Yet, she tired. How unfortunate that her opponents had been blessed with limitless endurance as well as numbers. They kept coming despite the thousands killed. Breathing heavily, she was determined to take the fight to them, though her solar rifle weighed heavy on her arms. But then, Horde crabs managed to overwhelm her, biting her multiple times. When Akerele saw his friend in trouble he became distracted, shouting her name in vain. A drone speared him through his abdomen from behind. Hawke managed to get to Zomo and slashed all the crabs. A nearby drone dissolved into five more crabs and lunged to attack him. But there were no match for the Black Guard. Skillfully, he out maneuvered them and slayed them with his swordsmanship. His blade seemed to have a mind of its own, bending or extending to claim more victims. Its ability to morph itself into various forms was intrinsic to Ariman weaponry.

"*Doctor!*" Hawke screamed, watching over Zomo's body. Zomo saw that Akerele had been stabbed. Taken by grief, she tried to move to his aid but Hatshepsut arrived and held her back. She tussled with the doctor until the neurotoxin caused her to convulse. Hatshepsut injected her with antivenom and Zomo silently screamed Akerele's name as the poison coursed through her veins. She watched him pull out a grenade only for another drone to tear his head away from his neck. The resulting detonation from his grenade and the mines he carried destroyed not only his murderers but it also devastated the Polymorph assault.

After being thrown off their feet by Akerele's explosion, Tronics, Adcox, Nanonramu and Jei'Gun had a much more easy time picking off the remaining Horde with them now in disarray. The Bird of Prey still provided crucial aerial support.

Adcox came by Zomo's side. "Is she going to be ok?" he asked Hatshepsut.

"I got to her in time to administer antivenom. The poison did not have time to set in. She should be back on feet soon."

"Ack is dead, sir!" Zomo said in a sedated, delirious voice. Hatshepsut passed her silver gloves along Zomo's forehead and short black hair to comfort her.

"I'm sorry, Zomo," Adcox replied.

Spontaneously the Ariman shield extracted outward from the shield handle Adcox still gripped around his left hand. It widened to form a two meter in diameter, protective curve. Without enough time to understand what was going on, a blast jolted him. Lowering the shield, he saw it had emanated from a Horde drone's bioblaster. The captain lifted his solar rifle with speed and shot it down. Adcox had battled through his nerves. He was tired, but found his courage.

"Oh no!" said Tronics as he backed away. They all heard him on the comms and stepped back themselves when they glimpsed at the source of his dismay. It was the large mass of a Horde squid. It stalked them using four of its tentacles to propel itself and lift it high off the ground. Its parasite insectoids crawled all over its ginormous, puss-secreting head. The squids were nowhere near as destructive as a mammoth but what it was, was hideous. A creature so utterly abominable should never have been given form.

"Do not look directly at the squid!" yelled Hatshepsut. "Hold breath!"

Too late, the rotten smell it gave off was enough to make Zomo vomit, a common side effect of its presence. Its other side effect hit Tronics and he passed out from fear.

Adcox fired his solar 506 assault rifle, trying to aim using his peripheral vision. On target shots sunk into its squishy bodily tissue, disappearing within and causing minor damage. Others took out some of its eyes, but hundreds more remained.

The creature's long frontal tentacles grabbed hold of Adcox and Hatshepsut. It began crushing Adcox's suit and he screamed out. In his agony the captain lay eyes upon Major Hawke on top of a levitating rock heading toward the creature's pulsing head. Hawke leaped and the squid opened its mouth wide to devour him. He extracted sword's blade. This time the blade broaden wider than the man himself and triple his length. He stabbed down on the creature and it unleashed a loud shriek, toppling onto itself. With Hawke disappearing within its large tentacled carcass.

Released from bondage, Hatshepsut used her medicine to revive Tronics and he opened his eyelids to the view of

Major Hawke appearing from the dead creature cutting through its tentacles to clear a path.

From the nearby cliff edge appeared a titanic hand which sunk into the ground as the weight of it came down. Rey'Jax reappeared. He still had his helmet but his upper body armor was gone, exposing his chest that was so thick and bulged a tank shell couldn't penetrate it. Cuts blanketed his exposed, toughened skin. Most of them instantly closed due to his superhoraxian healing ability. But he looked incredibly tired. The sight of the Ariman filled Adcox and Hatshepsut with joy. Rey'Jax unleashed a deafening battle cry, the sound would make the strongest bones of the strongest men stood armed in the greatest army tremble. It forced Adcox to cover his ears. Foolishly a lone drone scampered towards him and he clobbered it with such force it arced over two kilometers in the air. Horde crabs climbed over him in attempt to subdue him with poisonous bites. Penetrating his skin was a failure, they didn't possess enough venom to put him down even if they could. He crushed them with his fist against his own chest and leg.

Adcox picked off stray Polymorphs only to glance over his shoulder to see Hawke stabbing down at something. The sight of the Black Guard's victim caused him to stumble, though no one else had time to notice.

Rey'Jax ran at a herd of drones and they in turn rushed to meet him. As they clashed, the lucky victims that were not broken apart by the force of his blows were knocked so far into the atmosphere of the planetoid, gravity was unable to bring them back down and they floated away in dark space.

Jei'Gun had little time to gaze at the spectacle as he engaged multiple drones. Stabbing one of them up through its pectoral head, his blade became stuck inside the beast's cranium. Another Horde drone leaped on him and bit his hand, ripping it clean off. He roared from the pain and extinguished the drone with arm-cannon rounds.

Hatshepsut now witnessed the same horrific scene Adcox had glimpsed moments ago. It shocked her more than anything they'd faced since she arrived in dark matter space. The former Black Guard squadron officer commander, against all reason imaginable, had just stabbed Nanonramu with his sword through the chest.

The sweat-drenched Adcox was yet to snap out from his disbelief. Edging closer, he saw Nanonramu holding Hawke's sword blade and trying to dislodge it from his body, but it had pinned him to the ground. The Rogue extracted his arm blade. With more anger possessing him than pain, Nanonramu rocked back and forth, violently swinging his blade at Hawke. Purple blood spilled from his mouth as he snarled.

"Major, no!" Adcox's shouts alerted the team who finished fending off the last remnants of Horde and were making sure the wounded squirming creatures were dead.

"Tell Cagn he's next!" Hawke whispered and he placed his foot on the injured Horaxian's chest to hold him in place. Removing his sword, he plunged it into Nanonramu's forehead cracking his skull.

Fury consumed Jei'Gun at the sight of Nanonramu's demise. Blocking out the excruciating agony of his missing hand, he fired shots at Hawke but missed as the Black Guard pounced like a jaguar and rolled out of the way. The elite-shakan ran out of ammunition. He reloaded, preparing to fire again, but Adcox pushed his arm aside.

"No Jei'Gun, don't do it," pleaded Adcox, his armor indented and mangled at the waist-side from the squid's tentacle.

"Get away!"

"Wait, he must have a reason. And if he doesn't, then I won't stop you."

The Anubianite held his weapon arm high and in a rare moment he listened to the young marine and desisted from firing.

"Is there no end to your treachery?" Re'jax said, moving towards the major.

"No, your highness!" bawled Hatshepsut, she stood in his way, barely reaching above his waist. "Let him explain," she said, almost as if she knew more to Hawke's hideous actions. The team raised their weapons at the Black Guard.

"Nanonramu was a traitor," Hawke said.

"Lies!" bellowed Jey'gun.

"How do you think the Polymorph tracked us here from normal space? They never knew where the mothership was. He was giving away our position."

"How is that even possible?" asked Adcox.

"I found this on him." Hawke pulled out a small, flat creature similar in appearance to ancient echinoderms starfish. It wiggled around in his palm leaving an oozing residue. "It was generating the low frequency pulse that Rey'Jax's hearing was able to detect ever since we were caught in black hole's gravity. It's Horde."

"Why would he betray us?" questioned Adcox. "The Horde would kill him just as quickly. This doesn't make sense."

"Hawke's right," said Tronics, performing a frequency spectrum sweep on his slab. "I'm definitely picking up a trace trans-spatial frequency coming off it."

Hawke dropped the small wiggling creature and crushed it with his boot.

"They never attacked the Rogue," said Hawke. "He fired his weapon but yet he never made a kill. Eve established a baseline of everyone's vocal expressions since Kemeta. We noticed Nanonramu's speech patterns had altered. His tone lowered, his words changed and he began behaving differently. I think the brain Horde might have been controlling him. Must have got to him on Kemeta."

"What, you're saying this is some kind of extreme twisted Stockholm syndrome?" asked Adcox, his tone suggested to the group that he found Hawke's explanation ridiculous.

"Nonsense," said Rey'Jax. "Betrayal is all that fills his soul."

"How do we know that bug was not of your belonging?" asked Jei'Gun. "Why should we trust you, demon?" Despite his resentment, Jei'Gun himself was confused by Nanonramu's recent behavior; how he tried to prevent Jei'Gun from fighting the Black Guard commander, how he even referred to the Black Guard as "The Hawke," referencing him by name after the major told the story of the demise of his demon knights. But most damming of all was how he asked for the Black Guard's help on what to do against the Horde when they appeared on the planetoid.

Hawke bent down by Nanonramu's corpse and picked up two of his vault grenades from his side pouch. "You all heard him comment on how pleasant he found the smell of the dead rays. Then he hallucinated thinking he saw the ship."

"Rogues have poor vision fool," said Jei'Gun, "and are sensitive to smell."

"Yeah," said Tronics. "That, combined with the effects of the planetoid, hallucinations, as you said, Major."

"On us, that would be true," replied Hawke. "But he saw a mirage, *straight after,* we killed the rays. It was the smell of the rays on his acute Rogue Basarwan antennae that induced the illusion. It's called synesthesia."

"This is all starting to get a little farfetched," said Adcox, as he glanced around looking for signs of any more Horde. "Horaxians helping Horde, I can't buy it."

"Mr. Hawke speaks truth," replied Hatshepsut.

"My lady, how can you speak in defense?" questioned the elite-shakan.

Adcox too was stunned by what he heard.

"Synesthesia is a neurological phenomenon which affects humans and Horaxians. It is proof that his mind was being corrupted. Dr. Henry said brain Horde are able to psychogenically induce fear and we know fear has power to control. It is possible the brain took over Nanonramu's mind somehow."

"This is how they are able to understand our capabilities so well," said Hawke. "All are not always whom they appear to be!"

"But even though he was being controlled," said Hatshepsut, "did you have to kill him?"

"Yes!" said Hawke, she waited for more but that was all.

"Horde controlling Horaxians?" Tronics said. "This whole situation just got a whole lot scarier."

The voice of the Bird of Prey crackled onto the comms link. "Multiple Horde life forms approaching south of unit's position."

They all turned and saw another Horde advance in the distance. A look of despair engulfed them in view of the vast numbers.

"We can't hold them all off, we need to get moving," said Adcox. Like the rest, his face was dirty, his armored suit stained with alien blood and the weight of his rifle took a toll on his arms.

Jei'Gun broke the chain that linked his hefty shoulder pads and they fell to the ground. "We will not make it. Jei'Gun will buy us some time. Go!"

Adcox walked up to the elite-shakan. "Jei'Gun, you don't have to do this."

Jei'Gun looked to Hatshepsut and spoke. "Dying in service of protecting those whose bloodline commands imperial throne is not my decision, it is my duty."

"I don't want to lose another man out here, or Horaxian," said Adcox.

"Just leave!" urged the Horaxian knight.

"I'd rather leave my right arm," Adcox said. "Come with us, Alpha."

"In abundance I still dislike your kind but you have earned respect. You have proven yourself. Adcox, Captain!"

Hatshepsut walked up to Jei'Gun and placed her left palm on the elite-shakan's left cheek area of his helmet which concealed his supersized cranium and her right palm on his forehead panel. "I thank you, Power Made Flesh. If only I could have seen your face just once."

"You honor me my lady, but my oath forbids me." Jei'Gun was never to remove his helmet, one of the many privileges relinquished by an Anubianite warrior who chose knighthood. He turned towards Rey'Jax, "Jei'Gun fought alongside a living god this day, truly is he worthy."

"You seek what already possessed. You are already symbol of a true warrior." Rey'Jax extended his arms upright and performed an Ariman salute.

"Can you hurry this up?" said Hawke. "We ain't got all day."

Hatshepsut frowned at Hawke's words and the Anubianite spat on the ground. "My blade was robbed of your head, souwrak. But in the next life your cursed soul will be mine. Now, go!" demanded Jei'Gun to the team.

The rest of the team hurried along, except for Tronics who waited behind.

"Bird of Prey: protect Jei'Gun as best as you can."

"Command acknowledged, Corporal Manning!"

Tronics stared at elite-shakan and raised of his fist. "Respect, brother!"

"You are an annoying one. Be gone!"

As the team ran off, the elite-shakan pulled out five vault grenades one by one. He pressed a button on the side of each that generated a high pitched repetitive tone. Each of them levitated in the air by their own propulsion towards the oncoming Horde army, pulsing with an increasing frequency. Jei'Gun then unleashed every round his arm-cannon could fire as hundreds opposed the lone warrior. His robotic ionic plasma grenades floated until they came above the Polymorph ranks and activated. They rained their intense beam of superheated plasma on the onrushing aliens, killing close to a hundred. Yet they kept advancing.

He picked up the dead Akerele's solar assault rifle and fired it with the same hand he used to fire his forearm cannon. Still, the Horde closed in on him. Then, something happened, under his helmet he smiled, as if he was held in the arms of a long-lost friend.

***

The rest of the team hurried to the mothership. Zomo slowly recovered from the effects of the neurotoxins and Hatshepsut supported her by placing her arm over her shoulder. In the distance, they heard explosions and shortly after Adcox identified the distinctive churning of arm-cannon rounds. Then...no sound at all.

Chapter Seventeen - That Which Makes Men Extraordinary

As desperation crept in, all that mattered to the team was maintaining distance between them and their relentless pursuers as they journeyed on the metamorphic terrain. The landform altered from ravines to hills in quick succession, and morphing from a hard solid to pools of high viscosity liquid. Rocks, transformed into sharp spikes that speared a stampeding mammoth. Two of its feet were then swallowed by the ground which had transformed into black tar. Black vines wrapped around its body consuming it completely.

"The planetoid is turning against them," said Hatshepsut, finding it difficult to see through the rising black flakes of dust.

 The planetoid's surface rose to form a tall liquid wall that which curved like a breaking wave. It engulfed tens of drones as it crashed down. Immediately after the surface cracked open and scores of Horde drones and crabs fell in the rupture. Hatshepsut's foot slid and she almost fell in after them but Adcox grabbed her. Tronics helped to pull her up just in time as the ground closed again.

Tronics saw the horrible sight of another squid advancing and glanced down at his gravity weapon. Its magnetic coils were aligned once more. "Let's try this again." He fired the disruptor in front of the squid and a forty meter squared surface area collapsed under it, swallowing the vile creature. Again, the recoil propelled him. He slid ten meters across the dirt more comfortably than his previous tumble.

"Look!" said Hatshepsut pointing behind them. "They are retreating!"

They watched as the remaining drones scurried back from where they came.

"Yeah," said Tronics as he returned to his feet, "getting your arse handed to you would do that."

"Warning!" informed the Bird of Prey. "Aperture radar has detected an unidentified aerial anomaly approaching. High velocity."

"Anomaly?" Adcox said puzzled. "Distance and direction, Bird of Prey?"

"One hundred and three kilometers south of current position. Speed, three thousand seven hundred kilometers per hour and rapidly decelerating."

"Flock of rays maybe?" Hatshepsut pondered.

"Might be the Horde whale," Zomo said.

Tronics shook his head. "Whatever it is, it's moving at three times the speed of sound."

Hawke came to the middle of the group. "We've run out of time. It's MK1. It's here."

"What?" replied Adcox, the young man's spirit was broken. "The Mankiller? It can't be."

"Arh, come on, are you serious?" vented Tronics. He flung his weapon down and threw his arms in the air. "Are you joking? Is this for real?"

"Finally," Rey'Jax said, looking at Hawke, "the Wings of Death itself soars to claim its greatest prize," The Black Guard commander, as customary, hardly appeared surprised by MK1's presence.

Adcox tried to take control of the situation. "Bird of Prey: Obtain a visual of anomaly. Maximum safe distance."

"Command received, executing." The winged robot swung a wide arch and flew away in the Horde's direction.

"What we going to do now?" asked Tronics. "I mean if it is the Mankiller, entire armies couldn't kill that thing."

"We should never have come here," Zomo said as she broke down. "Akerele's dead, and for what? This is all your fault." Aiming blame at Hawke as the tears rolled down her cheeks.

"It's never over until it's over," replied Hawke.

"We can do this," said Adcox. "Let's complete the mission so that Jei'Gun, Akerele and all the others never died in vain. Major, if the mothership and the Mankiller came from the same origin then inside the ship may lie the power to stop it?"

"There is a way," said Hawke.

"All right let's get to this bloody ship," said Adcox. "Tronics, I need you sharp and focus..."

The Bird of Prey's voice sounded off on their comms link. "Status alert, visual confirmed, anomaly is cybernetic lifeform codename MK1."

Far behind them, the ultimate instrument of destruction closed in, leaving a wake of white energy behind it as it disrupted the air. There were loud, concussive bangs caused by its supersonic velocity. It arrived at the Horde whale, which still hovered high within the planetoid's little atmosphere, and circled once around it. In landing, MK1 caved in the surrounding area within a twenty meter radius. As the dust settled, the Horde gathered around it in cautious movements. All the drones bowed down to the cybernetic lifeform. Mammoths bended their six legs resting down. Even the rays dived and landed at its presence. MK1 rose and marched up to three brain Horde, one then pointed to the distant horizon and soon after MK1 took off in the air again in the direction the brain pointed.

It was in the direction of the team.

***

As Adcox and his men were making haste Rey'Jax halted, turning around to gaze behind them.

"What's wrong, Rey'Jax?" asked Adcox fearing the worst.

Rey'Jax's seventh sense, the vertical line inside his body, had detected a disturbance in the atmosphere's pressure. He saw, beyond normal sight, an object approaching. "We are too late. Death arrives." His voice, fearless.

"Eve, are you ready yet?" asked Hawke.

"Negative. Override code is not yet complete."

"I thought Eve was offline?" Tronics asked, short of breath.

"Activate the pod!" said the major, ignoring the marine.

Adcox also recalled Hawke's words that Eve came offline because of a malfunction but he had much bigger problems in view of the object as it created a white trail against the black sky. "This is where it all ends," he said to himself. His body accepted their doomed fate. His muscles relaxed. His breathing, softened. "Guys, whatever you've got left in you. Now's the time."

They formed a defensive line surrounded by newly elevated mountains on either side. Hope faded as their eyes latched onto the artificial comet crashing down on them.

***

The *Sword of Damocles* was stationary, still crippled from the Mankiller's assault. The bridge's crewmen hustled to the sound of repetitive alarms, tripping over themselves. The generals composing Earth Command were all assembled and in view on screen. General Baizan stood tall and addressed them. "Command, we need to mobilize the entire fleet for when MK1 returns."

The Lunar 1 general responded. "A strategic position within the solar system's Kuiper belt is the best chance we have. The icy rocks will create cover for the fleet."

"But that will leave Kepler-Terra, Biosphere-9 and all our outer territories defenseless," said Baizan appalled at what he heard.

General Burns responded in a stern voice. "We don't have the resources to adequately defend such a wide perimeter. For now, each outer world will have to fend for themselves with their planetary defense systems."

"Planetary defenses don't stand a chance," yelled Baizan. "You want to leave billions of people on two human colonies without any support of the fleet, or Command? Just abandon them?"

"Listen Baizan," Gen. Burns replied with more aggression. "Kepler-Terra's twelve hundred light years away. Yet the Polymorph's infestation on Gliese-Eden is only twenty-three light years from us..."

Baizan wouldn't let him finish. "I don't give a magic monkeys if the horde were camped outside *my bridge door*, I'm not...'

"Look James," Field Marshall Montgomery finally intervene to rein in the bronze man. He was the only one that could pull rank on him. "I'm sorry but it has already been decided."

Baizan paused in detestation of his colleague's sentiments. The man who was first to backup the Lunar 1 general's words of abandoning Kepler-Terra and Biosphere-9 was the commanding official of Kepler-Terra himself. Biosphere-9's commander, Gen. Maharaj, said nothing in defense of his colony. He realized the truth in Hawke's words. Humanity had become cowards, and the cowardice was the worst at the top.

"Not on my watch!" said Baizan, in the harshest tone.

***

The ground tremored like an earthquake with the Mankiller's landing, and they greeted it with a hostile reception. Conserving ammo was useless now. Each grenade round from Adcox's solar jolted MK1 upon impact but did little to stop its motion as it moved towards them. Zomo was back supporting her own weight and squeezed down hard on her trigger for a seven second semi-automatic burst. The presence of MK1 shocked her system enough to overcome the residual neurotoxins. Hatshepsut stayed close to her. It took standing face to face with the manifestation of destruction for her to believe in Hawke's words and she chose to fight. Grabbing Zomo's sidearm Hatshepsut fired haphazardly.

Hawke watched without action. He sensed Rey'Jax's intentions to engage in combat and placed his hand on his arm. "Not yet your highness, trust me...please."

MK1 fired a blast and it burnt a large hole straight through Zomo's torso killing her instantly. Adcox screamed her name. Hawke with his quickness of thought turned to Tronics and saw what he did not, firing at the robot with his sidearm in terror. The corporal's gravity disruptor's cubic coils had stopped rotating.

"*Tronics, hit the mountain!*" yelled Hawke.

"Hold me!" he said quickly to Adcox. Adcox grabbed him from behind by his waist and now supported from the kickback, he fired the gravity gun. The blast hit the lower part of the mountain causing it to break inwards. The upper section tumbled towards the Mankiller.

"Get out of the way, move it!" yelled Hawke, which made the team realize that the mountain was also falling above their heads too. Hawke then activated the two Horaxian vault grenades which he picked up off Nanonramu's corpse and they detonated above MK1.

While Hawke ran clear himself he turned to see the Mankiller emerging through the wall of plasma unaffected by the superheat. But it did its job, distracting the juggernaut long enough. The large mountain top crashed down on it. Certain death for any living thing.

They stopped in wonder of the destruction.

"We killed it!" said Hatshepsut.

"No, we have only slowed death," said Rey'Jax.

Adcox wasted no time and reloaded his solar 506 assault rifle. He checked to see that it was his last magazine left. He swore at himself for not picking up Akerele's rifle. "I've got ninety rounds left," said the captain.

Hawke glanced up at the mountain ahead of them and saw an opening. "Quick, get to the caves." They ran for their lives.

A burst of vertically focused energy shot out of the rubble of heavy fallen rock, then two more. The rubble began to move and a huge chuck of rock was hoisted high by the invulnerable robot and dashed aside. With no delay MK1 flew off towards the team. Hawke led the way one hundred meters inside the vast cave system. Although dark, electrical activity periodically illuminated the area. The electricity arcs from ceiling to ground, causing the floor of the cave to turn like marble from the intensity of the heat. The team were forced to jump out of the way of the energy spikes.

As the Mankiller entered the cave they recommenced firing. Hatshepsut's sidearm ran out of bullets and shortly after so did Tronics'. In hopelessness, he dashed his pistol at the robot. Adcox still fired for dear life as the robot strode towards them. The captain no longer had the rifle butt on his shoulder. Accuracy was meaningless now as he shot from the hip.

The Mankiller pulled its two arms together. Energy began to build up as it did when it destroyed the battleship.

"Again, Corporal. The grav gun," yelled Hawke.

"Everyone get down!" Tronics ordered, noticing the weapon had recharged. Leaning on Rey'Jax to support himself from the kickback, he fired the gravity gun and a gravitational distortion wave rippled through the cave and impacted The Mankiller at its center of gravity. Its body blew apart, only its legs and one arm remained partial intact. The left leg was connected to the left arm via thin vine-like strips of its body's metallic material.

The Mankiller released a sound of what can only be described as agony, flinging its left arm around. Its frame had fragmented just like on the neutron star, revealing its hollow insides and neon-blue strips of circuitry. The mangled pieces of its destroyed body however never fell to the ground, they remained attached to its legs, suspended in the air by hundreds of thin wires.

"You have injured it, extreme gravity must affect it," said Hatshepsut.

Adcox relaxed. "Being trapped in the neutron star for so long must have compromised it." He lowered his weapon.

"Keep moving," said Hawke. "The entrance to the ship is on the other side of this cave."

"Let me try reversing the g-force polarity!" Tronics said, he promptly removed his probe apparatus from his utility belt and began to make adjustments to the gun while it recharged.

Meanwhile, the Mankiller raised its left arm high and clenched its fist. Amazingly, the individual fragments swirling around pulled back in, reforming its body. All the cracks fused together, reassembling the glyphs that covered its entire body. Somehow it had mustered the power to make itself whole again and was ready to resume killing. It fired a blast at the team but missed, hitting the cave wall. Tronics' knee was injured by falling rocks from the impact.

As the corporal fell over, the advancing robot stopped for an unapparent reason. It seemed to have sensed something, and whatever it was, MK1 was troubled by it. The Mankiller spun to see the pod the team used to traverse into dark space bolting towards it. Placing both arms and fist together it fired its destructible blue energy but the pod kept coming at high velocity and unaffected. It tried to punch the pod back but it had no effect. The pod hit the robot nailing it to the cave wall. Despite using all its strength MK1 could not move the pod as it struck out at it. The cybernetic lifeform struggled furiously like a ferocious animal instantly trapped in a cage but all its attempts were futile. Its movement ceased, its arms dropped lifelessly to its sides. Witnessing the event, the team's tension eased once more.

"Good job Eve!" said Hawke. "Try destroying that!"

Hatshepsut's slender shoulders supported Tronics as they all began to flee the scene.

Moments later, the Mankiller's hands rose up and touched the pod. A blue energy sprawled from its palms and illuminated each of the hieroglyphic markings on the object.

"What's going on?" Adcox asked.

"Warning," said Eve. "Codename MK1 is severing my control link with the pod."

"Oh no!" said Adcox.

As the team dashed farther into the caves, they all heard the echoing thud of the pod dropping to the ground as the Mankiller punched it away from itself. It stomped once more towards the group. Their escape became blocked by two huge chunks of fallen cavern rocks at the end of their passage, entrapping them. Without prompting Rey'Jax started pulling them apart with his enormous biceps and made a narrow gap.

The exhausted Adcox fired once more as the Mankiller neared but his rifle untimely stopped; the ammo count on his solar was zero. All he could do now was grip his rifle by the muzzle-end and ready himself, hoping for one good parting strike.

"It's time, your highness," said Hawke.

Rey'Jax seized this moment to do what his heart wanted since the robot arrived. He released his hold on the rock and stepped in front of the group.

"I will end this," said the male of the first nation.

"No, Rey'Jax!" said Adcox.

"Titans must clash, young one," replied the Ariman, he then looked at Hawke. "Finish what you were chosen for, Urk'Tark."

"I will...brother! Everyone, let's go."

Making their way through the opening Rey'Jax created for them, they left the big male behind. With Hatshepsut supporting the injured Tronics they struggled to keep up and Adcox stopped to lend a hand.

"I will assist him. Do not lose Mr. Hawke," said Hatshepsut.

***

"Come demon, Ariman bones do not tremble." Rey'Jax stepped forward.

Cautiously, he and MK1 circled each other in a showdown. The robot seemed aware of Ariman strength by the manner of which it readied itself.

"Eternal torture my fate, if denied my fist its desire to clash against you."

As he said his last words both lunged forward left fists high and tightly clinched. Before their dual blows could land both bodies were struck by lightning arcs. Thousands of volts coursed through them and stunned both in their tracks illuminating their bodies, the Ariman much larger and wider than his cybernetic foe. Adcox turned to gaze as the combatants stood almost motionless for a moment in time, mirroring gladiator statues of ancient coliseums.

Mankiller broke free of the lightning's hold first and punched Rey'Jax, knocking him out of his hold. The two adversaries went blow to blow trading powerful punches no man could survive from, deafening impacts reverberated through the jagged walls.

The ground shook making Hatshepsut loose balance as she supported Tronics and they both fell over. The tremors intensified causing the cave's ceiling to collapse, trapping Hatshepsut and Tronics.

"Kevin! Hatshepsut!" cried Adcox, trying to move the fallen rocks. "Give me a hand, Major."

"We need to leave, Captain," replied Hawke's emotionless voice. He didn't move an inch.

"There's no way I'm leaving them."

"There's only one strong enough to move these rocks, and he's fighting for all our lives."

The ground beneath Hawke and Adcox tremored and rose up, pushing them out of the cave through an opening a hundred meters above.

In the treacherous caves, the robot's strength appeared to be matched by the strongest of Horaxians. They grabbed hold of each other and wrestled. Crashing into the angled walls and crumbling them in the process. A fight like no other, each of the destroyer's life-ending punches were answered by its unyielding equal and opposite. Then, the

Mankiller energy blasted the Ariman through the cave wall leaving a large gap. The robotic monstrosity made its way out to resume its assault.

Hatshepsut helped the injured Tronics out of the collapsing cave through the only way out, which was the opening the two colossal warriors had just created.

Now outside, Rey'Jax rose to the sight of the robot approaching. He removed his short metal stick from his waist and it extended, transforming into the large double axe last seen on Kemeta's battleground. "Yes, beloved companion," he said. "For too long have we been forced to restrain our power. Now longer. Grant me your strength. Let us make prey of them whom would make prey of men."

He swiped at the Mankiller, creating a wide laceration on his chest area and it staggered back, holding its chest as if in pain. Again MK1 released a high pitch sound which could only be translated as agony. However, the wound slowly closed back up and reformed its unblemished, metallic hieroglyphs. Rey'Jax landed more cuts with forceful swings powerful enough to rupture tank armor. MK1 staggered on the back trying to evade the Ariman's onslaught. The ancient Horaxian prince jumped off the ground to land a forceful double handed blow but the robot swung its metallic wings forward forming a shield and his axe crashed against it. The silver wings were less affected by the Axe's blade. Rey'Jax concentrated all his strength into his fist and hammered it into the robot's head. It crashed deep into a rock hill.

***

Hawke and Adcox found themselves high above on a newly formed cliff edge, separated from the rest of the team.

"Incredible! Rey'Jax is beating him," Adcox said as they spectated the battle.

"No...he won't."

"What? Then we have to get down there and help them."

"Maybe you have to."

"What are you talking about?"

"That is not our mission," said Hawke.

***

Meanwhile, Tronics and Hatshepsut watched on with horror from the ground, too tired and injured to move as the Mankiller returned, breaking through gigantic slabs of rock. Flying in with an uppercut, it fractured Rey'Jax's heavy helmet knocking it into the air, revealing the roots of his white, thick locks.

MK1's onslaught on the Ariman soul destroying. Each one of its punches would be a death blow if not for its victim's genetic might and endurance. The fight now turned one sided. Until missiles hit the Mankiller and propelled it off its feet, all courtesy of the Bird of Prey.

***

Back on top of the jutted rock, Adcox argued with Hawke.

"The mission? Are you nuts? We've got people down there, we've got..."

"...you have people down there," replied Hawke.

"So all you care about is the ship? Everyone's just collateral damage to you?"

"Our orders were to get the ship back home. Our protocol is to get that job done and we will complete our mission. Protecting the team was always your responsibility. You're their leader."

"Look, I understand you're here for the ship, but I'm ordering you..."

"The ship's entrance is right over there." Hawke pointed to an artificial structure buried in the ground, part of which protruded outwards merging with the black soil of the planetoid. Sporadic flashes emanated from deep within the openings. Major Hawke continued. "The Mankiller is distracted. This is the only opportunity we'll get. Only Eve can activate the ship, she and I are one. This is your chance to make that difference, isn't that what you wanted?"

"What chance, Major? I can't go up against that thing. I won't last a second."

Beneath the two men, the Bird of Prey continued to fire its remaining ordnance but it was soon forced into evasive maneuvers as the Mankiller fired numerous blasts at it. MK1 then lifted off and they both flew around low to the ground in a cat and mouse fashion until Mankiller was finally able to lay fist upon the bird and it free fell to the ground where it lay unresponsive.

"No!" Bawled Tronics. Enraged by sentiment and despite his injured state, he pulled out his particle accelerator laser which had enough time to cool down.

"Hold this!" Taunted the injured marine. He fired his weapon. The Mankiller's feet were back on the ground and they slid through the dirt rocketed back by the laser beam. It burnt a line deep into its hollow head. But the Wings of Death formed its wings into a shield to protect itself. The unbroken beam left a scar line across its metallic wings less deeper than the wound on its head which had closed itself. MK1 fired a blast back, missing Tronics but impacting the ground in front of him. It would have been a direct hit if Tronics' laser had not off balanced it. Still the force was enough to hurl the corporal backwards. His back slammed hard into a large rock at dangerous speeds.

Above, Adcox continued his heated exchange with the Black Guard commander.

"Don't give me that crap about the ship, or the mission. You don't give a damn, you're hanging us out to dry just like you did on Matelot-6 and Kemeta. You still don't have any value for life."

"No! Hatshepsut was right...all life is precious, that's why we must go. Eve and I, we can save both races. Jei'Gun, Rey'Jax, they sacrificed themselves for your cause. Because they believed in you. If you want to honor them, it's time to believe in yourself. If we can get this ship back home, we could end the war. If that's worth fighting for, is it not worth dying for?"

***

Below the captain and Hawke, Hatshepsut knelt by the injured corporal's side as he lay awkwardly on the floor.

"I can't move!" cried the marine, only able to marginally twist his neck.

"Your back is broken! Please elevate your calm, Tronics. Our lives now rest in fate's blessed hands."

The Mankiller paced forward to finish off Tronics and Hatshepsut. All Hatshepsut could do was wait for the end and be thankful it would be quick. But MK1 ceased moving, detecting something. It spun around and saw mighty Rey'Jax with a boulder larger than himself hoisted above his head. He threw it onto MK1. Its weight crushed the robot and sunk it into the black surface. It lay lifeless, with only one forearm above ground. Seconds past, and the robotic manifestation of death raised its exposed hand. It placed it on the side of the rock. An energy blast exploded the boulder into tiny pieces.

***

The explosion caught Adcox's attention, he turned back to Hawke. "We've thrown everything at it and it keeps coming. I...I can't do this."

"You were given all the tools you needed to defeat any obstacle. You were given them when you were born. You have honor and integrity, things that I lost long ago. Compassion, perseverance...that's all you need to do the impossible. To become inviolable. All you were missing was courage."

"All of that stuff's not going to help me right now, Hawke. Even Rey'Jax can't win. How am I supposed to defeat it?"

"You do not have to, Captain Adcox," said Eve. "You only have to slow it down."

Adcox could not help shake his head, he knew what Hawke was asking him to do. "You're asking me to sacrifice my own life?"

The major placed his hand on the young man's shoulder. "Diomedes, we're all just ordinary men. But we become extraordinary, by our beliefs and convictions."

Adcox needed a moment to contemplate the most important decision in his life. But a moment was more than they could afford. Hawke had to press him. "So what's it going to be kid? Attempt to save your friends and most likely die, or come with us on the ship and live?"

Adcox stared down at Tronics laying helpless and Hatshepsut, then turned back to Hawke. "I'd rather die, sir! When you get back home, just be sure to let everybody know, both humans and Horaxians died together holding that line, Major."

Hawke smiled at Adcox for the first time. "We are the sword. You are the shield, and in defense..."

"...lies invincibility." Adcox remembered his words on Kemeta. "I think I've got it now."

Both men shook hands. "It's been an honor serving with you, Major. Don't let us die for nothing, that's an order."

"Command acknowledged!" said Hawke and Eve simultaneously. Hawke saluted his commanding officer and then ran off towards the entrance to the ship.

A strong gust of wind blew on Adcox, he closed his eyes and embraced it. Glancing down at his shield handle he spoke the words. "Isih-lango, mighty shield of Arima. Honor me with strength so I may save my friends. I beg of you."

Once more he saw the handle's black markings shifted, like waves along its white metal.

Rey'Jax mustered his last reserves of strength, that thing which he thought he held in abundance, to trade blows again with the unstoppable robot. The Mankiller mercilessly assaulted him, bashing his skull in with the strength to crush reinforced steel. The carnage was too brutal for Hatshepsut to bare. MK1 then blasted the Ariman with an energy beam from close distance and he flew through the air, sliding across the ground close to Hatshepsut and Tronics.

The battle was over. Rey'Jax had been defeated. MK1 placed both fist together to release its most devastating blast. After a moment's pause to build up enough destructive power to exterminate the remaining team, it fired. Adcox rolled in front and his team. The shield extracted and generated a large, circular protective area. The Mankiller's constant energy beam reflected sideways. Then, the shield rapidly reformed and concaved, creating a parabolic shape that reflected Mankiller blast back onto it. Its effect was most devastating, almost its entire body had fragmented into floating pieces and it released a deafening sound.

"Diomedes!" Said Tronics in a battle to speak. "The grav gun, I reversed...the...polarity."

Adcox picked up Dr. Henry's weapon which lay on the ground glowing red instead of blue and fired it at the mangled enemy whose bodily fragments were still loosely held together by only thin wires. In an incalculable speed MK1 was shot into the depths of space with the force of stars. Adcox himself was thrown backwards from the kickback.

His ordeal was over. The young captain had defeated the Wings of Death. But without enough time to catch his breath, he heard a chilling scream. From the ground, he turned and saw Hatshepsut standing, frozen stiff. In front of her stood a brain Horde. Adcox screamed her name as he saw the creature, which appeared to have no eyes within its black, helmet-shaped skull. As it lifted its Scepter, its ten cranial tendrils suspended in the air. Hatshepsut's pink aura reappeared and she turned to Adcox. He could tell by her eyes that she was not going to fight her death. Instead, she uttered words contrary to the female he knew, words that should never be her last thoughts.

"The Sword in the Dark is the key!" she said.

The brain raised its hand and extended its fingers fully stretched. Its facial tendrils realigned upright. Hatshepsut turned to face it and her expression changed. Her arms dropped to her side and she fell to her knees as if in a trance. Adcox bolted to save her with desperation in his eyes. Nothing else in the universe existed. The monster's scepter ignited with energy and zapped Hatshepsut, totally vaporizing her.

"*Nooo!*" the captain screamed, teeth glaring. As he got close to the brain Horde, anger consumed him and left no room for fear. It could have been an entire swarm before him, *still* he would burst forward. The lanky brain reaching nearly seven foot lunged with its scepter and just missed the young man's face as he weaved back his head. Adcox threw a punch but the brain maneuvered behind him in an astonishing speed. The captain attacked again and again it moved inhumanly fast. Then it grabbed Adcox's skull with one hand and incapacitated his assault. Its claws dug into his scalp. His eyes rolled back.

His arms dropped to his sides.

His body went limp.

Chapter Eighteen - Sword in the Dark

The young man's thoughts became distorted by voices and indistinguishable visions, serenading calls for him to cease his struggle, to give way to an absolute force, the natural, universal order of the alpha and omega. Voices spoke truths to him, that the Polymorph were not a macroscopic virus spreading as would an uncontainable bushfire. They were the rise of a new civilization, and the old must make way for the new. To defy natural selection's divinity will only result in obliteration, unless he submitted to their will.

"Their will!" The words reverberated through his subconscious, striking emancipation's cord. "And what of his will?" Ideals that so recently were meaningless to him now served as anchors grounding his slipping psyche back to terra firma. His mind now only *partially* remained his. But he embraced Hawke's words and *partially* was enough reason to cling on to his will to fight. Still held by the brain Horde, Adcox's right arm began to rise once more. His body quaked. He punched the brain in the gut and it instantaneously extracted his shield, impaling the creature's upper and lower body simultaneously. The shield burst through its external rib cage and lumpy skin from the inside out. Spikes generated by the shield protruded outwards from all sides.

The brain's head dropped low, resting level to the captain's, and its dripping blood gave off an odorous, rotting smell. Adcox stared it dead in the blackness of its helmet-formed head. Never to have been recorded in history, two brown eyes appeared, human in form.

"We...are...legion!" said the brain Polymorph. It then fell to the ground.

Never before had the Polymorph been known to speak. The young soldier dropped on his knees overcome by grief. The immense responsibility which he was tasked had allowed him to rediscover his ability, to redefine who he was, but, its price was equally monumental. Caught up by duty, he never had chance to tell her how he felt. Nor despite how controversial, what he wanted for them. He thought of their brief moments together, from first encounter to sadden end. Then he pondered; of all the last words he would have wished parted her lips, why were hers an echo of his former colonel's?

Perhaps he heard incorrectly. Why would her voice of consistent condemnation for the Black Guard commander then change in her final hour?

"Diomedes!" a voice cried. It was Tronics. Adcox got up and came to his friend's aid.

"I'm here Kev, I'm here." Adcox reached into his belt compartment and pulled out his individual first aid kit. Taking out a small vile, he pressed it on the corporal's neck and it released a hissing sound. "The analgesic will start kicking in soon."

"I can't, I can't move my back. What do we do now?"

"I don't know! I think Hawke is gone. But don't worry, bruv. I'll think of something." Adcox looked around for ideas. "Here we are again. You know, all of this started because you got me transferred to special ops. Will you ever stop getting me into trouble?"

"That's like stopping a teenaged girl from having a crush. Which I got to figure out man, I've got two daughters."

They both laugh. Tronics always had the power to do that even in the grimmest of times.

"Let me go check on Rey'Jax a sec." Adcox walked over to the lifeless Ariman body. "Please tell me you're still alive, big guy."

Rey'Jax's eyes opened as Adcox drew near. His full head of long, thick-stranded dreadlocks, exposed with his helmet off, lay spread out along the ground, covered in his own purple blood. "I am here captain. We Arimans do not kill easily." Rey'Jax paused on every few words to breathe deeply. "And what of death?"

"The Mankiller is gone, let me give you something for the pain."

"I require no medical assistance. Though my injuries severe, my body will itself heal...in little time. Plus, you would need a cargo hold full of pain suppressors to have any effect."

"Is there anything I can do?"

"Elevate your calm, young one. My body is in agony, but thanks to you its soul belonging, has been healed. Urk'Tark was right about you."

"Right about what?"

"Why do you think he made you leader? He chose you to unite both people. He saw your strength internal through precognition honed through the master's teaching."

"Unite humans and Horaxuans? Me? That's too great a task."

"Yet you slayed what could not be slayed. What rests on your shoulders now, once rested on his. Master Uru taught him our ways and sent him back to mankind to be instrument of peace. But he did not have strength to complete task, the strength of heart. You must take place as Carijan, the one to unite both people. His actions today proved his path may once more be tru..."

Rey'Jax's words were distracted by his sixth sense. Then his electroreception was soon backed up by the sounds his acute hearing detected.

"What's wrong, Rey'Jax?"

"Horde!"

Adcox looked up and saw a multiple brain Horde creeping closer, at least twenty. He and his injured friends were surrounded, and with no means of defense. Yet the captain rose up. He rolled his neck and then clenched both fists.

The shield extracted by merely his thoughts. He will take the infernal creatures to the grave with him.

The captain noticed mysterious balls of green light encircling him. He felt though he detected heat radiating from the light yet he sensed no sensation as some particles bushed his cheekbone. The light intensified, spiraling around Rey'Jax and Tronics also like a snow storm of energy particles that grew brighter and their numbers swelled. They were forced to shield their eyes from the green light. Adcox opened his eyes to an incredible sight. They were within magnificently gigantic walls, metallic in composition, and covered in patterns completely alien. The main thing that stood out about the light-green lit surrounding area along with its indistinguishable yet beautiful hieroglyphics, was its remarkable vastness. The men and Ariman were dwarfed by its size as plankton would be floating past a blue whale. A bright light glowed amongst a corner of darkness—a small, round, blue light.

"Well well, look what we have here," said a voice originating from the same direction as the blue light source. From out of the shadows stepped Major Hawke, smoking his token luminescent electronic cigar.

"I didn't think I'd see you again, Major," said Adcox with relief in his voice.

"We get that a lot!"

"Engines activated," said Eve. "Seven minutes to normal space re-entry."

"So we were on top of the ship?" asked Adcox.

"We were always on the ship from when we landed," said Hawke.

"The vessel is over 17,611,230 km^3," said Eve. "Close in size to Earth's island of Madagascar on its x and y axis."

As the engines fired up, the entire vessel came alive with bright light illuminating the wall markings. Outside of the ship, the planetoid's rocky surface blasted away from an intense release of white energy. The rocks broke apart revealing a gigantic cuboid, rectangle in shape and almost identical to the pod in its form and external markings.

"The lion reveals itself," Hawke said aloud.

Adcox's awe soon transformed into a frown, he squinted his eyes at the major. "Don't lie to me, Hawke. Could we have gotten to the ship sooner?"

The major didn't answer and turned away.

"Eve, could we have got to the alien ship sooner?" His nostrils flared.

"Yes, Captain. Much sooner," replied Eve.

"You son of a bitch!" In his rage, he struck Hawke in the jaw, knocking the cigar out of his mouth. "Akerele and Zomo are dead because of you, Jei'Gun too." He went to punch him again.

"No, Captain!" Rey'Jax called out. His ruptured lungs gasping for air. His words paused Adcox's fists.

Hawke stood unfazed and without retaliating, instead he spoke to the captain with his usual blank expression. "Sir, we needed to find out who the traitor was otherwise they could have sabotaged the ship, the mission. We also needed to weakened MK1. We were already aware of its existence from when Eve connected to the mothership fifteen years ago, we were just unfamiliar with its codename. I also needed to buy Eve some time."

"Time for what?" asked the young captain.

"You'll find out in a moment. But most importantly, who we were waiting for was you, sir. The greatest treasure one can find is to find oneself."

Eve's voice replied with a flash of lights on the collar bone area of Hawke's suit. "It was I who overloaded the *Odysseus*'s string drive circuitry on Kemeta after you retrieved us from the Abyss."

"Why?" asked the puzzled young man.

Hawke replied. "To gather intel on Horde and assess their abilities. To find Rey'Jax and earn back his trust, and to prepare you for this mission, so that you could find yourself."

"In the presence of danger," Adcox uttered remembering Hawke's words.

"Affirmative."

"Hatshepsut...they killed her."

"No, they did not," Rey'Jax said, still breathing heavily on the ground.

"That was the other thing we had to wait for," said Hawke. "We needed to get her inside. She's alive, sir! Eve, replay a holographic projection of the digital recording highlighting the gravitational signature." Individual light particles converged above their heads and fused, expanding into a bright, rectangular visual display. "Captain, this is a replay of footage taken from the battle on Kemeta. As you see the trooper was blasted with the brain Horde's scepter. There, highlighted and superimposed on the image is a residual gravitational energy signature."

Adcox's eyebrows raised as his mind filtered out the Horaxian weapons fire and screams, and zeroed in on the trail of energy rising up to the sky. "The signature trails back to the Horde ship above. It's some kind of...they were teleported," said the astounded captain.

"Affirmative, sir!" said Hawke. "The brain's scepter manipulates dark matter's transmutable power to reduce a target to subatomic particles, teleport it, and then reatomise it back on their ship. They're then taken back to their home world. She's aboard the whale. Light it up, Eve!"

The entire area filled with spots of green light, engulfing the men. The spots were three dimensional stars.

"This is a map of the dark space universe, Captain Adcox," said Eve. "The area in red is the Polymorphs' occupied worlds. At this moment, they have populated one thousand two hundred and forty seven planets."

"We still can't decipher the rest of the map, but Baizan will find a way," said Hawke.

Adcox replied full of haste. "We can catch them before they get there. Quickly, let's go."

"Negative, Captain!"

The young commanding officer clenched his fist, his eyes flaring in rage. "Major, Eve, set off now in pursuit of the Horde vessel. That is an order."

"The plan was for Doctor Hatshepsut to get captured," said Eve.

"What?"

Hawke explained as he gazed at the encompassing stars. "We asked Hatshepsut to secretly scan everyone's DNA to find who had the largest genetic variation on the team, and it was her. We already speculated that the Polymorph were created with human and Horaxian genetic material. She said she would allow herself to be abducted to function as a mole behind the Horde lines on their home world once we could prove the xenogenesis to her. Rey'Jax's heightened hearing abilities overheard our conversations just after she analyzed the ray's DNA."

The confused and emotional captain shouted at Hawke. "No, we can't let her go through with it. You brainwashed her, you tricked her..."

"Urk'Tark tried to persuade her against chosen path," said the Ariman. "The idea, was hers."

"Why?" replied Adcox's broken voice.

"Captain, we've given her a tracking device," said Eve. "She will transmit information about their home world to us. If we go to save her now, all would be lost."

"If you had the power to end this war, would you?" Hawke asked him. "Well she does, and she sacrificed her life for something that was worth more to her, life itself. She made a choice to fight. You have your part to play too, we all do." He handed Adcox the digital glove that belonged to Hatshepsut.

"She gave it to us when the Mankiller was approaching. It has the data on the Horde DNA Hatshepsut collected as well as the information from her tracker. Get it to Baizan. We must know our enemy."

"It seems like we barely even know each other." Adcox's emotions began to overwhelm him. He would have preferred if the horde ripped the heart from is chest. In fact...they had done.

"Do not despair, Captain Adcox," said Eve, almost as if she could sense his sorrow. "She is not lost. We do not believe the xenogenesis is an immediate procedure and dark space is vast, over five times larger the normal space. It will be some time before they can get to their home system. Plus, we believe this ship has the capabilities to get their much quicker. You can get her back, Captain."

Adcox stared at Hawke, one eyebrow raised. "Sometimes...I don't know if I like you or if I hate your guts, Major."

"We get that a lot too. Wish we could tell you it will pass."

Both men released a smile at one another. The major then walked over to Rey'Jax after hearing his soul churning moans; Adcox went to check on Tronics.

"You've suffered massive internal damages," Hawke said to the Ariman. "If we can get you into a pod we could ease the pain."

"That is not my desire. Pain is a part of life we all must feel, Urk'Tark."

"Perhaps regret is another. I am sorry brother, to have wronged you. I had hoped to prove myself again in your eyes, even if it took an eternity."

"We cannot stray from the blood oath that was made."

"It is Ariman law," said Hawke.

"No, it is *our* law. As last of our people we must uphold their ideals...my brother." His punctured lungs required each of his words to be accompanied by deep breaths.

Hawke smiled. "I could have escaped the Abyss. I stayed for all of my shames and failures. But also for purpose, to make good on promises made. I have a message from master Uru, he's alive within the Abyss' depths."

Rey'Jax's eyes opened wide in disbelief.

Hawke continued. "He said, 'Through you our people live on, and for balance to be restored, the first nation must rise once more.' Live your majesty...our time has come."

Rey'Jax endured the pain necessary to raise his left arm as high as possible and he gave Hawke what the soldier had dreamed of in decades of remorse. Rei'jax performed an Ariman salute.

Adcox walked over to Hawke after seeing to Tronics. "I'm going to need all your help to get her back, sir," said the young man.

"We would have followed you into hell itself if you gave the order. But I can't go back home with you, Diomedes. I'm sorry."

"I don't understand."

"We have company!"

Eve interjected. "Codename MK1 is approaching. At its current speed it will be here in three minutes."

***

In the depths of dark space, a comet-like shape glowed ever brighter. Star systems away from the blast it received from the gravity disruptor, it soared with incredible speed. Soon it will reach the mothership.

***

Hawke relayed information to Adcox as he hurried in the direction of Tronics. "Eve has automated the ship's navigation systems to rendezvous with the *Sword of Damocles* while we deal with the Mankiller."

"No, wait Hawke. Eve, the ship must have the ability to defeat MK1," said Adcox.

"Unfortunately Captain," replied Eve. "I cannot activate, nor for that matter locate the ship's weapons systems. It may not have any."

"It has me!" said Hawke. "Eve, give us a visual of the outside of the ship where the Mankiller is predicted to arrive."

Eve complied, changing the image which the alien ship previously projected as a map to black nothingness.

"What are you planning to do?" asked Adcox.

"What's necessary."

Hawke arrived to Tronics' laying body. "Going to need your hardware, Corporal Manning, if you don't mind." The major picked up the gravity gun which lay beside the injured Tronics. Hawke also grabbed the electronic probe from Tronics' belt as he rested on the hieroglyphical indentations on the vessel's floor.

"What are you doing?" asked Tronics, unable to see because of his stationary neck position.

"I'm recalibrating it to implosion mode and for a g-force of nine point eighty-one meters per second squared." Hawke tampered with the settings with the help of the probe.

"That's the gravitational force of Earth," Tronics said.

He handed the gun to Adcox then extracted his sword blade with a double handed grip. "Blast me with it. Just trust me."

"This is crazy, but all right! Brace yourself."

The blast hit Hawke, bending his midsection backwards and his legs buckled. He dropped to one knee in pain then rose his feet.

"I'll go with you. We'll fight it together," Adcox pleaded.

"Leave him, young one," Rey'Jax said. "Titans must clash!"

Hawke glanced up at the view of outer space. Where once was complete darkness, a faint white light appeared and it grew brighter.

"Eve, can you alter a localized section of dark matter space at this side of the ship and change it to a solid state?" asked Hawke.

"I believe I can. Executing now."

"Thank you. You sure you don't want to sit this one out, darling?"

"How can I? We are one!"

"Wait Major!" Adcox called out. "We can use the gravity gun, set a trap for it somehow..." His eyes intermittently focused on the visual display of space and saw the distant white ball of energy enlarging.

Hawke smiled at him. "I knew you were special from the day we first met...all those years ago."

"Years?" Adcox said. He then took one big gasp of air. "Wait...I remember now. I saw you...on a ship."

"You were on board the *Ploiarion*, Captain Adcox," Eve said.

Adcox had no words for the revelation. He tried regurgitating memories of the ill-fated ark vessel, but there were none.

"They gave you advanced psychotherapy so you would forget," said Hawke. "We guess they feared that the traumatic events of the ark would have left permanent scars. Still, subconsciously, it did. Your fears were my fault, son. I'm sorry."

"Wait I've got questions I need to know..."

"Warning!" said Eve interrupting.

"There's no time. So long, Captain." Hawke activated his suit's head guard and it automatically extracted over his face clicking as it locked into place. His head raised to witness the ball of energy closing in, leaving a long white tail. "Ready when you are, Eve."

Captain Adcox could only watch as swirling light swallowed Hawke and ignited him with a burst of illumination that almost blinded the young man. Adcox looked to the alien display and saw Hawke's body rematerializing outside of the ship. He was standing still, in outer space. His feet rested firmly on what looked like...nothing, only blackness.

"*It's impossible!*" Adcox thought, refusing to believe his own eyes, forced to spectate as the comet shape of the Mankiller approached in the distance. But more amazingly he saw Hawke running in space along the nothingness just as you would on Earth, thanks to the weight provided by the effects of the gravity gun and the solidifying transmutational properties of dark matter. Hawke's Black Guard suit provided all the remaining biological prerequisites for his motion and survival in the void.

Adcox's last view of the man he will never forget, was of him and the Mankiller almost at the point of uniting. The mothership fired a focused beam of black and purple energy. At the focal point, the beam created a rupture in space. It then traversed through the tear and Hawke vanished from the captain's sight.

***

"Sorry to interrupt, General Baizan," said Commodore Hussein. Commander Xiao stood behind him. It was a lie. He was more than happy to disrupt Baizan's current argument with his peers on their next course of action. He prayed he wouldn't have to choose a side. Which could have meant either mutiny, or being asked to relieve the most respected man in United Earth forces. He grew annoyed that Dr. Henry seemed to find the exchanges amusing. "We're picking up unusual readings that I think you should be notified of."

Baizan turned away from the high ranking leaders on screen not respecting them enough to excuse himself.

The commodore continued. "There appears to be some kind of spatial anomaly building up fifty kilometers off our bow."

"Focus our hull sensors ahead and prepare weapons and fighter squadrons. It could be MK1 again."

A gateway opened and the alien mothership emerged. It size made the space carrier appear miniscule, like a small stone next to a mountain.

Dr. Henry dropped his contraption. "It is the ship. They have done it."

"Get me on a hail, all frequencies all channels!" ordered Baizan.

"Communication hail active. All yours, General," said Commander Xiao.

"This is General Baizan of the United Earth, is anybody listening? Can you respond? Over."

Nothing happened. Then, a radio response burst on the ship-wide comms network.

"General, this is Captain Adcox. Sir, we did it." Upon hearing Adcox's words, the *Sword of Damocles's* crew erupted in cheers. Adcox continued speaking above the noise. "Only myself, Corporal Manning and the Ariman made it back, sir."

"What happened to the Hawke, Captain?" Baizan asked.

"Sir, MK1 was coming for us. Major Hawke went outside the ship to engage it as we flew off and I've not picked up signs of either of them since."

"Repeat, he went outside the ship, did you say?"

"Affirmative, sir, I know it may sound ridiculous but, he was...he was running in space, sir."

"Negative son, it doesn't," said Baizan with an ever so near grin, a full smile was something the four star general could not perform.

The general turned to his bridge crew. "Divert all power to long range sensors. Look for any signs of MK1 or Major Hawke."

***

Somewhere throughout the stars at an unknown location, Kibu'Kan, the highest ranking knight of the imperial guard approached the High Apex, Commander Cagn, who sat in his throne room. The room was guarded by its green, monumental stone statues of legendary Anubianite Apexs of old. His throne itself, made of black metal laced with blue gems, hovered above its encircling steps within a dark-lit room.

"Master, surveillance has intercepted information from the Earth vessel *Sword of Damocles*," said Kibu'Kan, his deep voice distorted by his large helmet.

"They have the alien mothership?" asked Cagn.

"Yes, master!"

"And the...unholy ghost?" Cagn's leaning forward caused a slight dip in his throne's hover height, just before the levitation systems generated extra output to compensate.

"The Black Guard has disappeared. My lord, the *Wings of Death*, it..."

"...It has been freed?"

"Yes, master. It destroyed *The Virtuous Sword* and a feeble Earth warship. Death may be headed for us. We must prepare royal armada."

"No! All is as I have planned. But the Black Guard's body must be found. He is our biggest threat."

***

Some time had passed, yet the crew of the *Sword of Damocles* still searched for evidence of MK1 or Major Hawke. The commodore walked across the bridge against the view of the Earth Command generals who listened attentively on the viewing screen. "General Baizan," said the commodore. "We've been actively scanning every sector reachable by long range scanners but there's nothing. However, we'll keep monitoring."

"Truly astonishing," said Henry, "It appears Hawke has defeated MK1. I wonder how did he do it?"

A look of sorrow cracked through Baizan's stone demeanor as he looked down at the cloth he held. The white, Black Guard squadron's emblem embossed the black fabric. It was the same cloth which he had wrapped Hawke's sword hilt in. The inscription in the cloth read, "The beacon in the storm. The Sword in the Dark." Hawke embodied the motto, and now that he was gone Baizan realized they needed that sword more than ever. The general whispered to himself

"The most effective weapon is one that remains hidden. That strikes from the shadows, then disappears once again."

Within the alien ship's impenetrable walls, Adcox's thoughts lingered on his last moments with the mystifying man. He realized that being purged of the will to fight was in itself, like a virus, and Hawke had created the antibodies. Perhaps his death wasn't in vain.

Perhaps he could use those antibodies to help save both races.

Epilogue

In the unexplored cosmos of dark matter space, an obscure object drifted lifelessly amongst floating rocky debris. The innumerable rocks, ranging from minuscule to the gigantic, were the only remains of the planetoid's black surface.

From within the floating rumble two small blue lights appeared on the object, revealing its form in the surrounding darkness. They were glowing blue eyes.

And they belong to the Mankiller.

The Beginning...

I hope you enjoyed my little tale. Please don't forget to give this book a quick review on Amazon. Even just a two-word, "Liked it" or "Hated it" review helps so much. Positive or negative, I am grateful for all feedback from my readers.

Thanks for your support!

www.kassmith.com